THE SOMEDAY FILE

DEUCE MORA SERIES, VOL. 1

JEAN HELLER

This is a work of fiction.
Similarities to real people, places, or events
are entirely coincidental.

The Someday File

Second Edition August 2018
ISBN-13: 978-1-7327252-0-1

To the memory of the business as it used to be,
when integrity meant more than blind opinion,
and civil discourse quelled the shouting.

And in memory of Ray, who always inspired me.

PROLOGUE

L as Vegas works hard to maintain its reputation as the city that never sleeps.

Through most hours of the day and evening Vegas pulsates with multi-hued, neon-enhanced, electronically embellished energy that radiates an aura of action and risk. But in the small hours of the morning, before the deep darkness retreats from the displacing shoulder of dawn, Las Vegas steals a short interval to doze. In this seam in time, when awareness ebbs by an increment, nobody notices the assassin.

He swings the rented Ford off southbound Interstate 15 and down the ramp to Tropicana Avenue, the heart of The Strip. The hotels and casinos rise out of the flat, brown floor of the Mojave Desert, garish, surreal monoliths glazed in LED color so intense it overpowers the senses. The impact, the assassin thinks, is a hedonistic indulgence and a waste of a perfectly decent wilderness.

At 3:30 in the morning, he is just another motorist driving conservatively through the light traffic: taxis looking for late fares, cops looking for trouble, and ordinary citizens performing the city's worst jobs while trying to get through their graveyard shifts.

He drives a short distance on Tropicana, into the canyon between New York New York and the Excalibur, and turns into an Excalibur parking lot.

He circles the area once and pulls over under a "Do Not Park" sign against the turreted hotel building. Security won't tow the car, assuming it belongs to a guest. Management's first rule of business is to avoid pissing off the paying customers.

He flashes his headlights, kills the engine, and steps from the car into the chill of the desert night. He is of medium height and thin, but wiry strong. His short-sleeved, open-collar shirt reveals cords of muscle in his neck and arms. His hair is blonde, his skin fair, his Northern European features narrow, his eyes empty as a dead man's.

A burly man in the uniform of hotel security slinks from behind the landscaping but hovers close beside it, as if planning cover in case of sudden danger. The security guard has a pony habit, dangerous when you're not good at picking winners. Crushing debt owed to an unlicensed and impatient bookie makes him vulnerable to the lure of easy cash. But he is having second thoughts.

"You got my money?" he asks in a tone that suggests he fears the question will piss off the assassin. This is not a man whose patience he wants to test.

"Of course," the assassin says. He opens the trunk. Two items lie inside, an expensive leather hard-side case and a cheap duffel. He snaps on latex gloves, then reaches in and unzips the duffel. It lures the guard, who inches toward him, the way a hungry man might be drawn to a porterhouse sizzling on a charcoal grill. The man's tongue is nervous, running back and forth over dry lips.

There are two stacks of $100 bills, 250 bills to a stack, each worth $25,000. They are held with rubber bands. The assassin tosses one stack to the guard, who cradles it against his chest.

"Count it if you like," the assassin says.

The guard worries his lower lip with his teeth as he riffles the exposed edges of the bills. His eyes dart about, alert for witnesses. Finding none, he shoves the cash inside his jacket, the package hidden by the bulge of his stomach. The guard knows he will get the rest when the job is done. That's the deal.

The assassin lifts out the hard-sided case and the duffel, elbows the trunk lid down and nods to the guard.

"*Showtime,*" *he says.*

~

BY 7:13 A.M. the desert sun has risen high enough to reach the roof of the Excalibur and bathe the two men crouched beside an exhaust fan spinning out condensation from the roaring air conditioning system. The warmth of the sun is welcome to the assassin, but it pops an immediate sweat on the security man's upper lip.

At the same moment, across Tropicana Avenue, a tall, swarthy man with jet-black hair and a broad mustache emerges from a limousine in front of New York New York. He is a United States congressman, and four guards surround him. They eye the cheering crowd as if they were Secret Service agents protecting the president. The dark man reaches between the protective bodies to shake hands with political supporters. Then he disappears into the hotel.

The assassin knows the congressman's schedule to the minute. At 7:30 he will speak to a political breakfast and fundraiser. At 8:45 he will hold a strategy meeting with his political staff in a private suite and then give an interview to a local television station. Afterward, he will indulge television's unquenchable thirst for video by taking a turn on the famous New York New York roller coaster, named Manhattan Transfer. He and his party will be aboard the first occupied car when the ride opens at 10 a.m.

This will be the assassin's moment.

It would have been a simpler shot to take the politician as he entered the hotel. But the roller-coaster kill will create more confusion and buy more time for escape. And in a world where the assassin's talents are valued, such a daring kill will raise his profile.

"Why did we have to get up here so early if you ain't gonna do the shooting 'til ten?" says the security guard, who is resting his back against the roof turrets and sweating.

The question is too stupid to deserve an answer. How many more eyes could have seen them sneaking to the roof at mid-morning than in the deepest of night? The assassin stares at the security guard for a few moments, debating what to say. Then he points to the condenser and tells the man, "Go around to the shady side for a while, before you flood the roof with sweat. And stay low."

"Shudda brought donuts, or somethin'," the guard says as he crabs away.

At 9:30 the assassin consults the small temperature/humidity monitor he has set up to tell him how he must adjust his shot to compensate for the ambient conditions. He uses small binoculars to check out his telltale, a thin strip of torn green garbage bag snagged in a banner holder high on a lamp-post. City workers will remove the plastic strip when they take down the banner advertising the casino engagement of a well-known stand-up comic. But for now it serves the assassin well, allowing him to gauge wind speed and direction and the rise of air from the street. These, too, are factors that could affect the trajectory of his shot.

At 9:43 the guard returns from the far side of the AC condenser looking as if he has just awakened from a nap.

At the same time the assassin digs another pair of latex gloves from the duffel and snaps them on. Then he lifts out the components of a cheap Chinese knockoff rifle, assembles it, and lays it aside.

At 9:54, he makes his calculations and takes his good rifle from its leather case. An empty car rattles through the roller-coaster course, a security and safety sweep. The congressman's car will come up next. It clatters up the ramp at 10:07. The target is sitting in the right front seat. There is nobody between him and the sniper.

The image shudders in the riflescope as the car climbs. But as it slows near the top of the incline the shaking abates, and the scope's cross hairs settle over their mark. The assassin curls his finger around the trigger.

For an instant the car barely moves. The target's profile stands out in sharp definition. The assassin squeezes the trigger. The crack of the shot is lost in the roar of the condenser.

The assassin sees a blossom of blood explode from his victim's neck.

When the roller coaster begins its final terrifying plunge down the tracks the congressman has slumped sideways in his seat. The bullet has passed through his carotid artery, ripped through his throat and lodged in the chest of the city councilman sitting to his left. Within seconds the congressman is dead. The councilman, disoriented and confused, slips toward shock. Behind the two men, the protection agents become frantic, torn between tending to their charges and locating the sniper.

On the roof of the Excalibur, the pony-addicted security guard peers between the ramparts, immobilized by the coldness and finality of the execution. He doesn't notice the assassin move behind him with a handgun. Nor does he feel the quick double-tap to the back of his head that ends his life.

The assassin retrieves the stack of bills from the dead man's jacket and takes back all but $5,000. This is ample evidence to implicate the guard in the shooting, but it makes no sense to leave more than necessary. He also picks up the expended shell casing.

He drops the Chinese rifle beside the dead guard's body, a delaying tactic. He fired it out in the desert before driving to the Excalibur. There, too, he picked up the casing, which he now drops to the roof. This will lead the police to believe the knockoff is the assassination weapon and postpone for hours instructions to all public transportation leaving Las Vegas to examine checked baggage for a sniper's rifle. Meanwhile, the assassin's prized possession and $45,000 in cash will be nestled in the belly of a Greyhound bus speeding northeast toward Chicago on I-15. Back at the terminal, no one will have noticed that the man who checked the hard leather case onto the bus didn't board with it.

On the way to the airport, the assassin will toss the handgun and the latex gloves into a storm drain, the empty duffel bag into a Dumpster from which a homeless man will claim it within minutes.

By the time police helicopters are in the air searching for suspects, the assassin is walking toward an American Airlines gate on Concourse D at McCarran International Airport to board his flight for home.

1

"This Deuce Mora?"

The male voice exuded enough hostility that it threatened to flare through my phone and scorch my blouse. I keep an egg timer on my desk for such occasions. I knew what was coming: more of the same abuse I'd been enduring all morning. My tolerance for it had a strict three-minute limit.

The next sentence out of the caller's mouth delivered two curses. I flipped the egg timer. Fine sand trickled through its pinched waist. The indentation forming in the sand in the top mirrored the cone forming in the sand at the bottom. I found it soothing to watch the process.

In less than three minutes he called me a bitch four times, a dyke twice, told me three times to go fuck myself, and concluded I had all the writing talent of "a sock full of shit."

And I was fine with it.

Then he called my newspaper, the *Chicago Journal*, a "liberal, commie, pinko, butt wipe not even good enough for wrapping fish guts."

Honestly, I was fine with that, too.

My column in the morning's editions had hinted at the vague

possibility that guns kill people from time to time, a notion with which my caller had deep disagreement. He made his point several times, though I assured him I'd got it the first time. Repetitive tirades never persuade me.

The sand ran out, my three minutes of tolerance exhausted.

So I told him, "Sir, as much as I appreciate your having the interest to call, your cranky time is up, and I'm going to hang up now."

I did.

And then I laughed.

"God, I love my readers," I said to no one in particular.

In the next moment I was swept by the sense of unease that had been my sporadic companion for more than two years. I got up to go to the restroom, and it followed along, mocking me. Every time I left my desk I wondered if I would have a job when I returned. Today the feeling escalated to a mid-grade fear.

While I washed my hands, I checked my face in the mirror, scrutinizing details. People who had known her said I resembled my mother, even beyond the green eyes and auburn hair. She died when I was seven. If it weren't for family photos I don't think I'd recall what she looked like. I often found myself wishing I'd had time to know her. Now, with my future under siege and my temper short, was one of those occasions. I felt certain I would have learned from her something to help me deal with my current anxiety.

I fluffed my hair, which I had cut short a year earlier after wearing it shoulder-length most of my adult life. The change was a nod to Chicago's summer weather trifecta: heat, humidity, and wind. My hair still tended to coil into ringlets in hot, damp weather, but at least now it more resembled a style than a meteorological mugging.

I hurried toward the elevators and temporary respite from my unease. Cole Haan dress boots I coveted had gone on sale. A clerk at the Mag Mile store was holding a pair for me. I had told her I would be in early in the afternoon, and I didn't want to be so late that she put my boots back in stock. I could get there and back in my allotted lunch hour.

I don't overspend on clothes, but I never skimp on footwear. I'm six feet tall. I need two sets of shoes, one that emphasizes my height for work, when I need an air of authority, and one that doesn't, for times I meet an interesting guy who isn't six feet tall.

Pete Serrano, a copy desk editor I liked, intercepted me. "Good column this morning, Deuce," he said. "I liked the sarcasm."

"Thanks, Pete," I said. "I've been taking calls all morning from readers who don't share your enthusiasm."

"You gotta write those columns once in a while to be sure folks are still reading you."

"Gun control and birth control," I said. "The two subjects that absolutely positively will clog up e-mail and overload voice mail before noon. I'm thinking we'll take a circulation hit from offended gun nuts. Management won't like it."

"They knew what you were writing," he said. "It was on the news log all day."

I smiled at him. "That won't matter when the cancellations start rolling in. I'll be the one blamed for bad judgment. I could be the next expendable staffer out the door."

His face showed no mirth. "Speakin' of which, you see the bulletin board lately?"

"No. Why? Don't tell me we lost somebody else."

"Four people, including Kevin Clarke."

I felt actual pain. The newspaper economy was brutal. In many respects, the profession I signed on for no longer existed. With circulation and ad revenue in the tank, the *Journal,* along with hundreds of other newspapers, had been buying out and laying off people like crazy. If *Journal* cuts had reached Kevin Clarke, the situation was more dire than I had imagined. He was a Pulitzer Prize winner. Twice. Without our best people, we were nothing, a doomed shell of a nothing.

"Kevin?" I said, hearing heat in my voice. "I can't believe it."

"He took the buyout and jumped to the Internet," Pete said. "No specifics, but I think it's *Slate* or the *Huff Post.*"

I crossed my arms and frowned. "Tell me something, Pete. You think things are as bad as management says? I mean, come on. We've closed four bureaus, cut the staff system-wide by thirty-four percent, and those of us left have taken three pay cuts. Circulation is going up, and the economy is getting better for ad revenue. We're charging pretty good money for Web access. So why are we still crying poor?"

"If you get an answer let the rest of us know," Pete said. "Since it's a privately held company there's no way to look at the books."

I squeezed his shoulder and continued my trek in silence. I was standing at the elevator doors thinking about all the great journalists all over the country now unemployed or plying their trade on Web sites. I used to think finding a newsprint paper in a plastic sleeve outside my door every morning was as sacrosanct as the Bill of Rights. Everything had changed almost overnight. Was the Internet the future of journalism?

Was it my future? I didn't like the prospect.

When the elevator doors opened, Eric Ryland stepped out. If he wasn't the last person I wanted to see at the moment, he held a prominent spot on my list.

Eric was the *Journal's* metro editor. The *Journal* had several city editors who supervised the beat reporters who covered Chicago's 200-plus neighborhoods and 77 communities spread out over 228 square miles. It was Ryland's job to supervise and coordinate the city editors. He liked to describe himself as the big-picture guy. I often wondered how he and his ego squeezed into the same office at the same time.

Eric's face darkened when he saw me. I wasn't surprised.

"Deuce, wonderful," he said, his tone matching his expression. He came off the elevator clouded up. I expected him to rain on me momentarily. "Just the person I want to see. You headed out?"

Since I wasn't crazy about Eric to begin with, and since news of Kevin Clarke's departure had put me in a foul mood, I was tempted to reply that I always stood in front of elevators to hear the bells go ding and watch the doors open and close. Somewhere deep in my soul I found restraint.

"I'm headed to Michigan Avenue," I told him, "to see a store about a pair of boots, but it can wait. What happened with Kevin Clarke?"

Without answering me, he turned and walked toward his office. I sighed. I knew he expected me to follow like a well-trained puppy.

Eric closed the door. A flat-screen television on the credenza behind his desk was tuned to CNN. He turned down the volume until we could barely hear it. More conducive to a tongue-lashing. Or perhaps Ryland was about to dump me, too.

We sat, and he got right to the point. As it happened, he hadn't called me in to discuss a buyout. It was more unpleasant.

"We've been getting calls about the column today," he told me.

"Me, too," I said.

"They're not the sorts of calls we like to get."

"Me, neither," I said. "You could borrow my egg timer."

"Your what?"

"Egg timer."

"And what would I do with that?"

"Cook a perfect egg?"

He waved that off. He didn't understand and didn't want to.

"The fact is," he said, "I just left a meeting with the circulation people, who tell me they've taken forty-three subscription cancellations today because of your column and fielded a lot more cancellation threats. You know the economics. We're fighting for our lives. We can't afford . . ."

"What are you trying to tell me, Eric?" I said. "Don't circle around it."

"First of all," he said, "I'm not telling you what to write. But maybe you could cool it with the hot-button topics for a while until this settles out."

I could feel the heat rise in my face, and I was certain Eric saw me flush because he frowned and leaned away from me, as if anticipating an explosion.

"The story," I said, "was about a man who bought a gun at a gun show where neither he nor the seller complied with the required background check or the waiting period. He carried the gun home. In the heat of anger he shot and killed his girlfriend and her two-year-old son. He emptied a magazine into the woman, put in a new magazine, and emptied it into the little boy. The only hot button involved here is the one the state should push to lock the prison doors on him forever. Also on the idiot who broke the law to sell him the gun in the first place."

"So you said in the column. You do recall that Illinois abolished the death penalty some years ago?"

"Who said anything about the death penalty?"

"Subscribers who believe that's what you really want. This isn't your first trip into this briar patch."

"Eric," I said, "this state is making it too easy for anyone to carry a concealed weapon. We should be writing about it every time gun ownership is abused, keep the pressure on."

"You think you alone can turn around public opinion? That you alone always know what's best? That you can stir things up this way and still have a newspaper tomorrow willing to publish the next episode in this quixotic mission of yours?"

I heard my voice rising. "So you're telling me not to write on these subjects any more, that the fallout to our circulation is more important than the fallout on babies?"

"We have to consider everything," Eric said. "Do you want to keep your job? Because if the economics get any worse, the *Journal*'s headed for bankruptcy. We're an anachronism. We're holding on by our fingernails. We can't afford to take the occasional ad and circulation hits. We . . ."

But I had stopped listening sometime around the word "bankruptcy." Something on the television, words hardly heard, distracted me.

"Las Vegas . . . Assassination."

Adrenaline began trickling into my system. I strained to hear more and realized Eric's voice had stilled. I could feel him watching me, and I was certain he didn't approve of my lack of attention to his problems.

"Eric, turn that up," I said.

If he heard the urgency in my voice, it didn't move him.

"We're not through, Deuce," he said. "I want . . ."

I interrupted again. "Turn it up, Eric. Please."

First he grunted. Then he picked up the remote and thumbed the volume. I realized I was standing up, leaning toward the TV. I didn't remember getting out of the chair.

"To recap what we know," the anchor said, "eight-term Congressman Charles Reading of Nevada was gunned down by a sniper in Las Vegas this morning as he rode Manhattan Transfer, the roller coaster at the hotel casino New York New York. Reading, the ranking minority member of the House Judiciary Committee, was struck in the neck by a single shot, which Las Vegas Police believe came from the roof of a hotel across the street . . ."

The narrative went on but the ringing in my ears drowned it. The shock hit full force then, and Eric looked alarmed.

"Deuce, sit down," he said. "Are you okay?" He stood up and grabbed my arm, but I pulled away. I had to get back to a little duplex in Cicero where, the night before, I had dropped off an irascible 78-year old drunk after dismissing him as a head case.

"I have to go," I said. "I'm sorry Eric. I have to get to Cicero."

"Cicero?" he said. "What's in Cicero?"

"I'm not sure yet," I said, backing toward the door. "But today I think it's a whole lot more important than I thought it was yesterday."

2

I didn't remember leaving The Loop or getting on the southbound Dan Ryan or the westbound Stevenson. I kept seeing the face of the drunken old man named Vinnie Colangelo. He'd been sitting half in and half out of my Explorer the night before, preparing to stagger up the sidewalk to his house. He twisted around to face me and said, "Watch for sumpin' big happenin' in Vegas 'cause it's connected to me." The memory played in my head, over and over, like a closed video loop.

When I got to the I-55 exit for South Cicero Avenue, I turned north and pulled into a White Castle parking lot, where the odor of grease would have gagged me had I not been so distracted. I grabbed my cell phone and called Jerry Alvarez, the federal prosecutor who had sent me searching for the old drunk in the first place. Colangelo had an interesting story to tell, Jerry said. It might be a column for me.

I could feel beads of moisture bumping down my spine, even though the September temperature was in the high 60s, and even though I had the Explorer's AC set on Ice Age. The phone rang twice in Jerry's office before the secretary picked up.

"This is Deuce Mora from the *Chicago Journal*," I said. "I need to speak to Mr. Alvarez, please. It's urgent."

"I'm sorry, but Mr. Alvarez is in court until five," the secretary said. "May I take a message? I'll give it to him if he calls in early, and if not, I'll leave it on his desk."

"You think he'll come back to the office before he goes home?" I said.

"He always does."

"Okay. Tell him he has to meet Deuce Mora at Jo-Jo's in Cicero as soon as possible."

"He could have another engagement," she said.

"He has to cancel it, or be late, or something. This is urgent." I gave her my cell phone number and the address for Jo-Jo's and told her to have Jerry call me. "Tell him it's about Vinnie Colangelo." Then I added as an afterthought, "Tell him it's about Las Vegas."

"Are you certain that's the right address?" the secretary said. She sounded doubtful, and I couldn't blame her.

"Absolutely certain," I said. "It's not the best part of town, but right now it's the slam dunk center of the universe."

I pushed my Explorer north on Cicero and tried to remember where I'd left Vinnie the night before when it dawned on me I was driving in the wrong direction. He lived in a duplex south of the interstate, not far from Midway International Airport. I couldn't recall the street. I'd been focused on convincing him to tell me his story and trying to prevent him from booting all over my truck. He'd been throwing back Jo-Jo's house brand bourbon and Old Style beer for hours before I drove him home. I'd followed his directions to his house without paying attention to where we were going.

As I approached Midway, I recalled that I'd made a left at Vinnie's direction on West 55th Street. I tried to recall my other turns, but nothing seemed familiar.

I explored the neighborhood for half an hour. It looked better in the daylight. It was neat and tidy and working class all the way, block after block of yellow brick, single-story simplicity with two bedrooms and one bath each. At maybe 1,100 to 1,200 square feet, each home would have a tiny kitchen and smallish dining and living rooms. The yards were tended, red geranium flower boxes ubiquitous.

But I wasn't finding Vinnie's duplex until the piercing rotation of red and blue police light bars got my attention.

I had a bad feeling. The units attached to the light bars were parked in front of a single-story yellow brick structure I recognized as Vinnie's home. The building's condition set it apart from the rest of the neighborhood. Decades of imbedded grime stained the façade, and the front porch sagged. One of the two steps was splintered—a lawsuit waiting to happen.

I had to park a few doors down because two police cars, one unmarked, and a van belonging to forensics specialists crowded the curb in front of the duplex. I got my notebook and a pen out of my backpack and checked to make sure my press credentials still hung around my neck. Then I walked as close as the ring of yellow crime scene tape would allow.

I approached a uniform standing guard over the front lawn and flashed my best smile. It didn't always work, but this time it did. His eyes, set in a broad, flat Slavic face, glanced down at my credentials and then up at me. He returned the smile.

"I recognize you from the picture in the paper," he said, pronouncing it, da pitcha inna paypah. "Didn't realize youse is so tall."

"Hard to tell from a photo of my face," I said.

He looked sheepish.

"What happened here?" I said.

"You're gonna hafta talk to Detective Ramales, and he's still inside," said the officer, whose nametag identified him as Malovich.

"I'm not taking notes or recording this," I said. "I'm trying to find out what happened. I might know the person involved."

"Really?" Malovich said. "Inat case, you need ta talk to Ramales."

I sighed and looked disappointed, because I was.

"Old guy's dead inside," Malovich said.

"Is his name Colangelo?"

Malovich's eyebrow twitched.

"Yeah, or so says the landlady. Guess you do know 'im."

"How'd he die?" I asked.

"Wasn't natural, for sure. Beaten and strangled. That's how it looked to me. I was first onna scene. Terrible thing. The M.E.'ll make the call."

Beaten and strangled. After being seen leaving a dive bar with me. There had to be a connection, and the possibility made me angry. Malovich saw my reaction and added, "Aw, hell. He a relative of yours? Hey, I'm sorry."

"No," I said, "nothing like that. I barely knew him. How'd you find him?"

"Landlady called. She lives inna other halfa da house. Really, Miss Mora, any more you gotta get from the detective."

I didn't want to talk to the detective. Not right then. I would get in touch with him later. I got his full name before I hurried back to my truck. I needed to think, and I needed to be gone when other reporters showed up. They'd be curious to know why the killing got my attention.

I sat behind the wheel and thumbed the window down to get some fresh air.

Vinnie's parting words the night before swirled in my head:

"If I trust you, and I'm wrong, it'll get me killed. Tell you somethin' else. It'll get you killed, too."

I SAT THERE for a full ten minutes staring at the piercing lights on the police vehicles. I began to feel seventeen kinds of guilty. I also felt nineteen kinds of curious. Curiosity trumped guilt.

I had a strong hunch Vinnie Colangelo had been murdered because I went to that bar and sat with him while he drank cheap bourbon and cheap beer. I pumped him for information about his past in front of witnesses who must have heard. And then I talked Vinnie into leaving with me. The story I had asked about—the story

Vinnie in his drunken incoherency refused to discuss—must have frightened someone enough to silence Vinnie.

I grew even more determined to hear the story for myself.

But the guilt kept elbowing back in and paralyzed me in place. Vinnie said he was scared. He begged me to get away from him. And I ignored his pleas, chalking them up to alcoholic reticence.

I shivered. The breeze had turned cool and threatened rain, and my body was damp. The combination chilled me.

I closed the window, switched from high AC to low heat, and called Jerry Alvarez again. His secretary said she hadn't yet heard from him.

"You remember I told you it was urgent?" I said. She did. "Well, it just got worse by a factor of ten."

~

WHICH IS HOW, for the second September afternoon in a row, I came to be at the double front doors of Jo-Jo's Lounge in Cicero, Illinois.

The building looked like half the old corner bars in Chicago, weathered sandstone brick exterior and begrimed windows filled with neon beer brands and metal grating. The front door was angled to the intersection leaving it unclear which cross street gave the place its address.

I grabbed the door handle and paused. Why had I come here in the first place? It had been an unpromising mission, the hunt for an easy column on a day when I didn't have a better idea. And look what happened.

I write three columns a week. It's harder than it sounds unless you write the mindless ones, such as the top twenty-five uses for the plastic sleeve your newspaper comes in, picking up dog shit being everybody's favorite. I prefer to think a little deeper. It's great when I'm brimming with ideas, which I am, usually. But every once in a while inspiration eludes me, and I find myself flat smack stuck for an idea. That's when I go to my "Someday File." It's a manila folder in the bottom drawer of my desk where I stick things I've heard about that I might check out, someday, if I'm ever flat smack stuck for an idea.

There had been many more misses than hits in my Someday File. Up to now, the most notable success led to the freeing of a convicted rapist-murderer who spent eleven years in prison for a crime he didn't commit because of the mishandling of DNA evidence by the Cook County Medical Examiner's office. Richard Palmieri, a high-profile civil attorney, sued on the innocent man's behalf and settled for $5.7 million.

It was my Someday File that propelled me to Jo-Jo's the day before. Nine months earlier, during a Christmas party at the U.S. Attorney's office, Jerry Alvarez had pointed me at Vinnie Colangelo as a possible story. Jerry had been a friend and a source for a long time, and I had learned that listening to him often paid off.

But then, for the better part of a year, the piece of paper scrawled with details of Jerry's tip had stayed in the Someday File, forgotten. Yesterday, I remembered it and decided to haul it out and hold it up to the candle of daily journalism to see if it held a good yarn. I wondered if things might have turned out differently if I had approached Vinnie when Jerry first told me about him in December. Or if I'd waited until he left the bar. They couldn't have turned out worse.

The double front doors of Jo-Jo's were made of weathered cedar, and each had a large pane of etched glass in the top half, displaying a beer logo. A neon Old Style sign glowed behind the pane on the left, a Coors sign behind the pane on the right. A twisted version of the classic Frank Stockton story came to mind: Behind one door lurked a man-eating tiger, behind the other a perfect lover in the form of a good story. Which door should I choose?

The day before I had pulled open the Coors door with no inkling that this small choice would come to convince me I had chosen the tiger, and I would have been better off going back to the office and writing a whole string of columns about gun control.

3

J o-Jo's had no dance floor and no bandstand. The lights were cranked down to a level between romantic and blackout. The place could boast all the ambience of the garage where I take my Explorer to get the oil changed.

A bar stretched along the right wall, fronted by eighteen soda fountain stools crowned in cracked, red naugahide and ringed with dull, scratched chrome. The walls behind the bar wore years of water stains. To the left, two pool tables sat with balls racked and ready. A third was in use by two men holding Budweiser bottles by the necks so their hands wouldn't warm the beer. God forbid you should spoil a Bud.

Eighteen booths lined the three walls surrounding the tables. Predictably, the jukebox played Frank Sinatra. Right now he was belting out, "My Way," which could have served as a municipal anthem for Cicero. It was a city where officials had been known to run things freestyle. Convention and law were considered "suggestions."

While both Cicero and Chicago were located in Cook County, they were separate municipalities. Cicero's ties to the Outfit, the Syndicate—whatever you chose to call the mob—were't as storied as

Chicago's, but Cicero's ran just as deep. It was Al Capone's first head-quarters and the place he holed up when the heat in Chicago became too high. Cicero was a city tied to organized crime tighter than a corset on my grandmother.

Half the booths were occupied with patrons who ignored me. Two men sitting in the booth nearest the door turned to look at me, both about 30, dressed in identical worn blue jeans, running shoes, t-shirts and black leather jackets, their hair slicked straight back with some of the oil from my Explorer garage. The goombah twins. You could find guys like them all over Cicero.

One of them gave me his best imitation of a seductive smile and arched an eyebrow. A silent proposition. I get that a lot. I run and work out, so I'm not impossible to look at. And some guys like tall girls. That actress on "The West Wing" made us fashionable. I owed Allison Janney for helping me realize more than a decade ago that my height didn't make me a circus freak.

My eyes found the stool at the nearly empty bar where I'd discovered Vinnie sitting the day before. I wondered if the others in the place knew Vinnie was dead.

I sat at the end of the bar nearest the door. One other stool, at the far end, was occupied. The bartender, a man I knew as Percy, walked over, his muscled torso shrink-wrapped into a black t-shirt. I had left him a hefty tip the day before, so he smiled at me.

"Old Style?" he said. A little joke.

I had tried Old Style the day before because Vinnie was drinking it. I thought it would help us bond. It tasted like soap, and Percy had been amused by my reaction to it.

"Club soda," I said.

Percy brought the club soda in a tall glass, lots of ice, lime on the lip. Set it on a cardboard coaster. "Vinnie ain't in yet," he said.

"Vinnie won't be coming in," I said. "He was murdered sometime last night."

Conversation ceased. The click of billiard balls ceased. The sound of bottles and glasses hitting tables ceased. Those who hadn't heard me were whispered the news by those who had. Several people looked at me with questions in their eyes, but nobody asked anything. The guy at the bar glanced at me, then at Percy, then back to his beer. Another Cicero tradition: mind your own business.

"Aw, geez," Percy said. "Aw, geez. Poor old guy. He never hurt nobody. Had a hard life, but never asked nobody for nothin'. Aw, geez. Do the cops know who done it?"

"I don't think so," I said. "Percy, I need your help."

One of the goombah twins climbed out of his booth, tapped on the bar and extended two fingers of his right hand. Percy indicated he'd come right back and turned to get two beers for the guy. Then he checked with the man at the far end, who indicated he was good.

"Don't know what I could do," Percy said when he returned.

"Was Vinnie ever threatened?"

"Not that I know of, not that he ever mentioned. 'Cept that guy who come in here after you left last night didn't look so friendly."

Percy now had my undivided attention. "What guy?" I said.

"Didn't know him," Percy said. "Big guy, built powerful. Not like a weight lifter. More like a dockhand, a stevedore. And mean-lookin'. Shorter than you. I'm guessin' he weighed two-fifty, two-sixty. Maybe Italian."

"What did he want?"

"Asked where Vinnie lived."

"You tell him?"

"Not me, no. I don't even know."

"Last night," I said, "when I was trying to get Vinnie to stop drinking and talk to me, you said his story wasn't worth listening to, that he'd been bitching—your word—about his twelve years in Leavenworth ever since he got out."

"Yeah," Percy said. "Yeah, I said that. 'S true."

"So you've heard his story?"

"Yeah. A dozen times. Two dozen. More."

"Tell me."

"It all happened more'n forty years ago. It ain't important now."

"I want to hear it anyway."

Percy shrugged. He had nothing better to do.

"Vinnie was connected. Small-time, but still . . ." he said, his hand palm down, making a yawing motion. "Drove a 'frigerated truck for a meat supplier over in Bridgeport durin' the day. At night, he'd boost stuff for the local organization. He did a little time. Longest stretch was maybe a year. But the semi was a serious beef. Him and two other guys broke into a warehouse yard somewhere on Port of Chicago and boosted a load of Scotch locked up in a truck. Laphroaig, a real good single malt. You know it?"

"I've tried it a time or two," I said.

"Vinnie always said it was an acquired taste. Truth is, I don't stock it. No call for it in a place like this. Too expensive. You know the history of Laphroig?"

I confessed I did not.

"It was the only booze the feds allowed into the country durin' Prohibition. The distillers marked it as disinfectant, and when the feds smelled it, they believed it." He laughed. "Like Vinnie said, an acquired taste. But that's a true story. You could look it up."

"So what happened after they took the truck?"

"They all got busted," Percy said. "End of story."

So far, I wasn't hearing anything to explain why Jerry Alvarez sent me looking for Vinnie or, more important, why anything about Vinnie's story was worth killing him to keep quiet. I asked Percy if there was anything unusual about Vinnie's case.

Percy shrugged. "Nah, not really. Maybe some technicality. According to Vinnie, somethin' about who had legal ownership of the booze when they stole it. It has to do with Customs rules. One way it was a state beef, the other way was federal. It made a big difference. I dunno the rules, but Vinnie always said the state wudda let him plead him out and given him a short stretch somewhere. The feds went to trial, convicted him, fined him, and sent him to Leavenworth for the max, a dozen hard years. All Vinnie ever talked about was suin' the feds." Percy waved his hand in a dismissive gesture.

"What grounds did he have to sue?" I said.

"None. He was just a sad, old man. The feds seized every-thing he owned to pay off his fine. Then, about four years into his prison stretch, the wife divorces him and disappears with their little girl. Never tells him where they're goin'. He never sees 'em again. Way he figured, he had grandbabies he'd never seen. He wanted to sue 'cause he thought he got railroaded. Sad case."

Sad, yes. A bitter, aging mobster with regrets. Jerry had sent me after a human-interest story. Maybe someone who read it would know the whereabouts of Vinnie's family and get them back together. But I would have had a hard time getting readers to shed any tears for Vinnie. He served his time, lost everything, started boozing. Would anybody care?

Somebody cared. Or Vinnie would still be alive.

"Did Vinnie ever speculate about why things went so hard for him?"

"Said somebody wanted him outta the way."

"Did he say who?"

"I asked him that. I think he knew, but he wouldn't say. I think it scared him."

"Did he ever mention Las Vegas?"

Percy's brow furrowed as he consulted his memory. Then he shook his head.

"Don't recall nuthin' like that," he said.

My mind ticked back to the night before.

"That guy who came in here looking for Vinnie last night, what did he do when you told him you didn't know where Vinnie lived?"

"He took off. A car pulled up outside and honked, and he left here and drove off with another guy. You took Vinnie home, right?"

I nodded.

"Maybe the other guy followed you an' came back for his partner."

I sat back and tried to breathe.

I already knew I led the killers to Vinnie. I didn't need Percy to remind me.

And I couldn't quite forget Vinnie's inebriated caution that violence against him could spread to me.

I felt my outrage, my guilt, and even my fear tick up another few notches.

~

I PAID for my club soda and moved away from the bar to talk to the patrons. Maybe one of them had been there when the thug asked about Vinnie. Maybe one of them knew who he was.

As I approached the two players at the pool table, the front door to Jo-Jo's opened and Jerry Alvarez walked in, his eyes looking for me in the gloom and not finding me right away. Jerry didn't look like a federal prosecutor. He had stopped growing vertically at the age of 15, when he attained five feet, five inches. But he had been growing horizontally ever since. He fought a constant battle against weight, and constantly lost.

What he didn't lose were cases. At fifty-six, Jerry was twenty-two years my senior, and he liked to say he had entered his "reclining years." But you couldn't tell that to defendants who faced his meticulous court preparation or his generous sense of moral outrage. In front of a judge and a jury, Jerry Alvarez most resembled an angry moose. A small, angry moose. Tenacious and effective.

Jerry was second generation Mexican-American and spoke his family's native language flawlessly. I envied him that, because he spoke English well, too, and my language skills would fit into a taco shell without spilling over.

His eyes found me, and he walked over.

"*No es su estilio habitual,*" he said. "This place isn't your style."

Jerry had a habit of making remarks in Spanish and then translating for the rest of us. Usually I found it amusing. At this moment, I wasn't amused by anything.

We stood toe-to-toe, if not eye-to-eye.

"Vinnie Colangelo's dead," I said. I kept the volume down, but I could hear the anger in my voice. "You remember Vinnie? You told me last Christmas to look him up?"

"Yeah, sure." Jerry looked confused. "So? He was an older guy."

"He was murdered last night within hours after he left this place with me. Percy, the guy over there behind the bar, he told me Vinnie's story, the one you sent me to hear, and it doesn't sound serious enough to warrant killing a fly. But the guy was overheard talking to me, seen leaving with me, and now he's dead. I want answers."

Now Jerry looked stunned. "I don't know the questions yet, kid. Could we sit down and order beers before you bitch-slap me?"

"Order an Old Style," I said.

"Is there an Old Style Light?" Jerry asked.

"Ask the bartender," I said. I sounded snappish. I felt snappish.

We sat in a booth away from other patrons. Percy came over to take our orders.

"Do you have Old Style Light?" Jerry said.

Percy looked at me, then at Jerry, as if Jerry had arrived from the Antares Nebula.

"Yeah, if you really want it," he said.

"Yeah," Jerry said. "An Old Style Light."

I ordered another club soda.

"*Que?* What story did the bartender tell you?" Jerry said.

I said nothing, preferring to wait for our drinks so their arrival wouldn't interrupt us.

Percy returned, set our drinks down and backed away. I watched Jerry sip the beer and waited for his face to wrinkle in distaste. Instead, he smiled. "It's good," he said.

I was disappointed but didn't say so.

I told him Vinnie's story as Percy related it to me, including the big man who'd come to the bar to find Vinnie.

"When I dropped him at his house last night," I said, "the last thing Vinnie said to me was to watch for something big happening in Las Vegas, that it was connected to him. I guess the assassination of a congressman counts as big."

Jerry looked surprised, then skeptical. "*Seguro?* Vinnie Colangelo said that?"

"Yes."

He thought a moment then shrugged. "It could be a coincidence."

"Then what was Vinnie referring to? Some blue-hair who won a jackpot at the nickel slots on Fremont Street? I don't believe in coincidence, Jerry."

"I don't know what to make of it, Deuce. But you should tell it to the FBI. They've got the Reading case."

"I'm not ready to talk to anyone," I said. "All I could tell the FBI is what I told you."

"I don't know what more to tell you," he said "To me, Vinnie was a possible column for you. Minor gangster. Went to prison. He did his time. Stayed clean. Grew old and poor. He missed his family. Probably deserved a break. Findin' the wife and daughter wudda been a good thing, I think. No big deal."

"It's a big deal now," I said.

"So what do you want from me?"

"Help."

"What kind of help?"

"Whatever it takes to figure this out."

"*O Dios mio.* No. And hell no."

Now it was my turn to be stunned.

"Why not? You got me started down this road."

"And I don't want the road to stop with your dead body at the end of it," he said. "If somebody whacked Colangelo because he was talkin' to you, and you press the issue, what do you think the odds are of you livin' long enough to learn anything? If you can't figure the answer, I'll do it for you. *Nada.*"

I whispered an epithet that expressed my frustration.

Jerry cleared his throat. "You been over to Colangelo's house?"

I nodded. "There were cops and crime scene techs all over the place."

"You meet the lead detective?"

I shook my head. "His name's Ramales, but I didn't talk to him."

"Yeah, Juan Ramales. I know him," Jerry said. "Let me finish my beer, and we'll take a ride over there. If he's still around and he's willin' to deal with you, I'll introduce you. Then it's between you and him, and I'm out of it. And I hope you will be, too."

4

"You drive," he said, as we left Jo-Jo's. "You know where we're goin'."

I pulled away from the curb and saw Jerry touch and then heft the brass monkey that hung from my rear-view mirror.

"*Que es esto?* What's this?" he said.

"His name is Darwin," I said. "An old boyfriend won him for me at the state fair a long, long time ago. Aubrey Sullivan. Our political editor. I'm guessing you know him."

"Know the byline," he said. "This is heavy. Could pull the mirror off."

"Hasn't yet," I said.

He forgot the monkey. "Deuce," he said, "this isn't your fault. Not even close."

"It feels like my fault," I said. "Or yours. Why would you send me to see a man if you knew that being seen with a reporter could be lethal?"

"Because I didn't know," he said. "And I still don't. Could be total coincidence."

"Coincidence is a myth, Jerry. I already told you that. Everything has an explanation. People use the concept of coincidence when they're too lazy to look for an explanation.

I pulled to the curb in front of Vinnie's duplex. The street had quieted down. Only an unmarked police car and the forensics van remained. Local TV trucks must have come and gone, if they'd come at all.

"*Espera.* Wait here a minute," Jerry said. "Let me go see who's inside so they don't freak when a reporter walks in. And put your ID on."

I had taken it off when I went into the bar and dug it out of my pocket. Jerry ducked under the yellow tape, walked with care up the rickety front steps and disappeared inside the house. I waited seven minutes before he stuck his head out the door and beckoned me.

"Watch that top step," he said. "And watch where you step in here. Don't want to mess up forensics."

He handed me a pair of booties, and I slipped them over my shoes.

What I found inside was a house that appeared not to have been cleaned since it was built. Dust covered everything. I patted the headrest of an overstuffed chair and freed a billow of dust that tickled my nose and made me sneeze. On the table next to a recliner, a succession of un-coastered beer bottles had sweated rings into the dust and the wood, and dead cigarette butts and ashes spilled from an overflowing saucer.

I saw Jerry watching my mission of discovery. He rolled his eyes.

"Don't pass judgment on the dead," he said.

Hard not to.

We moved into the kitchen. On a countertop next to the sink, four food-encrusted black TV dinner trays swarmed with lines of frantic pharaoh ants. Nearby, a cardboard plate held a scab of dried ketchup. Another was smeared with food remains I chose not to try to identify. On a whim, I opened the refrigerator. An odor assaulted me from within, suggesting something had died in there around the turn of the century.

"In here, Deuce," Jerry said. "*No toques nada.* Stop touching stuff."

I followed him into the bedroom, which was every bit as filthy as the rest of the house. But I stopped noticing when my eyes found the bed. The sheets were bunched and twisted, as though the last occupant had writhed on them. And there was blood everywhere. Two forensics specialists were on their hands and knees on the floor.

A wiry man in a good suit stepped out of the bathroom and extended his hand.

"Ramales," he said. "And you're Deuce Mora. Recognize you from the pitcha inna paper. I often wondered about your name."

"Mora?" I said.

He smiled again, almost laughed.

"I'm the second-born of twins," I told him. "My dad started calling me Deuce in the delivery room, and it stuck. It's not a nickname. It's on my birth certificate."

"What did your mother think of that?"

"She never said. She died when I was seven."

"If your father called you Deuce, what did he call your sister?"

"Brother," I said. "We're fraternal twins. His name is Gary."

Ramales looked amused. The story amused most people.

"What happened here?" I said.

"Your friend was tortured and murdered," the detective said.

"Tortured?" I sagged back against the doorframe and squeezed my eyes shut, swallowing to suppress my gag reflex. Vinnie had done nothing to deserve this.

"Yeah, tortured. How well did you know him?"

I opened my eyes and stared back at Ramales. "First of all, Vinnie Colangelo wasn't my friend. I only met him once, last night, at a bar near here named Jo-Jo's."

"I know the place," Ramales said. "Wouldn't have made you for a Jo-Jo's customer."

"I'm not, or at least I wasn't before last night. I went there to interview Vinnie."

"And how'd that go?"

"Vinnie was drunk and didn't want to talk to me," I said. "I drove him home and let him out at the curb."

"You're saying you didn't kill him?"

"No, I didn't kill him. I just wanted to talk to him."

"What time was it when you dropped him off?"

"Before five," I said. "Maybe four-forty, four-forty-five. He was wasted. He'd been drinking cheap bourbon with beer chasers for hours."

"You're not a suspect," Ramales said, "but you coulda done it. Drunken old man. You look strong enough to overpower him."

"Maybe I am, but I didn't."

"Any idea who did?"

I wasn't supposed to share with the police information gathered in the course of doing my job unless one of the newspaper's lawyers was present to arbitrate. My choice was to violate that rule or refuse to help the detective. Jerry rescued me.

"Talk to the bartender at Jo-Jo's," he said. "He can give you something."

"Tortured?" I said again to Ramales.

He looked at me with an expression that said I didn't want to know. But he told me: "Tied him to the bed, gagged him, cut his clothes off, cut him with a broken bottle, burned him with cigarettes, then slashed his throat."

"Oh, God," I said, almost a whisper.

Then Ramales made it worse.

"If Colangelo was killed because of what he might have told you, then you need to watch your back," he said. "This wasn't just a murder. It was a message."

I DROVE Jerry back to his car. He offered to follow me home. I declined and watched his tail lights recede into the darkness. The wind had kicked up. It whipped at the branches of the oaks and maples that lined the block in front of Jo-Jo's, dislodging a few leaves that had already given up to the approach of winter. I felt paralyzed again. It required a major physical effort to move my foot from the accelerator to the brake. The gearshift felt like it weighed fifty pounds.

I relived the night before over and over as I watched people come and go from the bar. I imagined one of those coming out was the guy with the stevedore build who'd asked about Vinnie's address. There were lots of barflies with stevedore builds in Cicero. Despite my attempts to stop it, my mind churned out scenes of what might have gone down at Vinnie's house when the two thugs found him. He'd still have been intoxicated and unable to defend himself. His terror, filtered through the mental gauze of booze, might have seemed just a nightmare at first. But the pain would have made it real enough, soon enough. My mind saw the attackers strip him and tie him to the bed and ... I tried to push the scene away, but it wouldn't move.

The sharp taste of bile filled my mouth, and I barely got the Explorer's door open before I retched. I hoped the cold, wind-washed air would bring me around, but the heaves kept coming. I sat in the truck, with the door open, gagging on guilt and anger.

I checked the rearview mirror to see if anyone was behind me, possibly with the idea of tailing me. Finding nothing obvious, I used the last of my strength to turn the ignition key and find my way home.

5

T he next morning I sat at my computer in the *Chicago Journal's* cavernous newsroom in The Loop, our building standing on ridiculously valuable real estate between North Clark and North Dearborn. I wondered why the owners didn't sell the property since they owned it outright. An infusion of cash that large might save us, and we could move into cheap space way over among the warehouses west of the Dan Ryan Expressway. Who gave a damn about the prestige of an address? We were dying where we were.

Half the staff cubicles were empty, devoid of computers, books, stacks of dusty documents, and people. The once-robust, boisterous, energized hall now felt like a viewing room in a funeral home. There was nothing left to do there but say our goodbyes.

A phone rang here and there, but I remembered when it used to be a cacophony. I heard a few people talking, their voices subdued. I heard no laughter, and that was the saddest of all. A newsroom should be full of laughter. And spirited debate. And people hustling about, stoked about what they were doing and where they were going. I wondered if I would ever see that again. Certainly not with internet journalism, should that be my fate. Cyber interaction wasn't my idea of human relationships.

Looking back on it, the downfall of newspapers had been inevitable. They had lost their relevance with the rise of 24/7 broadcast news. Who wanted to pay money to read at dawn every day the news they heard before going to bed the night before? Investigative and project journalism couldn't save the business. While they still were relevant for the most part, people had lost their attention spans, along with the desire and the time to read.

It was only a matter of years before printed newspapers disappeared completely.

I sighed and acknowledged silently that my morning funk could have been a hangover from the whole Vinnie Colangelo thing the day before.

On the other hand, perhaps it was time to think about another line of work.

I sat in silence in my own space, forcing myself to plan the column I had to write. I felt sleep-deprived and emotionally drained. But I still had a deadline. I had chosen to pick on the Illinois Legislature because it was an easy target, and I needed an easy target. I needed a few hours not to think about Vinnie.

Sometime in the next few weeks, the governor would decide to sign or veto an astonishingly bad bill passed this morning in haste and corrupt judgment by legislators beholden to special interests. I argued with conviction and magnificent reasoning for the governor to do the right thing and veto the bill, as his predecessor had done. The *Journal* circulated down in Springfield, and I knew the governor read my column because he told me so. I lived with the conceit that he cared what I thought.

I finished before noon and felt deflated. Now I had no reason to avoid thinking about Vinnie. I needed to talk about him, and there was only one person I trusted to be honest. I walked over to Aubrey Sullivan's cubicle, where a nameplate on the entrance identified him as the *Journal's* political editor. He was talking on the phone. I decided to wait at a discreet distance so I didn't seem to be eaves-dropping.

It also gave me a chance to enjoy looking at him and to feel a few regrets.

We broke in with the newspaper on the same day in the same suburban bureau nine years earlier, and he swept me off my feet. He was tall enough to be a point guard in the NBA, and had clear, mocha-colored skin inherited from his bi-racial parents, his father the head of the Department of Geophysical Studies at the University of Chicago, his mother a wicked smart litigator with Kirkland & Ellis, Chicago's top law firm.

Within two months we were involved, and I thought Sully might be the real deal for me. But it was not to be. He transferred to the state capital in Springfield, and I was promoted to the main office in The Loop. The distance hurt us. He often had to work weekends, and I didn't like making the seven-hour round-trip drive for a few hours with him. Eventually, Sully met someone else, got engaged, married, and now had two kids. I was devastated at first, but I should have expected it. I suck at relationships.

Although ours hadn't worked out, Sully was still my best friend.

"You have lunch plans?" I said when he finished the phone call.

"I was going to grab something and work on a weekender," he said, then took a hard look at me. "You look busted up. The weekender can wait a while. Where should we go?"

I mentioned a sushi place we liked on West Wacker, a few blocks north of the office.

I liked walking with Sully. At 6-foot-5, he made me feel proportional. We made five blocks worth of small talk. Mostly he told me tales of his twin sons, Jake and Max, who were eighteen months old and eating everything in sight.

"They take after their father," I said.

Sully was a prodigious eater. The quantities of food he could put away never ceased to amaze me. But his metabolism worked in high gear all the time, and he burned off the food as fast as he ate it. Long ago, I used to tell him that even asleep his body was hot to the touch. He chose to think I was talking about his sexual prowess.

After we got our ice teas and had ordered lunch, I related Vinnie's story from the beginning. Sully's handsome face betrayed nothing, but his gray eyes stayed fixed on me. Then I got to the part where I dropped Vinnie at his house, and he made his cryptic statement about Las Vegas. Sully started to respond but thought better of it, I guess, because he sat there with this quizzical expression and his mouth half open.

When I finished, he stared at me in silence for a few seconds, and then our food came, and we both busied ourselves mixing wasabi and soy sauce and preparing our chopsticks so we didn't eat wood splinters with the *unagi*. But instead of digging in as usual, Sully sat there and stared at me. I think he was trying to get his head around everything and finding the process difficult.

Tell me about it.

His first words surprised me. "You remember Peter Linsky?"

I knew the name. I couldn't place it.

"My fraternity brother from UNLV," Sully said. "He stopped in Chicago to see us when we were still together. He was on his way to take a new job in D.C."

I nodded. I did remember Peter. Tall, bookish, heavy features but not bad looking.

"Peter's new job was on Capitol Hill," Sully said. "He had just passed the D.C. Bar. Remember who his new boss was?"

I didn't remember, but because of the UNLV connection I had a pretty good idea. "Charles Reading?"

"Yep. I've been trying to call Peter for the last day and a half," Sully said.

"You think he'd know anything?"

"No doubt. He's Reading's chief of staff. Or was."

We ate then, with tension hanging in the air. Sully finally gave voice to it.

"Are you going to pursue this?" he asked. "It could be very dangerous."

"I have to, Sully. A man's dead because of me."

"Did you kill him?"

I flinched. "Not directly," I said.

"Then you aren't responsible at all," he said.

"Yes, I . . ." He waved his chopsticks at me, cutting me off.

"No, you're not. Not in any way."

"But . . ." He waved me off again.

"I have no right to tell you not to push forward, but you need to be very careful."

"I know that," I said, sounding bolder than I felt. "I'm not going to do anything stupid."

"I know you, Deuce. You're impulsive. You don't always think things through before you leap. Before you do anything, you have to talk to Eric."

I tried to deflect Sully's concern, more to calm myself than him.

"I'm going to chase it," I said. "That's a given. But the only plan I have right now is to visit the federal court clerk's office this afternoon to get Vinnie's trial transcript, see who the prosecutor and the witnesses were and what the evidence said."

"At least talk to Eric about it first," Sully said. "He's your editor, and he has an absolute right to know. If not for you, do it for me. I don't want anything bad happening to you."

The sweet look on Sully's face made me uncomfortable, so I met him part way.

"Tomorrow," I said. "I don't want to spend all afternoon in the office explaining things again. I want to get started on the transcript. I'll talk to Eric first thing in the morning."

That ended the Vinnie discussion, and I was glad of it. I had enlisted Sully's help, which is what I wanted. I didn't want to keep hearing other people's worries about perils to me. Being reminded constantly only escalated my own concerns.

At some point, if I allowed it, my fear would begin to choke my determination to pursue Vinnie's story. The dread would flow through the pores in my skin, where everyone could get a good whiff of it. My own emotions would betray me as a quitter.

My FIRST STOP after lunch was the aforementioned clerk's office. What would it require, I asked a customer service agent, to get the transcript of a trial from back in the 70s?

The lady looked at me as if she'd bitten into an under-ripe persimmon.

"Those records are warehoused out in the western suburbs," she said. "We need a written request to pull 'em. What's the year of trial?"

"I'm not sure," I said. "I know it was in the seventies sometime."

She adopted the classic look of the put-upon public servant. It was a look public servants have perfected over years and years of eating bad persimmons.

"I assume you don't have the docket number," she said. "That'd indicate the year."

"I have the name of the defendant," I said.

"Well, at least you got sumpin'," she said. She sounded miffed. She had a right.

"Vinnie, probably Vincent, Colangelo," I said and spelled the name. She had finished typing it in before I got to the last syllable. Even when I had information it wasn't useful.

"Nineteen-seventy-four," she said. "August." She wrote something down on a note pad, tore off the sheet and handed it to me. "The docket number, in case it comes up again."

"Thank you," I said, and slipped it into my pocket. "Can I get the transcript?"

"Yep," she said. She pushed a form across the counter at me. "Fill this out and sign it. It'll take about three weeks."

"Three weeks?" I said, frustration clear in my voice. "I could walk to the warehouse in two weeks. Isn't there any way to speed up the process?"

"Sure," she said. "You could walk to the warehouse and read it there."

"Could I maybe drive out there and have a copy made while I wait?"

"Nope. Copies have to go through this office."

So I filled out the form, a reluctant slave to the federal judicial bureaucracy. I passed the paper back to her and watched her scan it for neatness and completeness. Then I left and went upstairs to see Jerry Alvarez. Maybe he could help me speed up this process.

Jerry's secretary told me he was in a meeting scheduled to eat up the rest of the day.

I checked my watch. It was 3:37. The rest of the day on the federal clock consisted of about 90 minutes. I had nothing better to do; I said I'd wait.

Jerry appeared in about an hour, walking with another man. He smiled when he saw me, a reflex. Then he realized I'd probably come to talk about Vinnie, and he grew serious.

"I'll be with you in a few minutes," he said. "Can you wait?"

I had waited fifty-eight minutes already. I nodded. Then I went back to the *Florida Angler* article I'd been reading. If I ever had occasion to go to Florida to spear fish for cobia, I'd know what I was doing. On my list of things I was eager to try, spear fishing for cobia ranked either $1,901^{st}$ or $1,902^{nd}$.

When Jerry called me into his office, we talked about his social life for a few minutes. He had been divorced for a decade and now thought he had found the new love of his life. He wanted to improve his health and his appearance. He asked if I was still running. It was his way of avoiding the Vinnie discussion. In my anger, I'd come down on him pretty hard at Jo-Jo's. Now I decided to let him set the pace.

"Sure," I said. "I try to get out four times a week, but mostly I only make three. I lift weights a couple of days, too. I've been doing it so long I've forgotten how not to do it."

"Think it might help me?"

"Absolutely. You should start with a personal trainer. It helps keep you interested when there's somebody pushing you. There's a good gym in the South Loop, Roosevelt and Canal. Lots of pink spandex with pretty women inside to distract you from the pain."

He shook his head. "*No se.* I don't know. Between this job and dating, I don't have a lot of free time. And I'm not supposed to be looking at pretty women in pink spandex."

"Don't give up before you try," I said. "The workouts, I mean."

He paused, fresh out of ways to deflect the conversation.

"The reason I'm here," I said, "is I'm trying to get a copy of Vinnie Colangelo's trial transcript. But the clerk downstairs says it will take three weeks to bring it in. Could you speed up the process a little?"

"No," he said.

"You can't, or you won't?

"Both. Neither. *El sistema es el sistema.* I can't bend the system. Clerks rule the world. And I'm thinking three weeks is a good thing. Call it a cooling-off period. When it comes to tilting, you need to find a new windmill. These are made guys, Deuce. They hurt people for a living. They won't hesitate to kill you, too."

"Jesus, I feel like I've stepped into a *Sopranos* episode."

"That was Jersey, but you got the idea."

"What makes you think the Outfit killed Vinnie?"

"*Quien mas?* Who else would it be?" he said. "That was Vinnie's life. That was the story you wanted to hear. They didn't want him tellin' it, and they don't want you pokin' it."

"It could have been a home invasion gone bad," I said.

"In that wreck of a place? Maybe some guys tryin' to steal flies and dust?"

A valid point.

"There are consequences to killing a reporter," I said. "Not as many as killing a cop. But it brings a lot of heat from high places. Most bad guys won't even consider it unless they're desperate."

"The thing with Vinnie looks pretty desperate to me," Jerry said.

"Jesus, it's a forty-year-old case."

"Yeah, but the consequences are lingering like a foul odor."

"Which is why," I said, "you should be taking Vinnie's Las Vegas tip more seriously. It time-warps Vinnie's life right into this week."

He frowned at me. Then he said, "When did scales grow over your brain? You're a lot of things, Deuce, none of them naïve. But right now you're acting like you just stepped out of j-school. I know you don't believe in coincidence, but I've got ten bucks says the Las Vegas link is nothing more than a big one, the figment of an ex-punk's drunken imagination. And you know I might be right, or you'd be off to talk to the FBI quicker than Bears fans turn on their quarterback. Vinnie's tip is so thin I could read the Bible through it. The FBI would laugh you out of the office, which would damage your credibility. And that's something you don't want."

I nodded. "That's part of it," I said. "I need harder evidence. Which is why I'm here."

"Where Vegas is concerned," Jerry said, "there is nothing harder. What sent the killers after Vinnie is your forty-year-old case. What will send them after you is you pokin' around in it. You won't be able to hide what you're doing. You think the bad guys don't already know you asked for a copy of the transcript? They have ways of knowing these things."

"That's not the point," I said. "Vinnie wouldn't talk to me in the bar. He was scared. I talked him into leaving with me. If I'd walked away and left him there, everyone would've known he didn't tell me anything. He'd be alive today to drink cheap bourbon with bad beer chasers. But when I led him out of there, they couldn't be sure. So they did the expedient thing. I owe him closure."

"No, you don't. This is neither your fault nor your responsibility."

"Well, I think it is. But it's going to be hard to pull off. Vinnie could be a long project. With my column schedule, I don't have time for long projects. So I need a little help from people who know what's going on behind the scenes. Let me scan the room for someone who fits that description. Oh, there you are."

Jerry slapped his desk and stood up to look out his window with his back to me.

"I can't talk you off this ledge?" he asked.

"No," I said.

"You think you've got some responsibility to rescue every stray crosses your path?"

It was funny he should ask. I had discovered journalism in my junior year in college when a little voice in my head told me it was my responsibility to help save the world. I liked the idea of me saving the world. I mean somebody has to do it.

"Yeah," I said. "Kittens, puppies, the occasional song bird and lonely old ex-cons. Help me, Jerry. I need to figure this out."

He sighed.

"I couldn't, even if I wanted," he said. "I don't know anything more than you. If this was my case, I'd take a look at the people involved. They're a lot more important than a forty-year-old trial transcript. Who prosecuted the case? Who did the prosecutor report to? Where are these people now? What are they doing? How did they get where they are?"

He paused and then added, "At least that's my instinct."

"Your instinct's usually pretty good," I said.

"There were things goin' on in the old courthouse back in the seventies that weren't kosher," he said. "They were still goin' on when I got there a decade later. It was a daily source of quiet gossip. Man, the stories the old-timers told. Unbelievable."

"What sorts of stories?"

"Politics in the worst sense of the word. Certain people could get deals done that were way outta line. Evidence contamination. Jury tampering. Nobody could prove any of it. Nobody wanted to deal with the potentially lethal consequences of trying. But everybody saw the signs. Maybe Vinnie got himself caught up in something like that. But why him I don't know. In the hierarchy of criminal behavior, 'jackin' a truck doesn't rank so big. In the hierarchy of criminals, Vinnie wouldn't rate a second look. An' I got nothin' more to say."

6

I was awake most of the night worrying I might have made a mistake telling Jerry about Vinnie's claim to a connection with the Las Vegas assassination. Jerry dismissed the timing of Vinnie's claim as an odd coincidence but wanted me to take the story to the FBI, nonetheless. I declined because I had nothing of substance to support the tip. Since Jerry was an officer of the court, he might feel duty-bound to go to the FBI himself and point them at me. They would try to force the *Journal* to force me to give up everything I knew and everything I learned. They could get a court order. They could threaten me with jail. Then, ultimately, they could conclude that Vinnie's warning and the killing in Las Vegas were a coincidence best ignored.

And I'd be the only one who knew otherwise.

Meanwhile, the noise made by the Feds would alert the culprits, and they would go to ground, taking everything incriminating with them. And that would be the end of the story. I didn't have time to wait three weeks for the trial transcript. I needed traction now.

If I could identify even one person who'd been involved in Vinnie's case, it would give me someone to interview. That interview

could lead to another. With luck I would find the truth at the far end
—a step ahead of the feds and the hoods—without relying on Jerry.

The next morning, when I got to the federal court clerk's office, I
found myself facing the same woman who'd taken my order for the
trial transcript the day before.

"I was the one who ordered this," I said, pulling from my wallet
the slip of paper on which she'd written Vinnie's case docket number.

Her eyes examined the slip of paper, then me, then the paper
again.

"It ain't come in yet," she said. "I told you, three weeks.
Minimum."

"I realize that," I said. "I was wondering if there might be some
basic information in the files here, like who the prosecutor was."

She got the bad persimmon look again.

She took the slip of paper. "Wait here," she said.

I promised I would.

After what could have been a lunch break, she came back with
my slip of paper and the news that the prosecutor on Vinnie's case
was Richard Palmieri. As an extra-added bonus, she also brought a
second name, Simon Donovan. He had been Vinnie's public
defender. Donovan's name meant nothing to me. But Palmieri's did.

"*The* Richard Palmieri?" I said. He was the hot-shot civil attorney
who got the multi-million-dollar judgment for the convicted rapist-
murderer whose guilt was cast into doubt by one of my Someday File
columns.

She shrugged. Apparently she didn't know *the* Richard Palmieri.

I found Palmieri's number in my phone's contact list. When I got
to the street, I made the call. The receptionist put me through to
Palmieri's secretary. I told her I wanted to talk to her boss about the
Vinnie Colangelo trial. She had no idea what I was talking about.

"It's an old case of his," I said. "Back in the 70s, when he worked in
the U.S. Attorney's office. I have a couple of questions for a column
I'm thinking of writing."

"Mr. Palmieri's schedule is full, and he doesn't talk to the media,"
she said.

"What could it hurt to talk about a case that's forty years old?" I said.

She took my office and cell phone numbers and said she would check with Mr. Palmieri. I wouldn't have bet my mortgage on a call back.

I sat down on the courthouse steps to think.

I had nothing better to do.

"WELL, well. I'm glad to see the press sittin' down on the job in public, since I've always suspected it's all you ever do in private. How ya doin', Deuce?"

I knew the voice and smiled. Chicago Alderman Tony Estrada was one of the good guys, and one of the funniest pols I knew. I lived in his district, and I felt fortunate to have him representing me. His delivery was as low-key as Steven Wright's and his observations worthy of Yogi Berra. He once voted against spending several million dollars on solar-powered parking meters with the argument, "What are we supposed to do in the winter, when a string of blizzards comes through, and it's cloudy for weeks on end? We'll lose thousands of dollars in parking revenue when the meters run outta juice."

Tony was aware nobody would be coming downtown to park in the middle of a string of blizzards because the city would be shut down, but his point was well taken. Why spend a fortune to put in a high-tech system when the old mechanical system worked well? Then a former mayor privatized the city's parking, and the whole system went to hell anyway, in a hellishly expensive hand basket.

Tony also had a legendary temper. When another alderman made an idiotic speech against one of Tony's pet literacy projects, Tony told him, "When you die, they're gonna give you an enema and bury you inna matchbox."

"This seat taken?" he said, indicating the step.

"Help yourself, Alderman," I said as we shook hands. I was glad for the company. If nothing else, I could depend on Tony for a column idea. He always had some political news to share, and today proved no exception.

"You hear that Bobby Boldock's runnin' for mayor?" he said.

I hadn't.

"He spent one term on the City Council," I said. "How's he qualified to be mayor?"

"I didn't say he's qualified, I said he's runnin'."

"How's he figure he has a chance?" I said.

"Daddy's money," Tony said. "Daddy wants him to be mayor, and Daddy's willing to buy him the office. Thinks it might help his own plans for West Side redevelopment."

I snorted. "Please tell me the voters aren't that dumb."

"Never underestimate the gullibility of the voters," Tony said. He poked me in the upper arm with his elbow. "So how you doin'? And what are you doin' leaving your butt marks, cute as they are, all over my courthouse steps?"

"Feeling frustrated," I said. "I think I'm onto something interesting, but every time I get close to real information, it skitters away from me."

"Yeah, you sound kind of whiny today," he said. "Anything I can help with, in a constituent service sort of way?"

"I doubt it," I said. "It involves a federal trial forty years ago, something Richard Palmieri handled before he opened his civil practice."

"Before he got rich as the Roman Catholic Church, you mean?" Tony said.

"Yeah, that, too."

"You talk to Richard?"

"I called his office. I'm not holding my breath."

"He's something of an ass, but I know him. Maybe I could grease the skids."

I appreciated Tony's offer, and I told him so.

"I'd rather get to him on my own," I said. "If I accepted a favor from you, then I'd have to bury the story about the million bucks you embezzled from the city."

"It was five million," Tony said. "You think I'm a *cheap* crook?"

That was funny, coming from a Chicago pol who wouldn't steal a potato if his children were starving.

I had a sudden thought.

"You've lived in Chicago forever, haven't you?"

"South Side since I was five," he said. "Back of the Yards, then Pill Hill, now Pilsen."

"Who was the U.S. attorney back in seventy-four?"

"Don't even have to think about it," he said. "Seventy-four was right in the middle of the reign of St. John the Divine."

I should have remembered that myself.

"Now Congressman John Conti," I said. My mind whipped to Las Vegas, to a colleague of Conti's lying in a morgue.

"Yeah," Tony said. "He's a pretty good guy. Works hard. Twenty-two years in Washington and he shows no sign of slowin' down, even though he ain't getting' any younger. Not much of an original thinker, though. Never in twenty-two years introduced a successful piece of major legislation. He gets re-elected by payin' attention to constituent service. He's got the triad down pat." Tony counted them out on his fingers. "One, don't steal public money. Two, get lots of pork for the district. Three, work hard for your peeps."

I knew that already. When I was growing up, the Contis were our neighbors on West Jackson Boulevard. My father and John were friends. John and I still talked now and then.

"I think John knows his limitations," I said. "He does what he can. Do you have information to the contrary?"

"If you mean, do I have any suspicion he's crooked, the answer's no. He's been seen a few times with connected guys. But in this town, if you're Italian, Irish or Latino, it's hard to avoid. I've sat down with a few bad boys now and then, and I'm always pleasant to 'em. It doesn't mean I'm takin' their money or applyin' any grease for them. And neither does John. He's a man with a lot of ambition. He came up in migrant camps, worse poverty than me. And he's doin' okay for himself. That doesn't make him a bad person, or a dishonest one."

It didn't. It made him a pretty good person. Despite a hard start, he'd made an admirable success of his life.

I changed the subject. "Did you hear about the murder in Cicero yesterday?"

"Which one?" Tony said, and laughed. "Yeah, I saw it on the news last night, and the papers had short stories today. Everybody danced around specifics, but it sounded brutal."

"If you hear any buzz about it, would you let me know?"

"Sure. You want to tell me why?"

"I can't."

Tony didn't press me. "Got your number on my desk," was all he said.

WHEN I GOT to the office, I knew I had to talk to Eric Ryland. But I also knew he would start walking the story uphill to the managing editor and the executive editor. I decided to write my column first.

So I talked to Bobby Boldock. He confirmed the mayoral bid Tony had mentioned. I chatted up some party officials and a couple of political consultants and got a fair column out of it. Nobody thought Boldock should run, except Boldock, and nobody thought he could win, except Boldock. He wouldn't like my take on his candidacy, but I didn't care. I had filled my allotted space with information that readers needed to know.

I stood up with the intention of going for coffee to fortify me against the gauntlet of editors I was about to run. My phone rang. I presumed it was someone I'd called about the Boldock column. I was surprised when a sultry voice asked me to hold for Richard Palmieri.

"How can I help you, Miss Mora?" the lawyer said. No preliminaries.

"Do you remember me?" I said.

"The DNA case," he said. "Yes."

"I wonder if you remember a case you prosecuted back in the seventies," I said. "Seventy-four to be specific. A minor hood named Vincent Colangelo was charged with the theft of a truck load of Scotch from a warehouse on the Port."

"Only vaguely," Palmieri said. "That was a hell of a long time ago. I seem to recall I convicted him."

"You did," I said.

"I don't remember much else," he said. "The case wasn't anything remarkable."

"Well, it's been a while," I said. "I'd like to make an appointment to come by and see you about it. Maybe if we talk the details will come back."

"How could it possibly be important now?" he said.

"That's what I'm trying to find out," I said.

"Let me put my secretary on," he said. "If she can find the time, it's yours. Though I think it will be a waste for both of us."

Palmieri's secretary found the time, all fifteen minutes of it, at three the following afternoon. Perhaps between now and then I could come up with some intelligent questions.

I turned to the wires and read an update on the assassination in Las Vegas. There wasn't much new. The dead guard had been identified. Apparently, he was a man with pony habit who succumbed to the lure of easy money offered by a killer who needed an accomplice with keys to Excalibur's roof. No one had a clue who pulled the trigger. No one had a clue what the motive might have been for the shooting. Everything else was background on the congressman, none of it relevant.

I looked for Sully to ask if he'd reached his friend from Congressman Reading's office, but he was out.

I got my coffee and asked Eric for a meeting. We used his private office. While I didn't like Eric much, I trusted him most of the time, the recent dust-up over my gun-control column notwithstanding. He wasn't born into the business as an editor. He'd spent quite a few years being a reporter first, and he was sympathetic to our peculiar problems and points of view—as long as they didn't conflict with his own self-interest. He was, after all, an ambitious man. I couldn't fault him for that.

I started by telling him I had the most amazing story he would hear all day.

"Better," he said, "than the one about the idiot bank robber in Lincoln Park? He didn't get as much as he hoped from the teller, and when she told him she could mail him some additional cash at the end of the day, he gave her his address. Better than that?"

It was the last time Eric said anything until I finished. Then he scrubbed his hands over his face a couple of times, as if staring at me for half an hour had left his head numb.

"So Colangelo wouldn't talk to you in the bar," he said. "He told you to leave him alone. He was so drunk you were concerned for his safety and drove him the four blocks to his house. Do I have all that right?"

"Yes," I said.

"If he was so reticent and frightened, why would he mention Las Vegas? You'd taken him home. Why didn't he go inside, pass out, and forget he ever laid eyes on you?"

"Don't know," I said. "I'm sure he knew I didn't have a high opinion of him, that I considered him a pickled ex-con and a waste of my time. I think maybe he wanted respect. He'd lost everything else important to him. In his drunken state, maybe he figured I'd think better of him if he gave me this crazy tip that would turn out to be true."

Eric shook his head.

"He was afraid to tell you about his arrest forty years ago, but he wasn't afraid to tip you off to an assassination the next day? That doesn't track."

"He was drunk, Eric. Alcohol doesn't help the cognitive process. I imagine he thought since we were alone in my car the tip wouldn't come back to bite him. What he didn't realize—what I didn't realize —was being seen leaving the bar with me raised suspicions among people who wanted him to die with his secret, whatever it was."

"And Jerry Alvarez takes this seriously?"

"He thinks there's something going on."

Eric sighed deeply. "I have all kinds of conflicting thoughts," he said. "If this is a freakish happenstance, it's best left forgotten. On the other hand, it's almost too much of a coincidence to dismiss out of hand. But if I let you pursue it—which is not a given—it is likely to put you in harm's way. How do we mitigate that?"

I shook my head. "I think it's too early to worry about it."

Eric put up two hands to stop me. "No, it's not. The only other choice is turning this over to the FBI and letting them deal. It's their job."

"They won't pursue it," I said. "We don't have enough substance to offer them. And I'm not ready to give up the story. So how about just giving me the green light to move forward and worry about the other stuff later, if we have to?"

"Not an option," he said.

~

WHILE ERIC TOOK the story up the chain of command, I started a search for information on liquor importing with two local attorneys who specialized in maritime law.

While Lake Michigan lies entirely within U.S. borders, it's connected to the Atlantic Ocean by Lakes Huron, Erie, and Ontario, and by the St. Lawrence River and Seaway, all of which lie in whole or in part in Canada. The Chicago River, the Ship Canal, and the Illinois and Mississippi Rivers connect the city to the Gulf of Mexico. Matters of international waters and shipping, therefore, are not unknown in Chicago. But the lawyers were no help and referred me to the feds. I called Alcohol, Tobacco and Firearms. I got through to the regional general counsel. She was quite pleasant.

"It's complicated," she said. "ATF makes sure liquor importers have the proper licenses and pay the duties. The paperwork, that's Customs, and I don't know what their documents are. Our regulations simply say that all applicable Customs requirements shall be met. We don't go beyond that."

"So it's not just a matter of somebody signing for the shipment?"

"Oh, my, no. You've got all sorts of complicating factors, like free-trade zones and foreign trade zones. There are times when a shipment of something is sitting on a dock, on U.S. soil, but from a legal standpoint it might as well be floating 500 miles out to sea. When a shipment clears Customs, chances are the people who bought the goods aren't the ones who take initial possession. There are companies that act as middlemen. They're called freight forwarders and customs house brokers."

"And stealing a truckload of Scotch wouldn't necessarily be a federal crime?"

"Stealing it, no, not necessarily," she said. "But selling it untaxed would be."

My head hurt. Since misery loves company, I called Customs. I couldn't find anybody to answer my questions, and I understood why. If there's a list of overworked, understaffed federal agencies, Customs has to be right up there near the top. The personnel were spread too thin, especially in the tedious climate of anticipated terrorism. I left a message.

Temporarily stymied on that front, I called Chicago Police Department headquarters, got through to Sgt. Pete Rizzo, one of its press spokesmen, and asked to see Vinnie's criminal record. His entire adult rap sheet would be public information. Only juvenile records were sealed. Rizzo said he'd see if they had anything and get back with me within the hour. He was as good as his word.

"Couldja come over?" Rizzo asked me over the phone. "We got the electronic file queued up, but if you want hard copy, I'll have to print it out and fax it. File's pretty big."

If I sat down in front of the police computer, I could pick and choose the pages I wanted. I told Pete I'd be there shortly.

I discovered the charges growing out of the liquor theft were the most serious leveled at Vinnie throughout his criminal career. The rest consisted of grand theft/auto, grand larceny, burglary, and a couple of B&Es dating back to 1961. Nothing violent. Pretty much what I'd expect from a small-time mug.

I did the math. Vinnie was seventy-eight when he died, so twenty-five in 1961, the date of his first arrest. There was nothing on his sheet between the ages of eighteen and twenty-five. Why did he wait that long to take a criminal turn? Or had he been lucky and eluded detection in his younger years?

"Does this guy have a juvie record?" I asked Rizzo.

Rizzo was a police spokesman because the department refused to let him to return to the street after he almost lost his life out there. He had pulled over a kid for speeding and reckless driving on Congress Parkway. While he was writing the citation, a passing gangbanger in a truck rammed him. Broke both his legs and crushed his pelvis. He nearly bled to death on the side of the road.

Rizzo went through three years of surgeries and rehab and claimed he was good as new. The department told him if he wanted to stay on, he'd have to drive a desk.

I was certain Rizzo hated it, but I never heard him complain, and as a desk-driver, he was one of the best around.

"You want his juvie record?" Rizzo asked me. "You know it's sealed."

"I know, but you're allowed to tell me if it exists."

He thought about that for a beat.

"Yeah, I am," he said. "Be right back."

He returned several minutes later. If Vincent Colangelo had committed any crimes before his eighteenth birthday, they had been adjudicated outside the city of Chicago.

Rizzo looked at me through half-closed eyes with an expression of feigned disbelief.

"You're gonna ask me to check the sheriff and state police databases, aren't you?"

I shrugged. "It's two phone calls. It would save time while I copy some of this file."

"I expect a big tip at Christmas," Rizzo said, right before he slammed the door.

I turned back to the computer and started copying all the records on Vinnie's arrest for the liquor theft. While the file was printing I scanned parts of it and found something interesting. Vinnie had been charged by the state immediately after his arrest. It became a federal case later. During the time the state had the case, Vinnie's defense counsel was Charles Haight. I'd heard of Haight.

Rizzo returned. "Sheriff's office, state cops got nothin' on any Colangelo with a DOB that would make him seventy to eighty years old. No record at all, adult or juvie."

That struck me as odd. Either Vinnie had engaged in criminal activity only within the confines of Chicago, or he moved here as an adult from somewhere else.

"Could we check the national crime computers?" I said.

"NCIC ain't for civilians."

"You're not a civilian."

"You want me to access federal records like I'm askin' for the department and then give you the data? Are you nuts, or you got another job lined up for me?"

"It was worth a shot," I said.

"You know better," he said.

I nodded and shifted focus back to the file in front of me.

"Who's Charles Haight?" I said. "I know he's a lawyer. Isn't he linked to the Outfit?

"Oh, yeah," Rizzo said. "He's tied in goin' way back. He pulled out a chair and straddled it with his arms folded across the back. "Why're you askin'?"

"Well, originally, the state charged Vinnie with the liquor theft, and it says here Haight represented him. After the feds re-indicted him, he was represented by a public defender, someone named Simon Donovan. Why didn't Haight continue to represent Vinnie when the feds took the case?"

"Don't know," Rizzo said. "Haight practiced in state court, federal court, hell, maybe even traffic and family court. He's represented all the punks at one time or another. Jurisdiction's never mattered to him, long as he got paid."

"What's his story?" I said.

"You'll have to check me on the details, but as I recall Haight came up here from Tampa, where he was an understudy to Frank Ragano." That was a name I knew well. Ragano had been joined at the hip to Santo Trafficante Jr., the head of the Tampa mob for three decades.

"Ragano was Jimmy Hoffa's lawyer, too, wasn't he?" I said.

"So I've heard," Rizzo said. "You read a lot of books on the Organization?"

"Yeah," I said. "In Chicago, that's what we call history."

Rizzo smiled. "Anyhow, Haight was like Ragano's son, and down in Florida he picked up the crumb cases Frank didn't want or didn't have time for. When Haight got some experience under his belt, he came north—Cicero first, then Chicago. At that point, he'da had no time for a minor player like Vinnie Colangelo."

"But he did. He represented Vinnie on the state charge. So now we have two questions: Why was Vinnie important enough for Haight to represent him at any point? And why didn't he represent Vinnie when the case went federal?"

"Good questions," Rizzo said. "I haven't got a clue."

Neither had I.

I GOOGLED Haight and found nothing useful. I found no telephone listing for him in Chicago or any of its affluent suburbs. So I called the magicians who do data-base research for the *Journal* news staff. My favorite researcher, Lucia Sandoval, answered my call. Lucy, in her mid-forties, was a whiz with databases and search engines. She could find out anything. She verified that Haight had no property in Chicago, at least none in his name. He had owned a condo on Lake Shore Drive in the heart of the Gold Coast, but he sold it for $2.65-million in 1987. That was a lot of money in 1987. It was a lot of money now.

These days, Florida DMV records had him at an address in Key Biscayne, down in Miami. Another nice neighborhood. The mob lawyer had retired.

But he wasn't retired in 1974. Either he hadn't been able to get involved with Vinnie's federal charges, or he hadn't wanted to.

On a whim I asked Lucy to check the Lexis-Nexis database for Vincent Colangelo's name in any newspaper articles from anywhere in the country going back as far as the database would reach. I wasn't surprised when she came up empty. Vinnie, it seemed, hadn't been arrested for anything before his twenty-fifth year.

I resisted the urge to call Haight. The sort of questions I had required a face-to-face meeting, preferably as a surprise to him. I would have to go to Miami for a day if my editors would cough up the money for airfare, but I wanted to get all the information I could on Haight's involvement with Vinnie before I asked to make the trip.

7

M y muscles told me it had been too many days since I last exercised, so I stopped at the gym on my way home. I got my gym bag from the back of the Explorer and changed in the locker room. My cell phone rang as I was putting on my shoes.

"It's Rizzo," the police spokesman said. "There's no record of your guy on any police blotter in the country going all the way back."

"You checked the NCIC?" I said. "I thought you couldn't do that."

"I said I couldn't ask the feds. Other people have access. I pulled in a favor."

"And there's no Vincent Colangelo anywhere?"

"None that fits a guy in his seventies."

"I owe you, Pete," I said. "Thank you."

MY FAVORITE PERSONAL TRAINER, Kaylee Shearson, greeted me when I came out of the locker room. Kaylee was one of those women that all the other women in the gym wanted to look like and never would. Not grotesque, like the people who go after bodybuilding titles. Not like the 'roid junkies who want to see how big they can get. Kaylee had sculpted herself using only diet and exercise.

"Hey, Rat, haven't seen you around in a few days," she said. The nickname dated back to my first few months at this gym. I'd been on a mission then that went beyond fitness. I wanted a body like Kaylee's. I worked out every day, whenever I could find a couple of hours, regardless of the time. Kaylee started calling me a gym rat. Even after I got realistic and stopped lusting after serious muscle defi-nition, the nickname stuck.

"You're getting flabby, girl," I said. "What'd you do, eat a jelly bean?"

"Funny," she said. I was joking, and she knew I was joking, but she couldn't help a quick glance at the wall mirror to make sure she hadn't added an unwanted ounce somewhere. "Where've you been?"

"Work," I said. "Gets in the way sometimes."

"You runnin' today?"

"Yeah, then some free weights if I've got any strength left," I said.

"I don't have a book for a couple of hours," she said. "When you get off the treadmill, flag me. I'll spot for you."

I RAN five miles in 39:30, a little under eight minutes a mile. Not bad, though I had to sprint at the end to make five miles in less than forty minutes. I refilled my water bottle, drank it, filled it again and went looking for Kaylee. I found her among the free weights.

"You ready, Rat?" she said.

I was still breathing hard, but I could feel it coming easier. "Ready."

"Let's stick to core work and upper body," Kaylee said. "Your legs have had enough."

I was in the middle of my third set of shoulder presses when the gym's most successful customer walked in. His name was Herbie Taylor, a common name for an uncommon man. Over the course of two years, Herbie went from a 343-pound couch potato to a body more resembling vintage Schwarzenegger. His chest was so large he couldn't bring his arms to his sides.

"He just signed with the WWF," Kaylee told me.

"The World Wildlife Fund?" I said, straining under some serious weight.

"No, goof, the World Wrestling Federation, or whatever they call it now. If he scores with the fans, he'll retire a rich man before he's forty."

"A professional wrestler named Herbie?" I said and couldn't help but smile.

"Not when he hits the ring. They'll give him some moniker, like Doctor Doom."

A synapse flashed. "Change his name?"

Had Vincent Colangelo been born in 1961, at the age of twenty-five? Had Vinnie been somebody else before that? While it would explain a lot, it also would double my list of questions, including, at the top of the list, who had Vinnie been before 1961?

I wondered if the medical examiner had run his fingerprints.

I lost concentration for a few seconds and squeezed out the final lift with Kaylee tapping encouragement under my elbows. I grabbed my towel and dried off as best I could, fascinated by my new idea and eager to talk to Jerry Alvarez. He was the only one I knew with the clout to influence somebody to run Vinnie's fingerprints through all the identification databases before they put him in the ground.

The sight of Herbie doing leg presses distracted me for a moment. I'd never seen anybody move that much weight.

"Tell me the truth, Kaylee," I said. "Would you ask him out?"

"He's not my type," she said.

"Ah, he scares you. Well, he doesn't scare me. I could ask him out."

"He wouldn't go out with you," Kaylee said.

"Why? What's wrong with me?"

"Nothing's wrong with either one of you," she said.

"Then why wouldn't Herbie go out with me?"

"He came out a couple of years ago. I figured you knew."

"Ah," I said again. "So if I wanted to date him, I'd have to pretend to be a gay man."

"Think you could handle that?"

"Probably too much of a stretch," I said.

As soon as I returned to the locker room I called Jerry at home. I told him about my hunch that Vinnie wasn't who he said he was.

"You think his body's still at the morgue?" I said.

"Possibly," he said. "They usually hold onto a body for a while, in case there's any next-of-kin to claim it."

"Can someone ask the medical examiner to take fingerprints?"

"*No puedo.* I got no jurisdiction in the case," he said.

"But you know the lead detective, Juan Ramales, and you could ask him."

"You ask him. I told you I wouldn't help you."

"Let's say I'm going to write a feature on Vinnie so maybe his family will claim his body," I said. "Nothing more than that."

"Ramales is gonna ask why I care."

"Couldn't you tell him you're reviewing an old federal prosecution?"

"I guess I could do that. But what good will fingerprints do you, Deuce? If this Colangelo had no record before he was twenty-five, no one will have taken his prints before then, after he already changed his identity. You should go for DNA. At least you'd be able to link him to a blood relative, if you find one."

"Will you ask Ramales to get DNA?"

"Yeah, okay. *Christo,* Deuce. Remind me never to give you a tip again."

8

T he next morning I decided to attack the investigation
through a back door. The door's name was Simon Donovan, the man who took over as Vinnie's public defender
when the case moved from state to federal court. Maybe he knew
Vinnie's real identity. Maybe he knew why Charles Haight had quit
Vinnie's defense.

I checked for Donovan in every phone book and on-line directory
I could think of. He wasn't listed. I checked a database of Illinois
lawyers. Again, a blank. I went to the Martindale-Hubbell legal directory online and found one Simon Donovan, who had been admitted
to the Oregon Bar a year earlier at the age of 27. Finally I found the
man I was looking for, in an obituary in the *Journal*'s electronic
morgue. He'd been killed in a courthouse shootout in 1981.

The Public Defender's Office told me cases from the 70s, such as
Vinnie's, would be in their microfiche files. But because they involved
a client, the clerk wasn't sure they could be released. I pleaded that
Vinnie's death and time should mitigate privilege. She said she would
ask. Apparently she did a good job of arguing my point, because I was
cleared for a look and told I could come at my convenience, which
happened to be immediately.

A helpful young woman found the right spool of film and showed me how to thread the machine and make copies at a cost of fifty cents a page. I hadn't sat in front of a fiche reader for years, but I was soon buzzing my way toward the Colangelo file.

It was slow going. Donovan's reports were detailed and meticulous. They started with his assignment to Vinnie's case. He mentioned he was replacing a private attorney who had petitioned the court to withdraw after Vinnie was reindicted by the U.S. government. He didn't speculate about why Haight wanted to leave or why the feds cared about the case. The first interesting item was his account of his initial attorney-client meeting with Vinnie.

"Mr. Colangelo claims to have seen documents in the truck showing the shipment had been signed off to an agent for Binny's Beverage Depot stores," Donovan wrote. "If true, that would mean the Laphroaig had moved into local commerce. Resulting grand theft charges would be at the behest of the state and out of federal jurisdiction. Will check."

I was about to go on to the next page when a hand-written note in the margin caught my eye. "Ransom Camp." It was underlined three times. A place? A name? I had no idea. I would look for an explanation as I plowed my way through the file.

In his next report, Donovan said he had asked prosecutors about the legal status of the Scotch, and they showed him the paperwork file.

"The file ends before the shipment was signed off to Binny's agents," Donovan wrote. "There is nothing to verify Mr. Colangelo's story. However, I have ascertained that Binny's is the correct identity of the purchaser. Makes me wonder how Mr. Colangelo knew that if he hadn't seen the shipment paperwork as claimed."

So what knocked down Vinnie's story was not the presence of evidence but the absence of it. The file put into evidence by prosecutors lacked the paperwork Vinnie claimed he saw. Could someone have destroyed the material? What sort of conspiracy would that have involved? How dangerous would it have been to destroy evidence by tampering with Customs documents?

And what dark motive could justify such a risk?

Donovan's next report outlined the proposal for a plea deal he presented to Richard Palmieri, the federal prosecutor. Palmieri flatly refused to consider it.

"I find this hard to explain," Donovan wrote. "Colangelo doesn't deny his role in the theft, so why would Mr. Palmieri waste the time and expense to take the matter to trial? And why is Mr. Palmieri handling this case? He is the chief assistant U.S. attorney. It is the sort of matter that normally would be shuffled to a junior prosecutor."

Then I found a personal note to the file from Donovan:

"If Mr. Colangelo had the money to hire Charles Haight when this was a state case, why couldn't he afford another private attorney after Mr. Haight withdrew?"

The only answer I could imagine was that Vinnie couldn't afford *any* private counsel. Someone else paid Haight's bill in the early days and decided to stop, leaving Vinnie begging. Perhaps somebody didn't want Vinnie to have the best defense, after all. Perhaps someone wanted him at the mercy of an overworked, underpaid public defender. In this scenario, someone wanted Vinnie to go far away for a long, long time and seized the opportunity to make it happen.

So maybe it wasn't about the liquor theft. Maybe it was about Vinnie himself.

I finished the file and nowhere in it did I find a repetition of the Ransom Camp note or any explanation for it.

The way Simon Donovan died raised red flags for me, too.

The shooting happened seven years after Vinnie's trial, so perhaps there was no connection. Or perhaps Donovan became as obsessive about Vinnie's case as I had become and asked too many questions over too many years. I was told there was no one left in the PD's office whose career overlapped Donovan's, who might have known if he pursued a Colangelo investigation beyond Vinnie's trial. All institutional knowledge was gone.

But several people remembered the shooting at the courthouse. A defendant charged with armed robbery grabbed a cop's gun and shot at anyone who tried to approach him. Simon Donovan had been waiting in the hallway for a case to be called and became one of the six victims.

However, witnesses said Donovan had not tried to approach the shooter; he didn't move an inch off his seat. Yet he died, anyway. If he didn't threaten the shooter, why was he killed? Was he the actual target and all the others simply cover?

Was I becoming paranoid?

At least I had questions to ask Richard Palmieri, and they'd probably get me thrown out of his office in a most unceremonious manner.

I HADN'T BEEN EATING RIGHT, so I took time to get a fruit-and-vegetable smoothie with a whey protein boost at a health food store and appeared at Palmieri's office a few minutes early. His receptionist sat at a large table, its open front displaying her gorgeous legs to every visitor who walked through the door. I wondered if she knew she had been put on display. How could she not? I wondered if she cared. I didn't appreciate it, but then it was none of my business.

She drew her legs back as soon as she got a look at me. Apparently she had been expecting a man, a notion she confirmed when I gave her my name.

"That's an unusual name for a woman," she said.

"It's an unusual name for anyone," I said.

She announced me to a secretary. Yet again, I was told to wait. I was getting very good at waiting.

Instead of flipping through magazines—I already knew enough about spear fishing for Florida cobia—I took a tour of the waiting area. Palmieri's outer office had been designed to impress potential clients and opposing counsel alike. Every surface was covered with gleaming wood. I could tell it was expensive. I thought it might have been oak. Solid oak. No veneer for this lawyer.

The walls were lined with framed newspaper pages proclaiming

Palmieri's memorable court victories. I looked for one in particular and found it, the judgment of $5.7-million against Cook County for the mishandling of DNA evidence that sent an innocent man to prison for eleven years for a rape-murder he didn't commit, the case based on my column. Like Vinnie, Michael Kennedy wanted payback for his wasted time.

I knew Palmieri took his cases for a contingency fee, as do most personal injury lawyers. He only got paid if he won. With judgments this high, he could afford the risk.

"That was some of my best work," said a deep voice behind me.

"And I believe it was based on some of my best work," I said.

I turned to find an imposing man who stood three or four inches over six feet. He wore a million-dollar tan under a $90 haircut and a custom-tailored suit that cost more than I made in a month. He had his hands on his hips, pushing back the suit jacket. His dress shirt had his initials stitched beneath the left rib cage. He wore French cuffs stapled with jewelry that would have blinded me had it caught the light just right. He had to be in his late 60s, but he could have passed for ten years younger without anyone questioning him. His hair was full, his skin tight, and his blue eyes sparkled.

He extended a hand on which the nails had been manicured and buffed.

"Richard Palmieri," he said. "And I finally get to meet the famous Deuce Mora in person. Interesting name."

"Some people think so," I said. "It's mostly a pain in the ass."

"As a result of that case," he nodded at the newspaper page, "I read your column now." I started to say thank you when he smiled and added, "Occasionally."

I realized he had calculated the remark to put me off balance. It's what lawyers do. He led me back to his private office and pointed me toward a sofa. He went around to the leather chair behind his expansive desk. The sofa looked comfortable, the kind you sink into. If I sat in it, Palmieri's head would tower eight or ten inches above mine, an alpha position. I took one of the chairs in front of the desk, instead.

He flashed a smile of acknowledgment.

"What's so important about this old case?" he said.

"I'm trying to figure out why it was prosecuted in federal court. The defendant says he saw paperwork proving the Scotch had moved into domestic commerce, which would make the crime a state charge of grand theft, or something."

"The defendant was wrong," Palmieri replied.

"How can you be so certain after forty years?" I said. "You told me on the phone the details of this case were hazy."

"That was yesterday," he said. "I've since had a chance to refresh my memory."

"How?" I said.

He shrugged. "I asked other people who were around then and pieced it together."

"That's a lot of time to spend on a reporter's question."

"I wanted to be able to give you a definitive answer."

"I've done some checking, too," I said. "You were chief assistant U.S. attorney then."

"I was."

"So why did you try this? Why not hand it off to a junior prosecutor? It hardly seems a big enough deal to warrant your personal attention."

"Are you baiting me, Ms. Mora?" he said. "I'm not easy to anger, but I might have to stop reading your column."

"I'm only trying to find out what happened and why."

"I've told you all I know."

I went for it all, the consequences be damned.

"I don't think so," I said. "Why did you take this case to trial? The defendant admitted his guilt and wanted a plea bargain. In the scheme of things, it was a nothing case. No one hurt. No insurance loss. Nothing. It almost feels as though you went out of your way to make sure he got all the hard time you could pile on and served it as far away from Chicago as you could convince the Bureau of Prisons to send him."

"I believe we're finished here," he said, rising from his chair.

I sat still.

"John Conti was the boss of the office back then, wasn't he?"
I said.

"Yes." He continued to stand.

"Did you ask him for the Colangelo case?"

"Not that I recall."

"Did he ask you to take it?"

"I don't think so."

"Did he order you to take it to trial instead of pleading it out?"

"No, he wouldn't have interfered once I'd taken over the case."

Palmieri's hands fisted and relaxed and repeated, a sign of a fight
to maintain control.

"So it was your decision?"

"What?"

"To take it to trial."

"I imagine so."

"He was aware of the case, wasn't he?"

"Nothing happened in the office that escaped John's attention."

"And he never asked you why you were spending your valuable
time on it?"

"I pretty much had free rein," he said. "I took the cases I
wanted."

"Why did you want Vinnie Colangelo's case?"

"I honestly don't remember, Ms. Mora. It could have been something as simple as the office getting overloaded with cases so everybody chipped in to get the volume under control. That happened
from time to time. It was no big deal. When we got inundated, John
helped out, too. Everybody did." His eyes flashed now with unbridled
annoyance.

"See, that's what I don't understand," I said. "Think of all the time
you could have saved by letting him plead out."

I could see I had pushed too hard. Palmieri's fury flushed his face.
I had time for one more question before he threw me out.

"Did you have some special reason to go after Mr. Colangelo? Was
there something more than a truck hijacking? Was there something
special about Vinnie?"

"We're through, Ms. Mora," he said, his voice flat. "I'm sure you can find your way out."

I could, and I did, thinking Richard Palmieri definitely was hiding something.

∾

I WALKED BACK to my office through a rush hour just reaching its peak. I hauled out my iPod, slipped in the ear buds, found Mark Knopfler's album, *Sailing to Philadelphia*, and tried to lose myself in the melodies and guitar riffs.

When I got back to the *Journal* building it was almost six, and I couldn't think of a reason in the world to go back to my desk. So I collected my car and decided to take a spin up Lake Shore Drive, always a spectacular sight as the sun began to set. The slow traffic would give me ample opportunity to enjoy the views and try to make sense of my day.

I worked my way south on Michigan Avenue to Roosevelt Road and turned east, skirting the south end of Grant Park, then north on Lake Shore Drive, what we in Chicago euphemistically call the LSD.

I was disappointed that the Buckingham Fountain was down for winterization. I hadn't seen it lit up in a while. But my disappointment was tempered when I looked up into the city skyline, lighted in an array of dazzling colors against a blue-gray evening sky. It was a diverse, historic, endlessly fascinating skyline that managed to be stunning without overwhelming the senses, as Manhattan can do. On the Navy Pier the enormous Ferris wheel—modeled on the original built for Chicago's 1893 World's Fair—blazed with pulsing white lights.

I drove through the S-curve that separated the lovely Oak Street Beach from the legendary Drake Hotel and on up to Fullerton Avenue. I got off the LSD there and on again in the southbound lanes. So far, my tour of the city had provided no insights. I couldn't make sense of the fact that the U.S. Attorney's office hadn't accepted a plea bargain from Vinnie Colangelo that would have made his undistinguished case go away.

I hoped some random thoughts would click for me on the way home. But I was distracted by what is, hands down, the best part of this drive. The view from the southbound side of the Outer Drive Bridge over the Chicago River is an unobstructed panorama right up the gut of the waterway, with its river walks and serene surface reflecting the illumination of the skyline towering above the river's banks.

I thought about how the flow of the river had been reversed in 1900, so instead of emptying the city's sewage and other waste into Lake Michigan, a series of locks turned the river flow to the west, where sewage and other waste was channeled into the Mississippi watershed. Good for Chicago's neighbors on the lake. For those living west of the city, not so much.

Now, with the sewage problem resolved through modern technology, there was talk of restoring the river to its natural flow.

That thought took me back to my conversation with Richard Palmieri. My gut told me he was trying to divert the truth about the Colangelo case, and somehow I had to turn the story around until it found its true course again. But I had no insights on how to do that.

I needed to talk to Sully and find out if he'd heard from his friend in Reading's office.

When I let myself in the front door, my cats, Caesar and Claudius, were waiting. So, it turned out, was somebody else who had opened every drawer, swept off every shelf, and left my stuff scattered all over the floor. At the last moment, I saw movement out of the corner of my eye and had just enough time to raise my arm and deflect the blow, so the bookend that connected with my skull didn't deliver a kill shot. Nonetheless it knocked me to my knees and started the room whirling.

As I tried to make the spinning stop, I saw the intruder turn toward my open front door. I dove at his knees. He went down hard on his chest. I heard an explosion of breath and figured I had a few seconds to inflict some damage of my own while he sucked air. I grabbed the bookend, a brass dog sitting on its haunches, and swung for the guy's head. Fair's fair, after all. He raised an arm in time to catch the blow on his elbow. He howled in pain at the same instant I heard something crack in the joint.

I raised the bookend to swing again, but he rolled over and caught me on the temple with his knee. I groped for a handhold on his belt, but he slid away and scrambled to his feet. I got a good look at him.

Swarthy. Five-ten or so. Built like a stevedore.

And running out my door.

Had I been able to find the coordination right then to reach for the wallet in my backpack, I would have bet five dollars he was the same guy who'd been at Jo-Jo's asking questions about Vinnie on the night Vinnie died.

I would have to call the police. But not right this minute.

Right this minute, I was going to lie on the floor and sleep for a while.

9

The sound of a telephone ringing and the sensation of Claudius massaging my face with his sandpaper tongue woke me sometime later. Caesar lurked nearby to assist as needed. I was nauseated, and I had a raging headache. I knew these were not good signs.

The front door stood open. I pushed myself to my knees and saw a pool of blood where my head had been. I crawled eight feet across the hardwood floor and pushed the door shut. A steady stream of blood droplets marked my path. I put my hand to the side of my forehead. It came away wet and red and sticky.

I managed to stand using a chair for support. As I staggered into the kitchen I heard someone talking to my answering machine. I held some wet paper towels to the gash, then checked my voice mail. There were two messages, both from Sully. He sounded worried.

I called 911 while I wrapped ice in a clean dishtowel. I went to the bathroom where I swallowed four extra-strength pain things. Then I called Sully and told him what had happened. I think he was running out of the office by the time we hung up. I heard sirens and then somebody began pounding on my front door. The peephole revealed paramedics and the Chicago police. I let them in and collapsed into my favorite oversized chair.

The police hung back while I got medical treatment, including some butterfly bandages on the cut.

"It's not too bad," one paramedic said. "A couple of stitches will fix it." She suggested I might have a concussion and urged twenty-four hours of observation at a hospital.

It was a good idea, and I knew that, but I didn't want to go. I wasn't trying to be tough. I simply didn't feel like getting out of the chair, and I sure as hell didn't want to be carted out on a gurney.

Sully arrived then with Eric, and both of them lectured me on the wisdom of going to the hospital. Sully knelt beside me and put a hand on my arm.

"A concussion isn't anything to mess with," he said. "I think you should go with them."

The paramedic asked if I had developed symptoms of concussion – headache, nausea, or vomiting, confusion or blurred vision. I told her I already had the first two, and if I got confused, how would I know?

That's how I found myself in the emergency room at Rush University Medical Center and, a few hours later, admitted to a private room arranged by Eric. As people came and went, I saw a police officer standing outside my door.

A detective named Herrero came in and took my statement. I asked him if I sounded confused. He said I didn't. I felt better.

He asked if I had noticed anything missing from my apartment. Nothing obvious occurred to me, but I couldn't be sure given the mess left by the intruder. And the fact I'd only had two seconds to look around before the guy came at me with a fist full of bronze.

He asked what the intruder might have been looking for, and I couldn't tell him because I didn't know. I assumed it had been about Vinnie, but I couldn't be certain. So I said nothing.

Herrero asked if I had any idea how the intruder got into the building. I told him you needed the front door code or a key to get in, or a resident had to buzz you in.

I gave Herrero the physical description. He asked if I could describe the assailant's face, and I did the best I could. I had a good image of him in my head, but I was finding it hard to put into words. Herrero asked if I would look at some mug books. He told me they could run my physical description of the assailant through a computer database and bring printouts to the hospital of those who matched. I agreed. It would be something to do.

When Herrero finished, Sully and Eric came in. A neighbor was looking after the cats, Sully told me, and the forensics people were dusting for prints. So far they had found one set, certain to be mine. Perhaps the intruder wore gloves. I didn't remember.

Eric stood back, finishing up a phone call. He snapped the phone shut, then sat in a chair next to my bed. I think Eric avoided an upgrade to a Smartphone because he liked the sound of finality and authority the clamshell model made when he closed it.

"You're getting protection," he said. "Starting as soon as you go home."

The phone on the nightstand began to ring. Jerry Alvarez had heard what happened and called to find out how I was. I assured him I wasn't confused.

"Is there someone who can spend the night with you?" he said.

"I think I noticed someone in uniform standing outside the room."

"Good. If you're up for some news, I just got off the phone with Juan Ramales."

"Is he willing to ask for Vinnie's fingerprints and DNA?"

"He was, yes, but *es demasiado de tarde*. It's too late."

Even through the fuzz in my head, I knew that was a bad sign.

"Somebody claimed the body," Jerry said. "Ramales was done with it. Family showed up. ME released the remains. But the good news is, bless his perverted little heart, the ME kept a DNA sample. It'll be in his fridge if you ever run down a possible relative."

"Excellent. Do we know who claimed the body? Can we find out?"

"No, and we'll run into privacy laws if we try. They asked not to be identified."

"I wonder if it was the long-lost wife," I said.

"Maybe, but I doubt it," Jerry said. "If she cared about him enough to claim the body, she wudda been in touch at some point before now, don'tcha think?"

"We've got to find whoever it was," I said.

"No, we don't," he said. "We need to get smart and let this go, Deuce. What happened tonight should tell you to back off. *Cuidate.* Take care of yourself."

My head was pounding. I wanted to sleep. But even more, I wanted information.

I turned to Sully. "What did Reading's chief of staff know?" I said.

"He thinks the murder could have been tied to a new organized crime investigation."

I groaned at the thought, then eased my head deeper into the pillow, trying to find a position that would give me some comfort.

"What new organized crime investigation? Does it involve Chicago?"

"Would almost have to," Sully said. "But even though Peter was Reading's chief of staff, he says Reading never discussed the new investigation with him. And now all the data's been seized by the FBI, including the contents of Reading's safe and his computers."

"Is there anything to tie Reading to Vinnie?" I said.

Sully shrugged. "Peter never heard of Vinnie. But that doesn't mean anything."

I turned my head and looked at Sully. "You know, if there is a tie to Chicago, you might have a piece of this story."

"Oh, no," Sully said. "Organized crime's not my thing, though a cynic might suggest that in Chicago, politics is a subset of the genre."

"You need to go to sleep now, Deuce," Eric said. "We'll check on you first thing tomorrow. I want you to take a couple of days off and rest."

Sully squeezed my shoulder.

"Call me if you need anything through the night," he said. "Anytime."

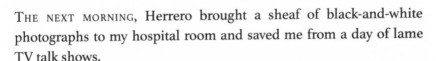

THE NEXT MORNING, Herrero brought a sheaf of black-and-white photographs to my hospital room and saved me from a day of lame TV talk shows.

"One of your neighbors let the intruder in," he told me. "The guy apparently called several units from the front door until someone answered. Said he was making a FedEx delivery, and they buzzed him in. There was no FedEx delivery to your building yesterday."

I looked through the photos. I found one thug who resembled the intruder, but he was too young by a decade. Since the picture had been taken only seven months earlier, it couldn't be the right guy. I apologized to Herrero and returned his printouts. He told me not to worry. They'd catch the guy sooner or later.

I rooted for sooner. What the hell was I doing messed up in something that had cost one man his life and might have taken mine but for a quick sidestep to avoid the shadow of something coming at me out of the dark?

Part of me, the conservative, cautious side, wanted to take seriously the warning written in Vinnie's blood. My instinct was to turn my back on the whole affair and hope there were no further ramifications. I could put on bravado for the world. But in the privacy of my own thoughts, I couldn't deny my id, that part of my personality where, according to Freud, "contrary impulses exist side by side, without cancelling each other out."

That was me, all right, a load of contrary impulses.

I was, at once, afraid, guilt-ridden, angry, and determined to get a full resolution for Vinnie. None of those impulses overwhelmed the others. Over all of this, my ego reigned. What would people think of me if I quit? One of the many neuroses I secretly share with other writers is the fear of being found cowardly or incompetent, or both.

The truth was, it didn't matter.

I wouldn't be able to face myself if I walked away. And walking away at this point wouldn't help keep the bad guys away from me if they really wanted me. That die was cast.

I laid back on the pillow and resolved to debate the issues more fully as soon as I'd taken a nap.

10

The assassin is growing weary of hearing Nicky Boy complain. He has no right. If he had done his job right, he would have been in and gone by the time the reporter got home, and the confrontation never would have happened. Now the fat fuck has elevated the profile of what should have been a simple burglary and shown his mug to a person trained to remember faces.

What if she goes to the police files? Will she be able to pick him out? Will they find and arrest him? And more important, if they do, will he give up everyone else?

The idiot! He needs a double-tap to the back of the head and a long bath at the bottom of Lake Michigan, preferably some place where voracious muskies feed.

The guy can't stop whimpering about his elbow and how it hurts like hell where the bitch hit him with a bookend. The assassin almost sides with the reporter. Hadn't she taken one to the skull with the same piece of brass? Good for her to have fought back. She should have opened up the imbecile's head for him.

The assassin's animus toward Nicky Boy has been growing since the night they killed the old man. It hadn't been necessary to torture him. The old drunk was helpless and whimpering. In the end, after he was burned *and cut up, he was crying so bad his nasal passages closed, and he would have suffocated if they hadn't taken the gag out of his mouth.*

So the old man's just getting his breath back when Nicky Boy climbs on the bed and opens his throat with a kitchen knife, after which the fat fuck has the gall to complain he's got the old guy's blood all over his pants.

He is definitely a piece of work. A dangerous piece of work. But the people calling the shots won't allow the assassin to take him out, and the assassin knows it. Too much history there. Too much family blood.

An accident, now that might be arranged. As long as there is no chance of discovery. A bad end for Nicky Boy with nobody to blame. A terrible, inexplicable tragedy.

The assassin smiles.

Nicky Boy will think it's out of sympathy for his pain.

The assassin walks to the window of his condominium in one of the Gold Coast's newer high rises. His building is a block back from the lakeshore, and he has windows and balconies overlooking both Lake Michigan and downtown Chicago. When he bought the place, he wanted something nice in a big building where no one would notice his comings and goings. But nothing so expensive it would call attention to the fact he had no apparent income. His street, mostly residential, is quiet, the way he likes to live between jobs.

But right this minute the assassin isn't enjoying it. They've been wait- ing, the assassin and Nicky Boy, for more than an hour for the boss to show up. The boss likes to keep people waiting. It's his power trip. But he's rarely this inconsiderate.

And then there is a soft knock at the front door.

The boss enters. His eyes take in everything. His head is turtled onto his shoulders, as if to protect him from danger. This posture causes his goatee to brush his collar with each pass.

He looks ridiculous.

His ample belly precedes him to the bar where he helps himself to a large bourbon without invitation or ice. This, too, is normal. He takes a healthy pull, then turns to the two waiting men. A drop of bourbon clings to the bottom of his mustache. Nobody tells him.

"What the fuck happened?" he says. His eyes are riveted on Nicky Boy.

"She came home before I got done," he says. "Couldn't help it, you know?"

"No, I don't fuckin' know," the boss says. "This is gonna make her more determined than ever. Fuck! What a fuckin' idiot move. She wasn't sposed to see you. She wasn't sposed to get hurt. You were sposed to be the fuck outta there when she got home. Take any fuckin' computers in the house, ransack the fuckin' place to make it look like a simple B&E, and get the fuck out. Shudda been a fifteen-minute job. You are such a fuck-up."

"What do you want to do?" the assassin says.

The boss tosses back the bourbon and winces as it burns its way through his esophagus.

"Stay fuckin' ready," he says and looks right at the assassin. "If it becomes necessary, we'll have to deal with her in a finalistic sorta way, if you get my meanin'."

11

I was released from the hospital on the morning of the third day with orders to rest. I went home and looked in a mirror. A square medical patch covered the stitches it took to close the gash at my hairline. A significant knot had formed beneath the bandage, but at least the doctors hadn't shaved my hair. On the other side, my head sported a compact bruise where the intruder's knee caught me as he scrambled to get out of my apartment. All in all, my face looked like a human train wreck.

My condo was equally messy. Someone had come in and cleaned up the blood, but the smudges of fingerprint dust remained everywhere. And my belongings were strewn about wherever the intruder tossed them. The cats dozed belly-up on the floor in the sun, burrowed into my underwear.

I took off the bandage and showered the blood out of my hair and the chemical hospital smell off my body. I swallowed three more extra-strength pain things. I was ready to deal with the office, although I had been furious the previous morning when I read the story of my assault in the online edition of the *Journal*. It would be in the print edition, too. I understood the paper had to publish something about the burglary, but the story was too long and too detailed.

I didn't like sharing my private life with readers. If the victim had been anybody else, the story would have been a tenth as long.

I ran a gauntlet of well-wishers on the way to my desk, and I no sooner sat down than Sully showed up with two cups of coffee.

"I thought you'd be at home resting?" he said, setting one cup on my desk.

"I'm planning to rest here," I said. "If you thought I'd be at home, why did you bring an extra coffee to the office?"

"Because I know you," he said.

"Thanks," I said. I took off the lid and sipped. It tasted good.

Sully smiled.

I didn't remember if I had told Sully and Eric about Jerry Alvarez's call to the hospital, about Vinnie's body being claimed by relatives, and the preservation of a DNA sample. Events of that night remained hazy. I asked Sully about it.

"We were right there when Jerry called," he said. "You really don't remember?"

I shook my head. I sipped coffee.

"You didn't happen to bring donuts, did you?" I said.

"You don't eat donuts, Deuce," Sully said.

"Oh, yeah, I guess I forgot that, too."

He looked concerned, and then he laughed. "Okay, maybe you don't remember telling us about the phone call. I'll buy that. But you do remember the relationship you have with fried circles of dough, right?"

"Something like that," I said with a smile. I couldn't digest donuts, and I hadn't forgotten. "I was thinking in the hospital, there has to be some record on Vinnie before nineteen-sixty-one."

"It's a long shot, but did you try Social Security?" Sully said.

I brightened. "You oughta be a reporter," I said.

"I am, but you probably forgot," he said, grinning. He laid a whisper of a kiss on my cheek. "I'm glad you're okay. I worry about you." And he walked away.

Lucy Sandoval, the ace data-base researcher, wasn't scheduled to start her shift until 10, so I tried to read the morning papers. I was a few minutes in when Eric Ryland walked up. He told me my protection would start that night, two armed private cops outside my condo from 6 p.m. to 8 a.m. I thanked him and tried to hide the fact that I felt relieved. Then I expressed dismay at the length and placement of the story about the attack on me.

"Come on, Deuce," he said. "There was a strong argument made to put it out on the front page instead of the Metro front. You're a public figure in this state. We don't ask permission from ordinary crime victims to put their stories in the paper. We're not going to treat you differently, and we're certainly not going to kill the story because it offends your sense of privacy."

He was right, and I needed a cooling-off period, so when I saw Lucy Sandoval appear behind her desk, I told Eric I needed to get a library search started.

"Okay," he said. "But if you start to get tired or start hurting, go home. You need rest."

As usual, Lucy greeted me with a big smile on her face.

"You okay?" she said with a hint of concern cracking her veneer of cheerfulness.

"Fine," I said. "Two nights in the hospital let me catch up on my sleep." I told her what I needed. There were no assignments waiting, so Lucy said she had plenty of time to check Vinnie's Social Security record.

I turned away and then turned back. "Would you check one other thing? I have no idea what it means, but see if you get any hits on the words, 'Ransom Camp.' It might be a place or a person or a state of mind. For all I know, it was Vinnie's favorite brand of canned peas." To me it sounded like a monumental request.

"Ooh," she said. "A mystery. Cool. I'm on it. I'll get back to you."

She came over and sat on a corner of my desk a while later. "Easy part first," she said. "Colangelo's Social Security card was issued in February 1961 in Chicago. Address in the Back of the Yards neighborhood. I can't find any record for him before that."

It was the same year as his first arrest, the year he turned twenty-five.

She continued. "About Ransom Camp. Just to cover all the bases I checked canned vegetables first. Found Van Camp, but no hits on Ransom Camp." She grinned.

I smiled back at her.

"So," she said, "I moved on to current real estate records. There is no place in Illinois that carries the name Ransom Camp. There is a little community in LaSalle County called Ransom. Just Ransom. No Camp. However," she paused, "I did find one reference in the *Chicago Tribune* archives to a place called Ransom Camp in LaSalle County dating back to 1957. The story would be huge today. Back in fifty-seven, not so much. Ransom Camp wasn't really a place. It was more like a bad acid trip."

I nodded. "Tell me about it," I said.

"I put everything on your computer."

I went to the newspaper story first. I raced through it once, then read it a second time, devouring every word. The story chilled me.

OTTAWA – At least 26 migrant workers died and another 17 were injured Saturday night when a raging fire tore through an enclave of old mobile homes and trailers about eight miles southeast of here. At least 16 victims were believed to be children. Police say the fires were caused by arson but have no suspects.

"It appears that someone snuck through the area some time after midnight and spread gasoline under two dozen different vehicles then set them on fire," said LaSalle County Sheriff's Deputy Coleman Blackwell. "People were literally cooked in their beds. They never had a chance. They burned down the school, too."

The heavily wooded area, several miles south of the Illinois River, is commonly referred to as Ransom Camp because of its proximity to the town of Ransom. The area is largely agricultural, so it attracts migrant workers who start their seasons along the Gulf Coast and work their way north as the growing seasons progress.

Police did not release the names of the victims.

"Most of those people don't carry much in the way of identification," Blackwell said. "Some are illegal aliens, and they don't want anybody knowing who they are. We'd have fingerprints on file somewhere if any of them were ever arrested, but the bodies are burnt up too bad to get prints. Most of them will go anonymous into pauper's graves. Too bad, but that's the way it is with those people."

THAT WAS IT. No follow-ups, no partial list of the dead, no official outrage. Nothing but the distant beat of racism. "Those people." Illegals. Stoop labor.

I felt the nausea return, and it had nothing to do with a blow to the head.

~

WHEN ERIC WALKED up I started to turn the computer screen so he could read the story, but he had something else on his mind.

"They want you to write a column about the assault, to personalize the sense of violation." He put a hand on my shoulder to keep me from exploding out of my chair.

"Who's 'they'?" I said.

"The collective editors who outrank both of us."

"Specifically."

"Ross." Ross Holt, the managing editor.

"Oh, Christ, absolutely not," I said.

"Write about the incident. Nothing about Vinnie. A random senseless crime."

"But it wasn't," I said.

"I know that," Eric said. "Ross knows that. Your readers don't need to know that. All they want to hear is what happened. Home invasion is everyone's worst nightmare. They want to know how you're coping."

"Bottom line, Eric, I don't want to do it, and it's my column."

"Bottom line, Deuce, it's your column, but it's Ross's newsroom.

You know how this works. Save us both a lot of time and grief by accepting gracefully what you can't change."

"And if I say no?"

"I'll tell him you refused, and there could be ramifications. You know, this piled on top of that gun column the other day. . ."

"He'd fire me?"

That caused Eric to pause. "No, not right now. It wouldn't look good after what you've been through. But there's always later. You carry one of the highest salaries in the newsroom. It's not a good idea to put yourself on Ross's radar."

Eric was right. I could do the piece in about forty-five minutes, then go back to more important things. But I'd be damned if I was going to swallow my displeasure in silence.

"Then I can go back to the Colangelo story?"

"There's some question whether you can handle Colangelo plus your column load. But until you prove it can't be done, Ross is okay letting you try. Stay on his good side."

"I will," I said. "But not cheerfully."

"Don't lose your temper in the newsroom."

"Somebody should tell you guys to stop jerking my column around."

"You can do that," Eric said, "as soon as you win the lottery and buy the paper."

Moving on, I told Eric I thought Lucy had identified the Ransom Camp reference scribbled in the public defender's case notes.

"If it's the right place, I have no idea how it fits into Vinnie's past, or what its significance is to the present. But it's one hell of a story." He sat at my desk and read.

"Dear God," he said when he finished. "Is there any more?"

"No," I said. "No follow-ups."

"How can something like this happen and then disappear after a day's coverage? It should have made national headlines."

"Not in 1957," I said. "You're talking about a time of serious racism, even in Illinois. Unless you were white, you were sub-human. The dead were, as Deputy Redneck informed us, just illegal aliens.

Disposable people. Who cares if they melted in their beds? There was no more coverage because nobody gave a damn."

"Fifty-seven was way back before my time, back during my pre-natal career," arson investigator Mark Hearst said with a chuckle when I got him on the phone. "Name Ransom Camp doesn't ring any bells. Not sure what I can do for you."

I had reached Hearst through the Illinois Fire Marshal's Office in Springfield, the state capital. Arson investigators weren't assigned to specific jurisdictions. They went where they were assigned to specific cases and worked from home. I was given Hearst's name because he lived in Chicago and was working on an arson case in the city.

"What you can do is a favor," I said. "You can say yes, or you can say no. I just want you to hear me out."

"Well, I'm workin' a warehouse arson investigation outta the firehouse on Pershing." He gave me the address. "When're you comin' over?"

"I'm leaving in five," I said.

I'd caved in and written a column on the assault. I hated doing it, and I hated the column when I finished it. What happened inside my home was my business, whether it was an assault or kinky sex.

Well, never mind about the kinky sex part. That was wishful thinking.

Before I left the office I called the LaSalle County Sheriff's Office and asked a clerk there to check on the whereabouts of Coleman Blackwell, the deputy who'd been quoted in the *Tribune* about the Ransom Camp fire. I left my cell phone number. She called back twelve minutes later. Blackwell had retired in 1969 and died in November of 1984.

I drove south with retreating expectations. From 1957 to 2014 was fifty-seven years, a long time. People forgot. People moved. People died. Records disappeared. I had lucked out at the PD's office. Vinnie's case file lived on fiche. I hoped for, but didn't expect, the same for the Ransom Camp file, assuming anybody had created a file back then.

Rather than deal with traffic on the Dan Ryan, I cut over to Halsted and drove south to Pershing, where I caught a red light. As I waited, I reflected on my surroundings.

I was at the northeast corner of one of the most storied neighborhoods in Chicago, Back of the Yards. A few blocks south, the great Union Stockyards gate was the only relic of the time when Carl Sandburg immortalized the city as "Hog Butcher for the World." Some of the rail lines were still there, the means of transporting animals in, sides of meat and waste products out. The meat fed the world. The waste products traveled only a few blocks west before being dumped into a stagnant branch of the South Fork of the Chicago River, an unfortunate little stretch of landlocked water that soon acquired the name Bubbly Creek.

Tons of animal waste went into the creek. Because the water had nowhere to flow, the putrefying byproducts stayed on the creek bottom, emitting bubbles of foul-smelling methane and hydrogen sulfide gases. Chicago lore suggests Bubbly Creek also became the disposal point of choice when Mob hit men had human bodies that needed to disappear.

Today, the waterway was pretty much done with its garbage. Both wildlife and boaters were returning. But when the temperature, humidity, and breezes were just right, hints of the old stench made themselves known. Some locals objected to the term "stench."

"We don't call it that," one told me. "We call it history."

The light had changed, and the driver behind me lost patience and let me have a quick tap of her horn. I turned right and found the firehouse.

Mark Hearst seemed affable enough, but wary. He didn't deal with reporters much. A press officer, Tom McMillan, was on his way, undoubtedly summoned to witness my interview. While we waited, Hearst and I traded small talk, and I let myself enjoy looking at him. He was about my age, maybe a year or two older. He was my brother's height, which made him six-three. The way his uniform shirt clung to him made his workout ethic obvious. He had a jaw that tended toward square, high cheekbones, clear blue eyes, light brown hair worn a little longer than Fire Department regs stipulated, and great teeth displayed by a brilliant smile that lit up his face. His only flaw was the scar running at an angle across his left eyebrow.

One leg danced on the ball of its foot, and he drummed his fingers on the conference table every so often. McMillen joined us in time to keep the situation from becoming awkward. He was a pleasant-looking redhead with healed burn scars on his neck.

He said he was hungry and suggested we grab lunch at a place called Morrie O'Malley's. O'Malley's was a quick drive from the fire house, over near U.S. Cellular Field, the home of the Chicago White Sox. When I longed for a real Chicago hot dog, I headed to O'Malley's. It had zero ambience, but the food was great, and it was a beautiful early fall day, so we could sit at one of the outside tables and enjoy the weather.

The guys each got two dogs and fries. I saw no reason to dilute the lunch with French fries, so I ordered two dogs and a bottle of water. If you're not from Chicago, and you've never had a real Chicago dog, you can't appreciate the amalgam of food sitting before me. Poppy seed bun. Vienna Beef dog. Bright green Rolf's relish. Yellow deli mustard. A kosher pickle spear, chopped onion, tomato wedges, sport peppers and celery salt. It doesn't get any better than that.

Of course it's hard to keep everything intact while eating it. But what falls on your plate you scoop back on the bun. Both Mark and Tom seemed to appreciate that I appreciated the cuisine at O'Malley's.

While I rested between dogs, I told the guys about the favor I was asking.

～

"WHY NOT ASK the LaSalle fire people yourself," McMillen said when I finished the story. "You have a right to the information."

"I know," I said. "But it will require some digging to find the records, if they even exist, and I don't have any clout over there. Chances are they'd ignore me."

McMillen said, "What makes you think we can get them to help?"

"The brotherhood. One fire guy asks another fire guy for a favor, the other fire guy's gonna try."

Hearst smiled and McMillen shook his head.

"You're talkin' almost sixty years ago," McMillen said. "Even if they wanna help, they probably can't. Even Chicago doesn't keep records that good."

"What's the big deal about an old fire, anyway?" Hearst said.

I slid the copy of the *Tribune* story across the table. Devastated would be an adequate description of the look on Hearst's face as he read it. He looked up at me with horror and slid the paper over to McMillen.

McMillen looked sick. "Oh, Jesus. Oh fuck," he whispered. When he looked up at me, I thought I saw his eyes glisten. "They butchered babies. Were there any follow-ups?"

"Not that we could find."

I chewed a bite of my second dog and washed it down with some water.

"You read the article about the old guy who was tortured and killed in Cicero a couple of nights ago? Vinnie Colangelo?"

"No," Hearst said.

"Yeah," McMillen said. "I saw it."

I filled in the blanks, including the events at Jo-Jos.

"The man who broke into my home the other night matched the description of the guy in the bar asking where Vinnie lived," I said.

"And Ransom Camp ties in how?" McMillen said.

I explained about finding the name, "Ransom Camp," in the margin of some notes made by Simon Donovan, the public defender who represented Vinnie in federal court.

"I'm trying to find out if there's a link between Vinnie and that fire," I said. "Assuming it's the same Ransom Camp. Donovan thought it was important."

"Did you talk to Donovan?" McMillen said.

"Can't. He was killed in a courthouse shooting in the 80s."

"Jesus God," Hearst said. "What a city."

I WAS SITTING at my desk the next morning wondering what the hell I was going to do with my day when Mark Hearst called and solved the problem.

"I talked to some of the guys over in Ottawa, the LaSalle County seat," he said. "The village of Ransom is still there – a quiet little farming community. They got no record of a Ransom Camp or a Ransom Camp fire. One guy said it's pretty common knowledge migrant workers used to squat around there, livin' outta their vans, campers, trailers, old school buses, whatever they could drive or pull with them. The fire marshal called a few guys retired off the job but still livin' in the area. Two of them had heard of the case. Neither of them remembered much about it, and neither guy had any personal involvement. But one remembered a Harold Bickerstaff, who might have been the lead fire investigator."

"Any chance Harold Bickerstaff is still alive?" I said.

"Yep," Hearst said. "He's eighty-nine, and he lives in a retirement home in Ottawa. I called him and told him a reporter might be comin' around. He seemed lucid enough, remembered the case right away. He said it was a bad one, and he'd be happy to talk to you. I sent his address and phone number to your email."

"I appreciate it," I said.

"I can't get that story out of my head, Deuce," Hearst said. "I dreamt about it last night. Off the record, I'd like to help you on this. If there's anything I can do, interpret evidence or circumstances, call me. You got the number."

"Thanks," I said. "Why do you want to get involved?"

"Somebody's got to get justice for those people, even if it is more than fifty years late. I wouldn't mind it bein' you and me."

12

I t was after 10:00 in the morning, the rush hour well over. Still, traffic on the Dan Ryan was stop-and-go southbound. By the time I got to I-55, the Stevenson, I was moving at the speed limit. I was glad of that because along the section of the Stevenson that ran from Chicago to the western border of Cook County—following the route of the Chicago Sanitary & Ship Canal—the scenery consisted of warehouses, mountains of tailings, gravel and rock, rusting industrial equipment, stacked rail cars, salt domes, and sparse vegetation covered in yellow dust. You couldn't see the water for the junk. This wasn't Sandburg's "city of the big shoulders." This was blight.

When hills started to roll, and grass turned green again, and trees began to show the first hues of autumn, I relaxed into the trip.

It took ninety minutes to drive to Ottawa, a historic place nestled south of the highway on the confluence of the Fox and Illinois Rivers. In the heart of the old downtown the place appeared not to have changed much since the 1930s. Some gorgeous old buildings sat high on the southern bluff overlooking the rivers. And the town square sported bronze statues of Abraham Lincoln and Stephen A. Douglas.

Ottawa, Illinois, was the site of the first Lincoln-Douglas debate, the one in which Douglas, leader of the Democratic Party, accused Abe of forming a secret, bi-partisan cabal of congressmen pledged to bring about the abolition of slavery. If that racist message played well here in 1858, it probably continued to resonate with some folks even 99 years later, in 1957.

By the time I found the retirement home, it was lunchtime. So I checked the dining room first, assuming Harold Bickerstaff would be there.

"Actually," the hostess told me, "Mr. Bickerstaff asked for his meal in his apartment today. He said he was expecting company and wanted privacy to talk. I suspect he was referring to you." She pointed me toward his address.

"Who is it?" a strong voice demanded from behind the closed apartment door.

"It's Deuce Mora, Mr. Bickerstaff," I said. "I'm a columnist for the *Chicago Journal*. Mark Hearst from the state Fire Marshal's Office called you about me."

The door opened to a man who supported himself on a walker. He stood about 5-foot-8 and carried maybe 140 pounds on his small frame. But he looked as if he'd been a tough guy once. Remnants of developed sinew corded along his arms, which extended from a clean, white t-shirt. He extended a hand and demonstrated a grip that still had plenty of strength behind it.

"Come in, come in, pretty lady," he urged. "Let me get you something to drink."

"I'm fine, Mr. Bickerstaff. Thanks anyway. I don't want to take up too much of your time. I understand you have lunch coming up."

"Already here," he said. "Put it in the refrigerator. Food's not as important as good company. I can eat any time. A conversation is rare, especially with a looker like you. You are very pretty, you know, and very tall. You married?"

"No," I said. "Still hoping."

He smiled. "Makes me wish I was seventy again," he said.

He rolled his walker into the living room, and I followed. The place was clean and bright, and the air coming in the open windows carried the aroma of the country.

"Sit. Sit," he said.

I chose the sofa. He sat in his easy chair. It had been aimed at the television set, but it swiveled, and he turned to face me.

"So you're a reporter, eh?" he said. "Looks like somebody beat you up."

"I'm a columnist, yes, sir," I said.

"A snoop."

"Yes, sir, sort of."

"Could be why you got beat up. Nobody likes a snoop. When you gonna get a real job?"

I couldn't help myself. I laughed. I'd never thought of my work that way, but Harold Bickerstaff had a point.

"But you didn't come for guidance counseling, did you?" he said. He nailed me with blue eyes. The color might have faded over the years, but they still glowed with intelligence.

"No," I said. "I came to ask you about an arson case from a long, long time ago."

"Which one was that?" he said. "I'm sure I've forgotten an awful lot of them."

His question stopped me. Mark Hearst said he mentioned Ransom Camp to Bickerstaff, and Bickerstaff remembered it. Now, apparently, Bickerstaff didn't even remember talking to Mark. That didn't bode well for me. Nevertheless, I took a small digital voice recorder out of my pocket and turned it on.

"Ransom Camp," I said, and Bickerstaff couldn't have looked more shocked if I'd slapped him. I could see him processing fragments of memory, and the process appeared painful. He pushed himself out of the chair and grabbed his rolling walker. He steered to a window that looked out over a garden. He leaned against the wall. He said nothing for a time, then sighed.

"Why now?" he said, his voice gone nearly inaudible. "Why after all these years? Why not let the dead lie at peace?"

"Because they didn't die at peace," I said. "They were murdered. And I want to know who did it and why."

He appeared more frail than he had five minutes earlier.

"Why?" he said. "That's easy. They were Hispanic, though that wasn't the word used to describe 'em back then. They were poor people trying to make a better life for themselves and their children than they had back wherever they came from. They worked for next to nothing and lived in squalor."

"Was there a lot of bigotry around here back then?" I asked.

"Logic and bigotry live in alternate universes, young lady," Bickerstaff said. "African American people know it. European Jews know it. Hell, the Palestinians know it."

"I found an old story from the *Chicago Tribune,* from right after the fire, but the coverage seemed to stop with that," I said. "Did your investigation uncover anything?"

"You ever see a burned up body?" he said. Then he looked off, as though at thoughts of his own, memories of his own.

I said I hadn't.

He turned back to me. "Unlike you might imagine, there's nuthin' fast about the way a human body burns. It's a slow process that causes the muscles and tendons to draw up and shrink, until the body's rigid, with the arms up and the fists curled into claws. Some call it a pugilistic attitude, like a boxer waitin' to throw the first punch. The mouth is open wide, lookin' like a final terrified scream. Course, it's all physiology, but that don't make it no easier to look at. Don't make it no easier to get out of your thoughts and your dreams and your memories."

Bickerstaff grimaced. "Now imagine that sight multiplied by twenty-six, the way it was down there that night. A lot of 'em children."

It wasn't a mental image I wanted to own.

"You figured out right away what happened?" I said.

"Oh, yeah. It was clear that gasoline was the accelerant. Whoever used it was vicious. They poured it under bedrooms, where people would be sleepin'. And if a home or a trailer had a propane tank, they poured it there too. They weren't new tanks. They were rusted and vulnerable. The heat from the gasoline fires exploded some of them, adding shrapnel and more fuel to the fires. Then the woods began to burn. Didn't get the fire under control until morning. If ever there was a vision of hell. . ."

"Did you figure out who did it?" I said.

"I had a pretty good idea," he said, "and there wasn't no bigotry about it. An Esso station up the road had sold forty gallons to a kid in the weeks leading up to the fire, and several witnesses saw the jugs stored in the woods near the kid's own trailer. He was one of their own, one of the residents of Ransom Camp."

I felt an adrenaline buzz.

"Who was it?" I said.

He looked at me, and I was glad to see that the light had returned to his eyes.

"Where were you fifty years ago when this information might have done some good?" he said. "Don't answer that. I know you wasn't born back then. I wanted to pursue the case, but in the end, it didn't matter."

He returned to his chair and used his still-strong arms to set his body in a comfortable position. He saw me notice.

"I still work out some with weights," he said. "Never too old."

"The name, Mr. Bickerstaff?"

"Ricardo LaPalma," he said. "Twelve-year-old punk. Twelve goin' on forty. I'll take his name to my grave. How do you turn a kid that young into a monster?"

"Was LaPalma charged?" I said.

Bickerstaff thought about that for a moment.

"Let me tell you about LaSalle County back then. We had a whole lotta prejudice. There was no minorities except for the migrants. The white locals tolerated them because they did the stoop labor nobody else wanted to do. Long as the migrants stayed in their place, the white attitude was live-and-let-live. Know what I mean? They'd have been run off quick as a whistle if they'd tried to climb out of their economic holes and take jobs the white boys wanted. Every once in a while, one of the migrants would get outta line. Next thing you know there's a dead body. My chief was one of those white boys, if you get my drift. Wouldn't give me the time to put a case together. Had other cases more pressing, he said. And then, like I said, it didn't matter any more."

"Why didn't it matter?" I said, fearing the answer.

"Somebody killed Ricardo LaPalma," he said. "Somebody took a pistol, put it to his head, and blew him away."

As Bickerstaff told his story, I'd found myself wondering if Vinnie, in his former life, had been the arsonist. Now, I was wondering if it had been Vinnie who killed the arsonist. Or maybe Vinnie had nothing to do with the fires at all.

"Harold, who killed Ricardo? Did you ever find out?"

Bickerstaff sucked a breath, his whole body seeming to shrivel.

"Wasn't a fire case," he said. "It was police business. And the cops didn't care. They couldn'ta found out anything if they tried. Most of the migrants who survived that night were scattered to the four winds by the next day, and those who stayed wouldn'ta said nothin' to the white authorities."

He looked at me for the first time in several minutes. "And really," he said, "who cared? In the end, Ricardo got what he deserved. End of story."

I GOT behind the wheel and drove south out of Ottawa, intent on taking a look around. Following Illinois Route 23, I tried to work out turns as they appeared on a map I'd downloaded from Google that morning. But the Internet directions didn't match up with reality. I drove back and forth, up and down, for an hour, alternating between paved and gravel roads.

For a while I wondered if I might be driving in circles. I was surrounded by endless fields of corn giving up the last of the year's crop, the leaves and stalks turning to a worn and tired yellow. The only things taller than the corn were hundreds of giant wind turbines, nearly all of them at rest.

Then, quite by accident, I ran into Ransom. A town of 400, the sign said.

Easy to miss.

The houses I passed were neat and clean with large, well-trimmed yards. But there weren't many people around, and there was no traffic on the streets.

I stopped at a place on North Lincoln called Jerry's Tap, a solid-looking red brick building that advertised itself as a sports bar and family restaurant. My mind needed information and my stomach told me it needed food and coffee. Jerry's Tap was dark, but clean and pleasant, with an entire wall devoted to big-screen televisions. Each was tuned to a different college football game played the previous weekend, all of them were muted with closed captioning activated.

Inside, a few people studied me, not in an unfriendly way, but certain in the knowledge I was a stranger. I smiled and nodded at them, and they smiled and nodded back, then returned to their meals. Ransom seemed, so far, to be an affable place. "So far" being the operative words.

I sat at a table alone and ordered coffee and a chicken sandwich. When the waitress brought my food and asked if there'd be anything else, I asked her if she had time for a question or two. She said she did.

"Did you ever hear of a place called Ransom Camp?" I said.

She looked to be in her thirties. If she'd heard of it, it was from her grandparents.

"Can't say's I have," she said. "There's fishin' camps north of here if you follow the highway up toward the generating plant. I don't remember nothin' called Ransom Camp, but there's lots of cabins and camp grounds back in the woods."

Her accent sounded more South Georgia than North Illinois.

"Ransom Camp was here a long time ago," I said. "Right here or nearby. It's where migrant workers stayed. It burned down fifty-seven years ago, in 1957."

"Never heard of it," she said. "Interesting coincidence, though. Fifty-seven in '57."

"North of here, not far," said a man's voice from the next table. "Sorry. Wasn't tryin' to be nosy, but I couldn't help but overhear the question. You know the power station?"

I admitted I did not.

"You have a map?"

I nodded and handed over what I'd copied from Google Maps that morning.

He looked at it and nodded. "Doesn't go far enough north," he said.

"I got a county map in the truck," said one of his companions. He got up from the table. "Be right back."

"I gotta warn you," the first man said, "the whole area's posted. I know a couple people snuck in to fish the lake and got theirselves shot at. If you're gonna explore, be careful."

As if to underscore the warning, a freight train crashed through town on tracks a half block north of Jerry's Tap. I feared for a moment it was coming straight through the restaurant. Everything shook and rattled.

The second man returned and smiled at me.

"Freight train startled you, huh? 'Round here the joke is, 'It sounded just like a tornado.' You get used to it after a while."

He handed a ragged map to his friend, who moved his chair over to my table. He unfolded the map, then moved aside utensils, my water glass, salt and pepper shakers, a bottle of hot sauce, and another of ketchup to make room for the map's footprint.

Now most of the restaurant was paying attention. It was the most interesting thing to happen in Ransom that day.

"Here we are," the man said. "And here's the east end of town. Illinois Route 170 runs north-south from there." His finger traced along the paper, following the road north around the Marseilles State Fish and Wildlife area. "Once you get north of the state land, there's a little road that goes back in toward the lake. It's gated and usually locked.

Behind that gate, that's the place used to be called Ransom Camp. Ain't nothin' left of it to see, though."

Another man commented, almost in a whisper, "Some say it's a haunted place."

The man sitting with me sat up straight and shook his head. "Seth, ain't nobody but you believes in ghosts," he said. "Just hush."

"Well, that's what they say, Charlie. That's what they say."

Charlie turned back to me.

"If you don't mind my askin', why're you interested in Ransom Camp?"

"I'm a history buff," I said. "I heard about what happened there and wanted to see the place. No special reason."

"They's just stories," Charlie said. "Nobody takes 'em serious."

"You don't think they're true?" I said.

Charlie shrugged. "No tellin'. Nobody I know of left alive around here to say one way or the other."

I took a bite of sandwich and a swallow of coffee. Both were excellent.

"I drove out here from Chicago out of curiosity," I said. "Might as well have a look."

"You can have that map if you want," said the owner. "I can get another easy enough."

"Thanks," I said, and gave him a big smile.

As I drank a second cup of coffee and studied the map, my mind picked at threads. What if Vinnie had been born Ricardo LaPalma and faked his own death? I did the math. Vinnie's police records said he was born in 1936. Ransom Camp burned in 1957, when Vinnie would have been twenty-one. Bickerstaff seemed certain Ricardo LaPalma was twelve. Nine years difference. What if Vinnie had lied about his age and DOB? Neat idea, but when I met Vinnie, he looked every one of his seventy-eight years and then some. Of course, prison could have done that.

My brain was turning to wet cement.

I paid my bill, returned to my car and followed the map. When I got to the little road into the private woodland I found the area posted, as I'd been told, and the gate closed and locked as advertised. Undaunted, I parked a quarter mile up the road, put on a pair of knee-high duck boots I kept in the back of the truck, walked back to the gate, and climbed over it. I had my story all ready if anyone challenged me. I'd hit a rabbit that scampered off into the woods. I wanted to try to find it and help it if it managed to survive. An injured rabbit might not move folks around here, but it was good enough to give my trespassing realistic cover.

Several feet into the woods, the fall-hued tree canopy blotted out the sun. I went as far as a fork in the road. Not having any clue what I was looking for, I headed downhill figuring that would take me to the lake.

I soon found a place in the woods where, over an area of maybe twenty or thirty acres, the trees seemed to be younger than the rest. And something in the weeds caught my eye. As I moved toward it, I realized it was the foundation of a building, the footprint too large to have been a house. I doubted it was the remains of any building attached to Ransom Camp. If it were, fifty-odd years of brush would have obliterated it by now. As far as I could see in all directions, this foundation was the only sign of the one-time presence of people.

The bristling hairs on the back of my neck warned of another presence as surely as the sharp snap of a dry twig in the underbrush.

I flashed back on the intruder in my apartment. I'd been an idiot to come here alone.

I spun around, alert for someone intent on arresting or harming me. I thought about running for my truck, but running in duck boots through the dense understory would be next to impossible.

"Who's there?" I called out. Adrenaline made my voice tremble.

I got no response but the call of a blackbird.

"If you want to talk to me," I announced, "show yourself."

I felt air move against my face, too warm to be the September breeze. And the brush around me wasn't moving.

Something touched my arm, but when I looked, I saw nothing.

"Hello," I called, somewhat louder. "Is anybody here?"

Silence.

The acute stress response kicked in. Fight or flight. Flight won hands down.

But when I took a quick step backward, I tripped over something. I fell on my butt in the weeds and scrambled to my feet. The world spun a little. My headache, once subsided to a dull growl, flared a bit now, as if warning it hadn't finished tormenting me. I looked around for the obstacle I tripped over and saw a pipe jutting from the ground.

I heard the sound of the wind, yet the leaves on the trees hung motionless.

It wasn't the wind. It sounded more like the murmur of voices, dozens of voices, all subdued, individual words difficult to identify.

I thought about the man back at Jerry's Tap. "Oh, shit. Damn it, Seth. I don't believe in ghosts, either."

"Maybe you should," a single voice replied. The voice was male, soft, non-threatening. It came from behind me, and I didn't imagine it.

I turned again to confront a weathered old man with a broad, flat face that suggested Native American blood. He carried a stout staff and draped himself over it. He wore faded blue jeans and a light-weight flannel shirt, its long sleeves buttoned at the bony wrists and the collar buttoned up to the neck. I couldn't come close to guessing his age. Over seventy? Over eighty?

"You startled me," I said. My throat was tight. I cleared it.

"I am sorry," he said, pronouncing the words with precision. English was not his first language. "What do you want here?"

"I don't know," I said. "Just looking around."

"Why are you here?" he said again.

"Is this the place that used to be called Ransom Camp?"

He didn't reply.

"I came to see something that isn't here any more," I said. "I guess that doesn't make sense to you. It doesn't make much sense to me."

His dark eyes held steady on my face. I thought I saw a warning there. I decided not to wait around, very much alone, for confirmation.

"I'll go now," I said. "I'm sorry if I intruded."

I took several more steps back. His voice stopped me.

"This is the place known as Ransom Camp," he said. "Why is it you want to know?"

I didn't answer but pointed at the building foundation.

"What was that?" I said.

"Many years ago," he said, "it is a school."

I remembered then the old newspaper story had mentioned a school burning.

"It burns with everything else," he said. "Now go. You disturb the spirits."

I thought the old man must be about two flowers short of a bouquet. Coupled with the eerie feeling of the place, my twitchy nerves were beginning to fray.

I needed to leave.

I retraced my steps to my Explorer.

I had found Ransom Camp, a discovery that left me shaken. I climbed behind the wheel, relieved to be off that land, but certain in the knowledge I would be back.

13

By the time I got back to my condo, two private cops were parked out front. I stopped abreast of their SUV and nodded. The man in the passenger seat nodded back and thumbed down his window.

"Ms. Mora?" he said.

I nodded.

"We got a pass key from your condo association. Your boss arranged it. We've already scoped out the garage and the lobby and they're all clear. We'll meet you at the elevator."

I frowned, but deep down I felt a touch of relief that somebody had my back.

They entered my condo first and pronounced it all clear. One of them handed me his business card.

"We'll be watching the garage and the front door all night," he said. "But if you need us, call immediately."

I poured a glass of wine and sat down to think about the day. I'd begun to wonder if I dreamed the encounter in the woods at Ransom Camp. The voices, the touch of something against my skin, they had to be illusions. I was still getting over a concussion. Perhaps blows to the head made me more suggestible. Maybe I'd be picking up messages from Antares next.

The old man who appeared out of nowhere, he seemed real enough.

It occurred to me the good folks of Ransom, Illinois, might have played a practical joke on a stranger from the city.

Nonetheless, I knew I wouldn't sleep, and my expectation became self-fulfilling. I gave up at 6 a.m., showered, dressed and headed all the way back to LaSalle County again, this time to the Regional Office of Education. Maybe if I could learn something about the burned-out school I would get some answers to other questions.

The Office of Education was located in Ottawa in the three-story courthouse on Madison Street, a great old building with high arches over the entrance, arched windows, architectural crown molding and an old clock mounted high on the front facade that kept accurate time.

Inside, I found the education office, identified myself and asked to speak to someone who knew a lot about the history of schools in LaSalle County. That person, the receptionist told me, was Kathleen Henderson, deputy superintendent.

Did I have an appointment?

I did not.

I should have called ahead. Someone would see when, and if, Ms. Henderson would be available to speak to me.

Fortunately, Kathleen Henderson turned out to be present and available right then. And she turned out to be a pleasant-looking, middle-aged woman who wore her gray hair in a bun. I guessed she had been an English teacher before she became an administrator.

"I'm trying to find out anything I can," I told her, "about a school that once existed a few miles north of Ransom but burned down a number of years ago."

"What was the name of the school?" she said.

"I don't know," I said. "I'm not sure it had a name."

"Wasn't it rebuilt?" she said.

"No, not that I know of," I said.

I pulled out my map and showed her where the school had been. "And I'm told it burned in 1957," I added.

"Hmm, no, that would be an impossible place for a school," she said. "Nobody lives there. The community of Ransom has a consolidated school right in town. The township has the high school, just south of here, near the river."

I pointed at the map. "I discovered the foundation of an old building on that land yesterday," I said, "and somebody from the area said it used to be a school."

"Perhaps they were mistaken."

"And perhaps not."

She picked up her phone and called someone who directed her to someone else. It was during the fourth call that she raised her eyebrows and gave me a little nod, which seemed to indicate she was getting somewhere.

She scribbled some notes and hung up.

"Ransom Camp School seems to fit the place you found," she said. "It was built for the children of the seasonal farm workers, and it burned in 1957, in June, after school let out. It definitely was arson, but our records don't indicate whether anyone was arrested. And you also are correct that we never rebuilt it. It was pretty informal as schools go. No defined grades. Grandparents and disabled parents served as teachers, from what I'm told. The county built the building, and the migrant laborers decided what to do with it. Some of them lived in it."

"Did the county have records on the kids who registered as students there?"

Henderson scoffed. "Not likely anything accurate. I doubt there was anything formal about the registration process."

"Still," I said, "I'd like to get a list of all the kids who went there in the fifty-six/fifty-seven school year, before the building burned. I know it won't be a comprehensive list."

Then I remembered Harold Bickerstaff's suspect, Ricardo

LaPalma, had been twelve. "Also, I'd like to get a list of students that same year who attended whatever schools the Ransom Camp School fed into."

"Tell me you aren't serious," she said.

"Actually, I am," I said.

"That's going to be a formidable list of names even if it is incomplete, and a formidable chore to find them after all these years," Kathleen said.

I nodded, unable to think of anything profound to say.

"It's going to take some doing," Kathleen said. "I hope for your sake that those weren't among the records that burned up in the fire we had here about fourteen or fifteen years ago. We lost a lot of paperwork."

"I hope so, too," I said.

"Leave me your card, and I'll call you when I have any information. Can you tell me why you're interested?"

"It's a long story," I said. "And right now I'm having trouble telling truth from fiction."

I scribbled my cell phone number on the back of the card and explained that I wasn't spending a lot of time in the office.

"I'll track you down," she said.

"I guess you hear this a lot," I said, "and I apologize for having to say it. But I do need the information as soon as possible."

She nodded and smiled. "That caveat is attached to every information request I get," she said. "I promise I will do the best I can."

I started to leave and then turned back.

"Were you," I asked, "a teacher before you became an administrator?"

"I was, as a matter of fact," she said. "An English teacher."

Bingo. I had nailed my first guess of the day. A good omen.

IT OCCURRED to me as I pushed through the front door that I'd never heard back from anyone at U.S. Customs. I called my voice mail to be sure. I had fourteen messages, all from readers. A man who didn't identify himself left one. No surprise there. His message, verbatim: "I wish that Good Samaritan who broke into your place had split your head wide open and then skinned you for good measure, you miserable Commie bitch. Your column is a waste of space, and you're a waste of breath."

I needed to shop around for an egg timer to take on the road.

I leaped to the conclusion that this particular caller was not from U.S. Customs, and that none of the others seemed to be, either. So I got the Customs number up on my iPhone and tried it again. There still was no one around who could answer my questions. I left another message and my cell phone number. At this rate, the whole world was going to have my cell phone number, and everybody could call me at their leisure and leave nasty little messages.

I was getting into my truck when the phone rang.

"This is Jack Collins with U.S. Customs," a deep voice said. "Sorry it took so long go get back to you. This is the first free moment I've had."

I told Collins I had some questions about the procedures used to move an import from international to domestic commerce.

"It can get complicated," he said.

"So I heard from ATF," I said.

I heard him flipping paper.

"I'm checking in an Air France flight from Paris at O'Hare Terminal Five at two this afternoon," he said. "Meet me at international arrivals and we can talk there for a few minutes before the passengers deplane."

I reminded him that only ticketed passengers could get to the gate areas. Journalists didn't rate exemptions.

"I can escort you," he said. "Meet me at the exit door marked 5C about 1:15. We'll go over together. Bring credentials and ID."

I had just closed the cell phone when it rang again. I hoped it was Sully with word from his source in Washington. It wasn't. But it was Washington calling in another sense.

"Deuce, I'm glad I caught you," said the rich baritone voice. "It's John Conti."

"Congressman," I said, feeling myself smile. "It's been a long time. How are you?"

"That's my question for you, Deuce. I can't imagine walking into my house and finding an intruder there, let alone one bent on doing me injury. I was going to call yesterday, but time got away from me. I hope you're doing well."

"I am, yes. And thanks for asking. How about you?"

He paused. I heard him sigh. "Remember those waves of grief we used to talk about?" he said. "They don't crash down on me as often as they used to. But sometimes they hit me when my back is turned, when I'm not even thinking about Carole."

"I know the feeling," I said. "Little things that remind me of my dad catch me up more often than I expected. I suppose it'll always happen."

"Story in the paper said you managed to strike a blow in your own defense after the intruder hit you. I hope you got him someplace where it'll hurt for a long time."

"I aimed for his head, but I think I got him on the elbow. Not quite the same thing."

"Are the police responding well? You tell me if they aren't."

"They left fingerprint dust all over the apartment."

Conti laughed, a pleasant sound. "Forensic procedure. I remember it. That stuff's the devil to clean up, too. You should get professionals in. I'm sure the *Journal* would pay."

"It's already in process," I said.

"Listen, as soon as we hang up, I'm leaving to catch a flight to Midway, a scheduled District visit," he said. "Perhaps we can help each other. The news along the grapevine is you're interested in an old case my office handled when I was U.S. Attorney, is that right?"

"Yes, it is. And I have some questions I'd like to ask you."

"Good. Because, as you so often do, you have piqued my curiosity. So let's interrogate each other. It's been too long since we got together, anyway. Let's have dinner tonight. How about seven? You know Rosebud, the one on Taylor Street?"

We made the date.

I took a meandering drive from Ottawa toward O'Hare and found a Starbucks in Elmhurst, south of the airport. I needed an infusion of caffeine. I settled in, fired up my laptop, and prepared to drain the Internet of information on the Trafficante crime family in Tampa. That was the organization that spawned Charles Haight, Vinnie's first attorney on the Scotch-jacking case.

I don't know what I hoped to find. Perhaps context for the mess I was trying to unravel. In the end, I came away more knowledgeable but devoid of new insights.

At noon, hungry, over-caffeinated and jittery, I shut down the laptop, bought two oat bran muffins, and headed to the airport. I lingered around the door where I was to meet Collins, and he showed up ten minutes later. He was hard to miss. He stood a little over six feet and looked to weigh maybe 250, little of it fat. He wore a full uniform, starched and pressed, and accessorized with a nasty-looking sidearm. So much for the image of the pudgy, desk-bound public servant.

We shook hands, and he studied the press credentials hanging from a lanyard around my neck. He seemed satisfied.

"Stay close to me," he said.

We approached security, where my credentials and driver's license got close scrutiny. After Collins assured the agents I was with him, both of us were waved through.

We reached a security door where Collins punched a code into the keypad and placed his palm against plate that matched him to a database of those authorized to enter. He got a green light, and we moved through to one of the passenger entry points where an Air France 777 soon would disgorge hundreds of people.

"Let's get this done before the people arrive," Collins said. "The plane's about twenty minutes late, and I don't want distractions when I start looking for bad guys."

While he set up his paperwork I told him I was trying to understand the process by which an import would pass from international to state commerce.

"And keep it simple for a dumb reporter," I said.

"Okay, what product are we talking about?" he said.

"A shipment of single-malt Scotch."

He nodded. "Well, first you have an agreement between shipper and consignee," Collins said. "The shipper is the seller. The buyer is the consignee. The shipper makes out a bill of lading. That's the contract between the parties. Once the Scotch gets to the U.S., somebody pays the freight and somebody pays the shipper, all done electronically. The receiver endorses the bill of lading. That right there is the execution of the contract. Then a Customs House broker takes the Scotch through Customs, which assesses duties and collects federal taxes. The broker signs a release-of-cargo document and turns the shipment over to the agent representing the receivers. That's the basic process."

"And once the release-of-cargo document is signed, the shipment has officially moved from foreign commerce into domestic commerce?"

"Yes, that's pretty much it, though I've oversimplified it," he said. "Importing goods to the U.S. involves something like twenty-two documents and forty-nine pieces of paper."

I wondered aloud how anyone ever came to understand the process.

"You get used to it," he said.

"Would copies of all these documents stay with the liquor shipment all the way to the buyer?" I asked him.

"No. The consignee gets a copy of the cargo manifest." He paused and thought about what he'd said. "It's not unheard of for a copy of the release-of-cargo document to travel with a shipment. Some consignees want them for the company records."

Collins looked at me then as if it had just dawned on him that he should care about my questions. "Where you going with this?" he said.

"I'm dealing with a situation where a man was charged with stealing a shipment of liquor while it was still in international commerce and therefore a federal crime," I said. "He claims he saw a form that proved the shipment had passed into domestic commerce, in which case it would have been a state charge. But when the shipping file was introduced into evidence, that document, the release-of-cargo form, wasn't there."

"That doesn't sound familiar," he said. "When'd it happen?"

"In nineteen-seventy-four," I said.

Collins shrugged, apparently relieved that the issue hadn't arisen on his watch.

"Well before my time," he said. "Your guy doesn't deny stealing it?"

"No, but he was charged with a federal crime and says he shouldn't have been."

Collins blew out his breath. "Well, if it *was* the release-of-cargo document he saw, that's pretty good proof to make his argument. If it was me it happened to, and I thought I'd been arrested unfairly on a federal charge, I'd beef about it, too. The federal charge is a big hammer with a serious swing in the penalty phase."

"That was his point," I said.

Beyond Collins I saw the big Air France Triple-7 rolling toward the gate. The plane was enormous.

"You handle that whole flight by yourself?" I said.

He glanced at the approaching aircraft and nodded. "The airport sends some folks to help check passenger paperwork, but the official stuff is all mine. The age of terrorism. More work and fewer people to do it." He looked back to me. "To finish up with your issue, the only way something like that could happen was if somebody made all the copies of the release-of-cargo document disappear. That would take a considerable and widespread conspiracy of corruption."

"But it could be done?" I said. "This is Chicago we're talking about, after all."

He laughed. "You got that right. But today, with all the federal security we got, I doubt it, even in Chi-town. Back in seventy-four, that was a whole different world. Yeah, it could've happened. But whoever put it together had some kinda balls, excuse my French. Can you imagine the risk involved? If it happened, whoever made it happen must've wanted to send your guy away real bad."

I thanked Collins and started to walk away.

"Hold up," he said. I turned back. "Where was the Scotch headed?"

"You mean, who was the buyer? Binny's Beverage Depot."

He shook his head and frowned. "That doesn't make sense. Binny's European shipments come through the Port of New York and then get trucked here. If your Scotch came through New York and was on a truck in Chicago, it has to have passed through Customs before it left the Big Apple. It's not a stretch that it might have had the release-of-cargo docs with it. It definitely would have been in domestic commerce."

Just as Vinnie insisted.

"Is that always true, that Binny's shipments come through New York?"

"No," Collins said. "Binny's is a big chain and buys stuff all over the world. Product from South America and Asia might come in through New Orleans or Los Angeles or Seattle. Generally, it's faster to truck from a coast than to bring it all the way by barge."

"How," I asked, "can I find out about this particular shipment?"

"You'd have to ask Binny's. And hope they still have the records."

~

AS SOON AS I got back to my truck, I began trying to reach someone at Binny's corporate headquarters in Skokie who could tell me about the shipment of Laphroig.

It was tough going. Everyone asked why I was asking. Everyone expressed dismay that I was asking about a shipment stolen forty years earlier. No one had that much institutional memory.

I finally got through to Howard Kaplan, the director of operations.

"I must say, Ms. Mora, that's the most intriguing question I've fielded all day."

"Do you know the answer?" I asked.

"Not specifically as to that truckload," he said. "But I might be able to help more generally. That was a tumultuous time in the East Coast ports. The ILA—the longshoremen—were rebelling against modernization and automation because it cost them jobs. The country was under almost constant threat of strikes and shutdowns that would have created economic havoc. Our solution was to avoid the East Coast ports entirely. We tried bringing our European products through Gulf Coast ports, but so many other companies were diverting those Gulf Coast facilities were overwhelmed. So we opted to offload our shipments to barges and bring them up the Mississippi and the Illinois Rivers to the Port of Chicago. I'm sure it cost us a lot of money, but at least we could factor the extra time into our ordering scenarios. I was an intern in the spirits department back then, but I remember we put in a lot of late nights trying to figure out shipping schedules."

"So nothing went through Customs until it got to Chicago?" I said.

"Nothing coming from Great Britain or Europe, no, not between May 1973 and the end of 1974. We used a lot of airfreight, but only from Asia and South America. Everything from Europe came up the Mississippi and entered through Customs at the Port of Chicago."

"Do you request copies of the release-of-cargo docs for every shipment entering the country, Mr. Kaplan?"

"We always have," he said. "It gives us a full set of papers tracking possession right to the doors of our warehouses."

"And since this semi in particular was still parked on Chicago Port property when it was stolen, what does that tell you about its status with Customs?"

"It's hard to say, Ms. Mora. Though my suspicion is the Laphroig had gone through Customs, and the truck was simply awaiting a driver. Give me the exact date of the theft, and I'll see what I can find out."

KAPLAN CALLED BACK the next day. Corporate records showed the Laphroig delivered to the company, but none of the documentation remained. All of it had been seized by the feds in the investigation of the theft. No one bothered to return it.

14

I heard John Conti enter the restaurant before I saw him. Murmurs of recognition and greeting. The distinctive, cordial baritone voice.

That was John.

His family and mine went back a lot of years. We had lived next door in the stately, old brownstones of West Jackson Street, in the Hospital District. When my mother died, John's wife, Carole, became a surrogate mother to the seven-year-old Mora twins. She and John had a daughter, but she was grown and lived in Oregon, and I didn't know her very well.

Years later, shortly after my father died of a stroke in 2012, Carole was killed in a hit-and-run crash on the Dan Ryan Expressway. John caved in on himself. He suspended his re-election campaign and talked about resigning from Congress. He was re-elected, anyway, but he didn't return to Washington right away. He holed up at home with the drapes drawn for months.

Although we weren't neighbors any longer, I went to see him as often as I could. We worked together to get through our shared losses.

Even after John returned to Washington, we talked from time to time by phone, and when he made visits back to the district we got together if he had time.

But people drift apart. I didn't think I'd seen John in eight months.

So far as I knew, the police still had no clues to the identity of the driver who killed Carole. I thought that lack of closure made her death that much harder on John. No matter how happy he seemed outwardly, I could see the enduring sadness deep behind his eyes.

I had secured a nice table by a window where John would have no trouble finding me. Sure enough, he turned up at my side two minutes later. I stood and shook his hand. He put a hand on my shoulder and drew me to him. He kissed my cheek and hugged me, gestures of familiarity and a long friendship.

John looked younger than his sixty-four years. He was tanned and fit and groomed as if for a photo shoot. His hair had gone gray, which made him look more distinguished. His dark brown eyes sparkled with warmth and interest. He drew back and squinted at my forehead.

"That musta hurt," he said. "I'm so sorry."

He ordered a double Johnny Walker Black on the rocks, and I ordered club soda, in deference to having eaten only a couple of muffins all day.

"Well, you're a cheap date tonight," he said. "I thought all newspaper people were drinkers. Bottle in the bottom desk drawer, and all that."

"I think that started dying out in the 60s, John," I said. "We're losing all the great traditions, booze in the desk, tulip telephones, people yelling, 'Copy!' and 'Stop the presses!' You've got to rent old movies to see that stuff now. The fact is, we're losing our profession to celebrity gossip, sound bytes, and the Internet."

He chuckled. "Bitter much?"

"Yeah," I said. "A lot."

"Things gotta change," he said. "Whole world's changing. But some things, like newspapers, I don't know, you expected there'd always be one at your front door in the morning. *Journal*'s lost a lot of good people, hasn't it?"

"It has," I said. "Earlier this week, they cut a Pulitzer Prize-winner loose."

He shook his head. "You think you're safe?"

I shrugged. "I don't think anybody's safe. It's a stressful way to exist day to day. Every morning I go to work not knowing if my job's still there."

Now he pointed a finger at me. "Anything happens to your job, your first call's to me. I'll help you find something corporate in Chicago. Or if you want to try government, we always need good people in Washington. I mean it, Deuce."

I appreciated it, and said so.

Our drinks came.

"I think about you a lot, Deuce," he said. "When I read your column, I look for hints about how you're doing emotionally. But you don't let people in much. I remember when your dad died you wouldn't talk to me at all about how you felt." He paused a moment. "Then Carole was killed, and we sort of crumbled together. It was the first time you ever talked to me about your feelings."

"That was a pretty extraordinary circumstance," I said, "both of us with such big losses coming so close together. I don't let many people know me. I hated writing the column about the break-in. I don't like sharing my private life. Makes me feel vulnerable. But my editors didn't give me a choice."

"When I read it, I realized how long it had been since I called you, and I was ashamed of myself. You must've thought I dropped off the edge of the world."

"No," I said. "We're both past the worst of our grief. We have to get on with life."

John sipped his drink and watched the amber liquid swirl around the clear ice.

"I still miss Carole every day," he said, his voice soft and sad. I noticed he wore a double wedding band, his and his wife's, soldered together edge-to-edge. Together forever. He saw me notice. "I still feel married to her," he said. "People ask me why I don't take the rings off. I tried it once, one night before I went to bed. I couldn't sleep. It felt all wrong."

"Then you shouldn't take them off," I said. "When the time is right, you'll know. And if you never take them off, it's nobody's business but yours."

"People want to fix me up on dates all the time," he said, and his face flushed. "I tell them I don't want to go out. I'd feel like I was cheating on her. Weird, isn't it?"

"I think it's sweet," I said. "I don't think Dad dated, either, after my mother died. And he lived another twenty-four years."

John ordered a second drink, and then we ordered dinner and changed the subject.

"So what got you interested in this old case of mine?" he said with a broad smile. "It's not only old news, it's mummified and petrified."

I explained it was supposed to be a human-interest story, meant to help an old guy find the family he'd lost years before.

"But Vinnie didn't want to talk about it," I said. "It scared him to death that I was even asking. I guess somebody wanted to make sure he didn't tell me, because they killed him that same night. Tortured him and cut his throat."

"Should I be leaning on the police?"

"In Cicero?"

He chuckled. "I know people in a lot of places."

"From what I know, the police are doing what they can."

"So you never even got to hear the old guy's story?"

"He wouldn't tell me anything. His bartender told me what he'd heard from Vinnie, but it didn't amount to anything."

"He got killed, and you got beat up over nothing," John said. "That's not fair."

"You think?" I said.

"But you're still looking into it?"

I shrugged. "I'm trying, but I don't think it's going anywhere. My editors won't let me take the time away from my column."

"What do you want me to do?"

"Maybe you could clear up a couple of things for me."

He nodded. "Sure. I will if I can."

"Why did this become a federal case when it started in state court?" I said.

"Well, not because we were looking for more work," John said with a small laugh. "Under most circumstances, we'da been happy to turn our backs on the case and leave it to the state. It was judicial clutter."

"Then why didn't you?"

"You're asking a lot of an old man with an old memory," he said. "When Richard Palmieri told me about your interest, we put our heads together. What Richard recalls is this Colangelo fellow had pleaded out any number of charges over the years, probably did a tenth the time he was liable for. When Richard found out the Scotch was still in federal jurisdiction, he decided to make an example of Colangelo."

He took a sip of his drink. "I was, after all, the law-and-order U.S. Attorney looking to run for Congress some day. Richard thought it would be a good conviction to have. So we prosecuted the heck out of the case – well, Richard did – and convinced the judge to send the guy away for the maximum. I guess it worked. I checked, and that's the last time he was arrested for anything."

"Why him and not his two partners?"

"They didn't have his history. I mean, they were bad actors, too, but not like Colangelo. It was a tradeoff. We figured they'd testify against Colangelo for consideration, and we'd get another crack at both of 'em later."

From John's view, I could see how it made sense. He was trying to pile up convictions to build a record he could run on. And he never made a secret of it.

"What else can I do for you, Deuce?" he said.

"I'm trying to get a copy of Vinnie's trial transcript," I said. "A clerk at the courthouse said it would take three weeks. Any chance you could speed up the process?"

John put his knife and fork across his plate of veal saltimbocca and sat back. He thrust his chin at my face.

"I can do better than giving you help," he said. "I can give you some good advice. Let it go. It's an old, old story. It's already landed you in the hospital once."

"There's an echo in this city. You're the third or fourth person to suggest walking away. But I can't do that. I owe Vinnie."

"No, you don't. And I don't want to see anything else happen to you. Deuce, I've lost too much, too many people I loved. If I lost you, too, and God forbid I felt as though I helped it happen, I couldn't live with it." He dropped his head and groaned. "That sounds pretty self-absorbed, doesn't it, as though this is all about me. Sorry."

"Nothing's going to happen to me from reading a trial transcript, John."

"It's what you do with the knowledge that worries me."

"Why, is there something that would send me off looking for dragons to slay?"

He smiled. "Not that I remember. I think it was pretty routine."

"Then what's stopping you?"

"Purely fear for your safety. As for rushing the process, clerks rule the world. But I can try." He took a small leather notebook and a pen from his pocket. "I'll make some calls. I can't make it happen overnight, but it shouldn't take three weeks."

"Thanks," I said. "I appreciate it."

We were interrupted several times by well wishers and hangers on, but John managed to keep the interruptions brief without offending anyone.

We watched the neighborhood slip by beyond the restaurant windows for a few moments. Little Italy was a good place, brought back from decay and rampant crime, an upscale wave of redevelopment working its way west along Taylor Street. Families were out in the evening. Young couples. Old couples. Gay couples. Tourists. Mexican, white, Asian, Greek, Italian, black. Having fun. Getting along fine. Enjoying a fall evening. Darkness was no enemy here. John and I savored the meal and enjoyed the ambience.

Over John's objection, I paid my share of the bill. Outside the restaurant we embraced, and John laid a soft kiss on my forehead. Then we went our separate ways.

I PULLED into my condo garage, and a pair of headlights washed over me from a giant vehicle pulling in behind me. I was blocked, my only escape on foot.

"It's all right, Ma'am," a man's voice said.

He killed the headlights, and I saw the Escalade with the rent-a-cop logo and the amber light bars, and I allowed myself to breathe again. These men were supposed to protect me, not scare me to death. We rode up in the elevator together. As I walked toward my door, I tried to stare through the walls to see if any living creatures besides the cats lurked there. Someone could have disabled the alarm and broken in during the day. As if reading my thoughts, the agents walked past me to my door.

"Let us have a look inside first," he said, taking my key.

My cell phone rang. It was Eric. I told him about my day.

"Good progress," Eric said. "It reinforces our decision."

"What decision?" I said.

"We're popping you loose from the column through next week. We want the story nailed down as fast as you can do it. So we're clearing some time."

"Really?" I said. I was both surprised and happy with that. I'd been feeling burned out on the column, anyway. This was my chance to rejuvenate. "Sounds like a plan," I said.

The security guard came out of my unit and gave me a thumbs-up. He handed me my keys as he walked passed. I mouthed, "Thank you," and turned back to the phone.

"I'm still waiting for the paperwork from the school district," I said. "And then I think I'll go back down to Ransom Camp and have another look around. Maybe I can find that old guy again. He's got some interest down there, or he wouldn't be so protective of the place. I wouldn't be surprised if he's the one who's been keeping the weeds cut back from the school foundation to preserve it. If he lived in Ransom Camp fifty-seven years ago, we might have ourselves a genuine witness."

"Maybe you should think about taking somebody with you," Eric said. "Are the security guys there? Take them."

"To ward off an old man?" I said.

"No offense intended," Eric said. "It's just that the old guy's got lots of backup."

"Who?" I said.

"You're the one who heard the voices of the spirits."

I sighed. "Good night, Eric."

As I WALKED through the front door the cell phone rang again. It was Sully.

"I'm on the campaign trail tomorrow," he said, "but you can reach me on my cell."

"More to the point," I said, "can your friend in Washington, Peter Linsky, reach you? I hope he's still trying to help us."

"Yeah, and he's got my number. Problem is, I'm not sure what he's going to get."

"Reading had to be working with somebody to develop information, Sully. Maybe he was using an investigator from some congressional committee, or even private help. Lean on Peter. Find out who it was. If Reading paid an investigator out of office funds, there has to be a record."

"The FBI will have him under wraps."

"Think positive," I said.

"Positively, Deuce. Think *positively.* Jesus, it's a good thing you don't write for a living."

I was two steps inside the front door when the phone rang a third time. It was Kathleen Henderson from the LaSalle County school district. She was working late.

"The good news is the information you asked for didn't burn up in the fire," she said. "The bad news is, it's so old we don't have it on the computer system. It's on fiche. We found the pertinent spools, but we have to make copies of the documents for you so we can redact personal information. If you stop by about ten tomorrow, they should be ready."

"That's great," I said. "Thanks."

I glanced around the condo at the mess. I hadn't felt well enough after the attack to clean up, and everything remained as the intruder and forensics guys left it, though someone had cleaned up the fingerprint powder and the blood. I didn't feel much like cleaning up the rest. It could wait until the weekend.

I had entered a mutual-aid pact with John Conti. I liked and trusted the man. But it was his office, after all, that prosecuted the hell out of Vinnie Colangelo under suspicious circs. If Richard Palmieri had reasons beyond the politics to go the extra mile back then, did John know? And if he knew, how far would he go to protect the U.S. Attorney's office and his old friend, Palmieri? I called the news library and got Lucy. Feeling guilty as hell that I had any doubts about John, I explained what I needed.

"I'd like to know everything there is to know," I said. "I'm sure we go over his background every time he runs for re-election, but I don't know the particulars. I need to know about his friends, his relatives, his associates—particularly Richard Palmieri. And Conti's finances. What does he own? Who does he owe?"

"You mentioned Richard Palmieri. You want me to do the same check on him?"

"Yeah, that would be great. Thanks."

I couldn't ignore Caesar and Claudius. They demanded to be fed and watered, which I took care of first. Next, I attended to their litter box. It needed fresh litter. I cleaned the pan and refilled it, and Caesar appeared seconds later to inaugurate the new sand pile.

My pet chores completed, I stretched out on the sofa to review the threads of my story. I realized a short way into the process that I had to use my living room wall to diagram the investigation or find a yellow legal pad somewhere.

I decided on the legal pad. It was easier to carry around than a wall.

Vinnie either foretold the assassination in Las Vegas or fabricated a story that became the mother of all coincidences. I didn't believe in coincidences. I've said that before.

I listed the people I'd interviewed with short synopses of their information:

Vinnie, the victim, a man with a long criminal history but no identity before 1957.

Jerry Alvarez, the prosecutor who tipped me to Vinnie and now refused to help me get to the bottom of Vinnie's murder.

Percy, the Jo-Jo's bartender who told me Vinnie's backstory.

Richard Palmieri, who prosecuted Vinnie in federal court for the theft of the Scotch.

John Conti, the congressman and my old friend, who had been Palmieri's boss at the time of Vinnie's prosecution but had no role in it.

Simon Donovan, the public defender who died in a courthouse shootout after he noted the name "Ransom Camp" in his file on Vinnie's case. Was there a connection?

The old man I encountered at Ransom Camp.

Sully, and by extension, his friend, Peter Linsky, the former chief of staff for the assassination victim, Rep. Charles Reading.

Harold Bickerstaff, the retired LaSalle County fire investigator, plus other assorted fire investigators and cops. And a cast of thousands.

So where was I?

I knew Vinnie Colangelo's story, his claims of over-prosecution, and the names of those who sent him away. I knew Vinnie was tortured and murdered after he was seen talking to me and leaving Jo-Jo's bar with me. It appeared the notation of "Ransom Camp" in Simon Donovan's file could tie Vinnie to a horrific crime almost sixty years ago. But if it did, I didn't know how. I suspected Vinnie had been killed to keep him quiet about something. But I didn't know if the topic was the Las Vegas assassination, the Ransom Camp fire, roaches in the kitchen at Jo-Jo's, all of the above, or none of the above.

In short, I didn't know very damned much.

15

I didn't feel rested when I woke up on the sofa the next morning. So I didn't feel up to putting a lot of effort into my appearance. I chose a pair of flared indigo blue jeans and a dusty rose V-neck sweater over a light blue t-shirt. A pair of black BØRN ankle boots completed the look, which I favored. I've always been a no-frills tomboy type, and if I didn't have to, I'd never get out of denim except to put on shorts.

Kathleen Henderson had the school records waiting for me when I showed up at ten. My anticipation had crawled so high during the morning I couldn't resist standing in her office and scanning the pages for familiar names. I found Ricardo LaPalma, the kid identified by fire investigator Harold Bickerstaff as the principal arsonist at Ransom Camp. According to Bickerstaff, someone had shot and killed Ricardo a day or two after the fires. There were seven other LaPalmas by my quick count, spread out over LaSalle County schools. I wondered if they all were related.

I checked the lists again. No Vinnie Colangelo on any of them.

I thanked Kathleen Henderson and returned to my truck to give the lists a closer read. I turned on the engine, plugged in my phone, and checked my email. Sully had left a note telling me Peter Linsky, his source in Washington, confirmed that Reading had been working with an investigator. Linsky didn't know the individual's identity but would try to retrieve it from pay vouchers.

There was a caveat. Peter had been picked up for a Senate staff job and wasn't sure how much time he'd have to help us. I emailed Sully back and urged him to guilt-trip Peter, tell him he had a moral obligation to help learn who killed his former boss and why.

My phone rang five seconds later. The caller ID read, "Ryland."

Eric didn't bother to say hello. "Have you looked at the school rosters yet?" he asked.

"Just a glance," I said. "By my quick count, there were eight LaPalmas in three schools in the fifty-six/fifty-seven school year. That includes the Ransom Camp School."

"Was Ricardo there?"

"Yes, along with five other boys and two girls stretching from the fourth grade to the ninth. I'm not sure how we're going to sort them out."

"So what now?"

"I'm going to head down south and look for the old man in the woods."

"Check in with me from time to time," Eric said. "After the other night, I'm not thrilled about you going down there alone."

"So you said."

"Well, I meant it."

I picked up the school list again, and a name jumped off the page. How had I missed it the first time? Mary Conti. I looked for other Conti names but found none. The congressman made no secret of the fact that his parents had been migrant workers, and that he lived in migrant camps as a very young child. But I didn't remember him ever saying exactly where. This wasn't surprising, since migrant workers start their seasons in the South and work their way north as the harvest year progresses. John Conti's family probably lived in dozens of camps in thirteen or fourteen states. Mary Conti was likely a coincidence with no ties at all to John. Conti was one of the most common Italian names in the United States.

To be certain, I pulled out my iPad and did a search of the name in Chicago. It came up more than 1,600 times. When I searched the whole state, the hits exceeded 5,500. Twenty-nine of them alone were in LaSalle County, right where I was sitting. Mary Conti was much more likely a member of the LaSalle County Contis than the Cook County Contis. Her name on my school list was interesting, but meant nothing.

The phone rang again. It was Lucy Sandoval, the *Journal's* researcher.

"Hi, Deuce," she said. "I've got Conti's financials for you, if this is a good time."

"Now's good," I said.

"Okay, this is your life, John Conti. Member in good standing of the Knights of Columbus and the Italian Catholic Federation. His election reports and financial filings with the House, all public record, show he's clean. No debt. He doesn't owe money to anybody."

"That's not possible," I said. "All politicians have debt, even if it's only stuff associated with their campaigns."

"Since his fourth campaign, he's been unopposed," Lucy said. "His election reports show a lot of political donations, and he uses some of that money in his campaigns. But he gives everything left over to charities in his district. He never borrows for campaigns. The personal financials don't show any debt. And his investments are true-blue. T-bills. Municipal bonds. Very conservative. No stocks. No possible conflicts of interest."

"Amounts?"

"About $730,000 total," she said. "Nice, but not extraordinary. A lot of members of Congress have investments worth millions. The AutoTrak database says he's got no boats, no airplanes. John Conti is a poster boy for fiscal responsibility."

"Cars?"

"He owns a new Mercedes convertible, the big one, an SL550 Roadster," she said. "There's more than a hundred-grand right there. But he doesn't owe penny one on the car. He paid cash. He has no credit card debt. His FICO score is 821. If he ever owed anybody anything for more than a month, it dates back more than the seven-year credit cycle. He has an American Express card and a Chase Visa. He pays them off in full every month."

"He has to have some source of cash to do that," I said. "Savings accounts? CDs?"

"Both," Lucy said. "He has $335,000 in certificates of deposit, all the long-term variety. He has $48,000 in a money market account, where he puts in $1,000 or so now and then but never seems to withdraw anything. He pays his bills straight out of an interest-bearing checking account, where his paychecks are deposited electronically. As of August fifteenth, he had $31,000 in there. That's a lot of money to keep in a checking account, even one that pays interest. But if you've got no debt, those congressional paychecks keep piling up."

"He gets paid pretty well for speaking engagements, too, and sits on some boards. Did he report all that?"

"Yep."

"What's his house worth?"

"His house on West Jackson is appraised for taxes at $795,000, which means the market value would be around $950,000, give or take. In a better market it might go for up to $1.5 million. Typical for the neighborhood. Isn't living without debt un-American?"

"My father was the same way," I said. "Paid off his house as fast as he could, never let a credit card bill slide even a month, paid cash for his cars. He was obsessive about it. I think it has something to do with growing up during or just after the Depression. It might not be the modern American way, but there's something admirable about it."

THE MORNING HAD TURNED into afternoon, and I was hungry.

I needed to go down to Ransom again. But I didn't want to spend time in Jerry's Tap answering questions from my new friends. So I bought a turkey sandwich, a bag of Sun Chips and a bottle of water from the little coffee shop in Ottawa and ate them in the car as I drove south.

Between the first half of my sandwich and the second, Lucy called again with the facts of Conti's personal life. I told her I was driving and couldn't write anything. She said she'd tell me what she found then drop the file in my computer. With her usual efficiency, Lucy already had all the angles covered.

"No real surprises," she said. "Moderate Democrat, Italian ancestry, widower, one daughter grown and living in Oregon. While he was U.S. Attorney he convicted a lot of people, but his critics said he was piling up numbers, taking on easy cases in order to create a crime-fighter platform for his House race. That was before he won a high-profile victory in convicting the psychopath, Roswell Parks. Parks kidnapped and killed two little girls from Cabrini Green. He raped them and stabbed them to death. Threw their bodies in a vacant lot. Conti stole the case out from under the nose of the local prosecutor, Harper Tealman, an idiot with a history of messing up big cases. Conti got the conviction and sent Parks to Death Row. He was executed in ninety-four."

"Anything else?" I said.

"He graduated from Bridgeport Catholic. Went to Loyola on a full scholarship and got a bachelor's degree in finance. Law degree from the University of Chicago. This guy's no dummy. He came up through the prosecutor's office and then headed off to Washington."

"Already knew all that," I said. "He serve in the military?"

"No. He registered, but they never called him."

I glanced at the name, Mary Conti, on the Ransom Camp school roster lying in the passenger seat.

"Lucy, do the records show Conti having any brothers or sisters?"

"Nope. He's an only child. Unusual for a Roman Catholic family of that era."

I needed to talk to John Conti again on the off chance he'd ever heard anything about Ransom Camp or had ever been there.

"Great work, Lucy," I said.

"I'll start on Richard Palmieri and call you back."

I RESUMED the circuitous trip back to Ransom Camp, my apprehension growing with each mile. I had been cavalier with Eric when he suggested I take someone with me. With each mile I drove, I found myself more and more wishing I'd taken his advice.

My concerns disappeared when I pulled my Explorer off the road in the same place I parked the first time. Sitting in front of me was a late-model red Dodge Ram crew cab 3500. It had the name and insignia of the Illinois Fire Marshal on the side.

I pulled on my boots, climbed over the gate, and walked toward the remains of the burned-out schoolhouse. I heard footsteps behind me, and my heart rate jumped. I turned and found Mark Hearst, the Chicago arson investigator, walking toward me. I was glad to see him again on two scores, one entirely unprofessional.

"I figured you were here," I said. "That big red truck was a definite giveaway."

"Couldn't get the place off my mind," he said. "So I came to have a look." He shrugged. "My day off. Got directions from the diner in Ransom. A waitress said I was the second person askin' about the place. Figured you were the first. Don't know what I expected to find. There isn't any evidence left after half a century."

"First time I was here," I told him, "I ran into an old guy who didn't take kindly to my presence. I was hoping for a second chance to convince him to talk to me. I have a feeling he knows what happened here."

"Haven't seen anybody," Hearst said. He looked around. "I did have the feelin' once or twice I was being watched, though. Could be your guy."

"So there's nothing here to see?" I said.

"Not much," he said. "Rusted out frame of a trailer. A couple of wheels, a few smaller vehicles, or what's left of 'em. Nature has long since turned everything man-made into weed planters. There's a few trails back in toward a creek that feeds and drains a lake, and a shack up on stilts. Shack looks like it's been here a while."

"So there's no reason for me to go poking around out there?" I said.

He shook his head. "There's nothin' you can make any sense of. Besides, you're not dressed for it. Lots of underbrush and mud and snakes. A rattler got me, but I took him on the back of my boot." He pointed to a spot on the leather. I saw two new pinprick scrapes and a smear of liquid, likely the snake's venom.

My own boots had steel reinforcement in the heels and toes, which would protect me as well as Hearst's boots protected him. But I saw no reason to test the theory. I wasn't here for a nature hike.

We stood in silence, scanning the bramble around us.

"Did you talk to the old fire guy in the retirement home, Bickerstaff?" he said.

I nodded.

"I'm sure he told you everything."

"Everything he remembered."

"Can you tell me?"

I did.

When I finished, we stood in silence. Between us, we'd seen all there was to see. Yet the place was oddly compelling and difficult to leave. When we made a move toward our vehicles, we came face-to-face with the old man, leaning on his staff. He'd come up on us without making a sound.

"You return," he said to me, his black eyes fixed on my face.

"Yes, sir," I said. "Something terrible happened here. We're trying to figure out what it was and who's responsible. I was hoping you'd help us."

"You disturb the dead before," he said. "Now you double the insult."

I assumed he meant Mark Hearst.

"We mean no disrespect," I said.

"We want justice for the dead," said Hearst. "My name is Mark Hearst. I'm an arson investigator for the state of Illinois."

"There have been your type here before," the old man said.

An opening. I took it.

"When were the fire people here before?"

"Back then."

"When the fires happened?"

"Yes."

"Sir, were you here on the night Ransom Camp burned?" I asked him.

His eyes held mine for a moment longer, and then he gave me a small, quick nod.

"Would you talk to us about that night?" I said.

"It was bad enough to live through it once," he said. "Why should I do this again?"

"Perhaps to help identify those responsible," I said.

"That will do no good," he said. "All of us who survived knew who they were. Nobody cared then. Nobody cares now."

"Are they still alive, the ones who set the fires?"

"*One* is still alive, yes."

"And you know who he is?" I asked the question with my heart in my throat and was stunned by the reply.

"Yes," he said.

The old man resisted saying anything more. I tried several approaches in hopes of convincing him that we could be trusted. Nothing worked.

"Is there a reason you won't talk to us?" I said. "We only want to help."

He hooked a weathered thumb toward Mark and said, "I know who he is. He belongs to the government, and the government never lifts a finger for us. No reason to trust him." He thrust his chin toward me. "About you I know nothing."

I realized I hadn't introduced myself during our initial encounter. I had reservations about telling the old man I was a reporter. Some people, especially those predisposed to distrust, don't respond well. But the paper had strict policies about this, so I came clean. He reacted in a way exactly opposite what I'd feared.

"You work for a newspaper?" he said.

"That's right," I said.

"You could put in the newspaper what happened to us?" he said.

"If you help me understand the truth."

He glanced toward Mark. "And you trust this man?" he said.

"I do," I said.

I saw him relax.

"Now that you know who I am," I said, "who are you?"

"Miguel," he said. "Miguel Astosso. I am Nicaraguan, of the Miskito Indian Nation. You think you can help us? After all this time?"

"Us?" I said.

"Some who survived fire decided to stay here. Built homes in the woods west of here. We don't bother nobody. Nobody bothers us."

"Tell us about Ransom Camp." I pulled out my digital recorder, backing up the technology with a pen and notebook.

"It is a long story," he said. "And my English is not good."

"We have time," I said. "And your English is fine."

He motioned us to a clearing where several trees had fallen. He limped along, putting most of his weight on his staff. He sank onto one log and motioned us to another, about three feet away.

"Ransom Camp," he said, and gave a snort that might have been a derisive laugh. "It even sounds evil. Full of snakes and people who act like snakes, always fighting each other for a little bit of work. Most were illegals who follow the harvests north from Texas and Lou'siana. They try to hide in these woods from the law that would send them home."

"But somebody built your people a school," I said.

"It is the city peoples who build the school in the early fifties. It has toilets and sinks and showers that work with big, uh ..." He spread his arms in a circle and moved them up and down, trying to pantomime the word he sought.

"Barrels," he said, finally.

"Cisterns," Mark said. "Rainwater capture. There's probably an old septic system around here somewhere."

"Yes," the old man said. "It is better from when everybody washes in the creek and lake and do their business where it suits them."

"I wonder if it was a school or a glorified outhouse," Mark said, glancing toward the burned-out foundation.

Astosso ignored the remark and continued. "The migrants supply own teachers, our own peoples who are too old to work the fields and don't know much more than the childrens they teach. Sometimes, though, city people come and help. Make records of childrens and check their learning and their health. Most childrens, they don't finish school. By the time they are ten, eleven, parents need the money they can earn in the fields. Sometimes a children gets born to parents who think education is good. One like this is Martin LaPalma. His mother and father, whose names I do not remember, come from Chicago during, what you call it? When whole country is poor?"

"The Great Depression?" Mark said.

Miguel nodded. "Yes. All this is three generations past. But it is important to what happens here. I was told of this by my grandfather, who was their friend. Martin LaPalma's parents lose their jobs and home. They got no place to go, so they come here. They hope for a future for their son, Martin. But they don't live to see nothin'. They die in a wreck coming home from the fields. Martin, their son, must leave school to work. He survives through the kindness of neighbors, including my family. But instead of thanks, his heart fills with bitterness. Instead of kindness for those who look after him, he shows only hatred. He wants the land of Ransom Camp for his own because he thinks being born in United States and being a citizen gives him rights the rest of us no have. In a few years, he marries a woman, LuAnne, who shares his hate for Ransom Camp peoples. It don't matter that the immigrants live in worse conditions, work too many hours for bad pay, have no medicine. The LaPalmas are crazy with hate. They should move away from this place, but it is like Ransom Camp justifi...justif..."

"Justifies?" Mark said.

"*Si*, justifies their hate. Their hate becomes who they are. They wear it like clothes. Reuben is one of their sons. Him and me, we are friends. He is not like the others. He wants to grow up to be a pilot in the Navy. But his parents, they kill his dream. They take him outta school. They put into his head that this country was made by white men, but the government lets it be lived in by trash like us who don't belong here."

Now I had to interrupt. I was thinking of those eight LaPalmas on the school board list.

"Reuben was one of the sons," I said. "What other children were there?"

He frowned. "Lemme see, my memory maybe not so good," he said. "There were two boys almost same age, Ricardo and Reuben. And the little girl, Emily. Very pretty. Very sad."

"That's all?"

"Maybe some cousins, but I don't know them so good."

I nodded for him to continue.

"Reuben tells me once," he said, "how him an' Ricardo watch from hiding when their father and three other men drag a Mexican from his pickup and beat him to death. Then they put the body back in truck, pour gasoline on it, and set fire to truck. The dead man say something in a bar about the LaPalmas. He is killed in revenge. Police don't care."

Miguel stared at me, as if to make sure I was getting it. Then he continued.

"After that, after Mexican gets beat to death, Ricardo and Reuben, they get mean. Is like they pick it up from their father and his friends. I can't even play with Reuben no more. He frightens me."

He glanced around, as though afraid of someone in hiding nearby. Then he looked back at me. "Reuben," he said," he frightens my grandfather, who doesn't want him coming around no more. Reuben, he talks about killing illegals, about driving everybody outta Ransom Camp and taking the land for his family. An' then one night, Ricardo and Reuben, they do it. They set fire to homes. Lotsa homes. Many peoples get burned up by Ricardo and Reuben. And then they set fire to the school. The woods catch fire. Everything burns." He paused and closed his eyes. "It was the night of screams."

I felt my eyes burn, and I had to swallow back the emotion trying to claw its way from my chest to my throat. "Your house burned, too?"

Miguel nodded. "With my grandfather an' my mother and my

brother inside. My sister and me get out right away. My grandfather an' my mother die in their beds. My brother escapes through a window, but he is burned bad and dies three days later. It is Reuben, who was my friend, who sets fire to my house. I see him do it."

He said this without emotion in his voice, but I could see in his eyes that he still felt the pain across the years.

"And then," I said, "sometime later, somebody shot Ricardo."

Miguel's eyes looked into mine with a ferocity that was almost palpable.

"Nobody shoots Ricardo," he said. "I shoot Reuben. For my burned-up family Reuben must die. But Ricardo? No. Ricardo still lives."

MARK HAD BEEN LETTING me ask the questions. Now he asked Miguel, "So, there were two arsonists?" Mark turned to me. "Harold Bicker-staff only identified the one."

"And he had the wrong one dead," I said. "He said someone shot Ricardo. Miguel says he shot Reuben. Assuming Miguel's story is accurate."

"It is truth," Miguel said. "What reason for me to lie?"

"None at all, Miguel," I said. "And the brothers, Ricardo and Reuben, they were close together in age, so Mr. Bickerstaff could have gotten them confused."

I heard a car on the gravel road above us. I looked toward the noise but saw nothing. I turned back to Miguel. The time had come for the big question.

"Where is Ricardo LaPalma today?" I said.

But Miguel was no longer paying attention to me. He was staring over my shoulder at the area where we'd heard gravel crunch.

"Miguel, where is Ricardo LaPalma?" I said again.

Miguel shook his head, then he stood, using his staff to pull himself up.

Without another word, he turned and melted into the underbrush. I called after him, but he didn't reply. I considered going after him, but it would have done no good. He knew the area too well and, as Mark pointed out, I wasn't dressed for the wilds of rural Illinois.

"I'll go bring him back," Mark said.

"You'll never find him. He's had decades to find every place there is to hide."

"I hate it," he said, "when a good story gets interrupted before the punch line. But it's time to get out of here. Whoever's up there has a key to the gate, and I doubt they're inclined to be friendly to trespassers."

As we set off on a roundabout route toward our vehicles, we heard a door slam and the sound of tires on gravel again, moving away from us this time.

"That's odd," I said.

"Let's see who it is," Mark said.

We began to run as best we could. We caught sight of the road in time to see a white car backing away, fast. At a wide spot, the driver executed a three-point turn, gunned the engine and headed west, toward the gate. Tinted windows prevented us from seeing who was inside, and by the time we got up on the road, the car was too far away to read any part of the license plate.

"It was a Chrysler," I said. "Did you get any details?"

"No," Mark said. "But now that they're gone, maybe Miguel will come back."

"I doubt it," I said, "but we can try."

We hurried back to the clearing and called for him, again and again.

We might as well have been calling to the wind. Mark put his arm around me. I felt heat through my clothes.

"I'm sorry," he said.

~

I TOLD Mark I would wait a day or two to let Miguel calm down and then come back and try to find him again.

"He said they lived in the woods west of here," Mark said. "We could go look for him. He has to be close by to come in and out on foot at his age, walking with that staff."

"Not today," I said. "If he's living among the survivors of Ransom Camp, they know by now that something spooked him. They'll protect him. Hide him if necessary. I'd rather give him some time to calm down and come back to us on his own."

As we walked back to our vehicles, the gate now wide open, Mark said, "I wonder why nobody ever developed this land. There's a nice fifty-acre lake down there and a couple of creeks that would've made nice spots for vacation homes. Pretty, wooded, secluded. Somebody could make some good money."

"Maybe," I said. "Maybe not. Miguel thinks the spirits of Ransom Camp live here. The land has a reputation for being haunted."

"All the better," Mark said. "Gives it a little cachet."

"Who'd want to live in a development called Ransom Camp?" I said.

He laughed. "Don't have to call it that. How about, Haunted Creek or Ghost Lake?"

"Or Sleepy Hollow?" I said, and we both laughed.

Still, his question raised one for me. Who did own this land? And what did the owners know of its history? I made a note to find out.

We approached our trucks, though Mark's dwarfed mine.

"I don't get it," Mark said.

"What?" I said.

"I know racism was never limited to the South. And I know there's a lot of resentment, even now, toward Latin immigrants, legal and otherwise. But I can't imagine two kids developing a hatred so intense they'd burn out an entire community and kill more than two dozen neighbors. They got all that from their parents?"

"Yeah, they could have," I told him. "I have an uncle who's a racist, the black sheep of the family. Uses the N-word every chance he gets. Doesn't matter to him what your ethnicity is. If you're not a white Christian, you're the N-word. He's well off, lives in a nice house, has all the comforts. But years ago, because of affirmative action, he didn't get some promotion he wanted. A black woman with performance ratings a little lower than Uncle Ted's got the spot instead. He went on to do fine, but he never got over that disappointment, and it grew and festered and boiled over into a really intense hatred."

Mark grimaced.

"And now," I said, "his kids are the same way. Only they hate without any reason at all, except they learned it from their father. Who knows what triggered the arson here. Somebody doesn't get his props and away you go. It escalates, much like modern gang warfare, I suppose."

"I can't imagine it on this scale," he said.

I had no answer for that, and we were quiet for a while. Then Mark asked a question.

"Would you have dinner with me some time?"

The proposal pleased me almost as much as it surprised me.

"I'd like that," I said.

He smiled a great smile. "Good. Let's check our busy schedules, and I'll have my people call your people to set something up."

I watched him drive away and missed him before he was out of sight.

I was putting on my seatbelt when Lucy called again.

"Richard Palmieri is pretty much a closed book," she said. "And his public record isn't very interesting. Law degree from DePaul, started in the U.S. Attorney's office at the bottom and worked his way up. After John Conti went to Washington, Palmieri opened his private practice, estimated to be the fourth most lucrative in the state. He has a jumbo mortgage on his home on Sheridan Road in Evanston, but no significant debt otherwise. No clue about annual income, but I think I'm safe in saying it's a bunch. Pretty dull."

"No hints of wrongdoing or Mob ties?" I asked.

"Not a thing I can find."

"Okay, Lucy, thanks for trying. As you have time, and there's no rush on this, you might run these names, all LaPalmas." I got out the pages of school rosters again and read off the first names of the eight LaPalma children. "One person told me Reuben is dead. Another said it's Ricardo who's dead. So run them both. The priorities are Ricardo, Reuben and Emily. The rest are cousins or no relation at all."

She repeated the names and spelled each one. She said she could get to the assignment first thing the next morning.

"I hope that's okay," she said. "Today's our twentieth wedding anniversary, and Vick is taking me to dinner at Spiaggia. I'm gonna need lots of primp time."

"Wow," I said. "Go. Enjoy. This can definitely take a back seat to a romantic evening with your husband, especially at Spiaggia. And congratulations. We'll talk tomorrow."

As I reached Ottawa, the county seat, I checked the dashboard clock. It was only 2:40. I had plenty of time to make the property appraiser's office before it closed.

I EXPLAINED to the clerk that I had no plat map or folio or anything else that would pinpoint the property or define its size. The best I could do was to show her on a map where the land was. She said we could muddle through with that.

We did. The one large parcel that encompassed Ransom Camp was 2,551 acres, including the unnamed lake and the creeks that ran through it.

"If that land's ever developed, the lake and creeks would be a big draw," the clerk said. "Large lots, mandatory shoreline setbacks, a couple of waterfront parks. It would be quite attractive and appealing to buyers."

"How's it zoned now?"

She frowned at her computer screen. "Agricultural. So the taxes are low. There's about 300 acres classified as flood plain, prone to flooding in heavy rain. That's maybe the reason nobody's snatched it up. It would take some serious and expensive re-engineering of the land contours to fix the problem. The law requires that the creeks and wetlands be protected or mitigated in the process. Might not be worth the expense."

I asked who owned the land, and the clerk ran a computer program.

"A company called Creek Enterprises, Inc.," she said. "No address. Just a Post Office box. The property tax bills go there, and it looks from these records as if they're paid promptly every year."

"Who signs the checks?" I asked her.

"These records won't say, but let me access corporation records." She tapped a lot of keys. "All we have is the name of the agent. Uh-oh, this won't help."

"What?" I said.

"Cal Miller," she said. "He's a professional agent. Works for a bunch of landowners in five or six counties around here. Makes sure their property is managed right and all the bills are paid on time. Mostly his clients are corporate farms."

"Where would I find this Cal Miller?" I said.

She wrote something on a piece of paper and slid it to me.

"He's in that office building right across the street," she said. "Convenient to get over here as often as he has to. Here's his phone number. Don't count on getting anything from Cal. He's not the most forthcoming person I've ever met."

I called the number from the street as I waited for the light to change. Cal Miller answered himself. He was in, but he had a client in the office and couldn't speak with me right away.

"I'll be happy to wait," I said. "I'll be there in less than five minutes. Stick your head out when you're done with the client."

I rang off. It was an old trick. Confront reluctant sources with your inevitable presence, and they tended to open the door.

They also tended not to tell you anything of value.

I hoped it would be different this time.

Miller proved to be a stereotype of the breed of people who do grunt work for others and get paid for it. They relieve the powerful and the overworked of necessary details of life for which they have neither the tolerance nor the time. Keeping all the details straight took a toll, however. Miller had a paunch and a stoop and a pair of wire-rimmed glasses that wouldn't stay set on his nose. As his stomach had grown, his hairline receded, and he styled what was left in a comb-over.

He greeted me with a weak handshake and indicated the chair in front of his desk.

"Sit and tell me quickly what you want," he said. "I have an appointment in an hour."

"An hour's more than enough time," I said.

"My appointment is forty-five minutes away," he said.

"Oh, well then, I'll get right to the point. I'm trying to find out who owns a piece of property listed to Creek Enterprises. It's southeast of ..."

"I'm quite familiar with where it is," Miller said, his tone displaying some tension.

"Who is Creek Enterprises?" I said.

"I'm not at liberty to disclose that information, and the law does not require it. If the owner wanted to be known, the information would be part of the public record. He, or she, doesn't, so it isn't."

"Why would this he, or she, want to hide his, or her, identity?"

"Ms....Mora, is it? If that's the information you came here to learn, then I suggest it's time for you to go. All legal and financial aspects of Creek Enterprises' ownership of the land in question are above-board and quite proper. That is all you will learn from me."

So I left. I had learned nothing. Cal Miller's attitude might have reflected his personality, or lack of one. It did nothing to satisfy my curiosity.

IT WAS a little after four when I drifted back toward Chicago. I had forgotten to check in with Eric after the encounter with Miguel Astosso. So I called. He scolded me, a mother act that had grown tiresome.

"I had a lot on my mind, and I forgot," I said. I told him about running into Mark Hearst, the conversation with Miguel, and the abrupt manner in which the interview ended.

"Damn, so close," he said.

"I'll talk to him again," I said.

"No idea who broke up your tea party?"

"Somebody driving a white Chrysler. Late model."

"Well, that narrows it down to twenty-thousand or so in the state."

When I finished with Eric, I called Sully. Before he became the *Journal's* political editor, Sully had been a whiz at stories involving real estate deals. Major deals, shady deals, deals inspired by politics. Maybe he could think of a way to get through the secrecy surrounding the true ownership of 2,551 acres of real estate I knew as Ransom Camp.

We agreed to meet at GT Fish & Oyster in River North. The neighborhood had been a lethal slum when the Cabrini Green project dominated it. Now those high-rises were gone, taking much of the crime with them, and River North had transformed from an area to be avoided into a trendy, upscale place to drink ginger martinis made with artisanal gin and eat great oysters at places like GT.

We ordered drinks, and I told Sully what I learned about the ownership of the Ransom Camp property. I said I thought Creek Enterprises was a front for someone, and I needed to know who. The property appraiser's office could give me only the name of the agent, and the agent wasn't saying squat. I didn't know where to go next, and I thought he might.

"And you checked the corporation records?" Sully said.

"The clerk in the appraiser's office did that," I said. "The agent's name was the only one on the documents, and the agent says he doesn't have to tell me anything."

"He doesn't, that's true," Sully said. "I don't think I can do anything tonight, but let me make a couple of calls in the morning."

He took a long pull at his beer as our waiter placed a large iced platter of assorted raw oysters on the half shell in front of us. When the waiter departed after identifying the region for each of the oyster pairs, Sully stared at me for a moment.

"You mind me asking what you'd gain from knowing who owns

the land? It seems almost symbolic, unless there's illegality involved, and I'm not hearing that."

"It feels important," I told him. "This is one of those stories where any little thing might be important. Why would somebody buy more than twenty-five-hundred acres when the most desirable three hundred acres are so wet the property would cost more to develop it than you'd be able to take out of it? It defies logic and therefore raises questions."

He sat back and put on what I called his "teacher face."

"Deuce, sometimes when a reporter gets into a story, the way you are with this one, you get to thinking that every little detail is earth-shaking. You start chasing these little details, and when you don't get anywhere, they start frustrating you and sapping your strength. Pretty soon, you find out the details that derailed you weren't important to the big picture after all. You're dead in the water, you've used up your energy, and you've got nothing to show for it. You have to guard against that."

I knew this, but I didn't think it applied in this case.

"I'm feeling pressure," I said. "This vacation from my column is finite. What if they decide I have to go back to it before I resolve anything, and the story floats off into the cosmos? Or suppose they give the story to somebody else."

"The editors want the story," he said. "As long as you make progress, they'll stay the course with you. And the pressure is all the more reason to use your time wisely."

I slumped back in my chair.

"Deuce," Sully said, "you're wound up way too tight. Let yourself breathe. Draw charts. Connect the dots. I'll make a couple of calls on that land. You have the legal description?"

I had made a copy for him and pushed it across the table.

"Thanks," I said. "You might be right. This might be one of those details that doesn't matter, but it doesn't smell right. If this land ownership is so righteous, why is all the ownership information being held so close?"

"It could be nothing more than an owner who doesn't want to be bugged by developers," Sully said.

"That would be easier to accept if the land were worth acquiring," I said.

"Eat your oysters," Sully said.

16

My armed guards were in place when I pulled into my garage. As usual, the younger one came for my keys so he could sweep the condo before I entered. Once again, he reported all clear.

I fed and watered Caesar and Claudius. I tried to watch reruns of *Seinfeld* and couldn't concentrate. At 10:30 I gave up and went to bed. But I couldn't sleep.

My mind kept wandering to Vinnie Colangelo, his brutal death, and my level of culpability. I would never look at my Someday File the same way again. Knowing my entry into someone's life could bring that life to a bad end was an awakening of the rudest kind.

And everything was about to get worse.

I gave up on sleep and tuned the television in my bedroom to a local 24-hour news channel. I'd never had much use for television news, local news in particular. The giggling and happy talk drove me nuts. Where was Walter Cronkite when we needed him?

The first story involved a shooting on the Far South Side. The second concerned a dustup at City Hall between the mayor and the city council. The third a fatal wreck on the Dan Ryan. The fourth story involved an ongoing investigation of public corruption in Cicero, a place that had honed public corruption to a fine art.

I got up to go to the bathroom when the next story stopped me in my tracks.

"A tragedy in a far western suburb tonight," the female anchor intoned. "An elderly man from LaSalle County died when his woodland home south of I-80, near the tiny community of Ransom, caught fire and burned to the ground in a matter of minutes."

The picture cut to an amateur video of flames pouring from windows and blasting through the roof of a small building.

Tightness began building in my chest.

The narrative continued. "Police and fire investigators say they suspect arson. The name of the victim has not been released, and the investigation is ongoing. We'll be back after this."

Cut to commercial.

I collapsed onto the side of the bed, certain I knew the identity of the dead man.

My cell phone rang. I grabbed it from the charger. It was Mark Hearst.

"You hear?" he said.

"Was it him?" I said.

"Yeah, it was," he said. "Deuce, I'm so sorry."

I felt my throat constrict.

"Shit," I said. "Shit. Shit. Damn and fuck."

"Off the record," Mark said, "it appears he was shot in the head first, and then the place was torched. Gasoline as accelerant, just like all those years ago. No effort to hide the fact it was arson. Whoever did it wanted us to know. More specifically, Deuce, I think, they wanted you to know."

"Oh, God, was he tortured, Mark?"

"That's something the M.E. will have to determine. But I think because he was shot to death before the house was burned, probably not. If they wanted to torture him, they would have let him burn alive."

Miguel Astosso thus became the second person to die because somebody wanted to send me a message.

Mark and I talked a few more minutes. Then I went into the bathroom and got sick. I seemed to be doing that a lot lately.

I BEGAN AN ALMOST maniac effort to clean up the days-old chaos left by the intruder. It was as if by cleaning my apartment I could clean up the hash I'd made of my world: If I put everything back in its proper place inside, maybe things would be normal again outside, and Miguel would be alive. And Vinnie.

It made no sense. But I became compulsive about order.

I was too wired to sleep, anyway.

When I had the place more or less restored, I poured a glass of wine and sat down to think. But I couldn't get my mind to focus.

My phone rang. It was Sully.

"I just saw the news," he said. "Please don't tell me ..."

"Yeah," I said. "What are you doing up at this hour?"

"I have two little kids, remember? They can't tell time yet." A moment's pause, then, "Are you okay?"

"No."

I felt myself losing composure. Sully waited for me to settle myself.

I continued. "Mark Hearst says Miguel was shot in the head first, and then the house was set on fire. How many people are going to die before I resolve this? And what if I can't resolve it? What if I keep getting people killed?"

"So what are you going to do?" Sully said.

"I want to rip out somebody's heart. But, Sully, to be honest, I'm scared. For me and everybody around me. I don't want anybody else to die, including me."

"Deuce..."

"I'm jumpy all the time. The guilt is making me physically ill. Right this minute I don't even want to be in journalism any more."

Sully was the one person on earth to whom I felt comfortable making those admissions. Revealing my feelings wasn't my style.

He was quiet for a moment. Then he said, "I don't want to see anybody else killed, either, especially not you. I want to tell you to quit blaming yourself for Vinnie and Miguel, and yet I know you can't. I couldn't, either. But try to imagine living the rest of your life with this story preying on your mind, with two murders gone unexplained and unpunished, on top of the twenty-six from 1957."

He took a breath. "I'm not telling you not to bail, Deuce. It's your life and your career, which makes it your decision. But don't do anything on a whim. Are you sick of the story? Are you sick of journalism? Or are you running away? And if you're running, where will you hide from yourself?"

Exactly the argument I had made to myself in the hospital after the home invasion. I had been right then, and Sully was right now. But at the moment, the rightness of the position didn't make much difference. I was sick of being me.

"Could you use some good news?" Sully said.

"Please," I said.

"I heard from Peter Linsky. I was going to wait until morning to call, so I wouldn't wake you up. Then I figured you might need some good news tonight. The investigator working for Reading is retired FBI. Peter is sure he can get a name. When I hear, you'll be the next to know."

"That's great, Sully, except even if we find him, he won't talk. So what good is he?" I didn't want to sound so skeptical, but I couldn't help myself.

"Maybe he will," Sully said. "You can be persuasive."

Yeah, I thought. And then he'll wind up dead, too.

17

The next morning, Eric called a hasty meeting with Sully and me. I had slept briefly and badly, wrestling with a decision. I came to the office with the intention of telling Eric to put my column back in the paper. If he wanted to assign the Colangelo story to someone else, fine. If he wanted to let it slide, fine. I was done. I wouldn't be responsible for any more death. Then, after I calmed down and caught up on my sleep, I could decide what to do about my future.

But Eric's reason for calling the meeting put my plans on hold.

Sully, he told us, was leaving the campaign trail for the weekend and going to Washington to schmooze his friend, Peter Linsky. The higher-ups figured Sully would get farther in a face-to-face with Peter than by waiting by the phone. The least I could do was wait to see how the weekend played out. Maybe Sully could get the FBI agent's name, and maybe the agent would decide to help us. Having an FBI agent to lean on might make me feel a little more competent.

"Give me a list of what we need to cover while you're gone," Eric told Sully. "Then get the first flight you can to D.C."

"Not a problem. There's not much going this weekend," Sully

said. "Hey, Deuce, I'll catch you later. Maybe tonight, after I've had a chance to see Peter."

"I'll be around," I said.

Sully left without mentioning our conversation the night before. It didn't surprise me. The decision was mine, and if I decided to pull out the timing would be mine, too.

I brought Eric up to date on the events of the night before. He had read about the fire. He hadn't realized its significance.

"What do you think this is really about?" he said.

"I wish I knew," I said.

"Any time this gets too scary," he said, "there's no shame in saying so."

There it was, my opening. And I couldn't bring myself to walk through it.

"Thanks," I said. "What about my column? The week's hiatus is up."

"We'll take it day-to-day," he said. "As long as you're making progress on the story and want to stay with it, you can."

"Have any readers asked about it, where it went, the column, I mean?" I said.

Eric had started reading and didn't look up when he said, "Not that I know of."

My ego shriveled up and ran off to hide inside one of my sinuses.

JOHN CONTI'S press secretary confirmed that the congressman was still in town—he was finalizing federal funding for the rehab of three bridges over the Chicago River. He would have some time to talk to me but not until early Sunday afternoon, if that was okay. It was. We would meet at his University Village office on South Halsted.

I had just taken my hand off the phone when I experienced a eureka moment, an instant when your subconscious links two apparently unrelated facts and rattles your brain to get your attention. Depending on whether Harold Bickerstaff or Miguel Astosso had the better memory, either Reuben or Ricardo LaPalma was dead. The other was in the wind. But there was one LaPalma sibling left, and if she was still alive, she might know where to find her living brother.

I wandered over to Lucy Sandoval. Again.

"Remember me?" I said.

"Vividly," she said with a broad smile. "What do you need?"

"First, I want to hear about Spiaggia. Was it as wonderful as its reputation?"

Lucy rolled her brown eyes. She looked radiant, from which I took it the after-dinner activities had been as pleasurable as the meal.

"It's heaven on earth," she said. "The price is insane, but if you're in a mood to celebrate, oh baby."

"So it was good," I said.

She squealed like a little girl remembering a hot-fudge sundae. And I had to laugh.

"So," she said, "back to business."

"Right. Did you ever have a chance to research those other LaPalma names?"

"I'm part way through the list. The work's been nuts the last couple of days."

"No problem. Did you get to Emily LaPalma?"

Lucy searched through some papers.

"I've already searched Reuben and Ricardo," she said. "I couldn't find either one of them for sure. Too many guys with those names all over Illinois. I haven't had a chance to search for Emily yet."

"If you have time, I'd appreciate it if you could check her now."

"Okay. Let's find Emily LaPalma."

"If she's married and took her husband's name, will that be a problem?" I said.

"Not if she hasn't completely abandoned her maiden name. Most women don't."

"She's older, so she's probably more old-fashioned about using her husband's name."

"Still won't be a problem. Was she married in Illinois?"

"I'm not positive she's married," I said. "I'm not even positive she's still alive. But if she is alive, and if she is married, I'm guessing she got married in Illinois. I'm winging it here."

"If she got married anywhere in the state, no sweat. I can find her in the marriage records. After that, we can find out if she's still alive. Don't go anywhere."

I watched her computer screen flash images and tried to follow along, but Lucy was into databases I knew nothing about.

"Is this her?" Lucy turned her monitor so I could see it more clearly and tapped it. "Emily LaPalma Humphries. DOB is August seven, 1947."

"So in 1957, she'd have been ten. That would be about right," I said.

"And, lucky for you, she lives in Bucktown."

I saw the address and started to write it down, but Lucy stopped me. "I'm printing it out for you," she told me.

"You're amazing."

"Piece of cake," she said.

I went to the GoogleMaps bookmark on my computer. I found the address on West Homer Street.

Bucktown was another of those neighborhoods west of the north branch of the Chicago River that had fallen into serious crime and disrepair and then made a comeback. It was now one of the trendy places to live. I suspected Emily LaPalma Humphries and her husband had bought their home back before the upturn began. Unless they had some serious money, a home in Bucktown now wasn't all that affordable. On the other hand, if they bought in the bad old days, they were now sitting on an urban gold mine.

When I pulled up a Google photo of the smallish three-story, it confirmed my guess.

The home had been remodeled outside. A wrought-iron gate surrounded a landscaped and manicured front yard and a brick patio ran down the left side of the house. The first level was half above and half below ground with a few steps leading down to the lower front entrance. Another few steps lead up to the porch and the main door.

Owners of homes like this often used the lower level as self-contained rental or guest space.

There was a third floor, too, an attic or a single room under the high, peaked roof. It had one window that held a unit air conditioner. That either meant no central AC or insulation insufficient to deal with the heat of the summer sun beating on the roof.

I took the six stone steps up to the main level, which had a stylish new wooden front door beside an elegant picture window.

During my drive north the sky began churning with heavy slate clouds. As I mounted the front steps, drops the size of small-caliber bullets began to pop against the porch roof. At least I had cover.

It had grown dark enough that I saw lights go on in the Humphries's home. I rang the bell. The man who answered appeared to be about Vinnie's age. He cracked the door just enough to speak to me, leaving a chain lock attached.

I introduced myself.

"What's a newspaper reporter want with me?" Verne Humphries said. "I ain't done nothin' worth puttin' inna paper."

"It's actually Mrs. Humphries I'm here to see," I said. "It's about her brother. I only have a couple of questions. It won't take long."

I saw his facial muscles tighten. I attributed it to fear, and perhaps hatred of Ricardo LaPalma. If Ricardo the adult remained as vicious as Ricardo the teenager, he had likely threatened his family into keeping his secrets. I was assuming here that Ricardo was the surviving brother, trusting that Miguel knew best which LaPalma he had shot.

"I'll see if Emily wants to talk to you," he said, "but this ain't the best time."

He closed and relocked the door, and I was left standing on the front porch in an increasing crossfire of wind-driven rain. The porch roof wasn't helping.

When the front door reopened, a smallish woman peered at me. Her white hair fell to her shoulders. I guessed she normally wore it up. Sun and age had lined her skin. At one time, the lines had been defined. Now they hung on slack flesh. She looked infinitely kind, the way I imagined my grandmothers would have looked had they lived long enough for me to know them. The thick lenses in her glasses magnified her warm brown eyes. A tide of tears filled the lower rims, and her cheeks were damp.

She had been crying, about what I couldn't imagine. The way her husband laid his hand on her shoulder, and the way she leaned into his touch, made me pretty sure he wasn't the problem.

"Yes?" she said.

"Mrs. Humphries, I'm Deuce Mora, from the *Journal*. Could I ask you some questions about your brother?"

"I don't want to talk to you about anything," she said. "Please. I don't mean to be rude, but it's a difficult time for me, and I'm not up to this."

"It's important that I find Ricardo."

"Ricardo?" she said. She squinted at me through those thick lenses.

"Yes," I said. "Do you keep in touch? Can you tell me where he is?"

"Please," she said, entreaty thick in her voice. "You have to go away. You have to go away right *now*. *Please*."

Before I could counter that, Verne reasserted himself.

"If you aren't off my property in ten seconds, I call the police," he said. "I won't have you upsetting my wife."

"I'm just asking a few questions," I said. "I'm looking into what happened at Ransom Camp." I looked back at Emily. "Do you remember Ransom Camp?"

Now tears overflowed those old, magnified eyes. Emily began to sob.

"Please, go away," she said in a soft, trembling voice. "Let the dead lie in peace."

"Nine seconds," Verne said. "Eight."

"Okay," I said. I handed him my business card. "In case you change your mind."

And I left.

～

BETWEEN THE RAIN and the Friday afternoon rush, it was early evening by the time I negotiated my way back to Pilsen. I allowed my guards to enter my apartment ahead of me and thanked them when they reported all clear. The older one smiled and told me the place looked nice all cleaned up.

I considered what to do with the weekend. I made the appointment with John Conti on Sunday for two reasons. With Miguel Astosso dead, I needed a way to approach others who had survived Ransom Camp and gain their trust. Because John came from a family of migrant workers, I thought he might be able to offer some suggestions. I didn't enjoy the prospect of putting more lives in danger over the Ransom Camp story, but if I was going to find out what Miguel hadn't had a chance to tell me, it was an unfortunate necessity.

For the moment, I decided to sit down with a glass of wine and do nothing.

Absolutely nothing.

I read a Nelson DeMille novel once, in which he wrote: "The problem with doing nothing is not knowing when you're finished." I laughed when I read it. But now I realized it wasn't entirely true. You know exactly when you're finished doing nothing. It's when you start doing something.

My phone rang. I answered it. Answering the phone is doing something.

It was Sully. He was calling from Washington.

"I just had drinks and dinner with Peter," he said. "The retired FBI agent, the one working privately for Congressman Reading, his name is Carl Cribben. Peter didn't try to contact Cribben. He thought it would be better if we approached him cold. Cribben used to be special agent in charge of the Las Vegas field office, which is how Reading knew him. He's retired now. You won't believe this. He lives up in Rogers Park, near Loyola University. Teaches a couple of criminal justice courses there."

"You know, my mileage reimbursements on this story could bankrupt the paper."

"So take the train."

Rogers Park was Chicago's northernmost neighborhood. It was crowded with old trees on good streets and bad. And it boasted Loyola University. Cribben lived near Loyola on one of the good streets.

If I drove up to see him the next day, I would have to plan with precision. FBI agents, even retired ones, didn't much like reporters showing up unannounced at their doors. I'd have to guilt him into talking to me, let the horror of what happened at Ransom Camp hook him the same way it hooked Mark Hearst.

Or maybe I'd spend Saturday trying to perfect the art of doing nothing.

I could go to the Oak Street beach and do nothing in the sun. Or I could go down to the Midway Plaisance in Hyde Park and do nothing in the shade. Or I could do nothing in the privacy of my own home.

Not an idea in the bunch that put anyone's life in danger.

So I WAS NOT a little surprised to find myself headed north toward Rogers Park the next morning. The weather had dried out and cooled off, and the sun blazed from a cobalt sky dotted by lines of small white clouds.

Cribben's street was pretty. The houses were three- and four-bedroom units with garages or parking in the rear. Nearly all were of a style called American foursquare. A few seemed to imitate Frank Lloyd Wright's prairie style.

Cribben's home on Touhy Avenue was one of the former: a simple box shape with two and a half stories, low-hipped roof with deep overhangs, a large central dormer on the third level, and a broad front porch with wide stairs. It was brick and well kept.

I found Cribben in cargo shorts and bright blue rubber flip-flops in his driveway washing what appeared to be a brand new metallic bronze BMW X5 Sport. It was, to my eye, the coolest sport utility vehicle on the road.

My Explorer wouldn't show well beside the Beemer even with Darwin, the cool brass monkey, hanging from the rear-view mirror. So I parked by the curb and tried not be obvious about carrying my notebook and voice recorder.

Although he was stripped to the waist and wet and standing in silly blue rubber flip-flops with a garden hose in his hand, Cribben looked FBI. Maybe it was the aviator sunglasses, or the razor-cut gray hair, or the well-toned muscle mass. Or maybe it was the whole package.

"Good morning," I said. I gave the Beemer an admiring look. "Beautiful vehicle."

He looked at me but didn't respond. At least I thought he was looking at me. Behind those dark glasses he could have been harboring disparaging thoughts about my Explorer.

Then he spoke. "Whatever you're selling, I'm not buying. Go away."

"I'm not selling anything, Special Agent Cribben," I said. If the use of his title surprised him, he didn't show it. I handed him my card. "If you can spare a couple of minutes . . ."

He looked at the card and pocketed it. At least he didn't hand it back or throw it on the driveway and squirt if into oblivion with the power nozzle.

"What is it you want?" he said.

"Is there someplace else we could go?"

"Right here'll do."

I lifted my notebook and handed him a printout of the Ransom Camp story. He wiped a wet hand on his shorts, took the paper and glanced at it.

I couldn't read his face at first, but after a few seconds a small muscle began to jump along his left jaw. He appeared to skim down the sheet then return to the top. When he finished, he handed the story back to me.

"I don't recall reading anything in the paper about that," he said.

"It happened in nineteen-fifty-seven."

"I was three at the time and living in Memphis," he said. "Horrible story, but what's it got to do with me?"

"It might be tied to the death of Congressman Charles Reading," I said.

He took off his sunglasses then and stared at me for several seconds. Then he massaged the bridge of his nose. When he looked back at me, his expression had mellowed.

"Let's go inside," he said.

THE INSIDE of Cribben's home looked as if he always expected company. We entered through the orderly laundry room off the garage and moved into the kitchen. With the exception of a coffee cup on a drying rack, everything was stowed and spotless.

We were leaving the kitchen for the lanai when Cribben's wife showed up. She was as well-turned-out and as fit as her husband. I knew this because she was dressed in barely sufficient tennis shorts and a tank top.

Cribben introduced us. He didn't have to refer to my card to remember my name. I was impressed. Nancy Cribben shook my hand with a firm, dry grip and said she read my column. That quickly, I had found something else about her to admire. Then she asked if I would like something to drink. I accepted a glass of water. Cribben took two bottles of water from the refrigerator and handed one to me.

"I hate to run off," she said, "but I have a tennis match. I'm sure you two are talking business, anyway. It was nice to meet you, Deuce."

She sailed across the kitchen to her husband. They kissed, unselfconsciously, as if they meant it. I liked that. I hoped I looked that good when I hit fifty. I hoped when I hit fifty I had someone to kiss like that.

We walked onto the lanai where a big black Labrador retriever was swimming laps in a pool. When the dog saw us, it swam for the steps and burst from the water.

"Shiloh, stay!" Cribben ordered.

The dog stopped at the top of the stairs.

"He and I are both from Tennessee, and I'm a Civil War buff," Cribben said, by way of explaining how the dog came to have the name of a famous battleground. "I want him to stay there until he shakes off. Otherwise, he'll soak you."

As if on cue, Shiloh began to shed the pool. It started with a rapid rolling of his head that traveled down his body to his rump. When he finished, Cribben said, "Good boy," and Shiloh trotted over. I let him sniff my hand, then scratched his ears and massaged the skin on the back of his neck. Shiloh put his head on my leg and his eyes went glassy.

"You like dogs," Cribben said, a statement, not a question.

"I grew up with goldens," I said. "Retrievers are great."

"You have one now?"

"Two cats. They're easier when you have to be gone a lot, and they're pretty good company when you get used to the fact that they're not, well, they're not dogs."

As Cribben smiled, Shiloh ambled off toward a patch of sun, where he stretched out on his side, heaved a huge sigh, and went to sleep. He left the smell of wet dog on my hands and a smudged area of dampness on my slacks. I didn't mind a bit.

"So how does that story affect me?" Cribben asked.

"I know you were doing some work for Charles Reading when he was killed, an organized crime investigation that was off the official House books."

"And you know this how?"

I remained silent and Cribben nodded.

"Okay, I get it," he said. "It doesn't matter who told you. I can't comment. I can't confirm an investigation, and if there was one, I couldn't talk about it."

I held up the old newspaper story about the fire. "Let's leave the investigation aside for the moment. Did you ever hear of a place called Ransom Camp?"

"Not until you showed me that paper."

"Did you ever run across the name, Ricardo LaPalma?"

For just a second, I thought I saw something flash in his eyes. Then it was gone, and he said, "Not that I recall."

"Nobody with that birth name now operating within organized crime using an a.k.a?"

"Not that I'm aware of."

"Have you ever run across *anybody* named LaPalma?"

He drank some water. "Deuce, I'm not at liberty to discuss anything about this investigation, whether it's something I know about or not."

"Miguel Astosso?" I was pressing.

"What is this, Twenty Questions? No, not him, either."

"Vincent Colangelo?"

Cribben shook his head. "Same answer. No comment. Deuce, I can't comment on anything you're asking."

I trusted Cribben. I knew he wouldn't tell me anything unless the trust worked both ways. Government agents and the press have a built-in adversarial relationship. They want to keep secrets that we want to know.

I had to get past that with Cribben, make him an ally. So I told him the whole story, leaving nothing out, widening the circle I had wanted to keep tight. He sipped his water and listened without interruption until I finished.

"That's quite a tale," he said. "So you started out with a human-interest story that seems to have spiraled out of control."

"Is somebody going to pick up the Reading investigation?"

"Off the record?"

I nodded.

"Not to my knowledge. This wasn't authorized. It wasn't official. No funds were appropriated to finance what I was doing. Mr. Reading paid me out of his own pocket."

"But it was all legal?"

"Absolutely, though a few old friends in the Bureau helped through back channels. Not strictly by the book, but like me, they thought Reading was on the side of the angels."

"Is there anything you can tell me, any guidance you can give me, that would point me in the right direction to get to the nut here?"

He shook his head. "Not really. I don't think my investigation and your story overlap."

"They might, if Ricardo LaPalma is alive and hiding somewhere inside the Chicago or Tampa organizations."

"Even if that's true, I couldn't help you. I'm part of the official investigation of the assassination. I'm under strict orders to keep quiet. Two reasons for that. The Bureau doesn't want the investigation to play out on television or on the front page of the *Chicago Journal*, and they don't want those responsible for the congressman's death to know where the investigation stands at any given point. That's not unreasonable."

"No," I said. "Not from their point of view. But I have a job, too."

"I know, and I like your attitude," he said. "I like the fact that your eye is still on getting justice for this guy, Vinnie, though I can't endorse his old life style." He thought about something for a moment, and then he made my day. "You know, there might be a way I could give you some help where Colangelo's case is concerned. The Bureau's got no official interest in an old mobster, so I wouldn't technically be violating any confidence. I'm not sure what I can do, but I'll give it some thought."

"Anything would be helpful," I said. "And appreciated."

We shook hands, and in that moment, I felt better than I had in days.

18

I woke up Sunday morning a little after seven with a face full of cat fur. Caesar and Claudius knew they weren't supposed to be on the bed. I glared at them. They stood up and stretched fore and aft at a most leisurely cat pace. Claudius then tiptoed to the bottom of the bed and jumped to the floor with a soft, almost inaudible plop. He acted as if it had been his idea to leave. Caesar chose to walk across my abdomen and up the mattress to the night table and then to the floor. It was a morning ritual that amused all of us.

I had seven hours until my appointment with John Conti. I tried to decide what to do with them and couldn't come up with anything. So I got out of bed and made a full pot of coffee and two slices of seven-grain toast with cream cheese. I gathered the newspapers lying at my front door. It took me almost three hours to finish them, and at that I skimmed the *New York Times*. I would be reading sections of it for most of the rest of the week.

I missed seeing my usual ramblings stripped down the left side of the Metro/State front of my own newspaper. A news story occupied my space, instead. At the bottom of the page, a small announcement promised that my column would resume soon.

By the time I finished the papers, I felt ready for some exercise.

I dressed in shorts, T-shirt, and running shoes, stretched out and headed over to Lake Shore Drive for a run along the water.

As I pumped along, my mind sifted all I'd learned since I met Vinnie Colangelo. In addition to what I'd written on my yellow legal pad, I now knew about all the LaPalma kids in LaSalle County schools in the 1950s. I knew two of them—Ricardo and Reuben—had set the Ransom Camp fires, and that Miguel Astosso had later killed one of them, leaving the other still alive. I knew the LaPalma sister, Emily, was alive and well and scared half to death in Bucktown. And I knew Astosso had been murdered after he told Mark Hearst and me about the night of the fires. I also knew the Ransom Camp property was owned by a mysterious someone who didn't want to be identified.

Nothing made any more sense today than it had in Jo-Jo's.

When my pedometer said I'd gone three miles, I took a break, walked out on some rocks and stared at the water, hoping for a eureka moment. But eureka moments don't always happen when you need them most.

I needed to be more proactive. I needed to stop running in place, hoping a break would find me. After I talked to John Conti, I would stop procrastinating and take a whack at Charles Haight, the attorney who initially defended Vinnie. His departure from the case remained a key imponderable.

If I flew down to Key Biscayne and arrived at his home unannounced, I might discover he was gone on a round-the-world cruise and wouldn't return for a year. If I called first, I'd put him on notice that the *Journal* was snooping around a case he'd rather leave buried. It would give him a chance to circle the wagons.

But a dozen people already knew we were snooping around. There was an absolute zero chance that word hadn't reached Haight. I decided on a course of action and finished my run. I felt fine. Six miles of roadwork will do that.

I fixed peanut butter on a rice cake and peeled a banana. While I nibbled I accessed my office computer from my laptop and found the file on Haight as compiled by Lucy Sandoval. Haight had an unlisted number in Key Biscayne. But there are some things you can't do in this world without providing your phone number. Among them is opening utility accounts, and that's where Lucy had found Haight's number. I dialed it.

A woman with a Hispanic lilt in her voice answered on the second ring. I asked for Charles Haight. She told me he wasn't in and asked who was calling. I asked if he would be in later in the day or perhaps the next day. She said she expected him later in the afternoon, and he would be in the following morning. I said I would call back.

I reached Eric on his cell phone in the middle of a round of golf. I told him I hoped I hadn't screwed up his putt.

"You couldn't screw up this round any worse than I'm screwing it up myself," he said.

I told him what I wanted to do, and he approved the trip.

No sooner had I hung up than Sully called.

"I've gotten everything from Peter there is to get," he said. "I talked to Eric. He agrees I should come home."

"Well, your trip wasn't for nothing," I said. I told Sully about my meeting with Cribben, and the chance that maybe I had him on board. I also mentioned I was flying to Miami the next morning to see Charles Haight. He wished me luck.

I ARRIVED at John Conti's University Village district office 10 minutes early. It occupied one of several empty ground-floor commercial spaces in a nearly empty apartment complex north of the Halsted Art District and south of the University of Illinois/Chicago campus on the city's Near South Side.

Former Mayor Richard J. Daley had committed hundreds of millions of dollars to gentrifying the area in hopes of proving the city could provide sufficient housing to support its bid for the 2016 Summer Olympics. When that dream died and the bottom fell out of the nation's real estate market, thousands of housing units and commercial spaces like this one were left without tenants. I'm sure

John got a great deal on the space and took pride in the belief he was helping his district's real estate economics.

When I let myself in his front door, a little bell jangled. I felt as if I'd stepped back into the 1930s. Several small offices used by district staff opened off the reception area. Today, they were empty. The door to the largest office stood open. John sat behind the desk and looked up when the bell sounded. He smiled and waved me inside.

John's private office was spacious but modest. There must have been a hundred photographs on his walls, but behind the desk, between the flags of the United States and Illinois, three photos had the most prominent places: Barack Obama, Richard J. Daley and Rahm Emanuel, a Chicago triptych. Family and personal photos sat in frames on top of a credenza along with a modest display of civic awards.

John moved from his desk and hugged me. Then he inspected the cut on my forehead.

"Better?" he said.

"Better," I said.

He had dressed in blue jeans, a raspberry-colored knit sport shirt and black leather chukka boots. A good look for him, overall, one that emphasized his fitness and vigor.

He motioned me to a cluster of sofas and chairs. I took a chair; he took a sofa.

"I made that call we talked about," he said. "I wouldn't be surprised if your trial transcript showed up a little earlier than advertised."

I thanked him.

"Is the Colangelo case still our topic of conversation?" he said.

"Yes, but only tangentially for the moment," I said. "I wanted to ask if you'd ever heard of a place called Ransom Camp."

That got a quick response from him. The color drained from his face, and I saw moisture glaze his eyes. He leaned forward, rested his elbows on his thighs and stared at the carpet between his boots for a long thirty seconds. One tear fell before he could raise a hand to his eyes to stop any more.

"Oh, Jesus," he said, his voice a whisper. "If you'd offered me a million dollars to guess what was on your mind, that would have been my last guess," He looked up. His face was damp. "Why now? What in God's name brings that hellhole up after all these years?"

"You obviously know of it."

"Know of it? I spent parts of the first six years of my life there. Yeah, I guess you'd say I know of it. That was a long, long time ago. A bad time. Ransom Camp was a brutal place to grow up and a brutal place to die."

"I knew your parents were migrant workers," I said, "but I never knew where."

"Hell, Deuce, there was no 'where.' We lived all over, from Texas north. When my parents worked northern Illinois, it was always around Ottawa and Streator, and the only place to squat was at Ransom Camp."

"You were there for the fire?"

He dropped his head again and took a deep breath. Then he nodded.

"After our old wreck of a motor home burned up that night, we went over and stayed in Streator with some friends my folks met years before I was born. They lived in a trailer that wasn't big enough for all of us, and after a few weeks we had to leave. I never had a real home until we came to Chicago. It was a one-room slum apartment, but it was beautiful to me." He shook his head. "When I saw the bathroom, I asked how many other people used it besides us."

He raised his head and his eyes locked on mine. I assumed he was sifting through the horror of fading memories. I was wrong.

"I don't remember your eyes being such a dark green," he said.

"Same eyes you've been seeing for years," I said. "Maybe they look darker in here."

"Green eyes don't run in your family. Your dad's eyes were sort of gray."

"I'm told my mother had green eyes," I said.

I let this bizarre conversation play out. I knew John needed to deflect the Ransom Camp conversation while he pulled himself together. His next words confirmed it.

"Ransom Camp," he said, "isn't a subject I ever wanted to visit again."

"Do you need to get some water?" I said. I could still see moisture in his eyes.

He heaved himself off the sofa. "Yeah, I do," he said. "I'll be right back."

He returned a minute later looking better. He had brought two bottles and handed one to me. "I never drink alone," he said, and we both smiled.

"Can you tell me why you're asking about this?" he said. He cracked the top off his bottle and took a long pull while his eyes and his attention focused on me.

I explained how I'd found the cryptic mention of Ransom Camp in the case notes left by Vinnie Colangelo's public defender.

John frowned. "And he never explained why he'd written it?"

"He's dead," I said. "And there's no explanation or any other reference to the place. I thought maybe Vinnie grew up there, too. But there is no Vincent Colangelo on any school records for that period. I did find a Mary Conti as a student at Ransom Camp School."

He nodded. "My sister."

That surprised me.

"I thought you were an only child."

"I am now," John said. "The night of the fires, Mary had just finished her second year in school. She loved it so much. She couldn't wait to go back."

I waited.

John cleared his throat and took another pull at the bottle.

"She disappeared in the fire," he said. "If they found her body, I never heard about it. Maybe my parents knew what happened to her, but they never told me. When I got older, I asked my mother several times about Mary, and she'd just start crying. Eventually, I stopped asking."

His voice caught, but he continued. "Lots of kids died that night. Nobody could have sorted them out. There was no DNA science back then. For a long time I imagined Mary got away, and somebody found her and took care of her. But there's nothing to support that. It's just a fantasy."

"Why haven't you said that instead of claiming to be an only child?"

He shrugged. "It was easier than reliving that night every time someone asked me about siblings. You know how we talked about waves of grief, Deuce? That when the death of a loved one drifts deeper into the past, the waves crash into you less and less often, but they never stop completely. Every once in a while I remember my young life with a sister, and it's still hard."

"I didn't mean to rekindle bad memories."

"I was six the night of the fire. I would have started school, if you can call it that, in the fall. I remember being excited about it because Mary was so excited. But it wasn't to be. Instead the family from Streator drove us over to Chicago and left us on the steps of a Catholic church near the stockyards. St. Mary of Perpetual Help in Bridgeport. At the time, I thought it must be the most magnificent building in the world."

"Then what happened?" I said.

"My dad got a job in the yards. My mother took in laundry. And I got shipped off to parochial school."

"I'm sorry, John."

He swallowed hard. "It was a long time ago," he said. "I've never been ashamed of my roots, and I've never made a secret of the fact that my parents started out as migrant workers. It was what it was, and we were who we were."

He sat back and sighed. "Most migrant workers these days are Hispanic. But it hasn't always been that way. My Italian grandparents were destroyed in the Great Depression. Both of my grandfathers died very young, one of a stroke, and one committed suicide. My grandmothers lived on charity. My parents wound up in the produce fields. A lot of folks took whatever work they could get. My parents were no different. I finally broke the cycle, but it was too late to help my family."

John's eyes were glazed and unfocused, almost haunted.

"You don't talk about it much," I said.

"I never talk about it. I was born into poverty and overcame it. I consider myself one of the lucky ones. But I don't find any particular honor in it. It's not something to brag over. And I ask again, why does any of this matter now? Just because of a notation in a public defender's case file?"

I nodded.

He held his hands wide, palms up.

"That I can't explain," he said. "I think you're the only living soul, other than Carole, I ever talked to about Ransom Camp. I don't know how a PD would've found out about it, or what it had to do with Colangelo's case. It's meaningless."

I was beginning to agree.

"Did you know either of the boys who set the fires?" I said.

"The LaPalmas, Reuben and Ricardo, if I recall correctly. I knew them. Not well. They were a lot older. They couldn't be bothered with me, unless it was to taunt me as a 'Dago.' I think they believed Italians were higher on the social hierarchy than Hispanics, and the way to make themselves equals was to drag us down. So stupid. So useless."

He paused and sighed. "There was a time when I looked up to them, admired their toughness. Hero worship, I guess. I approached Reuben once and tried to ingratiate myself. He punched me, knocked me to the ground, and kicked me in the ribs. I bawled like a baby. Hell, I was a baby. After that I avoided him. If our paths crossed, he'd either look right through me, or worse, he'd look at me with complete contempt and utter some ethnic slur. I always ran the other way. I heard he got shot after the fires. I guess it was tough justice."

He paused and resumed staring at the carpet beneath his feet. He didn't raise his head as he said, "I never knew why they set the fires. I didn't care. Ransom Camp was a place of constant violence. It wasn't as if the LaPalmas invented it. But they raised the bar, for sure. I didn't care that somebody killed Reuben. I was relieved, to tell you the truth."

"How about Ricardo?"

He raised his head. "What about him?"

"Do you know what happened to him?" I said.

He shrugged again and shook his head.

"No idea. I never heard of him again. And, like I said, that was fine by me. He was one mean sonofabitch, that kid."

"I heard he was still alive. I thought maybe he was still in the area."

"I wouldn't know. It's been too many years, Deuce. I wouldn't recognize him if he walked in that door. I told you, I didn't know him that well to begin with. Didn't want to then, don't want to now. He's part of my life I'd like to forget."

"And you never heard of anyone in the camp named Vinnie Colangelo?" I asked him.

"Never heard the name at all until we prosecuted him, and never in the context of Ransom Camp until right now. How old was he?"

"According to the birth date he gave, he was 78 when he died."

"Fourteen years older than me," he said. "I have no recollection at all of anyone by that name. If he was living in that shit hole, he'd have been twenty when I was six. Part of the code to staying alive was to stick with your own kind and your own age. We wouldn't have known each other."

I asked him then if he had any tips for winning the trust of the Ransom Camp survivors who still lived in the area.

"It would probably help to talk to them in their own language," he said. "But since you don't speak Spanish, you should take someone with you who does. They won't speak the pure Spanish we teach in the schools, so your translator will have to be flexible."

I thanked John for his time and got up to leave.

As we shook hands he said, "Let me know if you don't get that transcript pretty soon. I'll rattle some more cages. And Deuce, take care of yourself. Watch your back."

19

I avoided the sprawl and inconvenience of Miami International Airport by taking an early flight into Fort Lauderdale and renting a car for the drive to Key Biscayne. I would be at Haight's front door by late morning unless I ran into heavy traffic and road construction.

What did I mean, *unless*? South Florida was nothing *but* heavy traffic and road construction. People there would get up at three in the morning so they could be the first drivers to take part in a traffic jam.

I put on blue jeans and boots and a red long-sleeved cotton V-neck sweater with the sleeves pushed up to the elbows. I looked good and felt comfortable. I prepared the cats for a long day without attention. In addition to extra food, plenty of water, and clean litter, I left the radio on, tuned to NPR. I didn't know if they were soothed by the combination of good music and human voices, but it made me feel better.

As my Southwest flight from Midway glided toward southeast Florida, I began to consider Sully's caution about spinning my wheels on details of no consequence. Maybe Ransom Camp was peripheral to events surrounding the liquor hijacking. Perhaps it was something

Vinnie mentioned to his public defender in passing and had no real significance to his case. So why had the name even come up during an attorney-client conference? That question nagged at me.

As for Vinnie's prosecution, John Conti had been forthcoming about the reasons for going hard on Vinnie, and all his reasoning made sense. Richard Palmieri, on the other hand, had been fuzzier, and he hadn't been thrilled about discussing the case.

A synapse flared, another Eureka moment.

Ricardo is Spanish for Richard.

And LaPalma ... Palmieri?

If someone wanted to disguise his true identity, would he skate on ice so thin? If he possessed infinite hubris and conceit, he might. I could make a good case that Richard Palmieri had unlimited supplies of both.

Okay, he had been born Ricardo LaPalma, but after the fire, he changes his name to hide his identity. He becomes a top federal prosecutor. Somebody finds out about his past. Blackmails him. To appease the blackmailers, he takes a couple of strolls on the shady side, and his secret remains safe. While Lucy couldn't find that Palmieri had ties to the Organization, it wasn't out of the question for anyone who operated in Chicago.

I felt trapped on a broken wagon wheel without a rim. Vinnie was the hub. A dozen spokes extended out from him and then ended in nothing. Every time I crawled out a spoke to explore it, I simply took a header off the end.

I came out of my reverie as the flight attendant announced we had begun our descent into Fort Lauderdale.

When I stepped off the plane onto the ramp I was assaulted by humidity so thick it was like breathing through a pair of sweaty gym socks. I was way overdressed for late summer in South Florida.

I picked up a rental car with a GPS system to guide me to Key Biscayne. When it instructed me on the turns to make leaving the airport, I realized someone had programmed it with the voice of Homer Simpson. "In 200 feet, take the exit on the right and follow the highway. Doh!"

I zigzagged through construction and traffic that moved like sludge in December in North Dakota. The skyline of Miami glittered off to my left. The horizon filled with high-rise condos that stood shoulder-to-shoulder along Brickell Avenue—the old U.S. 1— keeping watch over Biscayne Bay and the Atlantic Ocean beyond. It was beautiful from a distance, but I knew all that glittered wasn't gold.

"Stay to the right," Homer said.

Then: "Prepare to exit the highway in one half mile."

"Prepare to exit the highway in one quarter mile."

"Prepare to exit the highway in 100 yards."

"Take the exit on the right."

"Prepare to turn left in 50 yards."

I had the steering wheel in a death grip.

"Prepare to die, Homer!" I said, and slapped the GPS off button. I missed. Instead of quieting the infernal voice, I knocked the receiver onto the floor, out of reach of my hand but not the guidance satellites.

"Turn left," Homer said, the voice only slightly muffled.

"Fuck you, Homer," I said, and then I laughed.

I left the interstate for the Rickenbacker Causeway, a low bridge that jutted east over the sparkling serenity of Biscayne Bay and stapled the mainland to two exquisite islands, Virginia Key and Key Biscayne. The northern half of Key Biscayne is Crandon Park, a municipal public facility with pretty beaches. The Town of Key Biscayne is draped across the island's midsection like a sash.

Wealthy South Americans own most Key Biscayne property. There is, however, a small and affluent American colony, which included Charles Haight.

The island had plenty of high-rise condos, where prices for the smallest units on the lowest floors started at $350,000. The largest, highest units with the best views went for millions. But Haight had opted for a single-family house, one of the big, new multi-million-dollar jobs. It was two stories, in Spanish style, with huge windows. It sat on Harbor Drive, in a cove off Biscayne Bay. An ornate balustrade ran around the flat roof, where the views would be spectacular in all directions. A sleek yacht rocked on the water behind the house. I saw a man aboard who might have been Haight. He appeared to be the right age, and his body language bespoke wealth and arrogance.

To reach the sea wall and dock I had to cross the manicured lawn and skirt a swimming pool with a circular spa set into the edge. The spa alone appeared large enough to accommodate at least eight adults. My movement caught Haight's eye. He looked up, the broad smile on his face reversing itself in an instant. It became a glare would have curdled milk, had I been carrying any.

"Whoever you are," he said, "I will thank you to get off of my property."

Undaunted, I took a few more steps and stopped at the bottom of the ramp that led up to the deck. "Are you Charles Haight?"

"If I were," he said, "I would have no business with you."

He tried to sound intimidating. He came close. After years of criminal lawyering he had the tone of disdain down pretty well.

"How would you know," I asked him, "before I tell you who I am and why I'm here?"

He waited in silence. I took that as a begrudging signal to continue.

"I'm Deuce Mora, a columnist for the *Chicago Journal*. I flew down this morning hoping for a few minutes to talk to you."

"I have nothing to say to you or to your newspaper. I never did."

"Mr. Haight," I said, "would it be okay if I came aboard so we didn't have to shout?"

"I'm expecting some friends momentarily," he said. "We're going fishing."

So am I, I thought. But what I said was, "I'll only take a few minutes."

He gave me a reluctant nod. "All right. Come aboard."

When I got to the top of the gangway, Haight stepped in front of me so I couldn't move farther onto the boat. He wore pressed cargo shorts, a yellow Polo shirt, and deck shoes.

"You should have called ahead," he said. "Another half hour and I'd have been gone for the day." He glanced at me over the tops of his glasses. "But of course you didn't want to do that, did you? I might have told you not to bother."

"You might have," I said.

He glanced at me again. "You're very tall," he said.

"So I've been told."

"And very attractive."

"Thank you."

"So what do you want?"

"I want to ask you about an old case of yours, back in the seventies," I said. "Vinnie Colangelo, and a shipment of liquor he was accused of stealing."

"Ah, yes," he said. "I was told your paper had been inquiring about that case."

"Who told you that?" I said.

He smiled and said nothing.

"If you knew I was going to ask about the case you've had time to think about it. Why did you take it as a state case and then back off when it went federal?"

He bent over a huge tackle box and began fiddling with an assortment of rainbow lures that must have cost a king's ransom.

"Are those for today?" I said.

"Oh, my, no. We'll be using live bait today."

"What are you fishing for?" I said.

"The big kings," he said. I had no idea what he was talking about. If he'd said cobia, I'd have been better prepared for a discussion.

"So why did you take the case then back off?" I asked him again.

"Another, more pressing matter came up. Besides, Colangelo's case was a loser. There wasn't anything I could do for him."

"What matter was more pressing than trying to help a client?"

"I don't recall."

"Sure you do," I said. "You'd represented Vinnie and others in his line of work before, probably in a lot of cases you couldn't win. What was more pressing this time?"

Haight stood and sighed. He looked out at the water with a

wistful expression that said he wished he'd shoved off an hour earlier.

"When I took the case, I hoped to get a plea bargain for Mr. Colangelo. The state prosecutors were amenable. All they cared about was avoiding a trial. When the feds stepped in, they told me they were going to send the man to federal prison for the maximum because he'd been getting away with murder for years. They wanted to make an example of him. Under the circumstances, staying with the case would have done the client no good and, frankly, would have damaged my reputation. All he needed was a PD."

"Who talked to you? Richard Palmieri or John Conti?"

"I don't recall. It could have been both, but probably Palmieri. Now we're done."

"I have just a couple of questions about the evidence?"

"No more," he said.

"The case is forty years old. Why can't you talk about it? What's the harm now?"

Now he looked me in the eye. "You ever hear of attorney-client privilege?"

"Vinnie voided that," I said. "He talked about the case and the evidence in public all the time. He never denied his guilt. And besides, he's dead now. He was murdered."

Haight smiled, but it wasn't a sign of amusement.

"Colangelo's not the client I was referring to," he said without looking at me. The disclosure was so sudden and stunning it took me a split second to process his admission.

"Can you elaborate?" I said. "Who was the other client?"

If he intended to respond, he never got to it. We both heard a door slam behind me. I turned to see two men beside a Cadillac Escalade, waving at Haight. They walked to the back of the SUV, opened the hatch and started rummaging around inside. My window of opportunity was closing.

"What did you mean . . . ?"

"I'm not saying any more. Get off my boat."

"Did you see the evidence against Vinnie?"

"Never looked at it."

Haight was watching his visitors. Their presence combined with mine made him nervous. He wanted me out of there, the faster the better. "Get off my boat!" Haight said again, with real conviction.

"Mr. Haight..."

"*Now!* Or I call the cops."

I left.

20

I woke up the morning after Miami feeling tired and befuddled. I was tired because of the long round-trip flight. I was befuddled because, without saying much, Charles Haight disclosed that he was taking orders from someone about defending—and then not defending—Vinnie. The who and the why eluded me. I had more questions now than before I interviewed him.

When I recalled my off-the-wall theory that Richard Palmieri might have started out life as Ricardo LaPalma, I rolled out of bed and called the *Journal*'s research library. Nobody was in, so I left a message on Lucy's voice mail that I needed some additional background checks on Richard Palmieri.

Along with everything else, I was unsettled by my encounter with Haight's two fishing buddies as I left the lawyer's property. When I passed them, they were carrying a large cooler, one man on each handle. It looked heavy. I guessed it was filled either with ice and beer, or a dismembered body they planned to dump at sea. Despite their burden, they paused to give me a thorough eyeballing, the way you do when you don't want to forget a face. They were Mediterranean, maybe Italian. The older one appeared to be in his mid-fifties, the other one a few years younger. I thought I recognized the older one, but I couldn't remember from where. I couldn't tell if he recognized me.

So my first order of business on this new day was a stop by the Chicago Police Department to see Sgt. Pete Rizzo again. I found him in front of the headquarters building, making like a talking head for local television reporters. The topic of the interview was a big haul of marijuana and the lowlifes busted with it the night before. I didn't care, so I leaned against an oak tree and waited. In addition to the Rizzo interview, television also would have the obligatory video of the feds and local police standing around their haul, looking serious and determined. It was all so predictable.

On the other hand, I prided myself on being unpredictable. When Rizzo wandered over to my tree and lit a cigarette, I said, "I think I met a real gangster yesterday. Maybe two or three."

"Ooh, cool for you," he said. "Care to mention who and under what circumstances?"

"In Key Biscayne," I said.

"Out of my jurisdiction," he said, inhaling deeply. "So why are you bothering me?"

"To give you a reason to stand out here and contract lung cooties."

"Thoughtful," he said.

"I want to look at some mug books. You still have mug books, don't you? I mean, computers didn't make them obsolete, did they?"

"We have mug books on computers," he said. "We also have traditional mug books."

"Redundant bad guys," I said.

"You looked at mug shots after the intruder in your condo. You didn't recognize anyone. If the guy you're lookin' to ID now is from Florida, he won't be in our books."

"I'm pretty sure I know the Florida guy from up here."

He looked me in the eye and shook his head. "You have strange hobbies."

I started with local books but didn't find either of the men I'd encountered in Haight's back yard. Then we went to the state files, and after forty-six minutes, I spotted one of Haight's fishing buddies.

His name was Richie "The Blade" Capelli. And I did know him from my early days at the *Journal*. I covered Capelli's trial for the torture slaying of a numbers runner caught skimming. He had been taken from a bar in Cicero and dispatched in a Sicilian variation on the ancient Chinese execution method called Death by a Thousand Cuts. It had culminated with some amateur surgery on the victim's genitalia. The sole eyewitness had recanted, fearing his own fate. But the forensic evidence against Capelli had been too strong for him to wriggle away.

A day after the jury went out to consider first degree-murder charges, Capelli agreed to plea to manslaughter. The prosecutor, uncertain whether the jury understood the forensic evidence, settled for a slice of pie.

I doubted that Capelli recognized me, since I was sitting behind him throughout the trial, and seven years had passed. On the other hand, being six feet did tend to make me memorable. I wondered if he had asked Haight about me. I wasn't too concerned. Capelli hadn't been close enough to overhear our conversation. And Haight had every reason to avoid mentioning that he'd been chatting with a newspaper reporter.

Near the end of the books, another mug jumped off a page at me. I had found the man who attacked me in my condo.

Nicholas "Nicky the Cig" Santori.

Why I hadn't recognized him the first time through the mug shots I didn't know. Maybe his mug wasn't in the stack the cops brought. Then again, I'd been in the hospital, injured and groggy, so perhaps his face didn't register. The moniker referred, no doubt, to his preferences when he indulged his penchant for torture.

Looking at his photo now, I remembered being struck in the head, remembered the wild scramble as we rolled around my living room floor, the satisfying smack of the brass bookend against his elbow. I jotted down the name for the Chicago police.

I checked my voice mail messages at the office. There were three that could wait. One couldn't. It was from the clerk at the courthouse. Vinnie's trial transcript had come in.

It hadn't taken three weeks to arrive. I smelled the influence of John Conti.

I owed him a Scotch.

~

I GATHERED up the stack of papers from the clerk. The pages were pristine.

"That's a hundred and thirty-six dollars," the clerk said.

That stunned me. "For what?" I said. "Postage?"

"Copying," she said. "You don't think we give you the original, do you?"

They wouldn't take my check, but they would take my Visa Card. I left with $136 worth of forty-year-old documents and wondered who had gotten the better of the deal.

I needed a quiet place to read. My condo would be best. I called Eric and told him I was taking the transcript home. I also told him about the meeting with Haight.

"I never expected any success with him," Eric said. "Good work."

"I don't know if you can call it success," I said. "We're still long on innuendo and short on corroboration."

"Keep working it," Eric said. "Call me if you find anything in the transcripts."

If I were reading the record of Vinnie's trial for news instead of clues, it would have put me to sleep. But I wasn't, and it didn't.

In the front of the federal file were records of the case's brief stay in state court. There were the usual pre-trial motions filed on Vinnie's behalf by Charles Haight, and Richard Palmieri's notification to the court that Vinnie had been re-indicted by a federal grand jury. The U.S. attorney sought jurisdiction, and the state court granted it.

When the federal procedures began, Haight was gone. He had petitioned the state court to withdraw prior to the federal indictment because a family emergency required him to be away for an unspecified period. The state judge acquiesced, even though the excuse reeked of deception. The federal judge asked Vinnie if he could get another lawyer, and Vinnie pleaded poverty. So the judge ordered the appointment of a public defender.

For some reason the judge never asked why, if Vinnie could afford Haight in the first place, he couldn't afford another private attorney after Haight withdrew. Naturally, I suspected that Vinnie wasn't paying Haight's fee, and whoever held the open wallet had told Haight to disappear. The wallet belonged, I suspected, to the unnamed client Haight was protecting during our conversation on his yacht.

Palmieri put on two witnesses, a Customs agent and an ATF agent, to confirm the chain of possession of the Scotch. Then he introduced documents to prove the shipment was in foreign trade when stolen. Finally, he put Vinnie's accomplices on the stand to nail down Vinnie's guilt.

That seemed like overkill. Why make plea deals with both when turning one of them would have been enough?

The whole setup smelled like a vendetta against Vinnie.

The public defender, Simon Donovan, tried to tear down the case by hammering on the fact that the accomplices had struck plea deals in return for light sentences.

"So what?" one of them said. "Happens all the time."

In the end, it was hopeless for Vinnie.

But I had four new people to look for—Vinnie's two accomplices and the two federal agents whose testimony proved so devastating.

I wondered if the agents had been influenced to perjure themselves. And by whom?

The Customs man was Samuel Griff, and the ATF agent was James Hagwood. I went to the Chicago phone book, the logical first reference. I didn't find any Samuel Griff, but there were dozens of other Griffs, and dozens of Hagwoods, but only four named James.

I called the local Customs and ATF offices and asked for the men. A secretary in the Customs office told me Samuel Griff had been killed in the line of duty in 1979. She wouldn't give me any information about Griff's family.

An ATF official reported that Hagwood no longer worked for the agency. He declined to tell me if any record existed of Hagwood's whereabouts.

"Is he retired?" I said.

"I have no information I can give you," he said.

I didn't have time to call every Griff in the phone book looking for the dead Customs agent's family. So I asked Lucy Sandoval to check for newspaper stories about the 1979 murder and to see if she could find anyone related to Griff. Since there were only four James Hagwoods I could handle those.

I checked for the guys arrested with Vinnie, Tommy Lazara and Sal Annuncio. No telephone numbers for either one, specifically, but lots of other Lazaras and Annuncios.

Crap. Couldn't somebody in this case have an unusual name?

I knew Pete Rizzo could supply police records for both Lazara and Annuncio, and identify their last parole officers. The parole officers would have their last known addresses and places of employment.

I was off and running again.

~

"JESUS, the city's gonna have to start charging you fees, the way you're monopolizing my time," Rizzo said when I appeared at his office door a half an hour before quitting time. He had his feet on his desk and had been reading something.

"Yeah," I said. "There's some other public servants been telling me the same thing. I'll tell you what I told them. Put it on my tab."

"You better not have anything that's going to take longer than..." He looked at his watch. " . . . thirty-five minutes."

"I need records on two guys and the names of their parole officers," I said.

He righted himself, one foot at a time descending to the floor. He looked at me with an expression that crossed resignation with amazement.

He smiled and shook his head. "Would you like me to order you a five-course meal while you're waiting?" he asked me.

I gave him the names, Lazara and Annuncio.

"DOBs?" he said as he jotted down the names.

"Don't have them."

He looked up from his note pad. "Of course not," he said. "That would be too easy. Gonna be hard nailing 'em down without dates of birth. Pretty common names."

"I can tell you they both struck plea deals with the feds in seventy-four, in connection with the theft of a shipment of Scotch. They got four months jail time and five years probation for turning on an accomplice."

"That would be your Colangelo guy?"

"It would."

"That helps," he said. "Wait here, and don't read any of my secret stuff while I'm gone."

I restrained my curiosity, which was a good thing because six minutes later Rizzo was back with several sheets of paper. He handed them over.

"The basic lineup of charges against your two guys," he said. He ripped a page from his notebook and gave that to me, as well. "And here's the names of their last parole officers. Lazara's gonna have a new one pretty soon. He's at Joliet doing fifteen for an armed robbery in '99."

Driving down to the state prison to interview an inmate was right above spear fishing for cobia on my want-to-do list. I'd go if I had to, but I'd prefer finding Annuncio alive and in the area and willing to talk. So I would focus first on him.

I thanked Rizzo.

"See?" I said, "that didn't take thirty-five minutes."

"Yeah," he said, "but you ain't out of my office yet."

21

The assassin watches an oily skim swirl across the surface of his espresso, the extract of the small curl of lemon peel he twisted into the brew. He finds the interaction of coffee and citrus oil more stimulating than the debate crackling around him in the back room of a restaurant in Little Italy. The boss is dribbling minestrone and bread crumbs on his tie, which is laid out over his ample belly as a sacrifice to gluttony. He is discussing murder with several associates. The assassin isn't sure why the boss insisted he sit in on the meeting. Usually the group decides what they want him to do and let him know and it gets done.

The air in the room is filled with words, some of them angry. They punctuate the scents of garlic and pasta steam that define the restaurant at lunchtime. There is sentiment to put an end to the killings lest they draw too much law enforcement attention. The boss waves the objections aside and pours himself another glass of Chianti Reserva.

One man's death has already been ordered. He will die by the hand of someone other than the assassin. There is no debate involved. The death is a given, and the others are simply being informed. He is an older man, out of town. There is no reason for anyone to tie his death to those in Chicago.

Two others, however, are locals. They will be the assassin's responsibil-

ity. Both must be taken down as soon as possible. Neither is of any consequence.

There also is discussion about the reporter. No one talks openly of killing her, but the discussion hugs that line as closely as possible without stepping over it.

If it comes to that, the assassin will try to refuse the assignment without getting his own head handed to him. He told the boss in the beginning he would walk away any time he perceived an assignment too risky or too stupid. Killing a high-profile reporter would qualify on both counts.

He suspects the next two killings—an ex-con and a retired ATF agent —will be his last for this bunch. He will move on, develop associations elsewhere, and put this collection of miscreants behind him.

The decisions are made. His assignments are given.

He swallows the rest of his coffee and nods.

22

I showed up first thing the next day at the parole office. It was bustling and noisy and filled with a lot of people I wouldn't want to meet on a dark night in an alley. The woman at the reception desk asked me what I wanted, exhibiting little inclination to care. I referred to the note Rizzo gave me the previous afternoon.

"A parole officer named Randolph Janofski," I said. "I hope I'm pronouncing that right."

"Ye-ah," she said. "But he ain't in at the moment."

I looked back at the paper. "How about Robert Pendleton?"

"I think he's back there," she said, jerking her head to the left. "Who's asking?"

I gave her one of my business cards. She looked from my name to my face and back.

"Oh, yeah, I know you," she said. "You're the woman from the newspaypa."

That's what it says there on my card, I thought. But what I said was, "That's right."

She picked up the phone, talked to someone I presumed to be Robert Pendleton, and nodded. She pointed down the hall.

"Sixth cubicle on the left," she said. "He's expecting you."

Pendleton's little cubicle office was the cliché that defined all little cubicle offices: files stacked on every flat surface that would hold them, including bookcases and file cabinets, including the chairs, including the floor. More files stood on their spines and leaned against the inexpensive metal and particleboard furniture. Pendleton extracted himself from behind his desk, shook my hand, and apologized for the clutter.

"I'm gettin' better organized," he said, "but it's slow going. What can I do for ya, Ms. Mora?" Pendleton was portly and fiftyish with a full head of hair gone almost white, and old-style bifocals that had a reading circle near the bottom of each lens.

"You can call me Deuce, for starters," I said. "I'm here about a parolee of yours named Tommy Lazara. I know he's at Joliet for a while longer . . ."

"You didn't hear," Pendleton said. "Tommy got shanked inna shower last night. Nobody got any idea who did it or why. He was sixty years old, tryin' to do his time and keep his nose clean and get out and retire from trouble. Had a parole hearing next week."

And that, I thought, is why somebody killed him. And it meant Sal Annuncio, wherever he was, could be next on the hit list. Somebody was systematically wiping out everyone who had anything to do with Vinnie's trial.

"Can you help me reach Randolph Janofski?" I said. "I think one of his guys might be a target, too, and he's going to need some protection."

"Can you tell me what this is about?" Pendleton said.

"Yes, but after we get Mr. Janofski working on protection for Sal Annuncio," I said. "Believe me, this is important."

"I'll page him."

When Janofski called in, I told him he had to find Annuncio fast. He was more forceful in demanding to know first why he should do this.

"Sal's not my responsibility any more," Janofski said. "I'm not his mother."

"If he's killed, his blood's on your hands."

The cliché was out of my mouth before I could stop it, but it got Janofski's attention.

"Lemme talk to Bobby again," he said.

I handed the phone to Pendleton, who listened and nodded.

"Yeah, I think it wouldn't hurt. Okay." He hung up. "Follow me."

We negotiated a gauntlet of people across the vast office space to another cubicle. It held as many folders filled with as many papers as Pendleton's office, but it was neater. Pendleton looked down a row of file drawers until he found the one he wanted. He opened it and found a file, which I presumed to be Annuncio's. He flipped through the pages until he found one with an address and phone number. I tried to read the writing, but Janofski saw me and moved his body between the desk and me.

"Why can't I have the address?" I said.

"First we gotta find out if the guy's still at this address," he told me. "If he is, I'll call him. If he's there, I'll warn him there might be trouble related to Tommy getting killed. Then you tell me what you know, and if I think it's necessary, I'll call the cops. But I can't give his info to you. Privacy laws."

"Fair enough," I said, though I was getting weary of bumping into privacy laws every time I turned around. "Let's get on with it, okay?"

Pendleton must have believed my urgency. Rather than returning to his own office to make the call, he sat down at Janofski's desk. Although he made sure I couldn't read the file, he made the mistake of leaving the telephone in plain view. I got the number as he punched it in and jotted it on the cover of my notebook.

Then I reached over and pointed to the speaker button.

"No," Pendleton said, pushing my hand away.

"Yes," I said. "If I don't listen, I don't tell you anything."

He glared at me over his shoulder, but he punched the speaker button and put the receiver down.

"'Lo?" said a woman's voice, out of breath. It sounded tinny.

"Yes," Pendleton said. "Is Mr. Annuncio there?"

"Who's askin'?" the woman said.

"Is this his residence?"

"I said, who's askin'?"

"He doesn't know me, but my name is Robert Pendleton. I'm with the parole office."

"Sally ain't on parole no more. Finished with you thugs a year ago."

"Yes, ma'am, I know. I need to speak with him for a moment. I'm working on some old paperwork, and I need an answer for one of the blanks."

We heard the phone clatter on a hard surface and a moment later, the woman calling out, "Sally, phone for you. It's the parole people." A pause and then, "I don't know. They said it was sumthin' they needed to ask."

A minute passed and someone picked up the phone.

"Yeah?"

"Mr. Annuncio?"

"Yeah."

"My name is Robert Pendleton. I'm a parole officer. I got your number from Randy Janofski. I hope I'm not interrupting anything, but this is important."

"Yeah?"

Not a man of many words, this Sal Annuncio.

"You remember Tommy Lazara?" Pendleton asked him.

A moment passed before Annuncio answered. "Years ago. Why?"

"Somebody killed him at Joliet last night. Stuck him three times. Nobody knows a motive, and nobody's got a suspect. But I got a newspaper reporter in my office says she thinks you might be targeted by the same people that killed Tommy. She says you need police protection. Can you think of any reason that'd be true?"

Now the silence ran longer. I could hear Sal's rapid breathing. He sounded frightened.

Finally, he said, "Leave me alone."

And then he hung up.

"Give me his address," I said to Pendleton.

"I can't. I told you. It's private."

"It's his life," I said.

"It's the law," he said. "And he told me to leave him alone, so I gotta leave him alone."

"You said you'd call the police."

"I don't hear you tellin' me why I should."

"His life being in danger isn't enough?"

"That's your opinion."

"Shit," I said.

I sprinted out of the office, grabbing for my cell phone. I called Lucy Sandoval.

"I've got something urgent," I said. "If I give you a phone number, can you do a reverse lookup and give me an address to go with it?"

"Piece of cake," she said.

THE ADDRESS TURNED out to be on the South Side, south of West 47th. As I walked to my car, I called Pete Rizzo, the Chicago Police spokesman. I cut him off when he tried to resume his complaints about the amount of time he spent on my problems.

"I'm calling you to try to prevent a murder," I said. I filled him in on Tommy Lazara's fate and told him I was headed to Sal Annuncio's house. I gave him the address.

"You gonna tell me what this is all about?" he said.

"No time right now, but you need to get a unit out there to protect this guy . . ."

"I'll call dispatch, but you owe us all an explanation real soon."

"I know, Pete," I said. "Please, impress on them how important this is."

"You stay back, okay. Don't go playin' junior G-man on me."

"G-woman."

"G-person. Just stay back."

"Yeah."

"I'll tell 'em to watch for you. What're you drivin'?"

I gave Rizzo a description of my car and the license number.

When I hit Western and 47th, a squad car pulled in behind me.

He flashed his headlights once, and I figured he was telling me he was headed the same place I was going. I pulled over to let him pass and fell in behind him.

We made a few turns and wound up in the old South Side neighborhood called Back of the Yards, not more than a few blocks from the firehouse where I'd first met Mark Hearst.

Back in the day, the area was settled by German and Czech butchers employed by the stockyards. Today, the neighborhood is predominantly Mexican-American. But the mix is sufficiently eclectic that an Italian-American like Sal Annuncio wouldn't stand out. On the other hand, until today, he didn't have any reason to hide.

The police unit pulled up beside a late-model Ford pickup, an F-350. I pulled in next to the officer and got out. The officer was pressed and starched and looked like a man who brooked no nonsense. He checked his notebook.

"You Deuce Mora?" he said to me. "Unusual name. I figured you for a man."

"A lot of people do," I said. "I'm glad you could get here so fast."

"Doesn't mean I'm stayin' long," he said. "You wanna tell me why we're here?"

I gave him a broad picture, including Vinnie's murder. He took no notes.

"At his trial," I said, "there were four witnesses against Colangelo. Two were federal agents and two were his accomplices. One of the accomplices got shanked in the shower at Joliet last night."

"And you think the killers are pointin' at this guy next?"

"Wouldn't you figure it that way?"

The cop snorted. "I think maybe you're giving this little investigation of yours a lot more importance than it deserves," he said. "Like you reporters usually do. I think it's crazy to believe what happened to the guy at Joliet is related to a forty-year-old case. If somebody wanted him dead, he'd have been buzzard bait a long time ago. You know what I think? I think you're grand-standin' to hype your story."

I looked at his nametag. Crandall.

"Officer Crandall," I said, "would you at least go inside with me and listen to what this man has to say before you decide whether I'm a self-important, self-centered, self-absorbed, manipulating bitch, or whether there might be a life here that needs protection? That is, I believe, part of your job description."

He pursed his lips, sighed, and nodded. I walked up the four concrete steps to the front door of the old brick three-story and knocked. A pleasant-looking woman, dark-haired and olive-skinned, opened it and peered at me through the screened door. I introduced myself and Officer Crandall and asked to speak with Mr. Annuncio.

"About what?" she said.

"About the phone call he got from the parole officer this afternoon," I said.

"I don't know about no call from no parole officer," she said. "Sally's not on parole."

"Are you Mrs. Annuncio?" I said.

She nodded.

"Mr. Pendleton called," I said, "not an hour ago. I was there with him. Please, would you ask your husband to talk to me?"

She turned away and used the front door to shield me from the other person inside and to keep their conversation private. Then she turned back.

"Sally'll be out in a minute," she said. "You wait there."

We did, and a few minutes later a great rotund man lumbered around the corner of the house. He must have been close to seventy. He wore his long gray hair back in a ponytail pulled so tight it seemed to stretch the skin on his face and hold his eyes unnaturally wide. He wore tent-sized chinos held up by wide suspenders that stretched like parallel runways over a sweat-stained white T-shirt. His feet had been inserted into unlaced running shoes, victims of pronation so severe the man practically walked on the sides of the soles.

"So I'm here," he said. "Whaddya want?"

I thought I smelled beer on his breath, and it wasn't even noon. He leaned his bulk against the brick wall of the house and stuffed his hands into his pockets. I offered him my card. He refused to take it. So

I asked him about Tommy Lazara and whether he remembered the job he and Tommy pulled with Vinnie Colangelo.

"We paid our dues on 'at," he said. "A stupid stunt. Shudda known better. But what's it matter now?"

"I started asking around about the charges against Vinnie," I told him, "and all of a sudden Vinnie is tortured and killed in his bed. Then last night Tommy was killed in the showers at Joliet, maybe to keep him quiet. A third man is also dead, over in LaSalle County. Somebody might try to kill you, too. Same reason."

"At's nuts," Annuncio said. "Who's gonna care now?"

I glanced at the deputy. He had the I-told-you-so look on his face. But he sucked in a breath and moved toward Annuncio.

"Sir, answer the questions, and we'll go," he said.

"Get the fuck away from me," Annuncio said. "I ain't done no fuckin' crime. Leave me the fuck alone."

Crandall took another step forward.

"We're done," Annuncio said. He heaved himself away from the wall and turned back toward the side of the house, moving with surprising speed for a man his size. A part of the house wall blew apart. Red dust and red chips of brick exploded out into the air. Annuncio yelped and fled, speed waddling around the corner of the house.

Crandall and I turned in time to see a man duck behind the house across the street. He was carrying a rifle mounted on a short tripod. He had used a picnic table as his shooting platform. Crandall drew his gun and ran toward the spot where the sniper had disappeared, calling on his shoulder-mounted radio for backup. I considered going with him, but I had nothing to offer in the way of help. Crandall didn't need his attention divided between catching the shooter and protecting me.

It wasn't lost on me, however, that it had been a sniper who killed Charles Reading in Las Vegas. If this was the same guy, he had to be pretty ballsy to attempt a murder here, now, in front of a cop.

I went back to the front door, which was still open, and called through the screen.

"Mr. Annuncio, he's gone," I said. "The shooter's run away. Now you know I was telling you the truth. Please come and talk to me."

His face appeared in front of me. He pushed open the screen. "Get in here," he said.

The interior of the house was dark and cool, and everywhere I looked there was a crucifix or a likeness of Jesus Christ.

Annuncio saw me looking. "The wife's religious," he said. "When you're married to a guy in my line of work, you need sumpin positive to fall back on, ya know?"

"What is your line of work, Mr. Annuncio?" I said.

"This an' that," he said. "Course, I'm retired now. No outstanding wants or warrants."

"Somebody wants you," I said, nodding toward the wall from which police would later recover a rifle bullet. "Could it have anything to do with Vinnie Colangelo?"

Annuncio moved to his chair, which had a motorized lift to help the occupant in and out. The seat cushion was up, higher at the back than in the front. Annuncio positioned himself against it, and a motor began to lower him.

"Thyroid trouble," he said. "I used to be thin." He waved his hand across breadth of the room. "Sit anywhere," he said. "But sit where I can see you. You're a looker, ya know?"

"Sal..." I said.

He waved me quiet. "Sure, it could be about Vinnie," he said. "Tommy and me, we knew what was goin' on. The bosses wanted Vinnie to go away, outta state, and doin' the max. Tommy and me, we helped wit dat."

"So you knew the Scotch had passed into local custody?" I said.

"Me, I never saw the paperwork, no," he said. "But Tommy told me he seen it in the cab, on the seat, when he hot-wired the truck. An' Vinnie mentioned it when he got up in the cab to drive, said we'd be doin' easy time if we got caught. Like a joke, ya' know?"

"But you and Tommy both testified at the trial you hadn't seen the paperwork."

Annuncio stared at me as if I were an idiot.

I heard sirens and assumed Crandall's backup had arrived.

"Why'd you do that?" I asked him. "Why'd you perjure yourselves?"

"We were told to."

"By whom?"

"By the guy we reported to, Georgie Cantolino. He told us what to say. But you can't ask him about it. He's dead ten, eleven years now."

"So you perjured yourselves."

He shrugged. "You gonna sue me?"

"No," I said, "but Vinnie's family might. He has a relative who claimed his body."

Annuncio opened his arms wide. "They can have all this," he said. "The rest of what I got's in an offshore account nobody's ever gonna find."

I took a gamble. "Sal, does the name Miguel Astosso mean anything to you?"

He curled up his mouth and shook his head. "Nuthin'. No."

"Will you give me a sworn statement about what you and Tommy saw and heard that night?" I said. "It can't come back on you. The statute of limitations kicked in years ago."

"I ain't givin' nobody nuthin'," he said. "When the wife's finished packin' up a few things, we're gonna put what we can carry in my truck. Then we're gonna get inna truck ourselves and drive to someplace where we're gonna to catch a plane to someplace else where nobody will ever find us. I got more'n enough money to cover us for the rest of our lives. For all I care, this place can burn to the ground. I know these guys you're after. Once I'm out of the picture, they'll stop lookin' for me. They want me to keep my mouth shut. They don't really want me dead."

"No?" I said. "They killed Vinnie and Tommy and an old man in LaSalle County, and they already tried to kill you once. Tell me who's giving the orders."

"I got nuthin' more to say."

"Sal, Vinnie deserves some closure on this. He lost his wife, his daughter, everything he owned. And eventually he lost his life. And you helped take it all away. It's a little late, but you could help make some kind of amends."

"I look like the fuckin' Red Cross to you?" he said. "Get out."

CRANDALL and the officers who responded to his call found nothing. However, two officers said they saw a white Chrysler speeding away. I would have bet it was the same car Mark Hearst and I had seen at Ransom Camp. I told Crandall about that incident and about Miguel Astosso.

Crandall insisted on knowing what Annuncio said to me. I told him Sal had confirmed Vinnie's story.

Crandall, ever the dutiful cop, went to Sal's door and talked to him for at least twenty minutes. When he returned, he told me I was going to lose Annuncio to the wind.

"There's nothing I can hold him on," he said. "He's committed no crime. He claims he didn't see who tried to shoot him and can't think of any motive. He insists he doesn't want police protection. We can't force it on him."

"So we let him disappear?"

"Life goes on," Crandall said.

"Damn it!" I said.

"Don't feel too bad," Crandall said. "This guy's testimony wouldn't do you any good. He's not the one who actually saw the documents you're looking for. He could only testify to what Vinnie and the other guy said. That's hearsay and inadmissible."

Crandall cleared his throat. "I owe you an apology for sayin' what I did earlier, that stuff about grand-standing. That shooter was real enough."

"No problem," I said. "You know you probably saved Annuncio's life. He got off that wall quick enough when you moved toward him."

"Yeah, maybe I startled him. I was just gonna get in his face a little, press him for better answers to your questions." He glanced across the street. "Or maybe he saw the shooter. Where the guy was set up he would have been visible over my right shoulder."

"Did you ask Annuncio why he moved?" I said.

"No, never thought to," Crandall said. "I'll have a lab team come out and go over the grounds here and across the street, dig out the bullet in the wall of the house, and put it in evidence. I'll fill out a report. Maybe somethin' will come up."

"Not for nothing," I said, "you might want to ask the FBI to check the bullet in that wall against the bullet that killed Congressman Charles Reading in Las Vegas."

Crandall's mouth dropped and his eyes went wide. I thought he was about to accuse me of grandstanding again, but he just nodded and walked away.

After Crandall and the other officers left, I sat in my Explorer and watched Annuncio's house. It wasn't fifteen minutes until he and his wife came out, threw two big bags in the back of the pickup and got in. Even with an extra step hanging under the running board, Annuncio had to use the steering wheel to pull his bulk up into the seat.

They drove away. I debated following them, but what good would it do?

23

I thumbed over the ignition, and my cell phone rang. It was Mark Hearst. Despite the distraction of watching my last living connection to Vinnie drive off into the sunset, I was pleased to hear from Mark. Maybe he was calling about the dinner he promised.

"Checking in," he said. "I hadn't heard from you in a few days. Anything going on?"

I told him I was going down to Miguel Astosso's house as soon as I could find someone who could talk to neighbors in whatever passed for their Spanish.

"That would be me, and I'd be happy to go with you," he said. "They know me a little."

That surprised me. "You've already been out there?"

"Yeah," he said. "I went out the day after the fire. I chatted briefly with the people next door, Miguel's relatives. They don't speak English. But we managed. I know some Spanish."

"How'd you get involved?"

"The LaSalle County Fire Department, the guys who gave me Harold Bickerstaff's name, invited me to consult on this case."

"They invited you?"

Mark laughed. "Yeah, well, after I asked. One of us state arson guys has to work it, and nobody else showed any interest. So, you want to take a ride down there?"

I met Mark, and we set out for LaSalle County in his official vehicle with the state fire marshal's logo on the doors. During the trip, I told him how the story had developed over the last few days and about my hopes for help from a former FBI agent named Carl Cribben.

On a whim, I copied Cribben's contact info out of my iPhone and gave the paper to Hearst. "In case something happens to me," I said. "Somebody needs to make sure he's kept up to date. I have a feeling he'd like to finish what he started for Reading."

Mark winced and started to object, then thought better of it and slipped the paper into his pocket.

We had arrived at the charred remains of Miguel Astosso's home.

Mark drove past the burned house and as close as he could get to the little structure behind it. Then he turned the truck so it stopped broadside to the front porch. Those inside couldn't miss its insignia.

"This is gonna be difficult," he said. "The people here are Miguel Astosso's sister, Maria Astosso, and her son, Tino. Tino speaks both Spanish and Miskito, the language of his mother's people in Nicaragua. Maria speaks only Miskito. So, assuming they agree to talk to you, you'll have to ask me a question, which I'll translate into Spanish for Tino, and he'll translate into Miskito for his mother. The answer will come back the same way."

"If that's what we have to do," I said. "You learn to speak Spanish back in school?"

"Ecuador," he said. "Peace Corps."

I cracked my door. "Miguel told us he escaped from the fire with his sister," I said. "What Miguel saw, Maria saw. If Miguel knew what became of Ricardo LaPalma, maybe Maria knows, too. Do I assume they use the name Astosso because Tino had no father?"

"Oh, he had a father," Mark said. "But Maria had no husband."

I dropped it.

Mark got out of the truck first. I fell in behind his right shoulder.

"Anybody home?" he asked in a voice loud enough to be heard

inside. When he got no answer, he repeated the question in Spanish. He got no answer to that, either.

We walked closer, and a man who might have been my age walked out onto the front porch with a rifle in his hands. It stopped us in our tracks. Tino, I presumed.

Mark spoke to the man in Spanish, reintroducing himself. Tino said he remembered Mark. Mark explained who I was and what I wanted. My Spanish isn't good, but I got some of the pitch: I was a friend of Miguel's, and Miguel had been helping me because I was investigating what happened at Ransom Camp. We thought that's why somebody killed Miguel, to stop him from helping. I saw a flicker of interest in Tino's eyes, and he motioned us to come up on the porch.

I turned on my recorder and opened my notebook.

"Is your mother at home?" Mark asked.

"Yes, but she is not well," he said in Spanish. "She tires easily."

Mark told me what the situation was and asked what I wanted to do.

"Maybe we could talk to her for a few minutes," I said, "and quit if she gets tired. Then we have to see about moving them to some place safe with round-the-clock armed guards. If somebody's watching the house and sees me here . . . "

I paused. "Well, we don't want a repeat of that." I nodded toward the burned out mess behind us.

Mark nodded and translated my request.

Tino showed us through the tidy house to his mother's sitting room. Maria was settled in a rocking chair, her legs covered by an afghan, her shoulders by a shawl. Her face was framed by a head of long, white hair. She held an open Bible and read it in a muttered language I'd never heard.

We got through the introductions and began the arduous process of asking questions.

Maria was clearly uncomfortable waking the horrific memories of the Ransom Camp fire. But she confirmed her brother's statement. She said the fires had been set by two of the four LaPalma children,

Reuben and Ricardo, and that Reuben had set the fire under her home. That was why her brother, Miguel, later killed Reuben.

I asked if she had any idea where Ricardo LaPalma was these days.

Her response was a quick, and frightened, shake of her head.

"Does she know if he's still living in the area?" I said.

That got another shake of the head.

I asked if she had ever heard of another Ransom Camp child named John Conti.

When the question got to her after two translations, she nodded.

Her reply translated, "He is like Jesus Christ." I knew a lot of people who liked Conti. But nobody ever compared him to the Son of God. At least not in front of me.

I asked Mark to confirm this was a correct translation. It was.

I asked if she could elaborate on what she meant. She shook her head again and began to cry. Her son asked us to go.

We did, after telling Tino we'd like to move them to a safer place and talk further with his mother another time. He didn't say no, but he didn't make any commitment either.

When we were in the truck headed back toward Chicago, Mark asked me what I made of Maria's reference to Jesus Christ.

"I don't understand it," I said. "She's an old woman, and not well. Her mind could be playing tricks. John Conti's a good guy. But not that good."

We drove in silence for a few minutes, lost in our thoughts. Mark spoke first.

"So this got you exactly nowhere," he said.

I considered that. On the surface, he was right. Maria Astosso hadn't added much. Except something was knocking at the edges of my subconscious just out of reach, as if I were swimming in murky water, and something I couldn't see kept bumping against my leg. I opened my notebook and flipped through the pages. I found nothing to add any clarity.

The rest of the way back to Chicago, I went over with Mark Hearst the options for keeping the surviving members of the Astosso family safe. He suggested the shelters that care for the homeless, and I rejected them.

"Too grim," I said. "Besides it would be too hard to give them protection."

"Where, then?"

"How about something like a safe house," I said. "A nice place where they'll be comfortable and under guard until this is over."

Mark turned from his driving to regard me with wonder. "You want me to talk the government into putting these people up somewhere, feeding them, caring for them, and providing a protective detail for the foreseeable future? Is that all?"

"For now," I said. And I grinned.

Shaking his head, he turned back to the road. "You don't ask much."

"Look," I said, "they could be material witnesses in two recent murders, Miguel's and Vinnie's. And twenty-six more dating back to 1957. That's worth something."

"How are they material to Vinnie's death?"

"In this case, everything's related to everything else."

"So you say. Proving it is something else."

He sighed the sigh of a man who wished he were elsewhere. "I'll see what I can do," he said. "If I can get them in a safe house and protected, will you have dinner with me?"

I started to say yes when my cell phone rang.

I answered, listened and severed the connection.

"Dinner will have to wait," I said. "My editor is demanding to see me right now."

24

When Mark and I got back to Chicago, I refused to get out of his truck until he swore he would find a safe house for the Astossos and that he'd mention them to no one, not even his friends in the department.

"I give you my word, Deuce," he said.

When I entered the lobby of the *Journal* building, a security guard at the reception desk waved me over. He rummaged through a pile of assorted packages and handed me a manila envelope on which someone had printed my name and nothing else. "This was left for you a couple of hours ago," he said.

"Who left it?" I said.

"I don't know. It was before I came on duty."

I figured it for something mundane, an invitation to speak to some group or a breathless press release from a public relations firm seeking publicity for a client. I carried it upstairs and tossed it into a corner of the desk.

I checked my e-mail messages first, answered a few that required attention, and deleted the rest. I checked my voice mail. Since my column was on hiatus, there weren't as many readers calling to tell me what an idiot I was. I had six messages. It would be days until I got to five of them because the first one blew me away.

As soon as the caller started to talk, the voice sounded familiar. Half way through the message, I realized it belonged to Carl Cribben, retired G-man.

"Your bad guys missed one," the voice said. "I left an envelope for you at your security desk. I think it might be helpful. If anyone asks, you have no idea where it came from."

I saved the message before I hung up and then tore into the envelope, taking enough care not to damage the contents. Two sheets of white paper slid out, copies of official documents. They were a little hard to read because the originals were old, almost forty years to be exact. The first document was a form attesting that all duties and taxes on a 1974 shipment of Laphroaig single-malt Scotch from Edinburgh had been paid in full. The second was the release-of-cargo form signed by the customs house broker who turned over the Scotch to the agents representing Binny's Beverage Depot.

It was Vinnie's missing evidence.

I tried to make out the signatures on the documents. The one on the release-of-cargo form was indecipherable, although a stamp below it read, "Port Chicago, Inc. Customs House Brokerage," with an address in The Loop. James Hagwood, the ATF agent who testified against Vinnie, had signed the duty form.

When he testified otherwise in court, James Hagwood had committed perjury.

"I'm sorry, Vinnie," I whispered to the old documents. "I wish you'd trusted me."

~

"WHERE EXACTLY ARE WE?" Eric said without preamble.

He wanted a logical story arc, to know who had done what to whom and why, and I couldn't give him that because I didn't have it yet. I described my encounter with Sal Annuncio, and the attempt on his life, my trip to see Maria Astosso and her son, and the newly discovered missing liquor documents. And I mentioned my notion that Richard Palmieri's name was eerily close to the English translation of Ricardo LaPalma. But I still didn't have a grand theory of the story.

I could prove Vinnie's claim, which is all I wanted to achieve in the beginning. But the evidence pointed to so much more. Trouble was, I couldn't define the nature of "more." I was foundering, and Eric picked up the scent of my doubt right away.

"So you've got proof of a forty-year-old miscarriage of justice done to a man now dead," he said. "He was, by his own admission, a crook. Why should anybody care? Okay, he did more time for that one crime than he should have, maybe. But it probably doesn't nearly make up for everything he got away with before."

I was forced to admit the truth of that. "But I have to keep digging," I said.

"Why?"

"Because some of the people involved in the case are still around, and they're killing people," I said. "Because there has to be a good reason they did this to Vinnie. And because of the Las Vegas connection."

"A connection you haven't made, by the way."

"And I keep coming back to Ransom Camp."

"An ugly, ugly story. But, again, we have no idea what it means, or if it means anything. The lawyer who made the notation never came back to it, so it might be nothing."

"I don't know that," I said. "Eric, are you getting pressure to take me off the story and put me back on the column?"

"The column is considered a key element of our coverage," he said, speaking editor gobbledygook. "But what really disturbs me is the alarming amount of violence swirling around you. Three murders —Vinnie, Miguel Astosso, and . . . " he stopped and consulted the hand-written note in front of him . . . "Tommy Lazara, the guy at Joliet. Then there's one attempted murder, Sal Annuncio, plus the assault on you. That lends credence to the theory that something is going on, but I don't see you making any progress in figuring it out.

Unless you can move the story forward pretty soon, I'm going to decide it's a police matter, more properly covered by police reporters, and put your column back in the paper."

I felt my temper rising and fought it down. There was a time, a few days earlier, when I might have stepped through this portal of opportunity to get away from the story. But I was over that now. I was committed, and I wouldn't give up the story without a fight.

"I'm not out of options," I told him. "Give me some time to wave these Customs documents in front of a few faces."

"How do we know they're legit? These things go missing for forty years dating back to seventy-four. But your source comes up with them in a couple of days?"

"I don't think there's any mystery to it," I said. "The fact is, nobody back in seventy-four looked for them. The prosecution's copy of the file was missing these two pieces of paper. We don't know if it was an oversight or evidence tampering. We do know the defense accepted the file as presented. There was no further investigation. It's entirely possible that every copy of this file has the two key documents *except* the one that made it into the courtroom."

"Vinnie never publicly accused anyone of altering the file?"

"He talked to his public defender about it. The PD tried to question the Customs agent during the trial, but the judge wouldn't allow it."

"And the PD didn't go looking to see if his client was right?"

"He asked the prosecutors about it. They showed him what they had. To dig deeper would have required a private investigator, and Vinnie had no money for that."

"Even if all your conjecture is true, it doesn't prove malice. Maybe somebody in the U.S. Attorney's office didn't pick up all the paperwork. That's unforgivably sloppy, but it's not criminal. And forty years later, with the victim dead, it's not news."

I held up the papers. "Except one of these documents holds the signature of a man who later testified in court, under oath, that the action specified in the document never happened. That's perjury, and there has to be a reason for it."

Eric considered that.

"Before we start charging people with felonies, we need to be absolutely certain the paperwork is real."

"The papers are dated and stamped," I said.

"That's not good enough, not in this era of technological possibilities."

"I don't know why you're skeptical. My source isn't a person who'd fabricate documents. He has no reason."

"My skepticism trumps your trust," he said. "Run them by that Customs agent you talked to the other day. Can you get his take without risking the story?"

"There's always a risk, Eric. I don't know the guy at all."

"Find a way," he said. He pursed his lips and put his palms together in an almost prayer-like gesture, lightly chopping the air in front of his chin. "Deuce, I have to ask the question no reporter ever wants to hear from an editor. Who is the source you're using, the one who found the missing documents?"

He thought I would be upset by the question. I disappointed him. It was his job to ask.

I said, "If this building had transoms, I'd say they came over one."

Eric smiled, the first time he'd done that during the meeting. "It did have transoms at one time, seventy or eighty years ago." He went silent, waiting for an answer.

"I'd rather not tell you who the source is," I said. "He's in a sensitive position, and he asked for my discretion."

"If you can't tell me his name, what's his situation? What puts him in a position to come up with these documents?"

"He's retired FBI."

Eric's eyebrows shot up as he considered that. He nodded.

"Okay for now," he said. "But I reserve the right to change my mind at any time. And as far as the story goes, you've got three more days. And the deadline's firm."

~

I HAD three lines of investigation I could pursue, and with so little time, I had to make my first choice a good one. Lucy had been diverted to another project, so she hadn't yet gotten to the search for information on the family of Samuel Griff, the Customs agent who testified against Vinnie. I set that aside for the moment.

I could call the four James Hagwoods listed in the phone book and ask at each home if I had the former ATF agent. There was no guarantee any of the four was the man I wanted, and if I did manage to hit the right guy, I didn't want to spook him. Cold calling at their front doors would take the better part of a full day of driving around the city. So I set that possibility aside for the moment, as well.

Third was Emily Humphries, Ricardo LaPalma's sister, living in apparent terror in Bucktown. I reasoned she was my best chance to resolve the Ricardo mystery.

It was close to seven in the evening. It would take at least thirty minutes to find my way back to the Humphries house. That didn't seem an unreasonable time to knock on someone's door, even someone who had made it plain once already that she didn't want to talk to me or ever see me again.

Is there any rule that says the second time can't be a charm?

I HAD a little trouble finding my way back to Homer Street in the dark, so it was closer to 8:00 when I retraced my steps to the front porch. This time, at least, it wasn't raining. The lights were on inside, so I assumed the Humphries family hadn't yet gone to bed.

I rang the bell. Verne turned on the porch light and pulled back the sheer curtain covering the vertical window beside the door to get a look at the person who had invaded his privacy at this hour of the evening. His face became a scowl when he recognized me.

He opened the door a few inches, the chain lock stretching across the gap. "I thought I told you to get off my property," he said.

"Mr. Humphries," I said, "please, hear me out, and then I'll leave,

I promise. Your wife, maybe both of you, are in terrible danger. I have to talk to you about it."

"Do you think we don't know that?" It was Emily Humphries' voice coming from behind her husband. Until she moved from the shadow of his back, I couldn't see her. "And there is nothing you can do. There is nothing we can do. But I know this: By coming here you're making it worse."

"Mrs. Humphries . . ."

"These are terrible people. When they want to frighten us, they break into our house while we're away and move things around, so we'll know they were here. Or they disable the alarm, and we wake up in the night and find them in our bedroom, watching us."

She was speaking faster now. "They don't hurt us. But they take great pleasure in letting us know they can reach us whenever they want, and we can't defend ourselves. There's nowhere to hide. They leave us alone as long as we don't threaten them. But you are a threat, and by coming here, you become a danger to us."

"I know people who can protect you," I told her. "All you have to do is give me a reason. Is it Ricardo who's threatening you? We can find him and stop him."

She pinched her lips and shook her head.

"Is it related to Ransom Camp?" I said. "You're one of the last survivors of that night. Are you in danger because of what you saw?"

Emily began to cry again, great wracking sobs that shook her whole body. Verne put an arm around her, but that caused her to cry harder. I loathed what was happening to this woman, and I loathed the people who were causing her this grief. But it frightened me more that I might be the source of danger for them. I decided to leave and not to return.

Verne glanced up and looked toward the street. His eyes went wide. I followed his gaze—just in time to see a white Chrysler slide beneath a street lamp and disappear down the asphalt into the cover of darkness.

When I looked back, the door to the house was closing. I heard a deadbolt click into place. Then the light went out, leaving the porch, and me, abandoned to the darkness.

As I was walking to my car, the white Chrysler made another round.

This time the front passenger window was down, and somebody was looking at me through a rifle scope.

I dove into the grass, using my car as cover, but the rifle remained quiet.

I thought I felt the ground shaking. Then I realized it was me.

25

When I left for work the next day I dressed for success, hoping it would lift the black mood I carried from the Humphries home the night before. A pair of Trina Turk pleated tan slacks fell from my hips, draped over my butt, and flared below the knee. A Casion red silk shirt fit as if it had been cut for me. And my new, brown Cole Haan boots finished the look. My hair bounced with a fresh wash, my makeup looked both good and subdued, and my impure thoughts focused on Mark Hearst.

Mark had called me at 6 a.m. to tell me about the arrangements he'd made for Maria and Tino Astosso. They were as good as I'd hoped. The Astossos were stashed under the watchful eyes of the U.S. Marshals Service. Mark lamented our missed dinner, and we promised ourselves we would try again as soon as possible. I told him about my deadline, and he offered to help move things along.

I presented myself at Sully's desk to ask if he'd had a chance to check on the ownership of the land beneath what had been Ransom Camp.

"I was about to call you," he told me. He scanned me from head to toe, looked embarrassed about it, and scanned me again.

"Wow," he said, "you look sensational."

I smiled.

"That's the good news," he said. "The bad news is we can't get those land records. They're in a family trust assigned to Creek Enterprises. We can't break into it. The sole purpose of Creek Enterprises seems to be as a holding company for the trust. Cal Miller, the agent you talked to, is the only name that comes up. It's sealed up tight."

I was disappointed, but I knew if Sully couldn't get the information, nobody could.

I moved to my own desk and placed a call to Jack Collins, the Customs agent who'd walked me through the importing process. His office said he was at O'Hare and would be back sometime during the afternoon. I asked if he had a cell phone. I was told he did, but that I couldn't have the number.

I looked back through the directory of recent calls on my cell phone, hoping when he returned my initial flurry of calls that he had used his cell. But he hadn't. He called from the office landline, the number I had already.

I couldn't see sitting around all day waiting for Collins to call back, despite Eric Ryland's insistence that I authenticate the import documents. So I decided to take a shot at the four James Hagwoods in the phone book and find if one of them used to work for the ATF. Not as good as going to their homes, but I didn't have time for that.

I hit gold on No. 3, a resident of Wrigleyville, who was most curious about my call. I told a terrible lie and said I was updating his personnel file.

I could hear in his voice that he didn't buy it. I thought I'd better drive up there and talk to him before he had too much time to think about it.

So I grabbed up the Customs documents, slipped them into my backpack, and started for the elevators, intending to confront Hagwood with them.

Then I had second thoughts about leaving the office with the only copies. I detoured by a copy machine, made duplicates, and gave my originals to Sully to hold.

"Put these in a safe place," I told him, "and whatever you do, don't lose them."

"If I sneaked a peek at them," he said, "would they mean anything to me?"

"They're the missing pieces of evidence that prove Vinnie's original story."

Sully gave them a quick scan. "Oh, wow," he said. "These are the documents Vinnie saw in the cab of the semi." He looked up at me. "Deuce, these validate everything you're doing. They're proof that somebody tampered with evidence."

"Not necessarily," I said. "They prove Hagwood perjured himself at Vinnie's trial. They suggest evidence and witness tampering but fall short of proof. It's possible the set of import docs presented in court was the only set missing this paperwork. It didn't have to be a broad conspiracy. It could have been one person stripping one file. Or it could have been accidental. Hagwood's perjury suggests a conspiracy but doesn't prove one."

Hagwood lived about four blocks from Wrigley Field. Convenient if he happened to be a Cubs fan. I found the house but had to leave the Explorer two blocks away to find a legal space. Most of the spaces in Wrigleyville were reserved for vehicles with resident stickers.

The man who answered the door was tall and paunchy and wore his gray hair in a brush cut. He appeared irritated by the interruption. The outfit I had put together with such care that morning didn't seem to impress him. I guessed his age at somewhere between sixty-five and seventy.

I asked if he were James Hagwood.

"What if I am?" he said.

"Are you the James Hagwood who used to work for ATF?"

"What if I am?"

I began to worry that I wouldn't be able to keep up with the conversation.

Then he got more expansive. "You're the one called me a while ago. You don't look like no clerk to me."

"I'm not, Mr. Hagwood. I'm Deuce Mora, a columnist for the

Chicago Journal. I'm looking into an old court case that involved you. A low-level gangster named Vinnie Colangelo was accused of helping steal a truckload of Scotch."

Hagwood stared at me as if he couldn't have been more bored.

"Do you remember that?" I asked him.

"What if I do?"

"You and a Customs agent, Samuel Griff, testified against Mr. Colangelo, right?"

Hagwood continued to watch me, and he continued to look bored.

"Could I come inside so we could talk about this?" I said.

"No," he said.

At last a straight answer.

"Okay," I said. "Well, Mr. Colangelo never denied his part in the theft, but he said he was tried in the wrong court, that the Scotch had passed into local commerce."

"There was no documentation to support that," Hagwood said. "The documentation ended before the tariffs were collected. "

So I had the right man.

"No," I said, "it didn't." I unfolded the copy of the tax-and-tariff form and held it so Hagwood could read it while it remained in my hand.

"That appears yours is one of the signatures on the tariff form," I said.

I will say this for James Hagwood, he kept his cool. I might have seen fear in his eyes for a nanosecond, but it was gone as quickly as it came. He looked back at the paper.

"That don't look like my signature," he said. "Maybe somebody forged it."

"It might not look like your signature today. People's signatures change, and I'm sure yours has changed over the last forty years. A handwriting expert could tell for sure."

"You're welcome to hire one," he said. "Nobody's gonna give a rat's ass one way or another, not after all this time."

That was a hard argument to refute, so I bluffed it. "I'm not so sure. I think I could convince a lot of people to care. I know the government can't touch you now. The statute of limitations on perjury and evidence tampering ran out years ago. But Vinnie's family can always file a civil suit. I'm not his lawyer, but I have a sense they might feel better about you if you helped set the record straight."

"How?"

"By swearing under oath what happened to the paperwork on the Scotch."

"Not a chance," Hagwood said. The hardness of his features had softened as he realized that pleading ignorance with me wouldn't work. "A civil suit's a lot better than what I'd get if I talked about this. Believe me."

"So you know, of the two accomplices who got leniency for their testimony, one was just killed in prison, and the other one has fled the country after a close call with a sniper. You could be next. I'd take some precautions if I were you."

Hagwood's eyes narrowed.

"Go away," he said. Then he closed the door in my face.

I'd been getting a lot of that.

As I approached downtown, I tried Jack Collins again and found him in the office. I swung by to show him the copies of the old documents. I still didn't figure a retired FBI agent would send me anything but the genuine articles, but I had my orders. Collins said the forms had changed over the years, but they looked like paperwork typical of the era that included 1974. The stamps, he said, were official.

Next I planned see if Lucy had made any headway on locating Samuel Griff's family, but a call from Eric Ryland changed everything.

"What's up?" I said.

"I want you back here immediately," he said. "There's trouble."

"Involving me?" I said. I felt my gut hollow out, a sensation of guilt I couldn't explain.

"What's it about?" I said.

"We'll talk about it when you get here."

When I presented myself to Eric's secretary, she told me to go in. None of her usual big smiles, no small talk or chit chat. Just a terse jerk of the head toward Eric's door.

I went in.

"Close the door," Eric told me.

I did.

"Jesus, Eric," I said, "who am I supposed to have killed?"

He handed me a fax. It had originated at the law firm that represented the *Journal*. I scanned the document, a temporary restraining order preventing me from going anywhere near Emily Humphries, her husband Verne Humphries, or any unspecified members of their families.

"I don't get it," I said.

"Then let me spell it out for you," Eric said. "In the supporting affidavits, Emily Humphries and her husband say you came to their door twice without notice, once in the middle of the night, and harassed them."

"Harassed them? That's not . . . "

Eric put up a hand to silence me. "They say you made unreasonable demands on them, threatened them, and that your persistence endangered their lives and their health."

I dropped into a chair, furious. This was the editor who wanted a story so badly he suspended my column to allow me to work on it, and now he sat there like a petulant child because there'd been a minor glitch. I'd done nothing wrong, and he should have waited to hear my side before he copped an attitude.

"I did not harass the Humphries," I said with total conviction. "The first time I went to see them was in the middle of the afternoon. Yesterday, I got to their front door around 8 p.m. All the lights were on inside, so I knew they hadn't gone to bed. I asked Mrs. Humphries a few questions. She didn't want to answer them and got upset. When her husband asked me to leave, I did. Both times."

Eric ran his hands down his face.

"When he asked you to leave the first time," he said, "that should have been ample notice. What possessed you to go back?"

"I don't believe this," I said.

"Believe it, Deuce. Why'd you go back?"

"To warn them that people who survived Ransom Camp have been dying, and they needed to be careful. I wasn't the threat. I was warning them about the threat."

"The problem, Deuce, is this is a public document," Eric said, rattling the TRO. "There are people at the courthouse who will trip all over themselves to get to a phone and call the *Trib* or the *Sun-Times* or a TV station and let this cat out of its bag. It's going to happen, and when it does, it will be a tremendous embarrassment for us."

"So that's what this is about?" I said. "It's not something I did wrong. It's about a possible embarrassment to the paper?"

I knew my words sounded impertinent and would only deepen my hole, but I couldn't keep my anger bottled up.

"It's like that column I did on gun control, Eric. You don't care about the truth, as long as nobody makes you look bad on the six o'clock news, as long as nobody cancels a subscription. When you think public response reflects badly on you, you duck and cover. And you're doing it again."

"Stop it, Deuce, before you get yourself in over your head," he said. "You know as well as I do that a newspaper's credibility is all it has to sell. Sometimes the public admires what we do. But more often they hold us in lower repute than cat burglars. Anything that causes the balance of public opinion to tip toward cat burglary is ground we never gain back. Restraining orders obtained by private citizens who claim harassment by a reporter tip the balance. This is publicity this newspaper can't afford, literally and figuratively."

"What was I supposed to do," I said, "not pursue the story? You've been pushing me to get it done. You're the one who gave me the three-day deadline."

"That doesn't justify scaring two old people."

I had no intention of cowering before Eric's indignation. He had let his asshole side loose on me too often lately, and I didn't intend to be intimidated.

There was a knock at Eric's door. He looked up to see who it was. I didn't much care.

I saw him motion someone to enter. It was Jonathan Bruckner, one of the lawyers who represented the paper. I figured Bruckner wanted a piece of me, too.

The lawyer pulled a sheaf of documents from his briefcase, the original court order and the supporting affidavits. He handed them to Eric, who scanned them. While Eric read, Bruckner turned to me.

"Tell me everything," he said. "Don't leave out anything or shade or embellish the truth. I want this order off the table, and I don't want surprises when I go to court to argue it should be lifted."

"Do you want me to start from the beginning?" I said.

"Beginning to end," Bruckner told me. "Everything."

So I gave it to him. Fifty minutes later, the lawyer and the editor knew every fact I knew, every suspicion I harbored, every theory I had formulated. In a way, it had been a good review for me. It served to reinforce my certainty that I'd done nothing wrong. I was grateful when Jonathan Bruckner reached the same conclusion.

"There's no legal basis for this order," he said to Eric. "I'll have it gone by the close of business today. I'll call you when it's finished."

"You can't go into open court to get the order quashed," I said.

"Why not?" Bruckner said.

"When the lead lawyer for the *Journal* goes to court for anything, you draw the local media like vultures to roadkill. You'll have to tell the judge a lot of what I told you. You'd be handing the story to our competition."

"You want the restraining order lifted, I've got to give the judge a reason."

"Leave the restraining order," I said. "For the sake of the story."

Eric cleared his throat. "If we leave the order in place, Deuce, you won't be able to approach the Humphries again for any reason. That could damage the reporting effort."

"You just said I shouldn't have approached them in the first place," I said.

"Without an invitation," Eric said, his voice rising slightly with exasperation. "There might come a time when we need to get back in touch, and now you can't do that. You're damaged goods. Maybe it's time for a change."

Bruckner came to my rescue.

"Taking Deuce off the story won't do any good," he said. "The order restrains all representatives of the *Journal*. You couldn't assign any reporter to talk to the Humphries without being in violation. Hell, you'd be in violation if you sent a circulation rep to their door to renew their subscription. And if they're already subscribers, you'd better hope their carrier doesn't go too far up the sidewalk to deliver the paper."

"I can finish this without Mrs. Humphries," I told Eric.

Eric thought about it for a minute. His eyes never left my face.

"All right," he said, finally. "We'll try it your way. If I get calls on the order, I'll say it was a misunderstanding. Deuce, if you get calls, refer them to me. Don't let anybody bait you into saying something stupid. I won't tolerate another misunderstanding."

THE FIRST CALL came early that afternoon from a television reporter named Harry Conklin. I tried to refer him to Eric, as instructed. But having gotten me on the phone, Conklin pressed hard. He was aggressive and obnoxious by nature. He professed suspicion of everyone and had an irritating habit of asking public officials the same question six different ways, trying to trick them into blurting out something they didn't mean.

"Did you know about the order?" he said.

"Talk to Eric Ryland," I said. "I gave you his number."

"What did you do to cause this?"

"Call Eric Ryland."

"Who are the people who went to court and got the order?"

"Eric Ryland." I picked up my egg timer and turned it over to start the sand trickling.

"Did you stalk and harass people?"

"Eric Ryland."

"So, I hear your job's in jeopardy. Is that true?"

"Eric Ryland would be the perfect person to ask."

"What story's so important that you'd stalk and harass people, Sweetheart? Hey, it's me, Harry. You know me. I'll protect you."

At this point I came close to telling Harry Conklin to fuck off, something I wanted to tell Harry Conklin every time our paths crossed. But I held my tongue and invoked Eric's name again. So Conklin tried a new approach.

"For God's sake, Darlin', help me out here," he said. "We're professional cousins."

"That's bullshit, Harry. You and I aren't related in any conceivable way. Furthermore, I am neither your sweetheart nor your darling. Call Eric Ryland. I'm hanging up."

And I did. The egg timer hadn't even run out.

Eric came by my desk fifteen minutes later.

"What'd you do to piss off Harry Conklin?" he asked me. "He bent my ear for ten minutes about what a bitch you are."

"You know Harry," I said. "He tried to get me to rise to his bait and say something about the court order, and I kept referring him to you. He's never been good at rejection."

"That's not the point. He's got a big audience. Do you really want him pissed off at you when he goes on the air?"

"Frankly, Eric," I said, "I don't care. I have better things to worry about."

He grunted. "Heard from anyone else?"

"Not yet. But if Harry knows, the *Trib* and *Sun-Times* know. *Chicago* magazine, *Time Out Chicago* and the *Reader* know. TV. Radio. I'm letting my voice mail screen calls."

He grunted again and turned away.

I wanted to get out of the office and away from the phone and away from Eric. I thought again about Samuel Griff, the Customs agent who testified against Vinnie and was killed on duty.

I turned around and saw Lucy Sandoval at her desk. I walked over. She looked up from her monitor and smiled.

"Hi there," she said.

"Did you ever find Samuel Griff's family, or have things been too nuts around here?" I asked her. "I know I've been taking up a lot of time."

"I found some info," she said. "Samuel Griff died a hero. He left a wife and son. Son's name is Adam. He's an architect. Lives in Evanston. Sheridan Road, right on the lake. I'd say he's doing well for himself. The widow's name is Jennifer. I found her in Oak Park." Lucy handed me a folder of printouts. "It's all in here," she said.

I headed out to find the Griffs. Just because Emily Humphries reacted badly didn't mean everyone would.

I hoped.

26

Oak Park was one of Chicago's western suburbs, just over the city line. The Village of Oak Park is best known as the community with the largest collection of Frank Lloyd Wright architecture in the world, including Wright's own home, which has been turned into a museum. I wondered if this was where Adam Griff got his career inspiration.

During the drive to Oak Park, the restraining order and my editor's reaction to it gnawed at my gut like rancid potato salad. The whole situation distracted me when I couldn't afford to be distracted. I was running out of options and time.

Whenever somebody who objects to a story says to me, "You people just print that stuff to sell newspapers," I always want to answer, "What's your point?" Of course we want to sell newspapers. Does Ford want to sell cars?

Yet as journalists, we aspire to so much more, we pretend to so much more, that sometimes we come off looking like pompous, self-aggrandizing jerks. That's why the cop back at Sal Annuncio's place had responded to me as he did. He thought I was trying to hype a story and myself.

Well, he had found out the truth. Most people never do.

And that, I knew, was the reason behind Eric's angst. The fabric of trust between a newspaper and its readers is a fragile one, and the way Eric saw it, I was fraying the fabric of trust at a newspaper where the future already looked dangerously fragile.

And here I was again, pulling up to another private home, about to ring another doorbell and confront another person who didn't know me, wasn't expecting me, and wouldn't like my questions.

The hell with it. I would deal with the consequences later. As I had told Sully, I could always opt out of journalism and go to law school. Or I could become a podiatrist. There were lots of older people in Chicago who needed help clipping their toenails.

Maybe even Emily Humphries.

The property that was home to Jennifer Griff was quiet, heavily treed, and expensive. I wondered how the Griffs afforded it and feared that I knew. I rang the bell to the left of the front door. I heard a double chime sound inside.

It didn't prompt any barking from a cooped up dog. It also didn't prompt the sound of footsteps approaching the door. I rang again. Still nothing.

I could circle the house and peer in windows. I could return to the Explorer and wait for someone to come home, which might be a week or two if Jennifer Griff were on vacation. Or I could go to the address I had for Adam Griff in Evanston and return to this house later.

As I walked back to the truck, I had a sudden, horrible sensation.

I was losing interest.

I'd been rolling along at a terrific pace. Now I found myself running on empty.

It hadn't happened the way Sully warned it might. I hadn't sweated the small details so much that I'd lost the energy to pursue the big picture. Instead, the combination of the court order, my editor's loss of confidence, and my own self-doubts had sapped my enthusiasm. They split my attention. I didn't have the emotional energy reserves to deal with the investigation and the office angst at the same time.

The misgivings had sprung up in front of me like a wall.

I had to find a way over it or risk losing everything.

ADAM GRIFF'S old stone home on Sheridan Road in Evanston—only a few blocks from the home of lawyer *extraordinaire* Richard Palmieri —was even larger and more gracious than Jennifer Griff's house in Oak Park. It was built on a large lot shaded by two dozen oaks, maples, and apple trees. I had to ring the bell twice before I got a response.

I introduced myself to the woman who answered the door, whom I judged to be about my age. Even without makeup, she was a stunning brunette, tall and lean. Her hair was dripping wet, and she wore a long terry beach robe. I could see a spacious swimming pool through the sliding glass doors at the back of the house. I suspected I'd pulled her from the water. It was a bit chilly for me to crawl into a swimming pool, but perhaps she was a member of the Polar Bear Club. Or perhaps her pool was heated.

"Are you Mrs. Griff?" I said. She confirmed it.

I identified myself as a columnist for the *Chicago Journal* and asked for Adam Griff.

"I thought I recognized you from somewhere," she said. "I'm sorry, Adam isn't here. He's on a job. I don't expect him home before seven. Maybe later."

"Can you tell me how to reach him?" I said.

"He's an architect," she said. "The firm is Ratliffe, Rutledge and Griff. Adam is the principal architect on a new mixed-use neighborhood in Skokie. Skokie Park Commons. He's been over there every day for weeks. You can find him there."

"Could you tell me one other thing," I said. "Was Samuel Griff his father?"

Her deep brown eyes narrowed a bit. "Why do you want to know? Your interest isn't with Adam?"

"It's about Samuel," I said.

"Well, yes, Sam was Adam's dad," she said. "He was a hero."

"Yes, his office told me he was killed in the line of duty. How did he die?"

"He was shot by a man trying to smuggle drugs from the Caribbean. Heroin. Sam went looking for it on a tip from a CI, a confidential informant. When Sam found it, the man shot him and tried to get away. Sam's partner shot the smuggler."

"Is Adam's mother the Jennifer Griff who lives in Oak Park?" I said.

She nodded. "Why do you want to talk to Jenny? Not about Sam, I hope. She still gets emotional about him, even after all this time. I hope you won't upset her."

I thanked her and assured her I would try to avoid disturbing Jennifer Griff's world.

Construction on Adam Griff's new development wasn't much out of the ground, but I knew I was in the right place because of the ornate sign that said I had arrived at Skokie Park Commons. I drove around in the construction dust until I found a man in a suit. I thumbed down my window and asked if he knew where I could find Adam Griff.

He was, I was told, over at Commons Commercial.

I had no idea where Commons Commercial might be located. I asked for directions.

"Go back to the main road," he said. "Turn left, then right at the second cross street. When you get there, look for a big, black Land Rover. Adam's never far from his ride."

The man was right. I found Griff leaning over the Land Rover's hood, going over architectural designs. He was in his early forties and dressed in form-fitting blue jeans, a red Polo shirt that clung to his muscular frame, and a white hardhat. He took off the hardhat as I approached, revealing a full head of sandy hair, longish but well-trimmed. He had an angular face with long, deep dimples, a square chin, and intense blue eyes.

I scolded myself for admiring a married man even as I was trying to arrange an evening with Mark Hearst. I couldn't have every good-looking man in the state. But that didn't keep me from thinking about it. It's good to have goals.

"You must be Deuce Mora," he said. "My wife called and said you were asking questions about my father. What's this about?"

Blunt. Right to the point. I followed his lead.

"I know you were a kid back in seventy-four ... "

I saw him doing the calculations in his head.

"Yeah, five or six. Why?"

"Even so, do you recall your father talking, then or later, about a federal court case where he testified against a man who was accused of stealing a shipment of Scotch in a truck parked at the Port of Chicago?"

I saw something flash in Griff's eyes, but I wasn't sure what.

"What's this about?" he said again, more insistent this time.

"It's about clearing up the possibility that your father and an ATF agent named James Hagwood testified mistakenly at the thief's trial, maybe knowingly, maybe unknowingly, and sent a man away for a lot more years than he deserved."

"Did this man claim he was innocent?" Griff said.

"No, he never claimed that," I said. "But he claimed he should have been tried in state court, where the penalties were less severe."

Griff wiped sweat from his forehead. Near as I could tell, the temperature was hovering near 70, and the sun wasn't that hot.

"Who cares?" Griff said. "So a thief did more time than he should have. A welcome reversal of form if you ask me."

Oh, well, looks aren't everything.

"So you don't know anything about the case?" I said.

"Not a thing. Like you said, I was a kid. My father wouldn't have discussed a case in front of me."

I extended my hand, and he shook it. I thanked him for his time and started to turn back to my car. Griff called after me.

"And stay away from my mother," he said. "I mean it."

TELLING a reporter to stay away is like a dare. We'll take it every time. It's a clear sign that someone has something to hide.

When I returned to Jennifer Griff's house, a white Cadillac SRX was parked in the driveway. My old Explorer was outclassed every time I parked it.

I rang the front doorbell again and heard the soft chime again. This time, I also heard the yipping of a small dog. Wherever Jennifer had been, the dog had been with her.

When the door opened, I found myself facing a woman who, given the age of her son, should have been around sixty, but she looked years older. She had iron gray hair cut short and unstyled. It was hard to tell where the faded hair ended and the faded face began. I saw a lot of hard years written there.

The small, fluffy dog in her arms bluff-barked at me, a kind of half-woof that came from deep in the throat, a pretend challenge. The woman stroked the dog absently, and it nestled its black head in the crook of her arm.

"Jennifer Griff?" I said.

"You're the woman from the *Journal*?" she said. "My son called me a few minutes ago."

"What did your son tell you?"

"Said I shouldn't talk to you."

I tried on a sympathetic smile. "How do you know if you want to talk to me if you don't know what I came to talk about?"

"You want to talk about my husband, and some old case where he testified," she said.

"I do. May I come in?"

She hesitated a moment, then asked to see some identification. I showed her my company and police IDs. She hesitated again, then stepped back to allow me to pass.

Except for a well-chewed white fleece doggy toy in the middle of the living room, the house was spotless.

Mrs. Griff indicated that I should sit in a big leather recliner with a footstool, a man's chair. It was old. I thought it must have been her husband's.

"Can I get you something?" she asked me. "Coffee? A pop?"

"I'm fine, thanks," I said. "This story I'm working on involves a man convicted in federal court of stealing a truckload of Scotch from the Port of Chicago." I went through the details of the investigation, the trial and the testimony, and she listened to every word. Then I asked, "Did your husband ever discuss the case with you?"

Jennifer had found a handkerchief somewhere and was winding it into something that resembled a vanilla Twizzler. She said nothing, so I pushed.

"This was a long time ago, Mrs. Griff," I said. "Back in 1974. Did your husband ever talk to you about his testimony? Did he ever say anything that made you think he had second thoughts about it?"

Her eyes filled, and she shook her head as if it hurt.

"You have no idea what you're doing," she said.

I nodded. "I sometimes feel that way," I acknowledged.

Without another word, she got up and left the room. I heard ice falling into glass tumblers in the kitchen. Ever hopeful, I set my digital recorder to voice activation and put it on the edge of the coffee table. When she returned, Jennifer was carrying two glasses of ice water. She set one on a coaster in front of me. I saw her notice the recorder. She took her glass and returned to her seat. I took this as a sign that she wouldn't be throwing me out of the house anytime soon.

"You're taping this?" she said.

"I'd like to," I said.

"Okay, I guess." She had something to say. I waited until she was ready to give it voice. The wait lasted nearly two full minutes. Her first words almost knocked me out of the chair.

"I never thought I would ever speak of this," she said, "especially to a reporter. But I have lived alone with Sam's secret for too many years. And Adam is old enough now to accept the truth."

She burrowed back into her chair, as if expecting the furniture to protect her. "My husband testified as he did because he was threatened and bribed."

I wanted to ask who was responsible, but she didn't give me time. The words, locked up for forty years, began to tumble out. "I had complications from my pregnancy with Adam, expensive complications that our health insurance didn't cover. Without surgery I would've lived the rest of my life as an invalid. Or I might've died. We couldn't afford the surgery on what Sam earned."

She took a long, shuddering breath. I waited.

She said, "They paid him $50,000 to collect copies of some Customs forms and destroy them. I imagine they paid the ATF agent something similar to collect copies of some other import forms. But I don't know that. I don't know the ATF man. Sam knew him some, from work, but I didn't."

"Who were the men?"

She took a sip of her water and looked at me over the rim of the glass. When she set it down again she asked, "Who do you mean?"

"Who were the people who threatened and bribed your husband?"

She stared at me a moment, then shook her head. She said nothing.

"You don't know, or you won't say?" I said.

"I've already said too much," she told me. "But at least you know the truth, and you can use it to help clear the name of that old man. I didn't plan to say anything to you, but then I remembered Sam wanted to set the record straight. Now's as good a time as any."

I shook my head. "What you've told me, it's all hearsay. Whoever made the threats and paid the bribes dealt with your husband, not with you. The court wouldn't allow you to testify to anything that you didn't personally hear or witness."

Then I had a thought. "Do you still have your banking records dating back to '74? If your husband made a deposit of $50,000, that would be evidence I could use."

She sighed and shook her head. "Sam put his paycheck into our checking account and paid the mortgage and my medical bills out of that. But he never put in a dime of the bribe money. We used the cash to cover everyday expenses and to buy clothes, stuff for the baby, and a new car. Sam said if anybody examined our books, it would look like we were scrimping by."

"The mortgage was on this house?"

"Oh, my, no." she said. "We couldn't have afforded this. We lived in Northlake, out near O'Hare. Adam insisted on buying this house for me nine or ten years ago."

"So you never saw this cash from the bribe?"

"No. When Sam told me about it, I said I didn't want to see it. I didn't want to know where it was. I would have preferred not even knowing it existed. I saw how the whole thing was eating at him, and I didn't want to feel the same guilt. But I did. I couldn't help it."

I took a sip of water, thinking over how to proceed.

Jennifer Griff started to cry.

"My husband . . ." She tried to unwind the handkerchief but had trouble, so the tears fell from her bowed head into her lap. When she had the handkerchief in useable shape, the floodgates opened and she sobbed. Her head bowed, her hand at her forehead, she sat there for a long time with her shoulders shaking. I watched, feeling ill at ease.

I caused too many tears lately. There was no more I could do for Jennifer Griff than I'd done for Emily Humphries because, once again, I didn't know what prompted the meltdown. I watched it ebb. I didn't push.

Minutes passed before she could speak again.

At last she said, "I don't think my husband died the hero they said he was. I think he was murdered, but not by the smuggler. I've always been convinced he told the wrong people about his plan to come forward with the truth, and they killed him before he could."

"Why do you think so?" I said.

"Sam told me that's what he was going to do," she said, "come forward with the truth."

"When was this?"

"A few years after he testified, a few weeks before he was killed. The whole thing was eating him alive, and he couldn't live with his lie. He was a very Christian man. He wanted to set the record straight. He told me he might be prosecuted for perjury. He said it would go easier for him if he came forward. I'm telling you this because it might help you, but I don't want you to print anything I've said. If any of this became public, it would ruin Sam's reputation, and he doesn't deserve that."

"But your husband wanted the truth to come out," I said. "He was convinced it had to, and he died for that conviction."

"But *I* don't want it," she said. "At this point, I don't care what Sam wanted. The old man you're trying to help is dead, so it doesn't matter to him. Sam has a legacy of heroism he left to his grandchildren. I can't allow that to be tarnished. Even if it's a lie."

"Then why did you agree to let me make the recording?" I said.

She began to cry again. "I don't know, I don't know," she said between sobs. "I didn't know I had a right to refuse."

That statement, also caught by my little machine, might throw the recording into legal limbo. But it didn't matter. I couldn't use hearsay any more than the courts can.

"What makes you think Sam told someone else about his plan to come forward?"

"Because after the man who shot my husband was shot and killed by another Customs agent, the dead man's picture was in the paper. They said he had ties to organized crime."

She paused, and I waited.

"I recognized him," she said. "It was the same man who came to our house at least twice, and each time he was here, it left Sam badly shaken. I think he was the man who threatened my husband. I think he was the man who delivered the bribe."

AFTER A BRIEF HIATUS, Jennifer Griff had jump-started my enthusiasm. Although she'd offered nothing but conjecture and hearsay, it fit. I called Carl Cribben.

I got his voice mail. I left a message, told him I had something urgent, and asked him to return the call to my cell phone.

Then I called the paper. I found Lucy Sandoval working the late shift again. I flipped to the page in my notebook where I'd written the date Jennifer Griff gave me, the date her husband died.

"If you get sick of me, let me know," I said when Lucy picked up her phone.

"I'm not going to get sick of your story," Lucy said. "It's a whole lot more interesting than the rest of what I've been doing. What have you got to break the monotony?"

"Back to the 1979 story about the Customs agent who was killed," I said. "I need anything you can find about the man who shot Sam Griff. His photo was in the papers, and the stories said he had mob ties. I need anything you can find on him."

"I'm on it. It won't take me long to find this."

I didn't want to go home and hang out there waiting for the phone to ring. So I went to the gym to run off some stress. Ninety minutes later, I was in the parking lot waiting for the Explorer's heat to come up when Lucy called.

"Sorry it took me so long," she said. "I got called off for something else. But I did get what you asked for. It's in your computer, in a file called, 'Griff'. There are photos with it."

Once home, I tended to the cats before I went to the laptop. Often, anticipation is better than reality. In this case, reality kicked ass.

The first story reported that a young killer named Nicky "Cha-Cha" Santori, known to be associated with elements of the South Side Organization, had gunned down Samuel Griff outside a warehouse at Iroquois Landing at the Port of Chicago.

Another Customs agent, Robert Delacorte, responded to the initial sound of gunfire, and when he turned a corner of the warehouse, he saw Griff on the ground and Santori with a handgun aimed at Griff's head. He ordered Santori to drop the weapon. Santori turned and fired at him, missed, and Delacorte dropped him. Griff was dead already.

I looked away from the laptop screen. Nicky "Cha-Cha" Santori. Except for the moniker, it was exactly the same name as the man I had picked from the mug books as the intruder at my condo, the jerk who clubbed me with my own brass bookend.

It was more coincidence than I could buy.

The story speculated that Griff caught Santori in an act of smuggling and died trying to apprehend him. That theme carried through all of the subsequent stories, the ones that hailed Griff as a fallen hero. Santori's death was ruled a justifiable shooting, and there the case ended.

I found photos attached to the e-mail. Griff's picture showed a handsome, smiling man with some sort of big fish in his hands. For all I knew, it might have been a cobia.

The photo of Santori showed a big man with a full head of dark hair, a day's growth of beard, and a deep scowl. It might have been a police mug shot. I knew the face. I'd gotten a good look at the man who wrecked my place and presented me with a concussion. With forty years separation, they could have been father and son, and they likely were.

I wondered how many generations of Santoris were tied up with the mob.

I also wondered why Carl Cribben hadn't returned my call. Perhaps he, too, preferred to be done with me. It would fit the recent pattern.

I discovered otherwise a little past midnight when the cell phone in the nightstand charger began chirping. It roused me from a fitful sleep filled with dreams of getting fired. I welcomed the chance to leave the nightmare behind.

"Sorry if I woke you," Cribben said. "You said it was urgent. I was on a late flight from Washington and just got in."

"Washington?" I said, trying to shake residual cobwebs from my head.

"Yeah. Don't ask. I can't tell you anything. So what's with you?"

First, I thanked Cribben for an unspecified favor, and he got the reference.

"Happy I could help," he said. "So is that why you called?"

I brought him up to date on Ricardo LaPalma, his roots at Ransom Camp, his role in the killer fires, and my conclusion that LaPalma still lived in the Chicago area.

"But our researchers," I said, "who can find anyone, can't find a trace of him."

"So maybe he's living under an a.k.a.," Cribben said.

"That's what I'm thinking," I said. "My hunch is he's hiding inside the mob. Or . . . " I hesitated and then told Cribben about the weird coincidence of Richard Palmieri's name.

"Did Palmieri ever come up in your corruption investigation?" I asked him.

"No, although we weren't that far in. Without a confession, we'd need DNA or fingerprints to prove Richard Palmieri and Ricardo LaPalma are one and the same. I don't know where we'd find DNA or fingerprints on LaPalma."

"There's a sister, Emily LaPalma Humphries, living in Bucktown," I said. "Her blood would have markers in common with Ricardo. But you'd have to compel a DNA sample from her. She is definitely not willing to get involved in this."

"And your hunch isn't sufficient cause to compel her coopera-tion," He said. "Anything else going on?"

Then I briefed him on my conversation with Jennifer Griff.

"None of that," he said, "will hold legal water without bank records or something in writing from Griff himself owning up to the bribe and the perjury. Did you get any indication from the widow that something like that might exist?"

"No to the bank records," I said. "We didn't talk about anything else."

I told Cribben I'd given his name, address and phone number to Mark Hearst.

"I'm not being paranoid," I said, "but Mark's pretty invested in this whole story, as you are, and if anything should happen to me, it will be important for the two of you to know each other."

"I thought I had stipulated my anonymity rather adamantly." Extreme irritation was clear in his voice.

"With Mark, you're as good as anonymous," I said. "He understands the circumstances. He's helping off-the-record, too."

"I'll be in touch," Cribben said. He hung up without saying good-bye.

27

I hadn't been at my desk five minutes when Eric Ryland's secretary came by and said Eric wanted to see me. She looked solemn.

I came to an abrupt halt at Eric's door when I saw that the other occupant was again the *Journal*'s attorney, Jonathan Bruckner. Eric looked up and made a wagging signal with his forefinger that I should come in. He did not invite me to sit.

"You don't learn, do you?" he said.

"I don't understand," I said. Instinct told me this was about the visit to Jennifer Griff.

Eric plunged ahead. "I have a complaint from an Evanston architect named Adam Griff that you went to his mother's house and interviewed her about her husband after he specifically asked you to stay away. He didn't want his mother upset, but you went anyway. You didn't call ahead to let her know you were coming. You just showed up and started asking questions. And to compound the problem, you secretly taped the conversation in violation of about a dozen laws. According to Griff, your visit devastated his mother."

I looked at him in utter disbelief.

"In the first place," I said, "I don't secretly tape conversations. Not ever. I know the law. Mrs. Griff's permission is the first thing on the recording, if you'd care to hear it. It would've been nice if you'd asked me before jumping to conclusions. In the second place, her son has no legal right to prevent me from talking to her. He isn't her legal guardian. I rang her doorbell. She answered the door. And she invited me in knowing full well who I was. She even asked to see identification, and I showed it to her."

My throat was tight with anger. I cleared the throat, if not the anger, with a cough.

Eric started to speak. I raised my hand to stop him.

I continued. "I was there for maybe half an hour. I asked some questions, and she volunteered the information about her husband. Yes, she cried a couple of times. Memories will do that. I didn't abuse her. Late in our conversation, she asked me not to use the recording, but she never withdrew her permission to make it. If she had, I'd have turned the recorder off. I have some sympathy for the son trying to protect the mother, but she gave me no sign that she needed or wanted anybody's protection. She talked to me willingly and openly."

Bruckner interceded and turned to Eric.

"I don't see any problem with Deuce interviewing the woman," he said. "You've got an angry son, that's all. I wouldn't sweat it. If the woman invited Deuce in, then neither she nor the son has any grounds for legal action."

"It was still a stupid thing to do, Deuce," Eric told me. "Dumb, blind, stupid. You have one restraining order against you already. If this leads to a second . . ." He threw his hands in the air, at a loss for words. He was seething. Then finished his thought. " . . . the damage to the paper could be irreparable."

Bruckner nodded, in a solemn lawyer way. "That might be a bit of an overstatement," he said, "but the first TRO could be cited in court as evidence supporting the need for a second. An attorney for the Griffs could claim you've got a history of acting irresponsibly. The fact that we didn't try to quash the first TRO could be viewed as a sign that we didn't disagree with the allegations. So if the Griffs go for a TRO, I'll have to try to get both of them quashed, and then your story has exposure in open court. You're not guilty of any misconduct, but aggressive reporting does have its down sides."

Eric turned from Bruckner to me. "I want to see you at two this afternoon," he said. "You'll be handing all your documents and notes over to Sully. You're done on this story, Deuce. You're a fine columnist, but investigative reporting takes finesse, and you've exhibited none of it. The story's going to someone who has."

I stared at Eric in anger for a few seconds, too worked up to risk saying a word.

Then I turned my back and walked out.

I'D WANTED to have lunch with Sully before the meeting with Eric, to discuss the situation in a place with no one to hear. But he was out of the office. So I went to a mediocre Italian place nearby and picked at a salad for an hour, feeling each bite sour in my stomach.

A part of me wanted to fight back, to lay down an ultimatum: Leave the story with me, or I walk. The sudden departure of the paper's highest-profile columnist would cause a big stink and mess up Eric Ryland's life for a while. But you don't quit one job until you have another, because it's easier to find work if you have work. Of course, if I took John Conti up on his offer of help, that would be as good as having another job.

The easiest action, and the best for my career, would be to crawl back into my column cave and let this whole experience fade from the paper's institutional memory over time. A couple of days ago I'd wanted to let the story go away. Now was as good a time as any.

Even after I finished lunch, I hadn't decided which outcome I wanted.

THE BIG CONFRONTATION took place in Eric's conference room. To get there I had to walk through the newsroom. Several colleagues gave me weak smiles of support. Bad news travels fast.

Eric and Sully both were in the conference room when I arrived. Eric looked angry. Sully looked miserable. He and I made eye contact, and Sully shook his head slightly, a gesture of sympathy and disbelief.

"What we're doing here," Eric announced, almost formally, "is passing the torch on what is potentially a good story from the reporter who uncovered it to a reporter in whom we have great faith to finish it off. Sully, you've done investigative reporting in the past, and you've done it well. This is a chance to do it again. There's nothing coming up on the campaign trail in the next month that we can't cover *ad hoc*. Deuce has been away from her column too long. We need her back in the paper three days a week. And, frankly, this story could take weeks more to see through."

"My political sources need to hear from me," Sully said. "I can't disappear for weeks, then pop up and announce I'm back and expect relationships to pick up where they left off."

"You can call them and check in," Eric told him. "Right now, this story needs you. You have investigative experience, and you know most of the details. It would take too long for anybody else to catch up. Deuce will turn over her files and notes. Feel free to call on her if you need expansion or explanation, but she will play no further role in the reporting."

He turned to me. "As for you, Deuce, if and when the story is published, you'll get a byline. Your *good* work will be acknowledged." He put a lot of emphasis on the word "good," as if to underscore his view that most of my effort sucked.

Sully shook his head. "Eric, I'm willing to work with Deuce, but I don't feel right taking over. We could make a lot more progress together."

"No, Deuce is a full-time columnist again."

Sully turned to me. "What about your sources, Deuce? "Will they talk to me?"

Eric spoke up as if I weren't in the room.

"Deuce will ask them to work with you," he said.

"Let me put my cards on the table," Sully said. "We all know what this is about. You want to rein Deuce in. You think she's stepped over the line on some things and maybe on some sensitive toes. Why not let the two of us work together—under the direction of an editor cut loose from all other duties, somebody with plenty of time to provide oversight?"

Eric turned his glare on Sully. "I don't give a rat's ass about sensitive toes," he said. "I care about having this story reported responsibly. It's my decision, not open for debate."

He focused his glare back on me, as if to verify I understood.

I stood, so both men had to look up at me.

"I'll make sure you're up to speed, Sully," I told him, ignoring Eric. "I'll ask my sources to cooperate, though one might not agree." Carl Cribben, the retired FBI agent.

I turned to Eric. "If Sully needs help, he can call me. But that's the limit to what I'm willing to do. I won't be returning to the column."

I took a breath.

"Eric," I said, "this isn't about bylines, it's about respect and trust."

He started to say something, but I cut him off. "I'd like to resign this minute, to be honest. But if I did, the newspaper's liability policy wouldn't cover me for whatever time it takes to complete the handoff."

I turned to Sully. "Stop by any time for my files," I said.

Looking shell-shocked, Sully could manage only a small nod.

I turned to leave the room.

"Deuce, wait!" It was Eric.

I turned back to him.

"Don't do anything precipitously," he said. "I want you to think about this. We value your voice in the newspaper. What you've done isn't a firing offense, it was a . . . an exuberant overreaction. Different people have talent for different kinds of journalism. Nobody is questioning your talent as a columnist. Nobody ever has."

I shook my head. "I think what you've just done here is an exuberant overreaction, whatever the hell that means. I've done nothing wrong. Jonathan Bruckner told you I've done nothing wrong. What you've done is display a complete lack of confidence in my judgment. I don't think your doubts will stop at the door to the columnist's room. Remember the gun-control column not so long ago?"

Eric blinked.

"Sooner or later," I said, "I'll do another piece that brings down the wrath of someone. We'll lose a few more subscribers. And your lack of confidence will resurface. Then it will be you pushing me out the door instead of me opening it for myself. I can't let that happen. I can't live every day with the Sword of Damocles hanging over my head."

Eric held up a hand, showing me his palm. "Look," he said, "take two weeks off. With pay, off the books. Get some rest. Think everything over. If you feel the same way when you come back, I won't argue. But don't do this in the heat of the moment."

"I thought you needed my voice back in the paper this minute," I said. "Or is it two weeks from now?"

"I'll . . . I'll agree to some latitude so we don't lose your voice permanently," he said.

Nice recovery.

Eric was right. Quitting a good job shouldn't come in the heat of the moment.

But I didn't mind letting Eric fret a while.

I would take the two weeks, but my demeanor remained noncommittal. I looked at Sully. "Let me know when you're ready to go through the files."

Then I turned my back and walked out of the room, the second time this day I had turned my back on Eric. I liked how it felt.

But other than that, I felt like shit.

"THAT WAS SOME EXIT YOU MADE," Sully said. "Eric was pissed."

We were sitting in the dining area of my condo, eating Cuban sandwiches, drinking Goose Island 312, and watching as a series of thunderstorms lashed the city. I didn't know why Sully insisted on bringing the Cuban sandwiches. He knew I didn't like them, even the good ones, which these weren't.

It didn't matter. I wasn't hungry.

"Eric was pissed coming in," I said. "He might have been more pissed by my abrupt exit, but on the Master Pissed-Off Meter, he didn't come close to me."

After I left the office, Sully tried to spend the rest of the afternoon reviewing my files and notes, but his phone wouldn't stop ringing. Members of the staff burned up his lines. Word of my abrupt departure spread with the swift force of a flash flood, with about as many variations on the story as there were people asking about it.

Sully had called on his way to my apartment. I didn't want company, but I needed to talk to a friendly face about the choice I faced: take two weeks off to cool down and then go back to the column, or walk out the door. So I told Sully to come ahead. He said he would bring dinner. I didn't know he meant bad Cuban sandwiches.

Though there was no sexual tension between us these days—at least nothing I felt comfortable acknowledging—Sully and I had a personal and professional bond that allowed me to be completely open with him. I told him I wanted his take on my future.

"I don't understand," I said, "how I earned a permanent place in Eric's shithouse. As we talked, I nibbled little pieces of my sandwich. It tasted the way I imagined wallboard would taste if you put mustard on it.

"He'll get over it," he said. "Once the Harry Conklins of the television world get past the glee of on-air gossip, the restraining order will go away as an issue. I figure Conklin's attention span covers one news cycle. That's about how long Eric will care. Take the two weeks he offered. It's a free vacation. It will give both of you time to cool down. Then come back. Your column is too good to disappear from the paper forever. Nobody's irreplaceable, but you're close. There's nobody around who can carry your pencils."

"I can't go back and pretend this never happened."

"No you can't. But you can come back rested and fit and eager to write again. Within a day or two, everybody will be back in the old rhythms."

"Except you. You'll be out there working on my story. And when you break it, all the barely healed wounds will crack open."

"Not true," Sully said. "You're going to get a byline. And I plan to insist that you do a lot of the writing. You're a better writer than I am. And I never met Vinnie. How am I supposed to put a face on him for readers? You'll be right in the thick of it."

"If Eric permits it," I said. "He's convinced I acted irresponsibly. Tell me the truth. Do you think he's right? Going to see Emily Humphries at eight at night? Was I wrong?"

"From what I remember of *All the President's Men*, nighttime visits to witnesses were legitimized as a reporting technique way back during the Watergate scandals. Woodward and Bernstein operated as much after dark as before."

"But Emily Humphries isn't a public official. She's a terrified old lady."

"You didn't threaten her or her husband?"

"Of course not. I left the first time when her husband told me to. I left the second time after he closed the door in my face."

"And he closed the door on you after he saw that white Chrysler?"

"Yes."

"He must have recognized the car. And it frightened him."

"Seems like it. It does seem to show up everywhere I go."

"You didn't threaten Jennifer Griff?"

"Not at all. I violated her son's instructions not to go near her. But she's an adult. He had no authority to order me to stay away. And when she opened the door, she invited me in. She volunteered the story. I didn't demand anything."

"Yeah, I think Eric's way overreacting," Sully said. "I don't know why."

I felt tears pressing behind my eyes and bit my lip hard to stop them. Sully saw this. He got up from the table and came around to hug me from behind, his face pressed into my hair. I smelled his aftershave. It used to drive me crazy. A few tears leaked down my face.

"This is crap," Sully said. "I'm sorry."

"Not your fault, Sully," I said. "Just don't give up on this. And please, do your very best not to get hurt."

"I promise," he said.

"Go home," I said. "It's where you belong."

Outside, the storm continued to rage. I told Sully to be careful driving.

He kissed the top of my head, and a moment later I heard my front door close.

28

The assassin knows she will recognize the white Chrysler he and Nicky Boy have been using, so he rents another car just for the day, an even more common and nondescript beige-gray Camry. He sets up half a block from her house, parking amid other cars so he doesn't attract the attention of her rent-a-cops. When she drives away from her building, he will follow and take the first good, clean shot he gets. The boss wants this done before she can conduct another interview. He wants it done today. She is getting too close to the truth.

The assassin hates this assignment. It is fraught with folly. It is the one kill he was determined to decline. Nothing good can come of it. But after botching the takedown of Sal Annuncio, the 350-pound slug in Back of the Yards, he owes his handlers a make-good.

He hasn't tried to make excuses for missing that shot. They wouldn't have understood or accepted that in the exact same fraction of a second it took a bullet to flash from his rifle to the target, the target had managed to get his entire body out of the line of fire.

Of course the assassin knew what happened. Just as the he pulled the trigger, a squirrel started harvesting acorns, throwing them out of the oak next to the picnic table where the assassin mounted his rifle. The first nut hit the table and startled him, and he lost the line of fire. There had been no

*time to get it back before the big lug disappeared around the corner of
his house.*

Fuckin' damn squirrels. Ain't nothing but rats with bushy tails.

*Now the assassin will do what he has to do. He has his reputation
to mend.*

*He follows her south on Damen to the Stevenson Expressway, east to
Lake Shore Drive and north to Monroe. Then west through Grant Park to
the* Journal *building.*

When she pulls into the office garage, he chooses to follow her on foot.

*He puts a counterfeit handicapped placard on his rear-view mirror. It
allows him to park in a metered spot indefinitely without paying parking
fees.*

*He puts on a plain black baseball-style cap and pulls it low, grabs his
duffel from the trunk of the Camry, hurries across the street and into the
garage stairwell. He searches floor by floor for the target's Explorer and
finds it on Level 3. Fortunately, he can hide behind a Chevy pickup truck
parked next to the stairwell door, making escape easier once his assignment
is done. He settles in to wait.*

Nothing about this job feels right.

*She is a high-profile target. Less so than the politician in Las Vegas, but
in Vegas he'd had time to plan. He took his shot from a well-concealed spot
where he had time to make a clean escape. Here, he will be working from
behind a pickup with the barrel of his rifle anchored on the truck's hood.
And the shot will have to angle through her windshield.*

It is a crazy chance.

But he has given his word, and he will keep it.

It is the honorable thing to do.

29

I drove to the office the next morning, planning to be in by eight, before anyone else arrived. I didn't want to see anyone or talk to anyone. But the heavy rain, which had continued all night, slowed traffic to a crawl, and I got in forty minutes later than intended.

I had dressed in a t-shirt, blue jeans, running shoes, and a light jacket, the apparel of leisure. No sense in dressing up to clean out my desk. I'd come for the originals of my files and notes. I had given them to a clerk to photocopy for Sully with instructions to put the originals back on my desk when she was through.

The fifteen hours that had passed since I walked out of the newsroom hadn't dulled my resentment. Bad timing, however, deprived me of my wish not to see anyone in the office. Eileen Holt, the deputy metro editor, was at her desk when I wandered toward mine.

"Deuce?" she said.

I turned to face her.

"I thought you were taking a couple of weeks off," she said.

"I am," I said. "I came in to get some of my things."

"I'm not sure you're supposed to be in the building."

Anger flared. "I haven't been fired, Eileen. Nobody's confiscated my security badge."

"Still."

I hated the newsroom at that moment. I turned my back on Eileen before I said something stupid and went back to my desk. My files were all there, stacked and waiting for me. I slipped out of my backpack and stuffed the folders into it. I glanced around the desk for anything else I might need. I found nothing. I wouldn't even need my egg timer.

I noticed my voice mail light glowed red. I had one message, from Carl Cribben. His FBI sources had done a general search of databases and found nothing that could tie a migrant worker named Ricardo LaPalma to a stellar civil lawyer named Richard Palmieri. They had opened up Palmieri's history all the way back to his birth, and there were no inconsistencies. Richard Palmieri and Ricardo La Palma were not the same person.

I was happy Cribben had gotten past his irritation about me sharing his identity with Mark Hearst, at least enough to continue helping me. But life would have been a lot easier had LaPalma and Palmieri matched up. Another suspicion gone wrong.

I was on a roll, a bad one. But there is something to be said for consistency.

I struggled to get the backpack on my shoulders. It weighed a ton. I left the floor using a route that wouldn't take me past Eileen's desk.

I saw several colleagues in the parking garage. One averted his eyes, pretending not to notice me. I got big hellos from the rest and an occasional word of sympathy. When I reached my Explorer I opened the rear hatch and heaved the backpack inside. As I lowered the tailgate, Sully pulled in beside me.

"Hey, wait up," he said as he got out of his Jeep. "I tried to call you this morning and got your machine. You get any sleep?"

"Not much. Why didn't you call my cell?"

He walked around to where I was standing and hugged me. I hugged back. "I figured," he said, "if you weren't home or weren't picking up, you didn't want to talk."

"Astute. Actually, I stopped by to pick up the originals of my files. I haven't the vaguest idea what I'm going to do with them, but I wanted to have them with me. Hey, you've still got the originals of the formerly missing Customs docs, right?"

"I do. In a very safe place. Want 'em back?"

"Nah, you hold onto them. I've got copies as good as the originals."

"I'll take care of them," he said. "You know the rumor mill's still going like crazy."

"I'm sure it is."

"What are you going to do?"

"I don't know. Go home. Try to keep myself from falling into a deeper funk. I need to stay busy. If the rain stops, I might go running. Lift some weights. Think about things."

"I'll call you later," Sully said. "Maybe we'll catch a drink."

"Whatever," I said.

I opened the Explorer's front door and got in. I ducked my head so I could see the ignition to insert the key.

The windshield exploded. Glass sandblasted my face and neck. Then searing pain ripped along my left arm. Sully pulled me from the truck. He was yelling, "Deuce, get down. On the ground. Now!"

I guess I didn't move fast enough because I felt hands drag me to the floor.

The commotion ended. I was flat on my back, assessing my pain, trying to find a spot that didn't hurt. My feet seemed to be okay. I raised a hand to my face.

"No, Deuce, don't," Sully said, pushing my hand down. "Lie still. I'm calling for help."

I heard him giving our location to 911, telling the operator that someone had been shot. It didn't register for a moment. Had I been shot or had Sully?

The side of my face felt as if it had been hit by a load of birdshot —or what I imagined the experience would feel like. I wanted to touch it, to assess the damage. But every time I raised my hand, Sully restrained me.

"It's okay," he kept telling me. "It's not bad. The docs'll fix you right up."

Then a lot of people crowded around us, everybody talking at once. I kept my eyes closed because I didn't want to deal with any of this, whatever it was. I wished everybody would go and leave me alone. I tried to shut out the world.

The wail of approaching sirens told me that wouldn't be happening any time soon.

I LEARNED EARLY on that I was neither critically hurt nor maimed for life. The paramedics who arrived even before the police told me my face and neck had been sprayed with pebbled safety glass when the windshield disintegrated. The pebbles left abrasions and little more. A few pieces imbedded themselves under the skin and could be removed in the emergency room. The paramedics told me I would look as if I had the measles, and then everything would heal up with little scars that would disappear in time. I was lucky none of the glass entered my eyes.

I also took some metal shrapnel to my left arm in the same general area where a bullet creased me. The bullet had torn along the deltoid muscle but didn't penetrate. Nothing to worry about there, either, at least not long-term. My tetanus shot was current. The wounds needed treatment and rest. I wouldn't be bench-pressing for a while.

The doctor who worked on me in the ER told me he wanted to keep me for observation for a few hours, and then someone could drive me home.

My first visitor was Det. Vernon Bronson, who told me the car glass exploded into me because a gunshot had blasted through the windshield.

"Guy must have been nuts to try a shot like that," Bronson said.

"Probably trying to scare me is all," I said.

"No, not so much. The slug that hit your arm might have hit your head except it was deflected by some metal animal thing hanging from your mirror."

"Darwin? Is he okay?"

"You're joking," Bronson said.

"No, I'm not. I love that monkey."

"Well, it gave its life for you," he said.

"Shit," I said, and I meant it. The important part, the fact that the metal ornament saved my life, hadn't quite sunk in at that point. Sully won it for me at the state fair when we were very much in love, and I cherished it.

Eric came in then and asked how I was feeling. I told him I felt like a pincushion. He didn't introduce himself to Bronson. I assumed the two had met outside.

Bronson would ask me about a motive for the shooting. I would be vague. I wanted Vinnie's story left out of the police report now even more than when the cops responded to my home invasion. Every local in the news business would pull a copy of the police report on the shooting. If I told Bronson the story, it would be like handing it to the competition.

This story was taking a hell of a toll, and I wasn't even working on it anymore.

"So what's this all about, Ms. Mora?" Bronson asked me.

"It's about irony, I suspect."

"Excuse me?"

I saw Eric watching me. He looked apprehensive.

"Irony," I said. "The opposite of wrinkly."

"Deuce." Eric's voice was low and serious.

"Okay, irony," I said. "The use of words, or in this case deeds, to express something opposite of the literal meaning."

Bronson frowned and looked impatient. "I know what irony is, Ms. Mora. How is it applicable in the case of this shooting?"

"I suspect the purpose of the shooting was to scare me off a story that I'm no longer working on. Hence, the irony."

"Deuce," Eric said again. Meaning to watch my step.

Well, the hell with him if he couldn't take a joke. It was me lying in the hospital bed. If I wanted to have a little fun with it, he could go screw himself.

"What's the story, and who wants you off?" Bronson asked me.

I saw Eric tense.

"I'm not going to discuss the story with you, Detective," I said. "Not because I wouldn't love to help you catch the guy who used me for target practice and murdered Darwin, but because telling you about the story wouldn't bring you any closer to catching the shooter. I have no clue who it is."

I went 'round and 'round with Bronson until he gave up and left. He told me there was nothing he could do to help me if I didn't try to help myself. I muttered something to the effect that my inability to help myself had become chronic. Bronson didn't hear. Eric did.

"Look, Deuce, I'm sorry about all this," he said. "I'm sorry how it turned out with the story, and I'm sorry you got hurt again."

"Yeah, sure," I said. "Thanks."

He crossed his arms over his chest. "What would you have done in my place? I've got a reporter who's turned into a loose cannon. What choice did I have but to set you down?"

"Why don't you take a close look at what I did and didn't do? I didn't harass Emily and Verne Humphries in Bucktown. I didn't do anything to warrant the restraining order, and even Bruckner said he could have gotten it lifted. I didn't harass Mrs. Griff in Oak Park. I asked questions. That, last time I looked, is what reporters do."

He opened his mouth to say something, but I barreled on. "How can you call me a loose cannon when I've done nothing but my job? Diligently, might add."

I saw nothing in Eric's eyes to suggest he understood, so I told him, "Go away, Eric. Go back to protecting your newspaper, and let me get some sleep."

I turned my head away from him. When I heard the sigh made by the closing automatic door, I turned back and he was gone. But I wasn't alone for long. The door opened again and Sully walked through with Mark Hearst.

"Geez, that'd make a great Halloween costume," Sully said, nodding toward my face. "How're you feeling?"

"I'm fine," I said. "But Darwin was killed. I'm sorry, Sully."

"I'll win you another monkey some day. Or somebody else will."

"Thanks for dragging me out of harm's way."

Sully waved me off.

Mark pushed past him and kissed my forehead. I thought it a sweet gesture.

"Had to find a spot that isn't raw," he said.

"How'd you get here so fast, Mark?" I said.

"Can't turn on the news and not hear about you. I wanted to find out if the prospect of having dinner with me is so grim you hired someone to put you in the hospital."

I saw a brief look of surprise cross Sully's face. Then his gaze fell on Mark and stayed there, as if he were an older brother evaluating his kid sister's prom date.

"You can both leave any time," I said. "The sooner the better, in fact."

"You are a poor sport, old girl," Sully said. "We just met in the waiting room, and already we've devised a plan for you and your wounded wheels."

"And what might that be?"

"I'm going to take care of the Explorer," he told me. "The police didn't impound it because there's no evidence in it, except for poor Darwin, and they did confiscate his remains. The bullet was found on the parking garage floor. So I'll call your insurance company and make arrangements to have the Explorer towed to a garage that can replace the window and clean up the inside."

He nodded toward Mark. "Fire Boy here is going to drive you to his place where you will stay until you heal up. My preference would be to change places, let Mark take care of your truck while I nurse you back to health myself. But Mark doesn't see this as a viable option. Neither would my wife."

"I've got a three-bedroom, two-bath condo," Mark said. "You'll have privacy."

I wasn't nuts about the plan. I didn't relish having Mark seeing me in this condition day and night.

"If you could drop me at my place, I'll be fine," I said. "Besides, my cats need me."

"The cat excuse won't wash," Sully said. "That lady next door, the woman who takes care of them when you're away, said she'd be happy to look after them for a few days. And she sends her best wishes. Meanwhile, she's packing up some comfortable clothes for you, which Mark will go pick up while the docs finish with you. By the time you're ready to leave the hospital, he'll be back to get you."

"So the two of you have this all figured out," I said.

"Trying to be of service," Sully said. "And a wonderful job we've done, too."

"Do me one more favor," I said to him. "Get the backpack out of the Explorer and give it to Mark. I don't want to leave it lying around."

Sully was grinning. "Way ahead of you, tall lady. Mark has it locked in his SUV."

I saw no advantage to arguing.

30

W hen I saw the story about the shooting on the *Journal*'s
front page the next morning, I cringed.

Once again, it was publicity I neither needed nor
wanted. The piece quoted Eric as saying that the shooting was being
treated as a random act of violence. Det. Vernon Bronson said police
knew of no motive for the shooting and had no leads. At least the two
of them had their stories straight.

I had company at Mark's place. He hadn't told me he had a dog, a
large Irish setter named Murphy. Murphy was friendly and the
antithesis of the breed's reputation as high-strung. He had rushed
toward me wagging a gorgeous feathered tail as soon as we walked in
the door of Mark's condo. Not wanting the dog to leap against my
injured arm, Mark told him to sit, and Murphy obeyed. He allowed
me to stroke him and lavish him with praise over his beauty and good
behavior, and he never made a move to leap on me again. As setters
went, Murphy was positively laid back.

Mark showed me which bathroom would be mine and then led
me into the bedroom. It was light and comfortable, furnished with a
queen-sized bed with a single nightstand, an easy chair and reading
lamp, a double dresser and a small, efficient desk. It was done in

earth tones, primarily taupe and green. Neither masculine nor femi-
nine. Just comfortable.

I sagged onto the edge of the bed, suddenly exhausted. Mark sat
down beside me, careful not to jostle. His reticence might have been
concern about hurting me. Or it might have reflected his uncertainty
as to how I would feel about him being on the bed that was now
mine. If he'd asked, I would have told him I was fine with it.

"You have a lot of pain?" he asked me.

"Surprisingly, no. It throbs a little, but the drugs are working."

"Are you going to be okay here?" he said, slipping an arm around
my waist.

I smiled. "Fine."

I turned to look at his face. Our eyes met, and his went dark and
smoky. He swallowed hard. I knew how he felt.

"If you'd feel better, I could sleep here with you, uh, well, on top
of the covers, of course. Or in the easy chair. If it would make you
feel safer."

I smiled at his unease and put a hand on his arm.

"I'll be fine," I said.

He didn't move his arm. And I didn't move my hand.

We sat there looking at one another for maybe thirty seconds, and
I'm quite sure we were sharing the same fantasy. Maybe someday we
could act on it.

He stood and began unpacking my small bag, stowing things in
the drawers of the dresser and hanging things in the closet, showing
no unease at handling even my most intimate garments. I told him I
could do it, but he didn't stop until everything had been put away in
the bedroom or in the bath. I sat on the edge of the bed and observed.
It was fun to watch him move around.

When he finished, he stood in front of me and cupped my face in
his hands.

He bent down and kissed me on the forehead, and then quickly
and lightly on the lips.

When the kiss ended, neither of us pulled away.

"Please," he whispered to me, "don't ever scare me like this again."

"I'll try not to."

After a moment, he kissed me again, now with an intensity that caused an instant arousal response in my body.

I stood and leaned into him. I discovered we fit one another perfectly.

I also discovered that there had been an arousal response in him, too.

I knew what he was asking when he ran the tip of his tongue along my lower lip. I shivered, and he pulled me closer. I opened my mouth slightly, and our tongues met.

When we parted, I felt as if the wind had been knocked out of me.

I knew it was brazen, but I couldn't help myself. I put my hand between us and laid it over the bulge in his jeans.

He moaned, and I shuddered.

He pulled back.

I think I whimpered.

"We can't do this, Deuce," he said. "Your arm ..."

"Is fine," I finished for him. "And besides, my arm isn't one of the body parts I care about right now.

"Are you sure?"

"More than sure."

Then he kissed me again, deepening the contact, and I started unbuttoning his shirt.

We undressed one another slowly, our eyes dwelling on what we uncovered. Mark was especially careful when it came to my wounded left arm. He slipped my uninjured right arm out of its sleeve and my head through the neck. Then he slipped the shirt down my left arm, lifting it over the bandages.

The shirt fell to the floor with a soft plop.

"Okay?" he asked me.

"Hmmmm, getting better all the time."

He kissed me lightly on the tip of my nose, my lips, the point of my chin, and the hollow at my throat. Then he pulled back again but not because of uncertainty. He was admiring the view. I didn't mind. I just felt eager to get on with the rest.

His eyes drifted from my face to my neck to my chest, lingering on my bra.

"May I?" he asked.

I nodded.

He reached around behind me and opened the garment as if he'd done it before.

The bra followed my shirt to the floor. He took in the view for a moment, then lifted his hands and cupped my breasts. They fit perfectly.

I moaned.

"You are perfect," he said, his tone almost reverential.

His gaze returned to my eyes.

"I have to get something," he said. "I'll be right back."

"What?" I asked. The thought of him leaving me at that moment was almost painful.

"Condom," he said.

I smiled. "Not necessary," I said. "Pill."

He winced. "Does that mean you're seeing someone? I never thought to ask."

"No," I said. "Just wishful thinking. And I think my wish is about to come true."

He kissed me again, his hands still fondling my breasts, and moved me backward until my legs came in contact with the bed. I sat.

"Lie down," he said.

I did.

He slipped my shoes off, then moved to my jeans.

After he thumbed open the button at the waist, he slid the zipper down slowly, generating a vibration as agonizing as it was arousing.

Then Mark reached a hand inside my slacks and laid it over the crotch of my panties.

Now he groaned. "You are so wet," he said. "Did I do that to you?"

"I'd like to think you did it for me," I said.

He had me raise my hips and worked my slacks off.

I was now lying across his guest bed in nothing but a thong.

He licked his lips. "I want to taste you."

I nodded.

He slipped the thong down my legs and discarded it.

He bent his head to me and spent a while teasing and arousing me with his tongue, his lips, and his teeth. My hands felt as if they had gone to sleep, and I had to knead them in the bedspread to get feeling back.

"So beautiful," he said several times.

I wasn't sure how much more I could stand and hold back my orgasm, so I thrust my hips at him to try to redirect his attention. He chuckled against the skin of my inner thigh and sent a jolt of sexual electricity through me.

"Please," I said. "Please."

He looked up and smiled, his eyes dark.

"What?" he asked.

"You know what I want," I said.

Without taking his eyes from me, he moved his hand to cover me and pushed his index finger deep into me, stroking and exploring.

"Oh, yes," I said. "More."

He slipped another finger inside of me and stroked.

My hips jerked.

I lost sensation in my hands again.

He caught my g-spot.

I lost control.

I began to writhe under him.

"Good?" he asked.

I glanced at him. "Oh, yes," I said. "I'm so close, and you're so overdressed for this."

"First things first."

He kept stroking in and out of me, and my arousal climbed higher and higher, my climax coiling in my abdomen.

His head dipped, and his mouth was on my clit, circling it and sucking it, nipping at it.

I came with a sound that was half scream, half groan. He kept his mouth and hands working, drawing out my climax for as long as he could.

When the aftershocks subsided, leaving me drenched in sweat and limp on the bed, he bent over and kissed me hard.

And then he stripped.

I saw so much about him to admire.

"Let me return the favor," I said.

"Another time," he said. "If you put your mouth on me now, it will be all over. I want to be inside you."

He moved between my knees and teased me with the purple head of his cock.

I felt new arousal and thrust my hips at him.

He smiled. And then he was in me, stretching me, making me gasp. I was quite sure I had never been more aroused.

He held himself above me with one arm planted on the bed, away from my injuries. I don't know how he lasted as long as he did, but he gave me plenty of time to catch up.

When I felt his balls tighten to his body, I wrapped my legs around his back and pulled as deep into me as I could.

My orgasm was gentler the second time. His was enormous.

When we caught our breaths, Mark rolled onto the bed beside me and held me with my head on his left shoulder.

After a time, he asked, "Would it be wrong to plead for you to spend the rest of your life with me, even though we haven't even been on a date yet?"

I laughed. "Maybe a little early. We're not sure we're sexually compatible."

He raised his head and looked at me. "How much more proof do you need?"

"Lots," I said. "Lots and lots and lots ..."

And we dozed off that way.

M ark slept in his own bed that night for two reasons: He didn't want to jostle my arm, one. And, two, there wasn't room in my bed for the two of us and Murphy. The dog was already feeling abused at being locked out of my room during his human's afternoon of fun.

A little after eight o'clock I was awakened by a titanic shift of my mattress. I opened my eyes, and Murphy was perched at the foot of the bed, awaiting my reaction.

I smiled at him. He moved up the bed and nestled in beside me with his head on my right shoulder, sniffed at the scuffmarks on my face, heaved a huge sigh and fell asleep. I had nothing to get up for. Mark told me the night before he left for work by seven. So I stroked Murphy's head and closed my eyes. It was nearly 9:30 when Murphy and I deigned to leave the bed.

By the time I finished reading two newspapers and had breakfast it was 11:00, and I wanted to take a shower. But the doctors didn't want me getting the arm bandage wet unless there was someone to change it for me, so a shower would have to wait for Mark to get home. I also felt a need to stretch my legs. My arm was beginning to throb, but I wanted to avoid prescription painkillers if I could. Instead, I popped Aleve.

The rain had stopped for the moment, though the forecast said the downpours would last another forty-eight hours, causing flooding in parts of the city. Taking advantage of the respite, I put Murphy on his leash, and we set out to visit all the hydrants in the River North neighborhood where Mark lived. I had a baseball cap pulled low over my face. It hid most of my wounds. My shirt hid the bandages on my arm.

We were strolling Kingsbury Street when my cell phone rang. I checked Caller ID.

"Hey, Sully," I said into the phone. "Murphy and I are having a wonderful time. Wish you were here."

"And who the hell is Murphy?"

I told him. "We're taking a walk. People are looking at me funny."

"Didn't they always?"

"Thanks."

"I didn't call to taunt you," he said. "I called to report insurrection."

"Really?" Insurrection always makes for good gossip. "Who's insurrecting?"

"Me."

"What are you insurrecting about?"

"I don't want to move in on your story."

I hoped Sully's actions didn't sink his career.

"You're scared you'll get shot, too," I said, but I didn't believe it. In my experience, Sully wasn't afraid of anything.

Murphy started tugging at his leash.

"Hang on a sec," I said. "I have to break up a dog fight."

I pulled an exuberant Murphy away from an alarmed Ipso Facto, or Lhasa Lipso, or whatever they call those hairy little dogs. Murphy was only doing the sniffing thing dogs do, and the woman seemed more alarmed than her pet. I separated the animals anyway. Then I smiled at the owner and got a glare for my trouble.

I shrugged. Next time her little fur ball could fend for itself.

I went back to the phone. "It doesn't matter what you want," I said. "The final decision is Eric's, and he's spoken."

"Eric also has the authority to reconsider."

"He won't."

"Don't be so sure. He's got to be hearing reports that a lot of the staff have concerns."

"Does a lot of the staff have concerns?"

"Hell, yes. Nobody feels safe. I made that point to Eric this morning."

"You didn't tell me you were going to do that."

"A spur-of-the-moment thing. You know how it is with me. What come up, comes out and deal with the consequences later."

Murphy and I got back to Mark's some ninety minutes later as the rain began again. I was surprised that the walk, which never exceeded a stroll, had tired me out.

Murphy settled onto the sofa for a nap, and I went to Mark's bookcases. I found a copy of David McCullough's award-winning biography of Harry Truman, which I'd read years before. I sat down, opened the book, and started to re-read it. I was a little more than one hundred pages into it when my cell phone rang.

It was Mark, checking to see how I was doing. I told him about the walk.

"Don't spoil my dog," he said.

"Yeah," I said. "Like that's work still to be done."

Mark paused. When he spoke again, his voice had changed pitch. "I've been thinking about you all day."

"Oh, my. Lascivious thoughts by any chance?"

"Oh, yes."

"Perv."

About ten seconds after we hung up, my phone rang again. I smiled when I saw the caller ID.

"Hi, Congressman," I said.

"Deuce, if you don't stop scaring the crap out of me, I'm going to have to whisk you out of Chicago and bring you to Washington, where I can keep an eye on you."

John Conti sounded serious.

"Yeah, this assault stuff is getting old for me, too," I told him.

"How bad is it this time?" he said.

"Painful. Not life-threatening."

"Have you got protection?"

"Well, no, not at the moment. But if the story I was working on prompted the attacks, the bad guys will back off now. I'm no longer working on it. I'm not sure, to be honest, that I still have a job. In either event, I'm no longer a threat to anyone."

"What? I'm sorry for that, Honey, but I'm happy you're out of the line of fire."

After I assured him I wasn't yet ready to accept his help finding new employment, he told me to heal fast.

I got another half page read when the phone chirped again. It didn't ring this often when I was working, so I might have been just a little testy when I answered. If I had checked caller ID and seen it was Eric Ryland calling, I might have been even testier.

"How're you feeling?" he asked me.

"Fine, thanks. Nice of you to call."

If Eric heard my sarcasm, he ignored it. "Do you feel up to a trip over here?"

"I thought you wanted me out of the office for two weeks."

"You came in yesterday."

"Yeah, and look what happened."

Eric changed the subject. "There's somebody here who wants to talk to you, and she won't talk to anyone else. I told her I'd call you."

"Who?" I said.

"Jennifer Griff. And, for the record, she says you were a complete lady at her house."

"Thanks. I already knew that."

IT OCCURRED to me after I hung up that I didn't have transportation.

I grabbed my backpack in the faint hope that I would need the files inside, and out of a new caution about leaving sensitive documents lying around. I hung it over my good shoulder and listed under the weight.

When I got to the street, I hailed a cab. I didn't have an umbrella, and I was pretty well soaked before one stopped for me. It wasn't until I reached Eric's office that I realized I still was dressed in cargo shorts, a T-shirt and deck shoes without socks. I hadn't thought to change clothes. Eric didn't seem to mind, though Jennifer Griff looked surprised.

"Come in, Deuce," Eric said. "Shut the door, please."

I did.

"Sit down," he said. Already he was more gracious than the last time.

I was grateful to slip the backpack off my shoulder. It was becoming painful.

Jennifer Griff didn't take her eyes from my face.

"Does that hurt terribly?" she asked me.

"A little. It will get better each day."

"Did it happen because of the story, the one you and I talked about?"

I smiled. She spoke conspiratorially, as if the story were a secret I shared with her but not with my editor. I half expected him to inject himself into the conversation, but he seemed content to let the two women talk by themselves.

"We don't know," I said.

"So somebody wants you dead," she said, "the same way they wanted Samuel dead."

"They were trying to scare me," I said, trying to reassure her, though I was no longer certain. I recalled what might have been without the brass monkey blocking for me.

"Still," she said, "I feel at least partly responsible."

"You're not responsible for this at all. I wasn't even supposed to be here yesterday morning. I walked into it."

She lowered her eyes and shook her head. "I don't know. Maybe if

I'd told you everything, you'd have been somewhere else doing something else."

That surprised me. "What didn't you tell me?" I said.

There was a pause in the conversation, and Eric filled it.

"Deuce," he said, "before we go on, you should know that a missing persons report was filed on James Hagwood last night. It didn't make any news waves this morning because his name doesn't mean anything outside this building. But Lucy caught it."

Jennifer gasped. "He's the ATF agent who ..." she didn't finish. "He'll never be found. Oh, God, this just doesn't have an end."

The news made me angry. Not so much because James Hagwood might have been kidnapped and killed – I wouldn't say he deserved it, but his perjury had helped doom Vinnie Colangelo. It made me angry because my living ties to the Scotch theft and Ransom Camp were evaporating.

All the more reason I needed to know why Jennifer Griff had come to my office.

"What is it you didn't tell me?" I asked her again.

Her fingers snaked around inside her purse, searching for something. She pulled out an envelope. It was old. Its corners were bent, its flap torn. It must have been white when it was new, but over time it had yellowed. She handed it to me.

I found two typewritten sheets of paper inside. I opened them and began to read the single-spaced text. Two sentences in, I stopped and flipped to the bottom of the second page. The signature, Samuel Griff, had been written in a strong hand. Beside the signature were the form and the old-style crimped seal of a notary public. I started reading again.

"To Whom It May Concern,

"My name is Samuel Griff. At this writing, on May 11, 1979, I am 38 years old and in full possession of my faculties. What I am writing here is an act of conscience. For several years, I have lived with a secret I can no longer bear.

In August 1974, I took the witness stand in a federal criminal case against a defendant named Vincent Colangelo. Although it doesn't seem like much, the case involved the man's role in the theft of a shipment of Scotch, shipped to Chicago from Edinburgh. I testified that when the theft occurred, the shipment had yet to pass out of foreign commerce.

This was not true. The taxes and duties had been paid, and the shipment turned over to a customs house broker and an agent for the assignee (purchaser).

"I was joined in this lie by a colleague at the Bureau of Alcohol, Tobacco and Firearms, James Thomas Hagwood. The circumstances of the deception are as follows:

"On the night of July, 18, 1974, I was summoned to a restaurant in Bridgeport named Andalucia by an informant who said I would be met there by someone with evidence of firearms smuggling at the Port of Chicago. When I arrived at the restaurant, I found Jim Hagwood there, as well. The two of us had been acquainted for several years and had worked a couple of cases together, including the theft of the Scotch by Vincent Colangelo and two accomplices.

"Hagwood and I had been summoned separately to the restaurant. We didn't immediately find this strange because smuggling and firearms could cross the jurisdictional lines of U.S. Customs and the ATF.

"We were greeted at the restaurant by one Tommy Picarella, a man Hagwood recognized as an enforcer for the South Side Organization. Picarella asked us to follow him to a back room, and this immediately aroused our suspicions. Why would an enforcer for organized crime be hustling snitches related to arms smuggling? When we tried to leave, Picarella showed us his gun and advised it would be in the best interests of our families and ourselves if we stayed.

"There were four additional men seated in the back room at Andalucia, two of whom I recognized as Organization associates, Almedo "Big Hands" Castellano and Joey "Two Fingers" Allegheri. One of the men I didn't know and never learned his identity. The fourth man introduced himself as Alfano Mustolli. Neither Hagwood nor I knew him. During the subsequent conversation, he talked for the group.

"There were 10 large stacks of $100 bills in front of Mustolli. He told Hagwood and me that the money was payment for our help in getting a dangerous criminal, Vinnie Colangelo, off the streets.

"We questioned how dangerous a small-time thief could be, but Mustolli said we only knew the half of it. It was important, he said, that Colangelo go far away and do hard federal time, and we were the ones who could make that happen. All we had to do was say on the witness stand that the Scotch was still in foreign commerce when it was stolen.

"I pointed out there was paperwork which would prove otherwise. Mustolli told me not to worry about it, that the paperwork would be made to disappear.

Hagwood and I both said we weren't comfortable committing perjury. Mustolli said that's what he was there for, to make us comfortable. He pushed four stacks of bills across the table, two to me and two to Hagwood. He said the stacks totaled $20,000 for each of us, and that we would get another three stacks each, or another $30,000 apiece, after we testified. And if we didn't take the money and testify as instructed, each of us would soon lose a family member to most unpleasant circumstances.

"We took the money and were escorted from the restaurant separately, probably so we couldn't talk about the situation. Mustolli said before we left that we should have no contact outside the courtroom, and we didn't. We both testified as instructed, and the back halves of the payoffs were delivered to us the following day.

"To all this I swear and attest on this day, May 11, 1979. I am sorry. It is my intention to come forward as soon as possible and tell the truth to the authorities. But as insurance in case I should disappear or die before I can do that, I plan to seal this document and give it to my wife, Jennifer Griff. My instructions to her are to turn this document over to the proper authorities at such time as she deems it will do minimal damage to our son. While it is not a legitimate excuse, I feel that Hagwood and I acted under extreme duress. May God forgive us both."

s/ Samuel I. Griff

I CHECKED the signature and the seal of the notary again to satisfy myself they were real. Then I handed the letter to Eric. Jennifer and I sat in silence while he read.

My mind was working overtime. From Griff's confession, it was apparent this Mustolli orchestrated the fix of Vinnie's trial. But who was he working for?

When Eric finished reading, he looked at Jennifer.

"Why give this up now? Did your son agree?"

"Adam asked me not to do it. I explained to him why I felt I had to. I am fulfilling my husband's wishes. My son wants to protect his memories of his father. I cherish those memories, too. But both of us have to see past this and accept that Samuel was a human being with human failings. What he did, he did to protect us and to help me."

"But why now?" I said. "When we talked, you didn't want this to become public."

She turned to me. "You told me my story wouldn't help clear that old man. Hearsay. Whatever. But Samuel's sworn statement will, won't it?"

"Yes," I said.

"When I read about you getting shot, I realized that after all these years, it was time to put an end to this. It's what Samuel wanted. It's what he died for. It's the right thing to do."

32

And that quickly I was back at work with the editor-imposed caveat that I was to take on only as much as my physical condition allowed.

"It has become readily apparent to me in the last forty-eight hours," Eric said after Jennifer Griff left the office, "that I'm developing a problem with the staff over my decision to remove you from this story. Everyone, it seems, knows you've threatened to quit. Even without knowing the facts, they feel I treated you unfairly."

"So do I. But you know that."

"At the very least," he said, "you should not have made the second trip to Bucktown to see Emily Humphries."

"I didn't think it would be a problem," I said. "And I felt I had to warn them."

"Which is why I stopped trusting your judgment. And, at the moment, you're giving me no reason to reconsider."

He paused to let this sink in.

I ignored his disdain because I had ceased to care. I guess he saw that in my eyes because he changed the subject. I didn't like the new subject any better than the old one.

"Deuce," he said, "I'm going to expand your police protection. We're going to have to guard you around the clock."

"It won't help," I said. "What if you'd had somebody watching my back in the parking garage? Could they have stopped the shooting? No. Could they have caught the shooter? Unlikely, since nobody was sure right away where the shot came from. Protection might make you feel better, Eric, but it won't help me. If somebody wants to do it, it will get done."

"You don't think armed personnel in a marked vehicle would act as a deterrent?"

"To a sniper? Not even a little bit. Remember Las Vegas? Reading was surrounded by professional security. Believe me, if I thought it would keep me safe, I'd agree to it in a cocaine heartbeat. Let's keep things as they were."

Eric didn't look completely happy, but then he never looked completely happy.

"Okay," he said. "The rest of this problem we'll chalk up to experience and call it history. I don't have a choice. Too many people are asking what you were working on that prompted the court order and the shooting. With others sniffing around, we don't have time for Sully to get up to speed. So what's next?"

"Do you know who this Alfano Mustolli is, the man in Griff's letter?"

"Never heard of him," Eric said. "Have Lucy run him."

"If he was a Mob fixer, we probably won't have much in our library that's helpful, but I'll have Lucy check, anyway. Meanwhile, I have some better sources."

And I hurried back to my desk.

CARL CRIBBEN, the retired FBI agent, had left another message on my voice mail, both an expression of concern for my health and safety, and a plea to call him as soon as possible on "a matter of utmost urgency." I returned the call immediately.

"I'm way out of line here," he said, "So you tell no one, I mean no one, who gave you this information. I wouldn't be saying anything except you need to know as a warning."

I agreed to his terms.

"After the shooting you witnessed in Back of the Yards, you told a police officer to dig the slug out of the side of the Annuncio house and send it to the FBI."

"Yes?" I said. My anticipation soared.

"It's a difficult comparison. The Nevada bullet went into Reading's neck, then through his throat and into the chest of the man next to him. It's pretty mangled. But an initial examination suggests key similarities with the slug from Back of the Yards. Now the Bureau's looking at the bullet that hit you. They think it will match the other two."

"Jesus," I said. I was almost breathless, the way I get when something totally improbable comes true. "So Vinnie was connected to the events in Las Vegas after all."

"It's looking more and more that way. You watch yourself."

I promised I would and hung up, turning back to the task I'd started earlier. Lucy had found two clips on Alfano Mustolli, one an old AP story that described him as the owner of a string of Chicago funeral homes and a murky figure in the shadows of Chicago politics and organized crime. A second announced his death, a short obit written off a notice from a funeral home, in this case the flagship of Mustolli's own funeral home empire. I thought it strange that a businessman of that magnitude didn't warrant a bigger send-off. The notice listed as survivors a widow, Eunice, of Chicago, and a daughter, Camella Whitman of Terre Haute, Indiana.

Lucy ran both women through a variety of databases and came up with nothing.

I called two political sources. Both were sufficiently intrigued that they juggled their schedules to make time to meet with me. We set up a lunch for 1:30 at The Kerryman, a lovely Irish pub on Clark Street. That gave me time to get home and change into clothes more appropriate to the occasion.

Eric gave me a company car to use—a Ford Focus—until mine came back with a new windshield. I stood in front of the mirror in my bathroom at Mark's condo and took most of the little Steri-strips off my face. I still looked like I had the measles, or maybe a bad case of acne, but the whole picture wasn't as weird as the white strips, which made me look like a Frankenstein monster held together with tape.

I arrived at the restaurant first. My federal prosecutor friend, Jerry Alvarez, showed up next, followed minutes later by Alderman Tony Estrada, both with wet raincoats and dripping umbrellas and nothing at all good to say about the weather. When I made the reservations, I asked for as private a table as possible, and got one on the second level that insulated us from what was left of the lunch crowd.

Tony shook a couple of hands on the way to the table.

"You okay?" he asked once we were seated.

"I'm fine, thanks," I said. "It looks worse than it feels. Except for my arm. That feels worse than it looks."

"Any idea who did it?" he asked. "You've been running with a rough crowd, I hear."

"Rougher than I guessed," I said.

Tony and Jerry shook hands. Neither had known the other would be there. But they were friends, so that didn't worry me.

"Glad to have company jumping into the rabbit hole," Jerry said to Tony.

We ordered iced tea and lunch. After the waiter brought our tea, I took over. I asked them, "Does either of you remember somebody named Alfano Mustolli hanging around politics back in the seventies?"

"Oh, yeah," Jerry said. "I never knew him, but I knew of him. *Una leyenda.* A legend."

"Yeah," Tony said. "He was no one to mess with from what I've heard."

"I only found one reference to him of any significance," I said, "a news story that called him a figure who moved in the shadows between politics and organized crime."

"He was before my time, and I'm grateful for that," Tony said. "He was a guy who'd muscle public officials to get things smoothed out for the Organization so they could do business without gettin' hassled. If there was a cop needed bribing, Mustolli got it done. Some public official needed persuading, Mustolli found the way. I've been told he wasn't above using violence when he deemed it necessary. I remember one old-timer told me after I won my first election that no matter how bad the pressure got on me, it would never be as heavy as in the old days, when Al Mustolli was pulling the strings."

Jerry added, "That fits with what I know. Remember, Deuce, I told you there was a lot of shady stuff going on back then, in the seventies, in and around the courthouse. If you were a fixer, that was the right era for you, and I heard this Mustolli was the best. Or the worst. He'd do anything for a price, and his specialty was corrupting the system."

"Who did he represent?" I asked him.

"To a large degree, himself," Jerry said. "He was a contract operator. *Trabajaba para cualquiera que pudiera pagar.* He'd work for anybody who could pay."

"Who did he corrupt?" I said.

Jerry waved his hand, a dismissive gesture.

"*Eso fue hace mucho tiempo.* That was a long time ago," he said. "Mustolli died in the early 80s. Most of those he reached have died since then, too."

"So none of the corruption he spawned still exists?" I said.

"I didn't say that. There's still corruption. Now it's *mas sutil,* more subtle."

I looked back and forth between them. "Can either of you give me names?"

Tony shook his head. "It's not a matter of pointing to any single individual as corrupt. If I could be that specific, I'd take the facts to the authorities."

Jerry took a long drink of iced tea. The cubes rattled up the glass. He set the glass down, nodded to the waitress who approached with a refill pitcher, then turned to me. "Unless you've sat with me," he said, "and witnessed inexplicable things transpire in the courtroom, you can't know. You see the unbelievable and unnecessary deals made with the worst criminal elements. You see cases botched, *probable-mente el objetivo*, probably on purpose, by prosecutors who know better. You see lists of witnesses who don't appear and can't be found. You see that for years on end, and then you know."

"How come nobody ever blew the whistle on Mustolli?" I asked him.

"He was buried way too deep," Tony said. "Anybody who knew enough about Mustolli to make a case against him was involved with him to the eyes. To give him up was to give up yourself. He was good at protecting himself that way."

"That's what immunity's for," I said.

Tony sipped his tea. "Immunity doesn't save you when the guns come around."

"The newspapers didn't know?" I said.

They both shrugged.

I had a hard time believing this sort of thing could go on without the courthouse reporters trying to turn over rocks. I said so.

"Different era," Jerry said. "Mustolli probably had the press in his pocket, too. Your professional forebears didn't make much in those days. They wouldn't have been immune to the temptations of free cash."

"That kind of cash is never free," I said.

"Oh, come on," said Jerry. "*No es estupido.* You're too old to be so naïve and idealistic."

"No," I said. "Guys like Royko, Algren, Herman Kogan—they never sold out."

"That we know of," Jerry said. "But you're probably right. They were the exceptions."

This was more reality than I could tolerate. I sipped my tea. "So Mustolli ran roughshod over the courthouse, peddling influence and doling out bribes?"

"And authorizing some rough stuff here and there," Tony said. "If somebody was pulling his strings, I never saw proof, and I never heard names except in speculation."

"Was Richard Palmieri or John Conti a part of Mustolli's rounds when they were running the U.S. Attorney's office?" I asked them. "Did Mustolli corrupt them?"

"Palmieri is a pompous ass and always has been," Tony told me. "I'd believe almost anything about him, but that's because I don't like him, not because I think he's corrupt. And, like I told you that day at the courthouse, I never heard Conti tied to anything serious. Then or now. If he was in somebody's pocket, I think there would have been rumors, courthouse talk."

Jerry said, "I heard both their names mentioned in casual conversation over the years. But that's all it was, casual conversation. I don't think you can run a U.S. Attorney's office in an era of corruption and not have people suspect you. *No significa nada.* It don't necessarily mean anything."

"But if the pressure was as bad as described to Tony, how could they have ducked it?"

"Couldn't have been easy," Jerry said.

"If they were so honest, and Mustolli was so corrupt, why didn't they go after him on public corruption charges?"

"Conti didn't take on the tough stuff," Jerry said. "He was into building conviction totals and running for Congress, not cleaning up the system."

"And that," I said, feeling miserable, "is a form of corruption all its own."

33

I drove to Palmieri's office. I figured he had a reserved spot in his building's garage, so I drove up and down the ramps until I found his silver Lexus SC convertible. I knew it was his because a sign on the wall said, "Reserved Palmieri Law." I pulled into a spot where I could watch the car. When he came for it, I would block him in. Then we could talk.

In the movies these things happen quickly. In my case, I had to wait for three hours and fourteen minutes. I saw the taillights on Palmieri's car flash when he used the keyless entry. I waited until he had one foot inside the Lexus and gunned my company Ford into position behind him. His expression morphed from surprise to fear to anger. He relaxed when he recognized me.

"Most people call for an appointment," he told me.

"I couldn't wait for your next free fifteen minutes," I said.

He extracted his right leg from the convertible and stood on two feet. "How's the face? I read about the shooting in the paper. Who'd you piss off? Besides me, I mean."

"I'm not sure," I said. "Maybe a case of mistaken identity. I need to ask a question."

"About what?"

"Alfano Mustolli."

"Jesus Christ, you do dredge up the unpleasant history. What about Mustolli?"

"Why didn't the U.S. Attorney's office ever go after him on public corruption charges?"

Now Palmieri's expression darkened. I don't think he liked the question.

"Because," he said, "you can't try someone based on rumor and innuendo. You have to have witnesses and hard evidence."

I took my shot.

"Or bribed witnesses and missing evidence," I said.

Palmieri frowned and looked perplexed. "What the hell are you talking about?"

"Vinnie Colangelo. I've got the missing paperwork."

I waited to gauge Palmieri's response. But he had no reaction at all and appeared to be waiting for my explanation.

I said, "I have the two documents that prove Vinnie was railroaded into federal court and federal prison. By your office. A case you prosecuted. I have a notarized confession of perjury from the Customs agent who testified at the trial that the liquor was still in federal jurisdiction. He says Mustolli is the man who arranged a big payoff for him and the ATF agent, who also testified falsely. The Customs agent was killed years ago. The ATF agent disappeared last night."

Palmieri frowned and shook his head.

"That's the first I've heard of this. I know Colangelo claimed there was paperwork. You and I talked about that already. But even if it's turned up, there's nothing to be done now."

"Did you ever have any dealings with Alfano Mustolli?"

"I met the man. If you held any kind of position of authority in the federal or county courthouses back then you were doomed to meet the man. He was everywhere."

"Ever do any deals with him?"

"Are you joking? No. Never. I did fire an assistant once for getting involved with him. But Mustolli never tested me. I'll be honest with you, Ms. Mora, I don't think I ever had a case he and his clients cared about. Which was fine with me."

He looked at his watch. "Now, if you don't mind, I'm running late for an appointment. Would you please release my car from your makeshift jail?"

I thanked Palmieri for his time and apologized if I'd made him late. Then I got into the Focus and left.

I WAS a hundred yards down the street when Sully called. My Explorer was ready. I drove the company car back to the office and took a cab to the garage. I paid the insurance deductible, making a mental note to put it on my expense account, and gave the truck a once-over. It was looking good again. Except Darwin was gone, and I missed him. I hoped the cops had saved the pieces for me. Maybe I could have him repaired.

On the drive home, I remembered that I'd disappeared from Mark's apartment without an explanation. I called him.

"I heard you were back on the story," he said. "Sully called me. I figured that would make you feel better. Uh, you're still going to stay at my place for a while, right? If you left, Murphy would miss you."

"And I'd miss him," I said. "He's wonderful. But I don't need distractions right now, and Murphy is a major distraction."

"*Murphy* is a major distraction?" Mark said with a smile in his voice. "Oh, thanks. Maybe instead of me, you'd rather have dinner with him and eat out of a dog bowl on the floor next to his."

I heard him sigh. "Please, Deuce. The thought of you alone at your condo scares the crap out of me. I'll only be a distraction when you need one. Please."

"I'll stay tonight, and we can talk about it."

"I'll take you out to dinner. Our first date."

"Yeah," I said, "we probably should get that out of the way."

He laughed.

"By the way," I said, "how are the Astossos getting along?"

"They're fine, physically. Guarded twenty-four/seven by marshals who want the overtime. Maria wants to go home. Tino is trying to keep her calm, but the day might come when she gets so agitated we won't have a choice. So the faster you can bring this to a resolution and end their exile, the better."

I thanked Mark and promised to see him later.

MARK WASN'T HOME YET when I got back to his place, so I took Murphy for a short walk. The big Hummer followed me, and I found myself grateful.

Once back inside, I tugged my files out of the backpack, wincing at the pressure on my left arm. I still couldn't shake the feeling that somewhere along the line I'd learned more than I realized, and that somewhere in the files a key nugget of information was hiding from me. I'd been through everything twice and found nothing. I might as well have another go at it.

I sat in the lounge chair in my bedroom and opened the first folder, and then the second, and then the third. When I hit the nugget, my eyes and my mind ran right over it, as they had before.

I was reading the transcript of the interview with Maria Astosso, thinking she had given me little to work with. I was predisposed to skim the words. I was three pages beyond the clue when it finally penetrated my consciousness. I turned back and there it was, Maria's reference to the LaPalma children. She said there were four of them.

I was certain when Mark and I talked to Miguel Astosso, he said there were three, two brothers, Reuben and Ricardo, and the little girl, Emily. I rummaged through the files until I found that transcript. Miguel had not said flatly there were only three LaPalma children, but he had only mentioned three.

I thought about my first encounter with Emily in Bucktown, when Verne Humphries told me it wasn't a good time to talk to his wife about her brother. I remembered when I mentioned Ricardo's name she looked surprised. Maybe she thought I was referring to a different brother, one I didn't even know about at the time. And I remembered that an unidentified family member had claimed Vinnie's remains.

Bells and whistles exploded in my head.

And pieces began to fall into place.

34

An hour later I was pacing ruts into Mark's oak floors.

I could be completely off base. If Maria Astosso's memory was faulty, my whole theory went into the toilet.

But I didn't think that was the case. There was a perfectly good reason Miguel hadn't mentioned a fourth child. That child was much older than the others and hadn't been involved in the Ransom Camp fires as either a perpetrator or a victim. Since Mark and I were asking Miguel about the fires, he had no reason to mention the fourth child.

I called Mark and caught him in his truck on the way home. I told him my theory.

"If I'm right," I said, "the answer to everything is with Emily Humphries. I'm sure Vinnie was the oldest of the four LaPalma children by quite a few years. He never lost touch with his younger brother, Ricardo, and he knew all the dirt. Ricardo's mob activities, his involvement with public corruption, and his responsibility for the Ransom Camp fire. Vinnie was Ricardo's Achilles heel, the only one with a motive to destroy Ricardo and the ammunition to do it. The more Vinnie shot off his mouth about his trial, the more nervous Ricardo became. And Emily knows all about it."

"How are you going to get past the restraining order?" Mark asked.

"In the morning I'm going to ask Eric to turn Jonathan Bruckner loose on it."

"You really want your lawyer talking about your investigation in open court?"

"I don't think we have a choice."

We were kicking it around when my call waiting beeped. I put Mark on hold and answered the new call. I couldn't have been more surprised when the voice on the other end of the connection said, "Ms. Mora, my name is Verne Humphries. I don't know if you remember me . . ."

I asked him to hold on for a moment, flipped back to Mark, and told him I'd have to call back. Then I returned to Verne Humphries and made certain he knew the terms of the restraining order.

"I don't care about that now," he said. "Emily's gone, and the cops won't help me."

My stomach convulsed.

"What do you mean, *gone*, Mr. Humphries?"

"Disappeared," he said. "I laid down to take a nap. When I woke up, she wasn't here. I thought she'd gone to the drugstore to pick up my prescription, but her car's inna garage, and the drug store said she never picked up the medicine. She's not inna yard or the house. I checked her friends and our neighbors, but they ain't seen her."

He was breathing hard now.

"The police say she hasn't been gone long enough to file a missing person's report because Emily isn't sick. She ain't got no Alzheimer's or dementia, so she didn't wander away and get lost. They won't do nothin' for another day or two."

"What can I do?" I said.

"You got her into this," he said, "all your snoopin' around. You gotta find her."

I couldn't take having more guilt heaped on me. It was already suffocating me.

"I'm coming up, Mr. Humphries," I said. "But to be clear, you're asking me to come, right? You want me there?"

"Yes, I do. Yes," he said. "But listen, I might not be here. I'm scared. I'm terrible scared. Maybe I'm going to some friends."

"What if Emily was kidnapped, and the kidnappers try to reach you?"

"No, no," he said. "She wasn't kidnapped, not for any ransom. We ain't got nothin' of any kind of value to trade for her. You know good as me what happened to her. Nobody's gonna be calling me about gettin' Emily back. And unless somebody does something fast, I'll never see her again."

"How can I reach you?"

"I got your number," he said. "When I decide what I'm gonna do, I'll call you."

I called Mark Hearst back. He said he'd meet me at the Humphries' house.

I gave him the address.

~

I called Eric and told him of the development.

"Mr. Humphries specifically asked you back to his home?" Eric said.

"He called me, Eric, I didn't call him," I said. "He was certain. He holds me responsible for Emily, and he wants me to find her and bring her home."

"And Hearst's going with you?"

"Yes."

"Do us all a favor. Get Humphries to say in front of Hearst that you are an invited guest. It might save a lot of grief later."

"Will do."

I knew I might not even see Verne Humphries if he made good on his decision to go into hiding, but I didn't want to get into that with Eric.

A few blocks from the Humphries home, the skies opened up again. The rain came in heavy waves, punctuated by lightning that lit up the earth and thunder that rattled it.

The Humphries house was dark, with the exception of a single light on somewhere in the back. Maybe Verne had decided to stay. Mark had used his lights and siren and arrived first. We ran to the porch. I rang the bell twice. No response. I hoped Verne was gone and not lying dead inside. I tried the front door. Locked.

I returned to my truck and rummaged through my storm gear for my utility light and rain jacket, wincing as I twisted my arm into the jacket sleeve. The storm had swamped the Humphries' yard. The ground was saturated, and the storm drains were overwhelmed. I slipped into my waders. On top of everything else, I didn't need wet, muddy feet.

I trudged back to the house. Mark was using his flashlight to examine the front door, and I mounted the steps to join him.

"I'd feel better if we had armed storm troopers with us," I said.

Mark pulled his jacket open and I saw a huge gun sitting on his right hip.

"I'll have to do," he said.

I reached around Mark and rang the bell again. I waited thirty seconds. Nothing. I turned on my light and tried to see through the thin curtain that covered the narrow window beside the door. I couldn't make out anything. I went down the steps and checked the lower entrance. It, too, was locked and dark.

"Hold up a second," Mark said. "Let's take this slow. We don't want to trample evidence." He started playing his flashlight over the house and the ground.

"What sort of evidence?" I said.

"Evidence of a crime, Sherlock. Let's go together."

Mark examined the two lower-level front windows for signs they'd been jimmied. He examined the ground under the windows for signs it had been disturbed. Both negative.

"What are you looking for?" I said.

"Anything out of the ordinary."

He led me around the side of the house.

We moved deliberately. He played the light over the side wall, the side windows, then slowly over the ground. He was looking for some sign of a break-in. None of the windows appeared to have been pried open. As he finished with each one, I used my light to scan the inside for anything out of order. I found nothing.

Our fortune changed by the back door. We found two sets of footprints in the muddy ground. One set was considerably deeper than the other. Both led away from the house into the yard of the house next door.

"They must have parked down the block," I said, "or on the next street over so the neighbors wouldn't see their vehicle."

"Excellent deduction," Mark said. "And I'd judge by the deeper impression of these tracks that this guy was carrying something that weighed more than a small sack of potatoes. The extra weight caused the deeper impression."

"Where are the entry tracks? All these are leading away."

"I'm guessing they knocked at the front door and forced their way in, then left with her through the back door," Mark said. "Knocked her out first."

"What if they killed her?"

"They probably didn't want to make a lot of noise. A gunshot or a fight might have drawn a neighbor's attention. It wasn't raining when I got here and hadn't rained in a while. There was no lightning and thunder to cover a commotion."

Mark continued to scan the tracks. "Wonder where her husband was through all this."

"He told me he was taking a nap," I said.

I played my own light on the tracks. The shallow ones looked familiar.

"Those are wading boots," I said.

"How do you know that?"

I cocked my right leg at the knee and played my light over the sole. "I recognize the tread. Mine are the same."

A brain synapse flared.

"I know where they've taken her," I said. "Ransom Camp. That's why they're wearing the waders. After thirty-six hours of rain, it'll be a swamp down there."

IT WAS A GIVEN that we needed backup. I suggested the LaSalle County Sheriff, but Mark said it was unlikely they would help, since there wasn't even an official missing persons report on Emily Humphries. And we were following a hunch. We would call the sheriff as soon as we had something concrete to offer.

I had one other idea, and it was a long shot. I made the call, explained the situation and was surprised at the quick, even enthusiastic agreement. Mark and I climbed back into our trucks and headed east. Since the lousy weather had cleared the streets, hooking up was a simple matter. Carl Cribben's X5 Beemer was waiting for us on the LaSalle Drive entry ramp to Lake Shore Drive.

We formed up a convoy, south to the Stevenson Expressway and west toward Ransom Camp. Mark led the way since he had the siren and light bars.

We had no idea what we were rolling into.

35

It was nearing midnight when we got to Ransom Camp, and I was exhausted. I'd been on an emotional roller coaster for days. I'd also been shot. Despite the adrenaline pumping into my system, my personal battery was being drained by my concerns for Emily, my guilt over Vinnie and Miguel, and my editor's on-again-off-again confidence in my work.

And then there was the pain. Once we got off the interstate, I had to wrestle the Explorer over the muddy, water-covered back roads. My arm was screaming.

The gate on the road into Ransom Camp was open.

And there was a white Chrysler parked inside.

We killed our headlights and drove in.

I pulled in front of the Chrysler and backed into its front bumper. Cribben pulled up along side it, almost touching the driver's-side doors. Mark pulled close behind it. The driver wouldn't be getting away.

Cribben and I walked back to Mark's vehicle. He was calling in the Chrysler's license plate. At least we would know who we were facing.

The answer came back seconds later. Avis. A rental.

"We still don't have enough to call for backup," Mark said. "We're on our own."

Standing in the shelter of my rear lift door, I slipped out of my rain gear, grateful when Mark stepped over to help me. I put on a fleece jacket for warmth, then the rain gear again over the top.

I wish you'd stay with the cars," Mark said in a low voice. "I'm worried about your arm and the danger. You promised you wouldn't scare me any more."

"I said I would try," I told him.

He looked at me with a pleading expression for a few seconds. Then he gave up.

I saw that Cribben, too, was dressing for the weather. And he, too, had come armed. We might not have a lot of firepower, but what we had was prime.

We closed our car doors gingerly and locked them manually to avoid the chirps of the electronics. The rain had stopped for the moment, and the sounds would have carried a long way through the night.

Mark gave us latex gloves. "Poison ivy," he said. "Place is loaded with it."

I hooked the strap of my utility light over my right shoulder. The act of undressing and redressing had further aggravated my injured arm. I tried to ignore it. I put my cell phone in a zippered pocket. I was ready.

A waterproof fanny pack nestled in the small of Cribben's back, probably filled with extra ammo clips. Mark hoisted a substantial backpack onto his shoulders. I had no idea what was inside.

"You think they're down at the lake?" I asked him.

"I'm betting they headed straight downhill for that shack," he said, his voice barely above a whisper. "We've got some rough going in the beginning, through a lot of underbrush. When we hit the trail things'll get easier."

Cribben stood beside me. Since this was his first visit to Ransom Camp, he had no idea where we were going.

"Watch where you walk," Mark said. "There's all sorts of debris hidden in the weeds. Leave your lights off. Mine'll be good enough. Stay close and pay attention. Don't make unnecessary noise."

Mark fitted a cap over his flashlight, and when he turned the light on it glowed a dull red. I didn't know how that was going to do us any good, but after my eyes adjusted to it, I found I could see well enough. The clouds parted now and then and let in a little moonlight, but those intervals were brief.

"Coming out here," I said in a whisper, "isn't the best idea I ever had."

"I sure hope not," Mark whispered.

We started off.

The first attack on us came from mosquitos. They didn't think my face was messed up enough and kept darting in to draw fresh blood.

It was slow going through the bramble. It entangled our legs and concealed nasty surprises. From time to time, each of us stumbled over debris we couldn't see.

Every fifty yards or so, Mark stopped to consult a compass. Only once did he alter course. I made a bet with myself that he had been an Eagle Scout.

What little moonlight passed through the clouds we lost when we moved into a stand of pine and large shaggy oaks.

Mark extended a hand. Cribben and I stopped.

Mark swept his flashlight along the ground.

"Over here," he said in a low voice.

We shuffled a dozen feet to our left, and I saw what he had seen. Two parallel tracks through the weeds and fallen leaves, gouged deep enough to expose bare earth.

Cribben crouched down and examined one spot.

"They dragged her through here," he said. "Easier to get through the trees that way. Probably one guy on each arm."

"Bastards," I said. I looked at the tracks with dread. "Is that dead weight?"

"Not necessarily," Cribben said. "Alive or dead, Emily would weigh the same. Dead weight's harder to carry, but not heavier. I'm thinking she's alive. If they were looking to dump a body, we've already passed plenty of good places."

We followed the tracks to the trail, where we could make out the clear imprint of two sets of boots that matched those at the Humphries house. The drag marks stopped.

"Somebody's carrying her again," Mark said. "See here, the waffle-pattern boots and the wavy pattern are nearly the same depth. Up here – " he pointed to a spot a few yards to the east " – the waffle prints get deeper."

Mark started forward again, but I stopped him. I took my cell phone out of my pocket and held it under Mark's light. A vertical bar graph on the left side of the screen showed three of a possible five bars. Acceptable, but not like being downtown.

"Let's hope the signal doesn't get weaker," I said. "Looks like we might need to call in the sheriff, after all."

"I have a hand radio," Mark said. "It should work even if the phone won't."

"The Lone Ranger never called in the sheriff," Cribben said and smiled.

"No, you're right, he didn't," I said. "And when he got shot it only hurt for a minute, until Tonto bandaged it up. That's how I know the stories were fiction."

My arm was throbbing. My workout regimen prepared me for the trek through the woods, but nothing really prepared a body to be raked by a bullet. The area of the wound felt wet. I hoped it was sweat, or leaking rain, and not blood.

When we came out of the stand of trees, I noticed we didn't get our moonlight back. It had grown cloudy again. All we needed was more rain. Mark read my thoughts.

"I forgot to mention the weather forecast," he said. "This whole area could get another two or three inches of rain tonight."

"Oh, great," I said. "We'll never find the bread crumbs I've been dropping."

A quarter mile farther on the ground became marshy with standing water everywhere, some of it several inches deep. We'd crossed into the flood plain. We slowed our pace, trying to keep our boots from sloshing or making sucking sounds as they sank into the muck and came out again.

A dim glow appeared ahead. I saw it first and put a hand on Mark's arm to stop him.

"That's the shack," he said in a whisper.

"It's occupied," Cribben said.

Mark doused his flashlight and we inched forward, crouching behind some brush to scope things out. The shack was just that, a simple box maybe twenty feet square, set up on five-foot stilts. A crude but effective shelter.

As if to emphasize the need for shelter, a heavy drop of rain hit my shoulder. I heard the slap of it against the nylon rain jacket as much as I felt it through the layers of clothing.

The storm bluffed a couple of times, starting, then stopping, then starting again. The third time it hit us with a vengeance, the rain so dense it blotted out the view of the shack. I pulled the hood of the windbreaker over my head, but the wind was blowing the rain sideways, and it found a route inside the nylon shell and began to soak the fleece pullover beneath. I was going to get cold.

"We need to move," Cribben said to Mark. "They're not going to be outside in this. So let's get down there."

Mark nodded.

We trudged forward and stopped again, behind cover, when the rain subsided. Now we were within twenty yards of the shack, and I thought I heard something.

"What was that?" I said in a low whisper.

"What?" said Mark.

"It sounded like a groan. Someone in trouble."

"The wind."

"Not the wind. I'm sure of it."

As if to punctuate my certainty, we heard a cry for help barely audible above the storm. It was Emily.

The men heard it this time, too, and we moved forward again

without hesitation. Now we were wading through water over our ankles.

Ten feet from the shack, we saw Emily, her body caught in the halo of light reflecting from the structure. My throat closed.

She was tied down, spread-eagled in the muck on the far side of the creek that drained the lake. Her captors had lashed her arms to two stout bushes. I couldn't see her lower body because it was hidden under the roiling surface of the water, which had risen to her chest. The upward slope of the bank held her head above water. If the rain kept coming, the creek would keep rising, and Emily would drown, a death orchestrated in prolonged terror. Just like Vinnie's.

I wanted to scream that we were there and would get her out. But I couldn't risk it.

The torrential rain continued. I thought I could see the creek rising as I watched.

"We've got to do something now," I said. "Let's go down and get her, and then we can tackle the guys inside."

"We can't," Cribben said. "If they're watching her, we'll be easy marks inside that arc of light. We've got to take them first, and we've got to take them fast."

He tripped the thumb break on his holster, and a Glock seemed to leap into his hand. "Okay," he said, "if there are only two of them inside I can nail them both with the element of surprise. Mark, you follow the brush line around to the other side and be ready to cut Emily loose as soon as I've got the bad guys secured."

"What do I do?" I said.

"You stay down," Mark said. "You're injured, and you're not armed."

Mark moved off, his gun unholstered and pointed at the ground. Cribben and I approached the shack, vigilant for someone hiding in the brush around us. We reached the steps that rose to the door. Cribben started up. I stood back. I hoped the steps were solid, but when Cribben hit the third one, it gave off the definitive croak of rotting wood. He froze.

Nothing happened, and he went on up. When he got to the front door, he leaned his body as far to the right as he could, trying to get a glimpse through a small window. He raised his hand to me with his index finger extended. I took it to mean he saw one person inside. That wasn't right. There had been two sets of tracks.

Right then is when something hard touched the back of my head, and a low voice told me, "You stand real still, or you die."

"YOU ON THE STEPS, put the gun down," the voice said, just loud enough for Cribben to hear. Cribben turned and sized up the situation. He set the gun down on the wooden railing.

I had the fleeting thought that Mark might return and get us out of this mess, but he couldn't have heard anything. He was on the far side of the shack in a driving rain beside a raging creek.

The man holding a gun to my head pushed me forward, toward the steps.

The shack door opened, and there he was, the man who'd broken into my apartment and sent me to the hospital.

Nicky Santori looked shocked at seeing Cribben in front of him and went for a gun. Cribben launched himself and body-slammed Nicky back into the shack.

"Ah, fuck..." the man behind me said.

I felt the pressure of his gun ease a little, and I made my move, too, ducking low, driving my good shoulder into the man's chest. His feet slid out from under him, and with a big splash, he went down onto his back in the water and ooze, taking me with him. He was shorter than me, but a whole lot stronger. And he had two working arms.

He must have lost his gun when he fell, because his hands came up empty. He reached for my throat. I couldn't let him get a grip – he would strangle me or flip me and hold my head under water until I drowned.

As hard as I could, I kneed him in the groin. He grunted and the focus of his attention changed abruptly. His grip loosened long enough for me to break free and scramble to my feet. He came up after me with amazing speed, and he had his hands around my throat faster than I could react. I felt my windpipe compress under his thumbs.

I thrashed and clawed at him. In my mind I was hurting him, but in truth, there was no strength behind the effort. Little lights danced in my eyes. I knew I was losing consciousness, and if something didn't change, I wouldn't wake up.

Abruptly, the man turned his head, startled by something over my left shoulder.

I heard a gunshot explode over the noise of the storm, and the man's head snapped back. A third eye appeared between the two he was born with. His hands slid from my throat, and he toppled backward into the swirling black water. It parted to accept his body, then rolled over him like a shroud.

36

"**I** should have shot her and walked away."
It is more like a flash of realization than a logical thought.
It is the last thing the assassin knows.

37

I rubbed my neck and gasped for air. I turned, unsteady, expecting to see Mark.

Instead I found John Conti, his head bare, his hair matted and dripping, the gun he had just fired still in his right hand, aimed where my attacker stood seconds earlier.

The hand was trembling.

"Enough," John said. "It stops here."

~

TEN MINUTES later we were all gathered in the shack, everyone except the dead man, whose body still lay outside under the floodwater. It would be recovered later if the raging creek didn't wash it away. Our paramount concerns now were to stay sheltered, to get warm, and to hope the little shed could withstand the fury outside.

Lightning blazed every few seconds, followed by terrifying explosions of thunder, as if our surroundings were ripping themselves apart to cleanse the horrors of Ransom Camp.

Whatever system brought this gale sat directly over our heads, and it didn't seem in any hurry to move on.

When Cribben body-slammed Nicky Santori, Santori fell into a wooden table and cracked his head. He was semi-conscious and unable to resist when Cribben cuffed his hands then stripped him of his belt to restrain his feet.

Mark Hearst, meanwhile, succeeded in freeing Emily Humphries and carried her inside, out of the storm.

John and I stood there at the bottom of the steps for a few moments, the rain drumming against us. He seemed to be in shock. Although he still held the gun, his hand had dropped to his side. He wouldn't make eye contact with me. I reached and took his gun in my good hand. He didn't pull it away from me, but he didn't release it, either.

"Thank you, John," I said. "You always seem to be looking out for me."

I tugged at the gun. He let it go.

"Let's go inside," I said.

He didn't respond at first. Then he turned his head and looked at me with dead eyes.

"You were never supposed to get hurt, Deuce," he said. "I never wanted any harm to come to you. But I wasn't the one controlling that guy." He cocked his head toward the spot where the assassin had disappeared under the water.

I took his elbow. "Let's get out of the weather, John," I said. I guided him up the stairs, his head down, his shoulders slumped.

He looked like a very old man.

MARK HAD BEEN CARRYING a supply of thermal blankets in his backpack. He spread one on the floor and laid Emily on it. Then he folded up his jacket and tucked it under her head. He stripped her of all the wet clothes he could without destroying her dignity and covered her with a second thermal blanket, creating a cocoon of warmth. She was incoherent and slipping in and out of consciousness, suffering from shock and hypothermia, a deadly combination for someone her age.

John Conti sat cross-legged on the floor next to her and took her hand under the blanket, whispering words none of the rest of us could hear.

None of us had cell phone service, so Mark used his radio to call for help. It would be a while coming. The storm was too dangerous for a helicopter to fly. The Sheriff's Office said it would send deputies and paramedics to a staging area on the road above the shack, but the lightning posed too much of a risk to let them slog through the trees to get to us. They would be close by when the storm abated.

I sat in an old straight-backed wooden chair, utterly spent, my elbows on my thighs, my hands drooping between my knees. I didn't realize I still held John's gun until Cribben came over and eased it away.

After tending to Emily, Mark cut off my fleece jacket and wind-breaker and cut away the sleeve and shoulder of the t-shirt beneath. My wound had started bleeding again staining all the clothes on my left side. Mark discarded the bandages and slathered a silver sulfadi-azine ointment on the wound to nip any infection I picked up in the floodwater. Then he redressed the arm and wrapped me in a thermal blanket.

He bent down and kissed my forehead. "Docs will put you on some antibiotics for a while, and you'll be fine. When you get out of the hospital—again—you get to be my houseguest—again. Murphy will be pleased."

I was too weak to protest. Besides, I didn't want to.

Cribben had retrieved his gun, dried and holstered it, and stuck Conti's gun in his belt. The ex-FBI agent stood guard over the scene with his arms folded across his chest. If he once took his eyes off John Conti, I missed it.

I mustered the strength to ask John some questions. "So what do I call you?"

His eyes caught mine then and held them. "You've always called me, John," he said.

"But that's not your name, is it?"

"It has been," he said, "for a very long time."

A bolt of lightning turned the night sky to noon, and the thunder detonated simultaneously. The strike hit right outside. Everyone ducked. We heard a tree fall and smelled the acrid scent of ozone.

"You want me to tell the story," I said, "or will you?"

"Deuce, do we have to do this now?"

"I think we do. You said it yourself outside. 'It stops here.'"

John said nothing.

"Okay," I said. "I'll tell the story for you, and it's appropriate that we do it here, because this is where it started, in 1957, in Ransom Camp."

"Martin and LuAnne LaPalma lived here," I said, "two people who hated the lives fate dealt them with a passion that knew no limits. They hated their work. They hated their neighbors. Worse, they infused their hatred into their children. Well, maybe not all the children. The oldest son, Julio, might have been an okay guy. And the youngest child, a little girl, was an innocent."

I nodded down at Emily.

"But the two middle children, Reuben and Ricardo, they were vicious. Their hatred for their neighbors ran so deep that one night they torched Ransom Camp, set fires to trucks, trailers, mobile homes, the school even. A lot of people died horrible deaths. A lot of them were children. I have to figure Reuben and Ricardo were pretty pleased with themselves. They destroyed an environment they despised. It would never be rebuilt."

Except for the storm, the shack was silent, everyone who was conscious hanging on my words.

I continued. "But their joy didn't last long because a young man named Miguel Astosso had seen Reuben set fire to the Astosso family's trailer. He had watched in horror as his mother and grandfather burned to death inside, as neighbors carried his little brother away to a hospital where he died after several days in agony. Somewhere Miguel Astosso got a gun, and he killed Reuben in revenge."

Conti blinked at me. He looked drained and numb. In a way, I hated doing this to him. He had saved my life, twice, in fact. Once after my father died and again today, a few minutes earlier. But this had to be done.

"I figure," I said, "after Reuben was killed, the LaPalma family fled and ceased to exist. There must have been a family named Conti living at Ransom Camp. I found a record of a Mary Conti enrolled in school. I'm guessing she and the rest of the Contis were wiped out in the fire, and the LaPalmas assumed their identities. How am I doing so far, John?"

He looked off, continuing his silence.

"The family set up together in Chicago," I said, "except Julio. He was a lot older and went off on his own, reinvented himself, and emerged as Vinnie Colangelo."

Mark and Cribben were watching me. John was looking at Emily.

"So let's do the math," I said. "Ricardo LaPalma would be about sixty-nine today. You shaved five years off your age and enrolled in school as John Conti. You did well, because in age and maturity, you were five years ahead of your classmates. If anybody noticed you were big for your age, they never pressed the issue. You've managed to keep those extra years off, too. Exercise, subtle plastic surgery, and hair color work wonders, and in your case, they make you appear even younger than you claim."

Lightning flashed, and thunder boomed again. Rain kept lashing at the shack's walls. I noticed the beginning of a few leaks.

"The added maturity," I said, "got you through high school, into college, into law school, and then into public service. You got an appointment as United States Attorney and got elected to Congress. But you couldn't have done it alone. You were smart enough to make it through high school and college, law school, too. But you didn't have the juice to get an appointment as a U.S. attorney, certainly not a plum assignment like Chicago. You had big-time help."

Now John glanced at me, then away again.

"Organized crime recognized your ambition," I said, "and saw an opportunity to develop some influence. The Organization stepped up and made an offer, and you lusted after the money and power too much to say no. Or perhaps someone within the Organization found out who you really are and what you did, and blackmailed you. I don't know which. And it doesn't matter. Either way, you sold your soul."

Conti's face remained impassive, though I thought he'd grown pale.

"May I have one of those blankets?" he asked, and Mark handed it to him. He draped it around his shoulders and shivered. I didn't know if it was the cold or the memories.

The storm continued to boil and hammer at the shack.

When the noise abated, John spoke. "I have a birth certificate that says I'm John Conti, born sixty-four years ago."

"Birth certificates can be forged," I said. "I suspect your friends did that for you, a service that came with the package."

He didn't respond.

I picked up the story. "As your reputation grew, you realized you had two potential problems, the two people in the world who knew your true identity. Your parents were long dead. But there was still your older brother, Julio, whom we now know as Vinnie Colangelo, and your little sister, Emily."

John looked down at Emily again. He still held her hand.

"Emily wouldn't talk," I said. "She was too frightened. So was her husband. And maybe, for a little while at least, so was Julio, your brother. Vinnie. But in the early years, you didn't worry too much about Vinnie. He got involved in organized crime, too. If Vinnie had made a move to expose you, all you had to do was put him away, which you could do because you were the United States freaking Attorney."

I sighed. "Oh, wait a minute. That's exactly what happened, isn't it? When Vinnie got himself in a little bind after the truck hijacking, he came to you, his brother, and asked for help to beat the charge. You refused. Vinnie threatened you with exposure."

I pointed my finger at John. "You went to your handlers in the Organization. They arranged to steal the documents that would prove the Scotch Vinnie 'jacked had moved into state commerce. You had Richard Palmieri reindict Vinnie on federal charges. You told

Charles Haight to withdraw as Vinnie's big-shot attorney, leaving Vinnie to a public defender. You had Richard Palmieri turn down a plea deal. You used Alfano Mustolli to bribe two federal agents to lie on the witness stand, and you worked it out for Vinnie's two accomplices to rat out their friend."

John still sat on the floor. He was shaking his head with each new accusation. I couldn't tell if he was denying or regretting.

"You used Vinnie's bust," I said, "to shovel him into a federal prison out in Kansas. And some time before that, maybe even before his trial, you told him if he talked about you, you'd kill his entire family, including his wife and his daughter. You threatened your sister, Emily, the same way. Right?"

Although John's face remained immobile, a small muscle went into spasm along his jaw line. I was getting to him. I felt no triumph. It all made me profoundly sad.

"You were living a tenuous lie," I said. "If either your brother or your sister turned on you, it would've exposed everything, including your real identity, your relationship to Vinnie and the Organization, and your role in the tragedy at Ransom Camp. So Vinnie wound up in Leavenworth, where he spent a whole lot more time than he should have, in surroundings much more dangerous than he deserved. And Emily got the message. My guess is Richard Palmieri never knew why he was prosecuting Vinnie's case so vigorously. He was loyal to John Conti and did what the U.S. Attorney asked of him."

I paused, then leaned over so my face was close to John's.

"What was it you wanted, John?" I asked. "A—To put your brother in harm's way so some con might shank him and end your problem? It's not an outrageous idea. Julio was small and slight, no match for some bulked up gangbanger. Or B—To scare him so badly with a display of your power that he'd never threaten you again? I'm guessing you hoped for Plan A and were willing to settle for Plan B."

Conti continued to stare at Emily.

"It worked, too," I said. "Vinnie was silent for years."

"Now flash forward," I said. "As Vinnie begins to age, the resentment begins to grow. He wants restitution. He wants his family back.

He wants to know his grandchildren. He tells people he was railroaded. But nobody believes him. He's an old drunk. Maybe he's even deluded. You're able to dismiss him—until I come along. When I start asking questions, you decide Vinnie's got to go. So you tell Nicky Santori over there and the goon under the water outside to go over there and make it look like a home invasion. You don't want Emily to suspect you ordered Vinnie's death—she's a lady of principle and might go to the authorities despite your threats."

Emily groaned. John bent over and whispered to her. I thought he was being extremely tender toward someone he'd just tried to kill.

I kept going. "After Vinnie died it's me you have to watch, because I've found Ransom Camp, and I've found Miguel Astosso, and Miguel is talking. It has to be stopped, but killing me would bring too much heat. Killing a reporter always does. So you get someone to set a gasoline fire in Miguel's house to be sure I get the point that it's just like the massacre at Ransom Camp."

John shook his head again and sighed, his only response.

"I missed the truth for a long time," I said, "because Miguel Astosso told me there were three LaPalma children, Ricardo, Reuben and Emily. He'd probably forgot Julio, who was older. But when I talked to Maria Astosso, Miguel's sister, she said there were four LaPalma children. And when I asked her about Ricardo, she said he was like Jesus Christ. I had no idea what she meant. But it came to me eventually. It was a metaphor. Of death and resurrection. Someone named John Conti died in the Ransom Camp fire and came back in a second life. As you."

I stopped and let my words sink in for several seconds.

"At some point," I said, "you felt backed into a corner. You decided to risk the heat, and you gave the order to kill me. God, John, when I think about the way you fawned over me that evening in the restaurant, asking me if I could ID my intruder, if I got a good look at him, it makes me sick. You were pumping me for information, and it didn't even occur to me. I'm losing my edge."

He looked up at me. "I couldn't have ordered anyone to kill you even if I'd wanted to, Deuce. I didn't have that kind of juice, and I didn't want anything bad to happen to you. The contract on you came from much higher on the food chain."

He looked away from me again, and I took it as a signal to continue.

"Well," I said, "somebody decided to have Emily killed too, because I had found her, and she would always be a threat. But that sick fuck," I pointed my chin at Nicky Santori, "he couldn't just kill. He had to torture first, which gave us time to get here and pull Emily out of the water. And now everything's spiraling down the toilet for you. There will be legal consequences for you, John. And beyond that, there will be consequences with the Mob. You ready for that?"

John sat in silence for another moment, then he cleared his throat. "I didn't order anybody to kill anybody. That's why I came out here tonight, to save Emily. That's why I was outside with a gun when you were taken, Deuce. I was going to kill that sniper guy, then come in here and kill Nicky, grab Emily and make a run for it."

"Where did you plan to go?"

He shook his head. "A long way away."

"If you didn't give the kill orders, who did?" Cribben asked John. They were the first words the FBI agent had spoken in half an hour.

"I don't know," John said. "I really don't know."

"Then how did you know Emily had been taken?" I said.

"Verne, her husband, called me. I told him to call you." He nodded at me. "He'll confirm it if you ask him."

"I didn't see your car up there," I said.

"It's hidden in the trees," he said, "down the hill, on the other side of the road."

John got up stiffly, as though his years were working against him. The blanket slipped from his shoulders to the floor as he shuffled over to the shack's single window. Outside, the storm was letting up, but not fast.

John stood at the window, peering out at the slackening rain.

∾

"I DIDN'T ORDER ANY HITS," he said. "I didn't order anybody to kill Vinnie, and the way he died sickened me. Assuming somebody had reason to kill him, he didn't need to die so hard. He was a drunk. He could have fallen down a flight of steps, off a bridge, in front of a bus. It could have been so simple. I don't know who hired these two fuckups for the attempt on Sal Annuncio, or Emily, or you." He turned to me. "God, Deuce, I never could have ordered your death. I really am fond of you. Strange as it might sound, I'm really fond of Emily."

"Bullshit."

The word came labored from Emily. She was conscious and staring at her brother. He moved to her, squatted beside her and reached for her hand. She pulled it away.

"You've been hoping for me to die for forty years," she said. "And don't say you never threatened to do it yourself, because nobody in this room's going to believe you."

She coughed, the hard, racking cough of someone with breathing problems. She'd undoubtedly inhaled some water, which made pneumonia a risk.

Mark rushed to her, lifted her upper body, and slid his whole backpack beneath her to raise her up. The coughing abated. Mark wrapped a third thermal blanket around her shoulders and neck.

"I'm sorry, Emmy," John said. His voice cracked. "I'll make it up to you and Verne."

"Go to hell," she said and closed her eyes.

John sank into a sitting position and buried his face in his hands. He made no sound, but when he raised his face, it was wet, and his eyes were red. He fixed his gaze on me.

I had a visceral reaction split between pity and loathing. I wanted to believe him.

Without taking his eyes from mine, he said, "You have it wrong about the fires, too."

"Oh? How so?"

"It had nothing to do with our parents. Their hatred was generational. We didn't share it. It wasn't personal."

"Then what?"

"We were bored."

I stared in disbelief. "You were *bored*?"

He smiled sadly. "Crazy, huh? School was out. The harvest season was a couple of weeks away, so we had no work. We were kids, bored and angry."

"Angry at what?"

"At life. We wanted a different life, something better than the hard, barren existence in places like Ransom Camp. To be born there was to die there."

I waited for more. No one else spoke.

John gulped half the oxygen in the room with a sound that could have been a sob.

"Okay, you want the story of Ransom Camp, here it is." He paused for a moment, then he stood up again and began to pace slowly.

"I was twelve. Reuben was fourteen. Close enough in age to be close in life. We shared fantasies. In one of them, spun in our room at night, we burned the place down and ran away to new and better lives. At first it was just talk. Then Reuben mugged an old guy outside a store and stole his wallet. He got about eighty bucks. That was a lot of money for kids like us. We savored the possibilities for spending it the way an adult savors a fine Chicago steak. In the end, it validated our escape fantasy, and we felt destined to act on it."

He shook his head slowly, sadly, a profound gesture of regret.

"Gasoline was cheap. We started stockpiling it, hiding five-gallon containers in the woods under a lot of brush. Then one night, when we were down to our last few dollars, we blew it on a couple of sixpacks of cheap beer. Golden courage. Not a good combination for a couple of bored, angry kids. We didn't exactly have fully formed consciences. But I think if it hadn't been for the beer, we'd never have done it. But the beer was there. We got drunk, and we made our own fun."

"Fun," he said with scorn. "Can you imagine?"

He shook his head, as if trying to rid himself of the thought. Then he raised his eyes and looked at me steadily. "It was a long time ago,

Deuce. What we did should be punished and, believe me, over the years I've endured a gut full of self-inflicted suffering. But I reformed, made a decent life for myself as a public servant, helped a lot of people. That has to count for something."

He paused, apparently waiting for a reaction from me.

When he got none, he pushed on.

"After everyone was asleep, we sneaked out and hauled the gasoline out of the woods. We put the cans around the camp, and when they were in place, we poured the gas everywhere. Under people's trailers, cars, trucks, old school buses, even in the building that passed for a school. All the while we were doing this, we were drinking beer to keep ourselves pumped. When the gas had been spread, we stopped to plan. Reuben said he would start the fires with the Astosso's trailer, and he told me to start with the Conti's. I guess I hesitated, and he pulled his gun on me. Our father had given it to him, and it was his finest possession. He would never let me touch it, and he said he would shoot me with it if I backed out on him. So, we set the first fires."

He scraped his hands over his head, as if the action might drag the memories from his brain to be thrown away and forgotten.

"This is very hard," he said. "I saw Miguel Astosso break a window and start helping members of his family out of his trailer. He spotted Reuben, who was standing about 20 yards away, gloating. Then I heard a scream, and I saw the little Conti girl running at me, on fire. Her clothes had all been burned off, like that old picture of the child napalmed in Vietnam. She was reaching out to me, begging for help. I grabbed her and rolled her on the ground, but by the time I got the fire out, she was dead. She died with her eyes open, begging me for help. She never knew I was the one who set the fire under her home."

A sob wracked him. "I'll never forget her screams. I'll never forget her face. That vision from hell was enough to turn me stone, cold, sober. And sick. I didn't think I'd ever stop puking. I couldn't believe what we'd done. I looked around and saw Reuben setting more fires, one after another, and because of all the gasoline, the fires began spreading on their own. He screamed at me to get moving. But I was in shock. I just stood there, staring at him, shaking my head. All around me people were panicking, screaming. Then I began yelling at Reuben to stop. Instead, he ran toward me. He pulled his gun, and he shot me."

John shoved the sleeve of his t-shirt out of the way to expose his upper arm. The flesh was puckered by a ragged scar where a bullet had struck his left biceps muscle about three inches above the inside of his elbow. He turned his head and stared at the old wound for a long moment.

"The bullet's still in there," he said.

He lowered his head into his hands. He made no sound, but his whole body trembled. Perhaps a minute passed. When he lifted his head, his eyes were distant, peering through the fog of the past to a time he hoped never to visit again.

He stood and stumbled back to the cabin's window.

"I ran," he said. "I ran to get away from the fires. I ran to get away from Reuben. I ran in terror and shame until I felt dizzy from losing blood. I knew where there was a drug store, so I went there and found a tin of big bandages. I stuffed them in my pocket and put the empty can back on the shelf, in the back, for someone else to discover. I also stole some salve my mother used on cuts and scratches to keep them from getting infected. Then I went into the bathroom and cleaned and covered the wound. The bleeding stopped."

Absently, he massaged the scar with his right thumb.

"I should have kept running, but I went back to Ransom Camp and hid in the woods until morning. That was when I saw Miguel Astosso kill Reuben. As Reuben lay in the burned brush with the stench of burned human flesh everywhere around us, I went to his body and took his gun. I showed it to him, though I knew he couldn't see me. And he couldn't hear me. But I told him, 'You never let me play with it, but now it's mine.'"

He glanced toward Carl Cribben, who frowned and glanced quickly at the gun he had stuck in his belt, the gun I had taken from John and Carl had taken from me.

"That's it," John said. "A .22 Ruger Standard, I think it's called. Except for a little target practice in the woods around here and cleaning it, it's been locked in my safe at home for years. Nobody else knew it was there, at least not for a long time. Until one Saturday afternoon. Carole had an event, and she came home early and found me cleaning it. She hated guns, and she demanded to know where it came from. I didn't want to tell her. I tried to lie, but she didn't buy it. Eventually, I told her the whole story. With every word I uttered I saw the contempt in her face deepen until it broke my heart. She told me our marriage was a lie, our life was a lie, and she wouldn't live a lie. Her deal was, I go to the FBI and tell the truth, and she would back me up. If I didn't talk to the FBI, she would leave me and tell our daughter, Susanne, what I'd done, and I would wind up estranged from both of them."

Now John began to sob uncontrollably. Tears streamed down his face and merged with mucous from his nose. His words came out of his mouth punctuated with spittle.

"So I did it. I made an appointment with the FBI. I told Vinnie and Emily I was going to confess, but no one else. Emily probably told Verne, and I'm guessing he's the one who sold me out. The next thing I knew Carole was dead. Smashed beyond recognition when a semi crashed into her car and pinned it against the median concrete on the Dan Ryan. 'Certain people' told me to reconsider my chat with the FBI, or my daughter would be next."

He was leaning with both hands on the rough-hewn window frame and dragged his hands down the wood as he fell apart.

"They murdered Carole," he yelled, still sobbing. "They butchered the only woman I ever loved."

His grief turned to anger.

"That's what I got for trying to do the right thing," he shouted. "My wife was butchered, my daughter threatened. How was that fair or right or just? Damn Ransom Camp. Damn and goddamn Reuben."

He opened his mouth, and the scream he emitted sounded like a mortally wounded wild animal.

His hands, punctured by large splinters, left tracks of blood on the window frame. John seemed not to notice. He continued to shout, challenging the storm for dominance.

"I wanted to die. I wanted them to kill me. I wanted to kill myself. I tried. I must have taken that fucking gun out of the safe a dozen, two dozen times and put it to my head. But I couldn't do it. I'm a killer and a coward, and I couldn't even end my own life."

He wiped his face on his sleeve, but new tears started leaking.

"And then," he said to me, "by some crazy coincidence, you found Vinnie and Ransom Camp and all the rest of it, and I couldn't stand it. I haven't slept at night worrying about you. I knew when they took Emily, and when Verne told you Emily was gone, you'd figure it out and come after them. I couldn't let Emily die. I couldn't let you die. This had to come to an end."

It was several seconds before anyone in the room breathed again. Then John shocked all of us. He turned from the window, his hands slowly dripping blood on the floor.

"I'm going to ask you a favor, Deuce," he said. "Let me go. I'll take my chances with the storm. I'll go back to my car and disappear forever. I can do that. I've had arrangements in place for years, looking to the day when I'd need to get out. In the memory of your father and my wife, would you do that for an old man who's still a coward?"

For a moment, I was speechless. The magnitude of what John Conti asked was indescribable. That he should invoke the memories of my father and his wife was unspeakable, contemptible. Obscene.

I stood and gasped for air. The shack was closing in on me. I had to get out of there.

I grabbed the door and opened it. A gust of wind and a sheet of rain hit me hard.

I turned and looked at Conti and found my voice.

I shouted to be heard over the rattling of the storm.

"Fuck you, Ricardo."

38

When the storm dissipated, an air ambulance flew Emily
to the University of Chicago Medical Center in critical
condition. Cribben called in FBI agents who took John
Conti into custody. They had jurisdiction because the assassin, whose
body still lay underwater, was the presumptive Las Vegas sniper. How
Conti and the sniper were connected, if they were connected, was yet
to be determined.

Because of the uncertainty over who had ordered Emily killed,
her brother or her brother's mob friends, Mark and Cribben
convinced the Chicago police to put a round-the-clock guard on
Emily's hospital room.

I was admitted to the same hospital for an overnight stay so I
could get thoroughly dosed with antibiotics. Sully and Eric were
waiting when I was wheeled out of the ER and into my private room.
We had just started talking when Jerry Alvarez called.

"It's about the dead guy in the woods," he said. "He's the one who
shot you. He's the one who shot at Sal Annuncio. And he's the sniper
who killed Charles Reading. He lives, or lived, on the Gold Coast.
They found the rifle in his condo. His prints were on it, and all the
bullets match up. Open and shut."

"What's his name?" I asked.

"Jose Hermann. Ever hear of him?"

I hadn't. Neither had Jerry.

"What's going to happen to Conti?" I asked.

Jerry sighed. "Not for attribution. For the moment, he's being held incognito as a material witness. We won't be able to do that for long, but we gotta get jurisdictions and details worked out before we say anything to the media, if you get my gist."

I did. The feds would withhold the Conti story for a time, but it would be a short time.

I smiled. "Thank you," I said.

"Yeah, well, we expect a *quid pro quo* for keepin' your secret a while," he said. "It's only gonna be a coupla days, maybe a week, Deuce, so work fast. The state will defer to the feds for the time being. We're lookin' at public corruption charges and conspiracy to murder a member of Congress. I'll keep you informed, but in the meantime, keep it quiet."

I had a story to write and a short window to do it. If John Conti was indicted before we published, everybody would have the details. We wanted to be ready to put the story on the street the morning before the grand jury acted.

Putting together a project like this is an endurance exercise, a sprint for the finish at the end of a cross-country race. Dozens of interviews. Stacks of documents. Legal questions out the yazoo.

Eric turned over his private office to me, and IT created a secure file for my stories. For five days and five nights, fifteen or sixteen hours at a stretch, I wrote with Jonathan Bruckner draped over my shoulder. He vetted paragraphs as I created them, finding ways to say things so the paper would face no legal ramifications later, or at least none in which we couldn't prevail.

Eric put together a design team, which worked behind the locked doors of his conference room. He did all the editing himself. Lucy was pulled off her regular duties to be my personal researcher. One photo editor pulled old file photos and worked with one photographer to get new material.

The design team created the front page, the jump pages and the headlines. Nobody who wasn't on the team had access to Eric's private office or to the conference room. When we left work—usually in the middle of the night—both doors were locked. Even the cleaning crews were denied access. Documents went into a safe, trash into a shredder. Nobody talked about the project outside those two rooms. Others in the newsroom were discouraged from wandering past to see what they could through the windows.

Two FBI agents were positioned in the newsroom twenty-four hours a day, discreetly, to guard our work. By orders of the United States Attorney.

We brought Jerry Alvarez into the mix. As he said, we had a *quid pro quo* to pay off. We helped him coordinate his own investigation for the grand jury, but we did *not* give him access to my notes and interviews. That simply isn't done. He could have subpoenaed them, and our lawyers would have had the courts quash the subpoenas, and it would have eaten up time and exposed the story. To Jerry's credit, he didn't put us through that because, once he knew who to interview and what questions to ask, he had no trouble replicating the work we'd done.

As a result, John Conti—nee Ricardo LaPalma—was indicted by the federal grand jury on racketeering charges three days after we published our first story. Additional federal charges would follow. Charles Haight came out of retirement to defend him. A full circle.

Except I knew Haight wasn't defending Conti. He was defending Conti's handlers. He would try to play it so the wolves took Conti without collateral damage to the Mob.

At arraignment, the prosecution argued for remand. Haight cited Conti's ties to the community and got bail of $50 million. Conti left jail and surrendered his passport.

Two days later I got a call from Cal Miller, the agent for Creek Enterprises, owners of the Ransom Camp property.

"You wanna come over?" Miller said.

"Sure, if you've got something worthwhile," I said.

It was.

The trust had been unsealed by court order. The owner of the Ransom Camp property was revealed to be John Conti, a.k.a. Ricardo LaPalma. He'd bought the land for back taxes in 1968 and placed it in the trust. I wondered if Miller knew why.

"I don't," he said. "He never told me, and I never asked him. None of my business."

I wrote that story for the next day. The editors put it on the front page.

Everything I wrote about this case went on the front page. Neither the editors nor the public could get enough of the story.

Before I left the office I got a call from Mark Hearst. Emily's condition had been upgraded to fair, and probably would be upgraded again the next day.

"She's a tough old lady," he said.

"My role model," I said.

~

THE NEXT DAY Jerry Alvarez called.

"You know what they're gonna argue, right?" he said.

"Who?" I said.

"Haight and Conti. They're going to argue contrition, that Conti bought the land and had it set aside into perpetuity so nobody could ever defile it again with shit like houses and schools and 7-Elevens. They'll argue it was the act of a remorseful man. Furthermore, they're going to argue that Conti spent the rest of his life in public service in an effort to right that old wrong, and that his record in public service, while not remarkable, appears to be clean. It's a story Charles Haight could sell to a jury."

"That's not the way it was," I said.

"*Como sabes eso?* How do you know that?" Jerry said.

"The old man told me, Miguel Astosso. Despite what Conti says today about not hating the migrants, Ricardo and Reuben deeply resented their presence at Ransom Camp. Where those boys were concerned, the migrants were squatting on land that properly belonged to the native-born. They heard that from their parents often enough. They came to believe it. Maybe they burned the place to escape the life, but when Ricardo had the chance, he took back the land he'd always considered his birthright. Reuben didn't live to see the day, but Ricardo made it happen for himself. And then he hid the fact that he owned the land behind a legal seal. There wasn't one ounce of contrition in it."

"Miguel's dead," Jerry said. "Without his testimony, Haight will try to sell Conti's version of events."

"I guess you'll have to see the jury doesn't buy it," I said.

"Gonna try like hell."

"And what," I said, "about the racketeering?"

"I know Conti's tied to the corruption of the Colangelo trial and probably a lot of others. But it will take time to piece it together. We're going to have to be deliberate with this case. It has to be airtight. I've got an appointment with Haight and Conti right now, as a matter of fact. I'll get a feel for how they're gonna play things."

Jerry called back two hours later.

"Conti didn't show," he said.

"What do you mean, he didn't show?"

"Just what I said. Haight came in alone. Conti never showed up."

"What did Haight say?"

"A lot of nothing. He didn't know where his client was. His client hadn't called to say he couldn't make it. We waited more than an hour."

"Could he have gotten a new passport, a forged one, and skipped the country?"

"Maybe. But *Dios me ayude*. I got a bad feeling about this."

So did I. I also had a hunch. I called Mark Hearst.

"You want to take another trip with me?" I asked him.

"I don't know," he said. "Last trip we took together nearly got us both killed."

"Conti's disappeared."

"You know where he is?"

"I've got a pretty good idea."

"Shit. Let's go."

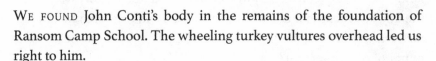

WE FOUND John Conti's body in the remains of the foundation of Ransom Camp School. The wheeling turkey vultures overhead led us right to him.

Conti was lying on the ground on his back. Insects already were having their way with his flesh. I felt the sting of tears behind my eyes. The vultures had found the body because the canopy of trees surrounding it was nearly empty now of the leaves of autumn.

Mark called the sheriff. We didn't want to walk into the clearing and risk messing up evidence, and there was nothing we could have done to help John. I could see from a distance of twenty feet that he'd taken a bullet to the head, and I thought I saw a gun by his right hand. I pointed it out to Mark.

"Poor bastard couldn't live with it," Mark said.

"I'm not buying that," I said. "I think some people were worried what old Ricardo would reveal to get out from under all the charges he was going to face."

"You think?"

"I think."

"You think we'll ever know who it was pulling his strings?"

"Maybe someday. It doesn't much matter now."

We heard sirens in the distance.

"You think we'll ever know for sure whether it's suicide or murder?" he asked me.

"The medical examiner will try to sort it out."

"Are we ever going to know who ordered all the killing? He denied he did it. Was that the truth, or wasn't it?"

"I don't know," I said. "I'd like to think it was the truth. The John Conti I knew didn't seem like a killer. The FBI is leaning hard on

Nicky Santori to give up his employers, but he's more afraid of retribution than prison time. He won't break. Since this started with Reading's death, the most logical bad guys are those who'd have most to lose from a new racketeering investigation."

Against my will I remembered John in earlier days, the kindnesses he showed me.

"It took a lot of time and effort and money," I said, "to set John up in high places. It would make sense to protect the investment. But in the end, when the scheme began to implode, John became a liability, and they took him out."

"But will we ever know for sure?"

"Probably not," I said. "If it was the Organization, they're good at this stuff."

I WENT to the hospital to tell Emily in person.

When I entered her room, I was stunned to find Richard Palmieri there, along with Verne Humphries.

"Counselor," I said, and Palmieri and I shook hands. Palmieri wasn't nearly as aloof as he'd been when we met in his office.

"Hell of a story, Deuce," he said. "I guess I'll be reading your column regularly when and if you ever get back to it."

"Oh, I'll get back to it." I turned to Emily. "I've got some bad news," I said. "Ricardo's dead. Shot once in the head. Mark and I found him down at Ransom Camp."

If I anticipated grief from the old lady, she didn't deliver. But I saw Verne Humphries tighten his grip on his wife.

"Mob got him," she said.

"You sure?" I said. "It could have been suicide."

"No, not Ricardo. He was too arrogant for suicide. No matter how bad things got for him, he always knew he could wiggle out. Not this time. I expected it, tell the truth."

"Maybe he couldn't live with the shame and the exposure," I said.

"What shame? He was incapable of shame. Can't say I'm sorry

he's gone, except it deprives me the chance to testify against him and give him a little of what Julio got."

I moved closer to the bed and tried to sew up the last loose thread in this saga.

"Do you know," I said, "how Julio knew ahead of time what was going to happen in Las Vegas, the Reading assassination?"

"Ricardo told him," she said.

"Excuse me?" I wasn't sure I'd heard her correctly.

"Julio'd been spouting off more than usual about his time at Leavenworth," she said, "and Ricardo went to see him at that bar. Julio said they sat in a back booth, where nobody could overhear, and Ricardo said certain people were about to remove a big thorn from their sides out in Las Vegas. Told him exactly what would happen and when. Ricardo said Julio should keep in mind that if they didn't squirm about murdering a United States congressman, they sure wouldn't mind killing a retired truck driver."

"Julio told you all this?"

She nodded.

"And you didn't tell anybody?"

"Who'd have believed me? You, of all people, know how crazy this sounds. And Julio told me in confidence. He said if I breathed a word, they'd kill both of us."

Emily had handed me the final answer tied up with a bow.

I was a little lost for words, so I turned to Palmieri.

"What brings you here, Counselor?" I said.

"An apology for a prosecution too vigorously pursued," he said. "I would have liked to convey it to Vinnie personally, but . . . "

"And he's my lawyer," Emily said.

"Your lawyer?"

Palmieri explained. "On behalf of Vinnie's estate, such as it is. He had a will. Emily is the executor and sole heir. The estate will sue the federal government for wrongful prosecution, witness tampering, evidence tampering, reckless endangerment. I'll think of some more if I need to."

"You're basically suing yourself," I said, "since you prosecuted Vinnie. What are you trying to do?"

"Get a judgment against the feds for Emily. Given her age, we don't want a protracted fight, so I've approached the Justice Department about a settlement. They're amenable."

"Wow," I said. "Can I ask a nosy reporter question? How much?"

"They put $1.5 million on the table," he said. "We countered with $15 million. We'll settle somewhere in between. And don't quote me or it could queer the negotiation."

I turned to a grinning Emily. "Emily, that's great," I told her. "You'll be set for life."

"First thing," she said, "I'm going to get me the best private eye in the business."

"What for?"

"I'm going to find Julio's wife and daughter. And his grandkids. Share the wealth with them. This whole thing cost them a lot, too."

I turned to Palmieri.

"And what do you get out of this, Counselor? Another front page on your office wall?"

He smiled. "I get nothing. This is *pro bono*. I told you, I came here with an apology."

"What do you know," I said. "A happy ending."

So why did I feel like warmed-over horse manure?

EPILOGUE

I t had been almost two weeks since the story broke. With the follow-ups, including coverage of John Conti's murder and Richard Palmieri's lawsuit on behalf of Vinnie's estate, I made national headlines every day. People were telling me I was a cinch for the Pulitzer. I won't say I'd turn it down if it came my way, but I wasn't going to obsess about it. I didn't even want to think about it. In the process of getting to this point I had taken a human toll that staggered me.

The good thing about the Vinnie experience was meeting Mark Hearst. Our relationship was deepening and comfortable enough that I never removed the personal items I left at his condo after I was shot. In fact, I added to them. I hadn't moved in with him exactly, but we found ways to spend a couple of nights a week at his condo. And a couple of nights a week at mine. He commandeered the closet in my guest room and the second bath. Even his dog and my cats found accommodation.

The Ransom Camp story offered me a stunning insight. I had gone into journalism to help save the world. If I was going to save the world one person at a time, I seriously needed to pick up the pace.

I mentioned this to Mark Hearst and Carl Cribben as we sat in a banquette at Shaw's Crab House on East Hubbard Street, just off the Magnificent Mile. They laughed.

Each of us had a Laphroaig. It seemed fitting.

"You know," I said, "this is the only liquor the feds allowed into the country during Prohibition. It came in labeled as disinfectant, and when they smelled it, they believed it. Percy, the bartender at Jo-Jo's, said Vinnie told him that story. I looked it up, and it's true."

Mark smiled. "Sounds like folklore," he said.

"Sort of like your story," Cribben said. "It's true, but who'd've believed it?"

"I couldn't have done it without the two of you," I said.

"I told you from the beginning," said Mark, "I wanted to help get justice for the victims at Ransom Camp. Though I never dreamed it would involve organized crime and a congressman with a gruesome mass murder in his history."

"And I got what I wanted," Cribben said. "Thanks to your stories, there's a House bill to open a formal congressional investigation into all aspects of organized crime in this country. It's already got thirty-nine co-sponsors. They're calling it the Reading Bill. And the House Judiciary Committee has hired me as a consultant to see the thing through."

"That's awesome," I said. "We ran a story about the new investigation from our Washington bureau a couple of days ago, but it didn't mention your involvement. You think you'll ever find out who ordered all the killing that surrounded John Conti, or who was controlling him?"

"That's pretty high on my personal priority list," Cribben said. He shook his head. "You know it's beyond belief that you were after a feature story and stumbled onto all of this."

The words came from memory: "Truth is stranger than fiction . . . because fiction is obligated to stick to possibilities. Truth isn't."

"The philosophy of Deuce Mora?" Mark asked.

"Mark Twain," I said.

We were all quiet a moment, then I said, "You know, I can't figure out why I'm not dead right now. Carl, too."

"What are you talking about?" Mark said.

"Well, the assassin was hiding in the undergrowth out there," I said. "He's a great shot. He could have taken out Carl and then me from hiding."

"He might be a sharpshooter, but not with the gun we found under his body," Cribben said. "It was a Smith & Wesson .38 Airweight. A nice piece but with a very short barrel, which means accuracy diminishes exponentially with every foot the bullet has to travel. Add the high winds and torrential rains, and the environment became his enemy. To insure a kill, he had to be very close. He knew better than to try it from any distance."

Cribben took a final sip of his drink, put fifty dollars on the table, and got up.

"First round's on me," he said. "I've got to get going. I've got to pack enough stuff to tide me over in Washington for a few weeks while we get this investigation off the ground. And if I don't do it myself, my wife will pack for me. This I need to avoid at all costs."

He shook hands with Mark, and then he hugged me and promised to stay in touch.

Mark and I gazed at menus for a few minutes in relaxed, contented silence. He was the first to break it.

"How are you doing?" he asked me.

"Relative to what?"

"You were taking a pretty heavy guilt trip. Vinnie. Miguel. John, even. Have you gotten past it?"

"No," I said. "I'll never get past it. My disregard for the danger to a couple of sources cost them their lives. You don't get past something like that. And John? Hell, I still don't believe it. I don't want to believe it."

The waiter brought us another round, and I sipped my Scotch.

"There's another thing I haven't told anyone. I had a relationship with John Conti."

"Yeah, you'd known him a long time," Mark said. Then he frowned. "Was there more?"

I smiled, knowing what he was thinking. "Nothing sexual, no, just a friendship. He and my father were close when we were neighbors on West Jackson. When my father died, John helped me get through it. And after his wife was killed, I returned the favor. We leaned on each other. It never occurred to me he wasn't who he claimed to be."

"But in the end, you got it right. That counts for a lot."

"It doesn't feel that way."

I sounded morose, and I willed myself to stop heaping my bleak mood on Mark.

"I heard you were thinking about leaving the business," he said.

"Sully tell you?"

"My lips are sealed," he said. "I protect my sources."

That forced a laugh from me. "You've got the jargon right."

"So are you? Thinking about quitting, I mean?"

"I was. I still am." I sucked in a deep breath to steady myself. "I had an editor once who said journalism wasn't a job. It was a calling, like the priesthood. It was noble and heroic. I don't see much of those qualities any more. And I miss them."

"Heavy thoughts," Mark said. "And you should think about them in a nice relaxing setting without a whole lot of distractions vying for your attention."

I smiled despite myself. "That would be good."

"Jamaica is a great place to think about things. I happen to have two round-trip, first-class tickets that aren't date-specific. We could go as soon as you wrap up the loose ends of the story. Eric says he could cut you loose in a few weeks. I, of course, would be offering my services as baggage handler, facilitator, tour guide, and uber distraction of the studly variety, if you were inclined to require the services of an uber distraction of the studly variety. Especially one who knows where to find the finest Caribbean sipping rums."

"Distractions of the studly variety are good," I said. "And fine sipping rum is good. Consider yourself hired. And thank you."

"I almost forgot. I have something for you now."

He had carried a brown paper bag into the restaurant. I hadn't given it a second look. Now he took from it a box about eight inches square, wrapped in bright red paper and tied with a big gold bow. He slid it across the table to me.

"What's this for?" I said. I realized I didn't sound very gracious, and moved to amend my response. "What's the occasion?"

"Us," he said. "The possibilities."

I liked that and opened the box. Nestled in tissue inside was a brass monkey, nearly identical to my poor, lost Darwin.

"If somebody asks the significance, you can say it was a gift from a new boyfriend. If you decide to name him Darwin the Second, I promise not to be jealous."

I started to laugh then, and I couldn't stop.

Until I started to cry.

Mark reached over and thumbed the tears from my face.

I mumbled something that amounted to a thank you, and that seemed enough.

When I regained my composure we lifted our glasses and sipped.

"To Vinnie Colangelo," I said.

"To Laphroaig single malt Scotch," Mark said

"I kind of agree with Vinnie on that," I said. "It's an acquired taste."

THE END

～

ACKNOWLEDGMENTS

First and foremost, I have to acknowledge all of those news organizations and the wonderful journalists who populated them for teaching me not only the business, but also curiosity and compassion, without which I would have had little success. The Associated Press. The *Cox Newspapers*. *Newsday*. The *Jackson Hole Guide* (honestly), and the newspaper formerly known as the *St. Petersburg Times*. Every single one of you I knew in those organizations touched me in some way that contributed to who I became.

To the city of Chicago and all of its denizens. Some cloaked version of each of you, will appear in the Deuce Mora series at some point. I couldn't make you up.

To Win Blevins, another great author and editor, who found the flaws and showed me how to fix them.

To Walter Satterthwait, a grand writer in his own right, who made some outstanding suggestions.

To Jean Gonzalez and Kathaleen Porter for their support.

To the denizens of Bacchanalia, who provided endless material and probably never realized that's what they were doing.

To all the hundreds of you encompassed in these acknowledgments, I thank you.

≈

WANT MORE DEUCE FOR FREE?

Sign up at JeanHellerBooks.com to join my mailing list and get *The Storm!*